THE MUSTARD SEED

ArcheBooks Publishing

THE MUSTARD SEED

Book One of the Mustard Seed Trilogy

By

Robert E. Gelinas

Copyright © 2003 by Robert E. Gelinas.
Trade Paperback Edition 2013

ISBN-10: 1-59507-247-0
ISBN-13: 978-159507-247-4

ArcheBooks Publishing Incorporated
www.archebooks.com

Trade Paperback Edition: 2013

OTHER BOOKS BY ROBERT E. GELINAS

Dead of Night

Touch of a Stranger

Dead Man's Run

Anticipation

Players

DEDICATION

This tale is delightfully dedicated to the truly abstract thinkers of the world, especially those unique souls I've had the privilege to know[1]: the oft scoffed at, ridiculed and disparaged unabashed askers of, "What if…?"

This story is for all those who've eagerly huddled together in coffee shops, taverns, dorm rooms, apartments, dens, basements and the like; plotting and scheming and conspiring and figuring and contemplating and debating and arguing and speculating and puzzling unto the wee hours of the morning, until your puzzler was worn bare; solving all of the world's problems, sober or otherwise, exploring the heights and breadths and depths of the multitude of permutations of possibility, fantasy, imagination, and raw creativity—where all of the most intriguing theories of the universe are found.

Namely, this book is dedicated to anyone who has ever dared give voice to the heresy: "Now, what if…it all didn't really happen exactly the way they told us?"

---

[1] You know who you are.

"Gods are born and die, but the atom endures."

Alexander Chase
Perspectives, 1966

PROLOGUE

Rub Al Khali Desert, The Empty Quarter
257 Statute Miles Southeast of Riyadh, Saudi Arabia

"We breached the chamber six days ago." Andrew Duncan adjusted the boom microphone closer to his chapped lips, allowing his thick Australian accent to be heard more clearly over the roar of the helicopter's rotors. "You won't believe the size of the complex. We've mapped it all out over the last several weeks. Most of it by hand, mind you. Even used composite infrared scans and low-level seismic and radar sensors, so we didn't miss any hidden rooms or passages. Obviously, GPS and satellite thermal imaging is bloody useless to us that far underground."

"So what went wrong?" Helen asked.

"Dunno. That's why you're here. We expected possible booby-traps, primitive self-defense apparatus and such…" He clenched his eyes shut. "…but what happened to the first team that went in there. It just isn't physically possible. Two of them died in minutes. The third isn't expected to make it through the week."

Dr. Helen Knight listened carefully, but her eyes remained mesmerized by the pale sterile bareness of the desert floor rushing beneath them a thousand feet below. As they cleared a long ridge of dunes forming the eastern horizon she squinted against the first harsh rays of the dawning sun glaring directly into her eyes, momentarily burning a bright cascade of yellow spots into her vision. She turned back to Duncan rubbing her eyes and yawning, still tired and stiff from the long journey from New York

1

that began fourteen hours ago.

"And there's no natural explanation for what happened to them?"

"No." Duncan shook his head. "Helen, I've been in the energy exploration business for over forty years. Sunk more than my fair share of wells. The only thing I'm aware of that can put out that much lethal radiation so fast is a few thousand active fuel rods reaching critical mass during a meltdown, or pure weapons-grade plutonium a few nanoseconds before the big boom. Every REM[2] counter we have gets pegged a few seconds after the chamber door is opened. It's like they walked right into the core of an unshielded nuclear reactor, but with no warning."

"Good God," Helen murmured.

"Dr. Cromwell, the only one of the team who's still alive, and *barely* so, mind you...he managed to uh...tell us how they all, like...began choking and vomiting within a few minutes after entering the chamber. And they also experienced, like this... Oh, how did he describe it?... Incredibly fast and intolerable rise in air temperature as well. Sounded to me like they got thrown into a fucking oven, combo convection and microwave! He said they couldn't have been inside for more than five minutes before he realized the danger, turned on his heels, and ran for his life. He only made it up as far as level five on his own. By then he couldn't walk...or see anymore. Helen..." Duncan swallowed hard, "...over ninety percent of the man's body is completely cooked. Inside and out. We don't know how he's still breathing, or why. The bodies of the other two are...presumably still in there somewhere. We couldn't find them."

Helen felt a tight twinge in her stomach. "Was that *Brian* Cromwell?"

"You know him?" Duncan asked.

A thick lump swelled in her throat. She nodded with some difficulty, recalling the faint memory of a lovely dinner after a nuclear regulatory conference in London years ago. It was a delightful night filled with laughter, followed by a slow walk hand-in-hand through a quaint little park on a chilly autumn night, highlighted by a brief and exceedingly rare, albeit most welcome, kiss good-night from a very sweet man.

"An old acquaintance. The Egyptologist from Cambridge, right?"

He bobbed a curt nod. "Right. The bloke that published all those landmark studies in the eighties on the sister cities of Heliopolis. The well known one in Egypt near Cairo, and the much older Baalbek site in Lebanon. He also did all the groundbreaking work on Tanis in the Nile Delta and Tilmun in the Sinai. Believe me, he's the best that money can buy. All of them were top leaders in their fields. With a find as massive and unique

---

[2] REM – Roentgen Equivalent Man, a measurement of radiation dose levels.

as this, we had to have the best." He shook his head in frustration. "Poor bastards."

Helen did her best to push the image of Brain Cromwell's kind face out of her mind and concentrate on the urgent task at hand. She could see the massive complex approaching as their pilot slowed the aircraft, banked sharply, then circled in preparation for landing. Below them lay a vast array of oil exploration machinery and industrial drilling equipment, all deployed around a central ten-story drill rig, an imposing iron skeletal obelisk painted fire-engine red. The rig was flanked by neat rows of metal Quonset huts, tilt-up warehouse facilities, a regimented encampment of beige tents, stacks of forty-foot steel cargo containers, and a generator plant that looked like it could support a small city. A small fleet of trucks and jeeps swarmed in all directions leaving clouds of dust in their wake. The bright red Duncan International logo was emblazoned on the side of each and every one. In an open sector near the south side of the complex, apart from all the machinery and other structures, stood a towering pyramid of sand, dirt, shale and pulverized rock.

The twenty-five acre site was surrounded by a gleaming ten-foot chain-link fence, topped with coiled razor wire. Elevated guard towers marked each of its four corners. Uniformed guards, who looked to Helen more like heavily armed Special Forces soldiers than mere sentries, patiently patrolled the perimeter. It resembled a prison camp. An oddly formidable sight, she thought, considering that the remote desert location was over a hundred miles from any semblance of civilization. What were they guarding? And from whom? On the other hand, there wasn't anything overtly recognizable about the place that indicated it was no longer an energy exploration operation, but had instead been transformed into the topside base camp of what was surely about to become the most significant archaeological discovery made in over a hundred years—located almost a mile below the earth's surface.

"Andrew, who else have you invited to this party?"

He licked his dry lips and offered a brief glimmer of a smile, the first one she'd seen on his face since he'd met her personally at King Khaled airport in Riyadh just three hours earlier. "Well obviously we've had to keep an extremely tight lid on everything that's happened here over the last several months. Hundred percent top secret, don't-cha-know, tighter than a frog's asshole. I mean, if the Saudis had any *idea* of..." He stopped himself and let out a wary sigh. "Well...let's just say we'd be shut down in a hummingbird's heartbeat. Guaranteed. Only two individuals, other than yourself that is, have been called in for now. One is an old friend of yours, I believe. Dr. Jason Wise, sharp young fellow out of Pittsburgh.

And I've also called in a subject matter specialist."

"Yes, I know Jason," she nodded, but with a puzzled look of recollection. "He's an A-List astrophysicist. Works a lot of NASA contracts. I first met him when I helped him with some of his dissertation research at Carnegie-Mellon. But that was almost ten years ago. I've consulted with him on a few projects since then, but we haven't really kept in touch. What's he doing here? And who's this...*specialist?*"

Andrew Duncan hesitated before answering, either choosing his words carefully, or lying. Helen wasn't sure. "The specialist is Dr. Else Friedrich, from Munich. She bills herself as an anthropological investigator. Also a top linguistics expert. Has her PhD in ancient cultures and languages. Bizarre bitch, I promise you. Gives me the willies, if you must know. But she comes very highly recommended in her field, with top references from everyone from the British Museum to the Vatican. They're both already on site waiting for us."

A pang of realization swept over Helen. The hairs were standing up on the back of her neck. "Andrew, wait a minute. You didn't fly me halfway around the world on a moment's notice *just* to help you contain this radiation phenomenon. You think you've found something else. *Something*—"

"Just stop right there, m'lady, and don't jump to any rash conclusions." He shrugged. "The fact of the matter is, we don't know exactly *what* the hell we've found. It's a complete mystery. That's why I've brought in the best minds I could find, in a variety of areas."

She started to say something in reply.

He didn't let her, explaining, "Look Helen, I've invested over ninety million American dollars in this dig over the last eleven months, and I'm prepared to spend that much again and more, if need be. Yes, we came here for camel crude. But I'll settle for high-concentrate uranium ore, the treasures of King Tut, the Tower of Babel, or even a goddamn flying saucer. Who knows, maybe all of the above. But I *don't* intend to walk away from this dig empty handed, or let some pimple-assed goddamned government bureaucrat steal it out from under me after I've taken all the risks and seen precious lives perish in the process. I'm telling you, I've hit more than my share of dry holes from Perth to Sydney, from Texas to the Ukraine, and all over the Sinai and Persian Gulf. My gut's telling me we've hit a big one here. *Something*. I don't know what it is yet, but *something*. And my gut's rarely ever wrong."

Helen's gut was alarmingly queasy at the moment.

Andrew Duncan's smile reemerged as he patted her knee with a wink of confident assurance. "As far as the radiation containment work goes, you're the nuclear expert here, my dear Dr. Knight. So that's one-hundred percent your department, no questions asked. Anyone gives you any shit about that, you come straight to me. As I told you, you'll have whatever resources you need to get the job done—bar none. Everything you requested when we spoke two days ago is already here on site, checked out, and ready to go. Even your Iron Maiden and its Chariot from Houston are here."

"Excellent," she nodded.

Andrew rested his hand on the back of Helen's. "Helen, your containment and clean-up work after those unfortunate incidents in Russia, India, and Malaysia over the last twenty years have been more than impressive. They're the stuff of myths and legends. Bordering on the miraculous. As far as I'm concerned, your creativity and genius in conquering all this kind of hazardous shit is second to none, and that's exactly what I need right now—a *bona fide* dragon slayer. Lives depend on it. One of whom might be my own. I'm confident that if it can be done, you're the one to do it."

Helen suppressed the broad smile that was yearning to bloom in the warm light of Duncan's flattery. Professional compliments and sincere appreciation were rare in her business. Compliments in general in her personal life were rarer still. She turned her gaze back to the intricate complex below as the helicopter gently descended to alight on the landing pad, creating its own minor sandstorm in the process. Helen's brain was already its own churning cyclone of conflicting thoughts and possibilities.

Like walking into the core of an unshielded reactor? A mile below the earth's surface? Impossible. What the hell could be down there?

In less than three hours, she would see for herself.

PART I
INT⊕ THE ABYSS

"Science without religion is lame, religion without science is blind."

Albert Einstein
Out of My Later Years, 1950

"Science and religion, religion and science, put it as I may, they are two sides of the same glass, through which we see darkly until these two, focusing together, reveal the truth."

Pearl S. Buck
A Bridge for Passing, 1962

"The supernatural is the natural not yet understood."

Elbert Hubbard
The Note Book, 1927

CHAPTER I

As the surface winch slowly lowered the two-man, yellow steel cage down through the first seven-hundred meters of pitch black earth, Dr. Helen Knight kept repeating the little mantra her therapist had given her years earlier to help keep her knees from shaking.

"Safe in a cocoon, we'll be out soon..."

So far so good.

Even after so many years, at age fifty-seven, Helen still painfully fought to restrain the percolating screams of panic bottled up tightly inside her. It wasn't a condition she could just wish away, nor something that even the seasonal rains of time itself could erode and wash away. It was her constant demon. She could feel the frightening thorny pressure building up behind her breastbone, moment by moment, foot by foot, as the creaking cage descended deeper and deeper into the heart of the earth. She squeezed her eyes tight.

She shuddered. "Safe in a cocoon, we'll be out soon..."

It was her own little dark secret, but the fact of the matter was, Dr. Helen Knight had been chronically claustrophobic since childhood. She bore the unfortunate emotional scars garnered one late summer afternoon spent with her younger brother, Aubrey. It was a simple tragedy. He was six. She was nine. They were playing too close to an abandoned wishing well. He fell in trying to retrieve the old wooden water pail. She tried to help get him out and fell in, too. Just like Jack and Jill. And there she lay on top of his cold, lifeless body, crying in pain and screaming for help for almost a day and a half before being found. His neck was broken, and so was her arm. The arm healed. Her soul never did. And from that day forth, finding herself in any dark enclosed space was potentially sufficient to trigger a most violent and traumatic episode.

"Safe in a cocoon, we'll be out soon..." she repeated quietly, over and over.

"Didn't copy that," crackled the jovial and energetic voice of Dr. Jason Wise in Helen's headset. "Please repeat, Helen?"

"Nothing," Helen replied, muting her chant to a faint mumble.

She was alone, of course.

It only made sense for her to go down by herself for the first radiation risk analysis. Besides, they only had the one EVA suit onsite. The special Extra-Vehicular-Activity (EVA) space exploration suit she wore was comfortable, despite its phenomenal weight. Many elements of the suit were of her own design and specification, developed as part of a classified project she had completed for NASA two years prior. The suit was completely self-contained, was forced-air and liquid nitrogen cooled, electrically heated, and crafted as impervious as modern science could conceive to protect its wearer from extreme temperatures, heat or cold, X-Rays, Alpha and Beta particles, as well as gamma radiation. The simple lead linings of earlier generations of radiation protection apparel had been radically updated with a unique new alloy of depleted Uranium-238, one of the densest of all metals, fused with a multi-layer fabric of lead combined with fibers of twenty-four karat gold, interlaced with pure iridium.

It wasn't physically possible to move about freely in the suit except in zero gravity environments. Thus, it was mounted in a gyroscopic transport unit—a high-tech, battery powered one-man chariot with two triangular-shaped belts of titanium treads, one mounted on each side of the vehicle instead of wheels. The gyro-unit allowed movement in any direction, inclusive of climbing stairs up to a fourteen inch tread rise, merely by the rider leaning slightly in the direction one wished to travel. Actually, the only thing Helen could move freely inside the suit was her hands, which hovered above two specialized control panels and micro-keyboards, also contained within the suit.

Even Helen's face and head were completely protected. That is, there was no face mask or porthole from which to peer out. She could only see by wearing a pair of heads-up display goggles beneath the shielded helmet that was sealed to the torso of the unit at the neck, like a deep sea diver. An array of exterior cameras and sensors fed her real-time images of what it looked like outside the suit. She had a variety of viewing choices from Hi-Definition full-color video images to Infrared Thermal Imaging, or the pale greenish and ghostly white images of Night-Vision. Any combination of the two could be divided or overlaid between her left and right eye, as desired. The binocular camera array gave the illusion of unfettered three-dimensional sight, which helped assuage any perception of being locked inside a lead sarcophagus or an Iron Maiden, hence the suit's nickname. Everything she saw, heard, said or did was relayed to the surface and recorded. Presently, there was nothing to see or hear but the blur of earth and stone rising around her as she descended down the long, dark shaft.

Temperature readings read forty-seven degrees Fahrenheit. She was just over halfway down.

"How you doing?" came Jason's cheerful voice again. "How about a quick system check for me?"

Helen interrupted her mantra for a moment. "All systems five-by-five. Rate of descent still smooth at five feet per second. Temperature rising slightly. Now at fifty-one degrees."

"Any radiation?"

Helen punched a button on the control panel. A green meter appeared in her vision. "Nominal."

"Good to hear," Jason noted. "Keep an eye on that one."

"Roger that." She closed her eyes and her lips began their quiet ritual once again. *"Safe in a cocoon, we'll be out soon..."*

•

The abrupt echoing impact of the yellow steel cage reaching the stone floor at the bottom of the mile long, forty-eight inch wide shaft popped Helen's eyes open with a start and a quick gasp. The monotony of her chant had helped her doze off. It had taken twenty minutes to complete the journey from the surface.

She checked her readings and yawned, her neck popping as she cocked her head to the side. "OK, base, I'm down. Temperature is...*wow*, a balmy seventy-six degrees. Radiation levels...still normal."

"Copy that," Jason replied. "Good God, look at that."

"Look at what?" Helen was still looking at a smooth stone surface.

"Queue up your aft cameras," Jason replied. "Or turn around."

Helen leaned to her right and backward. The gyro-unit's servos hummed as the left and right treads moved in opposite directions, rotating her one hundred and eighty degrees. Her breath stilled yet again, eyes wide.

Before her lay a great cavernous hall.

It was oval in shape, roughly the size of a large aircraft hanger. Evidently, the drilling shaft had penetrated the hall at one extreme end, along a wall. The thought occurred to her that if Andrew's crews had dug a few feet further to the north, they might have missed it entirely. To her immediate left was a portable electric generator and a rack of digital radio relay equipment, all bearing the bright red Duncan International logo. Helen could hear the gentle hum of the generator. Tethered to it, via long black power cables, were a series of industrial halogen light banks. The work-lights were positioned along both sides of the hall at about ten meter intervals, brightly illuminating the entire expanse. The smooth stone interior was obviously no natural phenomenon. No, this was no cave, no volcanic bubble nor fissure. These walls were crafted of uniformly hewn and dressed rectangular stones, tightly fitted and seamed without mortar, clearly the product of skilled masons and stone cutters.

Every square inch of it was covered with pictographs and glyphs.

Andrew Duncan's voice broke in, "Helen, all the maps of the complex are loaded into your NAV system. If you punch up series one, it will indicate your current location in real-time with a red dot. But for now, just exit the main hall on the far end, and go straight ahead. Through the arch at the other end you'll find a central junction point of five corridors. Take the second one on your left until it ends. There you'll find a utility lift we've hung in what appears to be some kind of vertical air shaft. That will take you directly down to level seven. That's where you want to make your way."

"Roger that." Helen activated the gyro-unit's mechanical arm to lift the yellow cage's safety gate. When the arm was fully retracted she leaned forward. The gyro-unit rolled ahead, padding its way across the great hall on its miniature tank treads.

It took another fifteen minutes for Helen to navigate down the tall stone corridor as instructed, find the utility lift, and then ride it down to the lowest subterranean level. Visibility was extremely limited. After leaving the great hall above there were no more portable work-lights deployed. However, Helen's Night-Vision imaging showed her that she was still completely surrounded by smooth stone walls. The corridor itself was approximately ten feet wide, but twice as high.

She glanced at her instrument readings again. "Temperature is constant at seventy-six degrees. Radiation still normal."

"It will be," Duncan added, "until you reach the chamber door."

"Is it sealed?" Helen asked.

"Not any more," Duncan replied. "Just closed. It took two days worth of cutting torches to get through it initially."

"Why did you open it in the first place?" she asked.

"Self-explanatory. You'll...uh...see for yourself," came Duncan's hesitant reply. "Just keep following the main corridor directly in front of you a bit more. You're doing great. When you reach the end, you're going to enter a large antechamber. More of a foyer, I suppose you'd say. A bit garish and ostentatious for my tastes. But that's where you'll find the chamber door. Can't miss it."

Helen followed the main corridor for another hundred yards, ignoring the unending series of elevated doorways, grand arches, recessed alcoves, niches, colonnades, connecting passages and side corridors passing by her on either side. At the end of the long corridor, as promised, stood a majestic stone archway, soaring up almost three stories. Its large stones were chalky white. Limestone, perhaps, she figured, each weighing maybe two tons or more. The room beyond the arch was equipped with another one of Duncan's small portable generators along with two additional banks of halogen work-lights. They were automatically activated by motion detectors, which illuminated as soon as she rolled into the room.

Helen's entire field of vision went white.

She squinted as she switched from Night-Vision back to Hi-Def-Video mode, blinking several times until her eyes adjusted. On the other side of the archway she stopped abruptly, again staggered by what she saw.

Holy shit! Now there's something you don't see every day...

The walls before her were no longer dull, cold, gray stone. They were unmistakably covered with gold. The antechamber resembled more of an extravagantly overdone baroque cathedral or shrine—or perhaps a king's treasure chamber. A series of wide tables or altars flanked either side of the room, covered with every manner of container and serving pieces. The artwork adorning everything in the room, including the walls themselves, was stunning: high relief branches and leaves, vines and grapes, date palms and olive trees, birds of prey and fishes, cattle and livestock, exotic sea creatures and...*oh, my God*...what appeared to be some type of winged humanoids bowing in supplication. Helen took a closer look at one such human-shaped figure. It certainly wasn't the cherubic fat Gerber-baby angels of the Renaissance. No, these renderings were larger than life-sized, perhaps seven or eight feet tall she surmised, had they been standing.

"Are you getting all of this?" she whispered.

"Roger that," Jason's voice confirmed. "Unbelievable."

"Can we get back to the task at hand?" Duncan's voice interjected.

Helen faced ahead and rolled forward. Twenty yards further, on the opposite side of the antechamber, stood "The Door." The massive portal was at least ten feet in height and almost that again in breadth, smooth and glimmering in brilliantly polished gold with no visible seams. A constellation of twelve large gemstones adorned its center, arranged in three even rows of four. The door itself was hinged to Helen's left by three gold exterior hinges, each almost a yard in height. On the right side of the door, she noticed the irregularly cut and discolored metal edge from Andrew's acetylene torches, as well as a broad pool of melted and re-hardened gold spread out on the floor.

"OK, what's the trick to get in?" she asked.

"Just pull," came Duncan's reply. "It's completely inset into its jam. The goddamn thing's almost a foot thick. Can't begin to imagine how many tons it weighs. But you'll find it's balanced on its hinges so precisely and smoothly you can move it with almost no effort. Picking up any radiation yet?"

Helen glanced to the display meter. "No, nothing. All readings normal."

"OK. Are you ready?" Jason asked.

Helen took a preparatory breath. "As ready as I'll ever be. Let's see what nasty things we can find."

She activated a control panel beneath her fingertips and with a hydraulic hiss the gyro-unit's mechanical arm reached forward. With the soft buzz of its servos, the motorized pincer stabbed into the crevice cut by the torches. She used a trackball under her right forefinger to manipulate the arm, prying it with as much leverage as she could muster from the angle she was positioned.

The door swung free with a deep whoosh of air.

As it came open, Helen felt a protracted series of dull, throbbing, low-frequency waves begin to pass through her—pulsing and pulsing, slowly rising and falling in intensity. It made her teeth and sinuses hurt. All sensor readings remained stable. She rolled forward slowly, cautiously crossing the wide threshold and entering the chamber. She stopped inside to look around, bracing herself mentally for the possible sight of two irradiated and decimated corpses. Only darkness and silence lay before her, save the low throbbing pulse, rising and falling.

She rolled forward.

"*Danger. Danger. Excessive Radiation,*" blared the robotic warning voice inside Helen's earpiece. She halted her advance and glanced at the REM Counter. The digital graph had gone from near zero to a reading pegged in the red zone. Temperature readings shot up to almost two-hundred degrees. She entered a quick command, resetting the sensitivity on the REM Counter down an order of magnitude. The levels stayed maxed out. She set the calibration down once more and the readings dropped to about three quarters of the scale.

"Oh shit," she sighed as she initiated an emission analysis program.

"How bad is it?" came Jason's urgent voice, crackling and somewhat distorted amid a hissing wave of static.

"It's bad," Helen answered. "I've never seen readings like these. No living thing could endure this. They'd absorb a lethal dose of gamma radiation in seconds. At these levels, even my EVA-suit won't give me any more than twenty minutes of safe exposure in here. And then I won't be able to come back for another twenty-four hours. Gotta move quick. Starting countdown now." Her fingers quickly punched in the stopwatch settings and hit the START button. The digital timer in her upper right peripheral vision began decrementing.

"Let's hope that's enough time to find out where it's coming from," Duncan added. "And how to stop it."

"Roger that." Helen looked around, surprised to see that the chamber was perfectly circular, roughly sixty yards in diameter. She angled her cameras upward, observing that it was a perfect hemisphere above a smooth, level floor, illuminated by a pale green light emanating from the walls and domed ceiling above, a light that grew brighter by the second. The chamber appeared to be empty, with the sole exception of a small dome in the very center of the room. It was another perfect hemisphere, approximately fifteen feet in height. She approached it. The throbbing low frequency wave intensified as she drew closer.

"Hey lady, how's your levels?" came Jason's garbled voice. The hissing static storm in her ear grew worse as she moved further inside the chamber.

"Radiation is holding steady," Helen noted. "Temperature is now over four-hundred and still rising. But I'm good up to eighteen-hundred degrees, before it all starts to melt and I burst into flames. There's no visible or apparent source of the radiation that I can see. I'm going to check out this convex structure in the center."

"Copy that," Jason replied. The static in Helen's earpiece made his words a buzzing garble of distortion.

Helen rolled forward. As she neared the small center dome, she could see its surface was smooth, softly reflecting the green hue of the walls. She made one full lap around it. It was opaque, with no other distinguishable features. A movement in her peripheral vision caught her attention.

"What the hell?" She looked at her instruments. The REM Counter was holding steady at its hyper-lethal levels, but the temperature was over eight-hundred degrees.

"What is it, Helen?" Duncan's voice cut through the hiss.

"I don't know," she replied. "Hang on a second."

She angled her cameras down, not exactly believing what she was seeing. All around the perimeter of the small dome were rising ribbons of steam. She moved closer, zooming in her camera's resolution on the dome's surface. Beaded drops and tiny rivulets of what appeared to be water were cohesively collecting and running off of the little dome, vaporizing the instant they touched the superheated stone floor.

"It's melting," Helen said out loud.

"What's melting?" Duncan again.

"The dome in the center," she replied. "It looks like this thing is either made of, or covered with, a thick layer of ice. The heat is melting it."

Helen moved closer still, extending the mechanical arm of the gyro-unit once more. She used the sharp pincer to peck and chip away a small section of the dome's surface, confirming her suspicion. It was indeed ice, several inches thick, but liquefying rapidly. Temperature readings were now approaching a thousand degrees. Large pieces of ice began breaking away and sliding off the convex surface, crashing loudly onto the frying-pan-hot floor—fizzling, dancing, seething, boiling, shattering, shrinking and popping until they were completely vaporized.

"How we doing on time?" Jason queried.

"I've been in here for..." Helen answered, glancing at her timer, "...eight minutes. Ten more and I'll need to head for the exits."

"Make it seven," Jason advised, his voice now almost gone.

Helen circled around to a section of the small dome that was now completely cleared of ice. "The inner dome appears to be made of a solid material. It's reflective in nature to light, but I don't think it's stone or metal. Actually, it looks a lot like..."

"Like what?" asked Duncan.

"Like glass," she replied.

As larger and larger pieces of ice continued to break off and tumble away, Helen saw the soft green glow of the room permeating the smaller dome. It indeed had a certain degree of transparency, like a giant glass bowl turned upside down.

A loud rumble and a distinct thump to Helen's left brought her attention back to the golden chamber door. It had slammed shut of its own accord. The floor beneath her trembled.

Oh no.

A flash of panic gripped her heart. She immediately started to roll back toward the door. The gyro-unit had a top speed of fifteen miles per hour. However, before she could reach the door, the dull low frequency pulsing sensation ceased.

"Are you guys seeing this?"

There was no reply.

The static in her earpiece was gone.

"Hey, Jason? Andrew? Anyone? Can you hear me?"

Silence.

Helen's eyes went to her sensor readouts again. Surprisingly, the temperature in the chamber was dropping fast. Radiation levels were falling as well. The Max-Temp indicator showed that the ambient air temperature had reached just over twelve-hundred degrees Fahrenheit, and yet it was now down to six-hundred degrees and still falling.

None of this made any sense to her.

Her initial sense of panic and deep desire to flee gave way to a disturbing wave of confusion mixed with no small measure of bewildered curiosity. She stopped, spun around, and looked at the small dome again.

How interesting.

The glassy exterior had begun to cloud over. Soon the green glow passing through it from the walls could no longer be seen. She knew what was happening. The evaporated water molecules in the air were condensing on the cold surface again and crystallizing. Soon its shroud of ice would be securely back in place.

"Hello, upstairs," she called out once more. "Can anybody hear me?"

No reply.

"Wonderful. OK. So let's just finish up our little look-see, and then get the hell out of here," she mumbled to herself as she punched up the Infrared Thermal Imaging camera. The room went bright red. The ambient temperature readings were still above two hundred degrees, but continuing to plunge.

"How cold is this thing?"

In her heads-up display the small dome appeared as a horizontal half moon of rich violet around its edges and inky black throughout the center, quite distinct from the bright red heat signature of the walls and floor—with one exception.

How curious.

From the very center of the dome shone a small speck of white light. Helen moved closer. It couldn't have been any larger than a pinpoint, like a distant star in the night sky, shimmering slightly, fading, pulsing, twinkling.

Helen's headset suddenly crackled in her ear, then squalled and shrieked with feedback.

"Oww!" She grimaced and shook her head in pain.

The shrill tone stopped as abruptly as it came. Her ears were ringing. Her teeth hurt. The painful pressure in her sinuses was building again, its sharp talons running down the back of her neck.

And that's when she heard it.

It wasn't an audible sound in her earpiece. No, it wasn't a sensation that touched her ears at all. But heard it she did, ever so clearly and distinctly. Yes, somewhere in the back of her mind, it came through vividly, like a triggered memory, leaping forth with a sudden rush of urgent recognition.

It was a plaintive voice.

Help me.

CHAPTER 2

"*What* just happened?" Andrew Duncan ran a nervous hand over his neatly trimmed gray whiskers.

Jason's long, nimble fingers flew across his keyboard. Alternate images from remote cameras in the underground complex flashed up on a separate bank of television monitors. There was no sign of Helen on any of them.

Dr. Jason Wise was an athletic African-American man in his mid-thirties with chiseled features, closely cropped hair and deep penetrating eyes—bedroom eyes, his last girlfriend had called them, if he could re-member back that far. He continued to stare at the blank video monitor before him, visibly just as surprised and dumbfounded as Andrew Duncan. As usual, Jason wore his favorite black and gold Pittsburgh Steelers bowl-ing shirt, faded blue jeans, and well-worn high-top tennis shoes. He pulled a half-gone grape Tootsie-Pop out of his mouth, nervously tapped his low-er teeth with it for a moment, then put it back in his mouth, rolling the soggy white paper stick back and forth from one corner of his mouth to the other, narrowly missing the clear plastic boom microphone of his head-set.

Jason's brow furrowed with annoyed concentration as his fingers con-tinued to enter combinations of keystrokes. "I don't *know* what just happened. All transmission was interrupted. Maybe an equipment fuck up, or a software glitch on this end. Hang on. Give it a second. Helen, come in. If you copy, please acknowledge. We lost you on this end. If you can hear me, acknowledge."

Duncan turned to Arnold McNulty, his operations manager. "Don't wait. I want you to get four of your men in our best RAD suits and get them down in that hole immediately. Alert Dr. Markham in the infirmary. I want her out of there! And I mean fucking *now*!"

"Right away, sir." McNulty, a heavy-set man in his forties with a clean shaven head, ruddy cheeks, and scrub-brush moustache, clad in neatly starched khakis, grabbed a radio off his belt and bolted from the command trailer, issuing terse commands to unseen minions.

Jason turned to Duncan. "Andrew, that won't help. The lift is sitting at the bottom of the shaft. If something really *is* wrong, it'll take forty minutes for the first two men just to bring it up and ride back down. And then another fifteen or twenty to reach the chamber. Helen doesn't have that much time."

"Why did she have to go down there all alone?" came a calm feminine voice, spiced with a prominent German accent. All of her words which contained a hard "th" came out sounding more like "z's." "This and that" became "zis un zat." The voice belonged to the only other person present.

Duncan and Jason turned to Dr. Else Friedrich. She stood leaning back against a tall rack of computer equipment, with her long, lean arms folded tightly across her chest, watching them both intently. Dr. Friedrich was in her early forties, tall and gaunt, with short cropped black hair. She wore no make-up to speak of, and dressed predominantly in black—black pants, black hiking boots, black tee-shirt. A pair of round, gold wire-rimmed glasses sat perched on a thin pointed nose. The whole Goth ensemble would have been made complete if her complexion were ghostly white, but the stereotypical image was somewhat distorted by her darkly tanned skin, taut and leathered, evidently garnered from her many years of outdoor field work.

Duncan answered her, sounding at first almost apologetic, but with a clear note of his own frustration festering as he rambled, "No choice, really. Couldn't risk anyone else down there without proper protection. Bear in mind, that special environmental suit she has on should be more than enough to protect her. She'll be all right. You'll see."

"But you have other protection." It was more a statement than a question.

"No, not really." Duncan shook his head. "At the radiation levels we've measured down there, our standard RAD suits hit lethal exposure in less than two minutes. Barely enough time to get in and out."

Jason looked down at his watch. "Yeah, but that doesn't matter. Even inside the Iron Maiden she only has five more minutes in the safe range."

The intricate watch on Jason's wrist befit the young prodigy scientist from western Pennsylvania, who held four separate PhD's and seven technology patents in four advanced sciences: Quantum Mathematics, Computer Science, Physics, and Astrophysics. The gold and platinum encased timepiece boasted a Hi-Res digital display which normally showed a 3-D image of three analog dials for two separate time zones plus Greenwich Mean Time, all digitally synchronized within fifty milliseconds via a satellite transponder to the atomic clock at the National Institute of Standards and Technology (NIST). With the flick of a MODE switch the intricate chronometer also functioned as a wireless PDA, scientific calculator, stopwatch, compass, altimeter, underwater dive computer, and GPS receiver. Another former girlfriend called it his Geekonometer. But that was several years ago.

"*So*—then you are saying, if this is anything other than a communications failure, your men go down for recovery, not rescue. Yes?" Else was coldly matter-of-fact, taking a second to glance down at her carefully manicured fingernails painted a deep metallic purple.

Andrew's chin fell to his chest. "I'd prefer not to think of it like that just now, if you don't mind."

Else added, "You must realize that there can be no further exploration, salvage, or recovery of artifacts until the radiation threat is fully contained. If your Dr. Knight should be lost, who else can you find for this task?"

Duncan just stared at her, speechless, somewhat in disbelief. His jaw clenched tighter and tighter, his nostrils flaring with every breath.

Jason jumped in, doing his best to sound convincing, while masking his own sinking sense of dread. "All right, guys, look, come on. You know, it really *could* just be a communications failure. The heat and radiation we were measuring down there could have easily melted some of the radio circuitry, fried a PCB[3], or maybe knocked out one of the relay repeaters just outside the door. Her equipment may be suitable for walking on the sun, but our traditional shit just wasn't intended for that kind of abuse. She may still be fine. Let's give her the goddamned five minutes before we start writing any more obituaries. All right?"

Duncan broke his icy gaze with Else and turned back to the blank monitor. "Yes. That's exactly right, Jason. I appreciate your clear thinking. We'll wait five more minutes and see what happens. Helen knows what she's doing. If she can't contact us, she'll know she has to get out of there, and fast."

If she can, they all thought in unison, though no one said a word.

•

Helen glanced at her decrementing stopwatch timer. It said she had just under five minutes remaining. However, the radiation levels had fallen almost to zero. The ambient room temperature was leveling off in the mid-nineties. *Beach weather!* She was about to leave the chamber, but was still strangely intrigued and momentarily mesmerized by the small ice covered dome. Through her Infrared-Thermal Imaging cameras, the walls and floor had dimmed from their bright red glare, through muted shades

---

[3] Printed Circuit Board

of orange, softening to a cooler greenish hue. The lonely little ice dome was completely black, as inky black as deep space itself. The tiny twinkling star was gone, obscured completely by the thick encrustation of ice.

Helen wondered if she had actually heard what she thought she heard. Did something really say, *Help me?* Her rational mind told her it was nothing more than her own potent and excitable imagination, or at worst, her own internal voice sounding an urgent note of panic, a simple cry for help, echoing a sense of initial alarm from the moment the door closed—potentially trapping her inside.

AM I trapped in here?

For some inexplicable reason, at that moment, Helen didn't feel especially alarmed, nor feel the need to suddenly turn and dash to the door to find out if escape was still possible. No, something kept her undivided attention firmly fixed on the small, cold, silent ice dome. She leaned forward, and with a hum of her electric motor, rolled towards it once more. The mechanical servos driving the titanium treads clapped against the stone floor with a crisp metallic patter.

A new sound arrested her progress.

It came through her earpiece, but it wasn't a radio signal. Rather, the sound came from the external microphones on the EVA suit itself. At first, it was merely the whispering hush of a light breeze, rising and falling, like the sound of a conch shell held up to your ear at the beach. But soon it accelerated in intensity swelling into a mighty, rushing wind. In only a matter of seconds, Helen could feel the external pressure of waves of warm air in the room buffeting against her left side, threatening to topple her over. The gyroscope stabilizers could withstand over a hundred miles an hour of hurricane level force without yielding, and she was strapped in securely, but the pressure of the gale could be physically felt roughly buffeting against the suit nonetheless. She was taking a pounding. A dark thought struck her: if she did fall over, there was no getting up, and no calling for help.

Oh, shit. She grit her teeth and hung on for dear life.

The swirling storm swept around the circumference of the circular room, growing stronger and roaring louder, a veritable indoor typhoon. Ice crystals from the central dome flew off its surface and were quickly caught up in the grip of the air currents creating a glittering conical cyclone, dancing and twisting high above the center of the small convex shell. The floor trembled once again for almost ten full seconds.

Then, as quickly as it had begun, the earthquake abruptly abated, as did the fierce fury of the wind. The gusting air currents diminished with a familiar decelerating whine, akin to a jet turbine being powered down.

All grew silent and still.

Helen swallowed once and waited, not quite sure what it was she was waiting for, but feeling overwhelmed with a palpable sense of anticipation that whatever was going on, wasn't over. Her entire body was soaking with sweat. She instinctively checked her instruments one by one. The familiar routine was calming. The room temperature was now down to eighty-seven degrees. No significant radiation detected. A strange, but welcome, wave of relief washed over her. Maybe it was over.

She half-laughed to herself, "OK. What now? Rain, thunder and lightning? Hail, frogs and locusts?"

Her earpiece crackled and popped with static once more.

And then it happened again.

Help me.

"Jason?" Helen startled. "Is that you. Can you hear me? If that's you, this isn't funny, you little son of a bitch. I'm going to beat your ass as soon as I get back topside. You scared the shit out of me."

Silence.

Free me, and I shall give you the desires of your heart.

Helen froze.

"Who *is* this?" She spun the gyro-unit in a full circle looking everywhere, searching, scanning. The room was still completely empty. "*Where* are you?"

Here, in this abode. Awaiting one to awaken me and set me free.

CHAPTER 3

The Massachusetts Institute of Technology (MIT)
Cambridge, MA

"We're talking today about the Theory of Inherent or Retained Energy, which is a form of vectored inertia—that is, energy of motion headed in a specific direction, propelled by a measurable quantity of force. This is where we shall find that the basic Newtonian concepts of Potential Energy and Kinetic Energy effectively become one and the same. And what we shall see from our study over the next few weeks is that many of the fundamental postulates and underlying complex mathematics of Chaos Theory and String Theory aren't as potentially random or arbitrary as one might think. But rather, these fields of study are merely conceptual constructs and models of motion acting in perfect accord to a relative, albeit unaccounted for source of nearly infinite energy and the underlying directional influences of that energy."

Professor Christine Jacobs scanned the panorama of blank, skeptical and/or confused eyes of her undergraduate students. Confusion and ignorance she knew could easily be dispelled with the healing balm of knowledge. Skepticism, on the other hand, was an entirely different animal. Without a doubt, some forms of skepticism were healthy, constructive, and as far as she was concerned, patently *essential* to the entire scientific process of analysis and discovery. But she also knew all too well how other more insidious forms of *pseudo*-skepticism were merely wolves in sheep's clothing, feigning thoughtful debate, but wanting nothing more than to taste the hot blood of infidels who would dare challenge the well-established dogmas and doctrines with their fresh insurrectionist ideas and creative thoughts of heresy.

Oh, what truly lay lurking deep inside her students' tiny little minds and hearts at that very moment? She wasn't sure. Was it the noble inherent skepticism that dutifully challenged any new concept and made it pay its dues until proven, or was it the never ending incredulity of myopic prejudice she was forced to endure from everyone who encountered their first eighteen year-old advanced physics professor—and who had been one for the last three years?

At the tender age of eighteen, Dr. Christine Jacobs knew she certainly didn't look the part of the wizened academic or tenured professorial scholar. Oh no, far from it. But it wasn't like she could wear a sign around her neck informing the general public that she'd won both the Max Plank award in Mathematics at age ten for her research in applied physics, along with the National Academy of Science Award in Mathematics at age twelve for her two groundbreaking discoveries in quantum cryptography. Granted, it didn't help that her extremely petite frame, soft-spoken voice, and cheerful giggle that involuntarily erupted when something was truly funny, as well as when she was nervous, made her look more like a junior high-school student whose top priority was boy bands and lip gloss than a professional young adult. But that, too, was part and parcel of the lifelong dilemma of conflicting messages and contradictory cultural idioms that Christine Jacobs was forced to deal with on a daily basis.

Without exception, everyone had told her from earliest childhood that she was "pretty." Some even said she was beautiful, with her long tresses of natural brown curls framing a genuinely cherubic face and big brown eyes. On the other hand, Christine was painfully aware of how such compliments merely perpetuated the endless propaganda of female vanity, reinforcing society's cruel obsession with ascribing human worth purely in terms of external appearance and physical beauty—most of which, she believed, was perpetuated by other women.

Or was it perhaps the leg that made their brows furrow so?

Dr. Christine Jacobs wore one prosthetic limb where her right leg used to be.

Her brilliant mind repeatedly tried to tell her that her physical appearance didn't matter to her—*shouldn't* matter to her—or to anyone else for that matter. Looks were simply superficial and without intrinsic value. They didn't define the worth of the individual. She earnestly believed that. But a dark part of her soul knew otherwise, reminding her that superficialities like skin color weren't supposed to matter either. But try convincing a person of color that it was irrelevant, that their experience to the contrary was just a figment of their imagination. Oh, yes, Idealism versus Existentialism. The eternal struggle between the right and the real, perfectionism versus pragmatism. Where did the truth lie?

Christine stood ramrod straight behind her small antique handcrafted cherry wood rostrum, which was reputed to have been owned and used regularly by Benjamin Franklin himself two centuries earlier. It was a cherished gift from her father. "Furthermore, class, we shall demonstrate conclusively how Einstein's theories of both General and Special Relativity, while conceptually useful in many respects, and illustrative of numerous key scientific principles, are in fact incomplete, and postulate a set of constants and barriers that are, in may ways, misleading, if not entirely false."

A low murmur mixed with a few scattered chuckles rippled across the tiered stadium gallery of fifty souls.

"Mr. Edwards," Dr. Jacobs addressed a portly young man with long unkempt hair wearing a once-black but now faded Aerosmith tee-shirt, sitting in the second row. He had just begun to doze off, in obvious recuperation from the previous evening's celebratory escapades. Christine liked Edwards. He was exceptionally bright and witty, but woefully undisciplined academically, as well as in character by her estimation, as were virtually all of her charges.

When would they ever get serious and learn?

"Yes?" He blinked to attention, glancing about with a momentary blush, wiping one eye with his fist.

Christine folded her hands behind her back at Parade Rest, tilted her chin up, and cleared her throat. "Mr. Edwards, let's pretend that you're flying in an airplane. And since we're pretending, let's say you're a passenger seated in first class."

A titter of laughter from the back of the peanut gallery put a hint of a smile back on Christine's lips.

"OK. First class. Sweet." The young man nodded, dodging the teasing elbow of the classmate to his left.

"And let's say you're traveling from your recent exotic Spring Break vacation in Rio De Janeiro—" She paused, glancing across the class as a whole. "That's in Brazil, boys and girls, in South America on the bottom side of the planet, for those of you who haven't taken Professor Grossman's geography course yet."

More giggles.

Back to Edwards. "That's right, Mr. Edwards, you're on your way to Cairo, Egypt to see the Great Pyramids of Giza. Your plane is traveling east by northeast with a ground speed of 600 miles an hour, or approximately 1,000 kilometers per hour. That's ten miles, or just over sixteen kilometers, per minute. Or one mile every six seconds. Or half a mile, almost a full kilometer, every three seconds. Everyone with me?"

Lots of nods and murmurs of assent.

"Good. In your hand, Mr. Edwards, you find a fuzzy yellow tennis ball. You toss your tennis ball straight up into the air and catch it. The tennis ball's flight takes exactly three seconds. The height of the toss is three feet above your hand, and your hand remains stationary until you catch the ball on its way down. So the question becomes, how far did the tennis ball actually travel in those three seconds, and in what direction or directions did it travel?"

Edwards straightened up in his chair and coughed, "Umm. Well...uh...since I'm in a plane going 600 miles an hour and not sitting still, then I think the ball went one kilometer, plus six feet in a shallow rise convex arc."

"You think so? It didn't look that way to you," she replied. "In terms of Relative Velocity, to you, it just flew up three feet, gravity arrested its ascent and pulled it back down, whereupon it traveled down three feet, for a grand total of six feet of total distance traveled. Right?"

"But that's not it's total movement," Edwards objected. "You have to take into account the movement of the airplane."

"Ah ha!" She raised an index finger. "The movement of the plane. OK. How many of you agree that we need to factor in the movement of the plane?"

Most of the hands in the class tentatively slid up.

"All right, now tell me this, all of you who think we need to factor in the speed and direction of the plane. Do you also think that this additional information will give us the truest perspective, the best and final answer, of absolutely how far and in what direction or directions our ball has traveled?"

A couple of the raised hands went down.

Christine's hands went to her narrow hips, at the waistband of her skirt, pulling her elbows slightly forward. She pursed her lips for second, then took a deep breath and launched into rapid-fire cadence, "I mean, if we're going to factor in the movement of the plane, both in terms of velocity and direction, then that's only going to give us an answer relative to what someone standing on the ground would perceive. Is *that* really our true path? I mean, what if we're on the international space station orbiting the earth? The earth itself is rotating. Right? So our airplane ride from Rio to Cairo along the equator should also take into account the full rotation of the earth, which when we're flying from west to east is coincident with the spin of the globe, which has a velocity of a little over a thousand miles an hour, considering the fact that the earth at its equator is a little over 24,000 miles in circumference and takes twenty-four hours to complete one full revolution, which we refer to as a Day. And that factor would also add a greater degree of arc to our flight trajectory factoring in the addition of the curvature of the earth's surface.

"*But*...the earth *itself* we learn is in orbit around the sun, moving at about thirty kilometers per second, or roughly 60,000 miles per hour. So depending on whether our trip is occurring during the day or night, that factor has direct bearing on whether we are benefiting from the speed of the planet moving in the direction of the solar ecliptic and therefore accelerating, which happens at night when our position on the earth at the equator is facing away from the sun, or decelerating when our position is rotating against the planetary ecliptic during the day, when facing the sun.

"And then there's the added effect of the balance between the forces of the sun's gravity offset by the earth's centrifugal force which sustains the Earth's orbit within the solar ecliptic, as well as the Earth's own gravitational force exerted on both the plane and the ball. But before we factor in all of that, we need to remember that the entire solar system itself rotates within the Milky Way Galaxy at 225 kilometers per second, or roughly 450,000 miles per hour. And the galaxy itself is part of a galaxy cluster, which rotates within the context of the known universe..."

Professor Jacobs paused to take a breath. All eyes were wide and most lips were parted. It was the desired effect she was hoping to achieve.

She smiled. "So needless to say, our little tennis ball may have traveled quite a long way and at a tremendous velocity in those three seconds, in a most bizarre and circuitous direction."

General laughter.

Christine walked with an almost unnoticeable limp to the blackboard and picked up a fresh stick of white chalk. "But two key points are most relevant here." The chalk clicked and screeched against the board as she wrote. "One. Within each closed domain of perspective, which I will refer to as a unique and separate universe, each domain represents a place where a uniform set of physical laws *appears* to apply. That is, laws which are thought to behave *normally* for those elements inside that particular closed universe, but in fact may behave completely different from any other domain or universe."

Debbie Crow threw a quizzical look at Edwards. He shrugged in reply.

"For with respect to Mr. Edwards sitting there in first class, the relative behavior of his tennis ball appeared to him to fly normally straight up and straight down, a simple six foot journey. End of story. No big deal, because we understand the basic concept of relative velocity. Yet, point number two is this." Her chalk went into crisp motion again. "All the other domain perspectives, or universes as we call them here, universes that are completely invisible to Mr. Edwards, are still very much acting upon the ball, even if he can't see it or perceive it from his perspective."

Debbie Crow's hand went up. "But Dr. Jacobs, if the concept of relative velocity means things behave as normal in a closed system or universe, then what's the relevance or relative influence of any other universe?"

Christine finished writing her second point, returned her chalk to the worn wooden tray and turned around. "Good question. All right, Ms. Crow. This time we're going to put you sitting in the back of a pick-up truck. Your driver is cruising down the highway at sixty miles an hour. You have a baseball in your hand. You're a pretty good pitcher, albeit not playing for the Red Sox. And on a good day, let's say you can throw a baseball at sixty miles an hour."

More giggles.

"Shut up," Debbie chastened the class over her shoulder with an *It Could Happen* tone.

Christine continued undaunted by the interruption. "So let's say you throw your ball out of the back of the truck, and the ball quickly accelerates away from you to its maximum velocity of sixty miles an hour relative to you. What does it *look* like to you sitting in the back of the truck?"

"Like I threw the ball normally." Debbie was confident in her answer.

"Exactly," Christine nodded. "But if a hitchhiker was standing on the side of the road and saw you throw the ball, what would it look like to him?"

Debbie frowned for a moment, then ventured, "Like I just dropped it out the back?"

"Close." Christine turned to the board again, picked up her chalk and illustrated the ball's flight as she spoke. "During the period of acceleration, it would have appeared to the hitchhiker as if the ball were trying to follow the truck for a moment, but losing ground quickly. But as the ball reached its top speed of sixty miles per hour, countering the full Retained or Inherent Energy of the truck's imputed velocity, it would have looked like it came to a stop, and then fallen to the ground, as pulled down by the earth's gravity."

Debbie was nodding. Others in the room were too, all scrawling notes.

"On the other hand," Christine went on, "had you thrown the ball in the same direction that the truck was moving, and for the sake of discussion here, let's presume wind resistance wasn't an issue, then the energy of your sixty mile an hour throw would have been added to the truck's sixty miles an hour of imputed velocity, or inherent energy, and the hitchhiker would have thought you were able to throw a ball at 120 miles an hour."

She had everyone's rapt attention.

"So from the perspective of our hitchhiker standing on the side of the road, depending solely on which direction you threw the ball, you either accomplished nothing, or you threw it faster than any professional major league pitcher. Yet to you, in both instances, the ball went from a position of rest, Point A, to some location, Point B, at sixty miles per hour, behaving just as if you weren't in the truck, but were throwing the ball standing on level ground." She turned to Mr. Edwards. "So I ask you again, Mr. Edwards, how far and in what direction did your tennis ball fly?"

"From who's perspective?" he asked with a smile.

"Exactly," Christine nodded. "Very good. Let's move on. You all know the basic law of physics which states: any object at rest will remain at rest unless acted upon by an external force. I contend for your consideration, based upon what we've just discussed, that this fundamental postulate is inherently flawed. For you see, ladies and gentlemen, the entire concept of 'at rest,' and I mean this in a very literal sense, is a complete and utter illusion. There is no such thing. The concept must be stricken from your thinking. For in fact, everything in this room, ourselves included, is moving through space at this exact moment at tremendous velocity due to the earth's rotation, added to the planet's movement along the solar ecliptic, added to the solar system's march around the galaxy, and so forth. And by definition, all movement necessitates energy. So even though an object may appear to be at rest, stationary to the naked eye in the local domain or universe, it still contains all the imputed inertia, that is, all of the relative inherent energy of all the other universes to which it is associated and moves within—the same as Mr. Edward's tennis ball and Ms. Crow's baseball did inside the airplane and in the back of the pick-up truck respectively."

Little lights of understanding were coming on in the students' eyes.

Christine turned back to Debbie. "Let's go one step further to illustrate the power of this imperceptible energy source. For example, Ms. Crow, if your pick-up truck were to meet with misfortune and run headlong into a solid wall at sixty miles an hour, despite you sitting there perfectly still in the back of the truck, you would in all likelihood be killed, even if nothing directly struck your body. The cause of death would be from the sheer force of the retained energy of the truck's velocity crushing your body, despite your senses having equalized to it and becoming unaware of it. The same is true for Mr. Edward's plane impacting with a mountain. In one moment, everything around you inside the passenger cabin appears still and normal. You toss the ball. You catch it. You are oblivious to the tremendous energy that every molecule of your body is retaining. And in the next moment, when a force capable of countering that energy is applied, like an immovable mountain, you suddenly experience its devastating effects."

Chins were nodding. More notes were being scribbled.

Professor Jacobs returned to her rostrum. "It is my contention that this retained or inherent energy exists within all matter in the known universe. I'm convinced, based upon my own research and analysis, that if properly analyzed and understood relative to the curved orbital vector influences of relative universes, that this very same inherent or retained energy can be *harnessed* and *employed* in the base universe, that is, from the observer's local perspective, literally used to defy the laws of three-dimensional Newtonian physics. We shall conceptually demonstrate this in our lab exercises in the coming weeks. And hopefully, in years to come, we'll find ways to practically apply and benefit from this concept."

The class was reverently silent.

Christine closed her lesson plan. "I want each of you to begin thinking about what we've discussed here today, and come to class next time fully prepared to discuss the following topics: One, how can Einstein's long held contention that the speed of light cannot be broken possibly be true, especially in light of the fact that according to his own theorem to do so requires infinite energy and infinite mass, and yet obviously the photons of light itself seem to accomplish this feat quite nicely without the need of infinite energy or infinite mass? This is a variation of the old quandary which asks: if you were flying though space in a rocket, and accelerated to the speed of light, and then turned on your headlights, what would happen?"

That merited a few giggles.

"Two, how can the speed of light therefore be broken using our pick-up truck and baseball throwing analogy? Three, is the shortest distance between two points *really* a straight line?" She paused with a mischievous grin. "And four, before you answer item number three, define the very concept of a straight line in light of the fact that, as we discussed today, no two points anywhere in the known universe are ever fixed, or are ever really at rest."

Christine felt good. Mission accomplished. She couldn't wait to blow their minds in three weeks when she shattered all their elementary notions of the space-time continuum, not to mention the very concept of time and the elemental nature of matter itself. She watched her students filing out of the lecture hall, all abuzz in inspired conversations, when her teaching assistant, Darren Kirby, came up holding out her cell phone to her.

"Who is it?" She was almost finished packing up her book bag.

"A Dr. Helen Knight. Long distance," Darren replied. "She said it was important, but I didn't want to interrupt your class."

"Thanks," she mouthed silently, taking the phone and exclaiming, "Professor Knight, is it really you?"

"Christine, I'm sorry to bother you at work," came the urgent, but familiar and welcome voice of Dr. Christine Jacob's very own advanced physics professor of four years ago. As usual, Helen Knight came right to the point. "I need you. How soon can you be on a flight to Saudi Arabia?"

CHAPTER 4

"I've already told you. As soon as I pushed the door open to leave, within ten seconds or so the radiation alarms in the EVA sounded again, and the air temperature began to rise, just like the first time."

Dr. Helen Knight sat in a molded plastic chair at one end of a stainless steel conference table with Andrew Duncan, Dr. Jason Wise, and Dr. Else Friedrich. She took a sip of water from her plastic bottle. The water hadn't been out of the ice chest for five minutes and it was already warm. The main Quonset Hut where they were assembled was the traditional Gomer Pyle USMC styled half-pipe architecture. The windows were nothing more than cutout metal flaps, hinged and propped open with a metal rod. Four oversized pole-mounted oscillating fans pushed the stiflingly warm dusty desert air around the room. The fans helped a little, but by late afternoon it was already well over 110 degrees in the shade, and nothing really helped. And they certainly didn't deter the hungry scavenger flies and clouds of gnats that swarmed to the scent of human sweat.

Andrew's shirt showed dark sweat stains in the armpits and in the center of his chest. His cheeks were flushed bright pink. "And you saw no direct source of the emissions?"

Helen shook her head. "Nothing. I'm certain it wasn't coming from the central structure, because it was completely covered in a thick layer of ice, melting from the outside in. It should have vaporized completely if something underneath wasn't keeping it super-cooled. I suspect the radiation was somehow integral to the construction of the walls themselves, something synthetic, definitely not a natural phenomenon. The walls possessed a greenish iridescence, which grew brighter in intensity as the radiation levels increased. Who knows, perhaps there really are some kind of enriched uranium-based control rods that are raised and lowered within the walls to start and stop the process. I just don't know."

Jason huffed, "If what you're saying is true, then that would indicate that there's an active detection and response capability functioning down there. I mean, we're talking about something really powerful, something that's still working after however many hundreds or thousands of years it's been sitting idle, buried down there."

Helen shrugged. "Well, if it's nuclear-based, the half-life of some materials just happens to be measured in thousands, if not billions, of years. So unless the passage of time alone caused some portion of it to malfunction, its longevity is not that miraculous."

"It's *not?*" Jason was flabbergasted. "Bullshit."

"It doesn't matter." Duncan cut them off. "The only thing that matters now is how do we contain it? What's the plan?"

"I'm not sure yet," Helen replied. "We need more data. But one thing is very clear to me. I believe the radiation system, however it operates, is there to serve as some kind of a self-defense mechanism, to keep any living thing from gaining access to the central structure inside."

"Why do you say that?" asked Jason.

"Because after the onslaught of the radiation and direct heat, which would have not only killed, but effectively incinerated anything inside the chamber, all that was followed by a powerful air stream that engaged for several seconds, maybe a full minute, which I could swear sounded very mechanical in nature, like an electrical turbine. I felt like I was standing in a wind-tunnel. It conceivably could have cleaned up and ventilated any evidence of an intrusion quite nicely. I never actually saw any open supply or exhaust vents, but that doesn't mean there weren't any in there somewhere. Regardless, it could explain why there was no trace of your other team members."

"Amazing," was all Duncan could say.

"So then what the hell is it protecting?" Jason walked over to an ice chest and pulled out a cold bottle of apple juice.

Helen was about to say something, but caught herself. Thus far, she'd not told a soul about hearing any "voices" in the chamber. She still wasn't absolutely sure if it had really happened, or if it was just a figment of her own claustrophobically influenced imagination.

Dr. Else Friedrich spoke up. "I may be able to help with this question. Since I arrived onsite yesterday, I have been studying most carefully some of the photographs taken over the last few weeks of the main entrance hall on level one, as well as analyzing images captured by Dr. Knight's cameras from the gilded antechamber on level zeeben...uh...seven. The language on the walls on level one undoubtedly predates that of anything contemporaneously indigenous to this region of the world. It isn't any form of early Arabic, Egyptian, Hebrew, or even Aramaic. It's very sophisticated. I think it's definitely Semitic in nature, but clearly predates Akkadian, Assyrian, or even Chaldean culture. I'd say it's more akin to the pictographs of the early Sumerians of Mesopotamia, pre-Babylonian, circa 4000 B.C."

"Four *thousand* B.C.?" It was Andrew's turn to be incredulous. "Oh, for fuck sake, you must be joking."

Else nodded, "Or older. Perhaps much older. It looks a great deal to me like similar writings and inscriptions I've seen on thousands of clay tablets and seals from my digs along the lower Euphrates in southern Iraq, specifically in finds at Eridu and Ur, in your biblical antediluvian Land of Ur. The mother country of Abraham. Interestingly, I must point out, is that the information found here at this site isn't the usual litany of epic tales of mythical heroes or some forgotten king's long-winded sagas of ambition and conquest, or epic poems, hymns and tributes to a pantheon of ill-tempered celestial deities, or the sexual misadventures of promiscuous demigods."

"Well, what is it then?" Helen sipped her water.

Else frowned, characterizing her observation. "I would have to say that this information seems to me to be more...*technical* in nature. Mostly long columns of numbers and complex calculations. From what I can decipher, there are many references to what I believe are star constellations, the movements and patterns of the stars, as well as the sun, moon, and neighboring planets of our solar system."

This topic was of great interest to Jason. "No shit? So what exactly do you mean by the *movements* of the stars and planets?"

"Just what I said," she quipped, as if irritated by the interruption. "They speak of the orbits, or *destinies* as they're called, of the gods of the heavens, which are detailed depictions of their comings and goings, with intricately plotted distance, bearing and azimuth measurements, and what appears to me to be some type of intricate calendar references with respect to the alignments of entire constellations. I would need to go down there myself and do a much more detailed study to tell you more."

"And so you shall," Andrew prompted.

"Oh no I won't," Else fired back. "Not until you can assure me it is completely safe to do so. Dr. Knight herself confirms that this place has the ability to detect intruders and defend itself with terrible force. How do we know when we are safe from *all* of its defenses? Perhaps there are more, as yet undiscovered."

"Well, perhaps some piece of information down there will tell us what we need to know on that very point. In case you forgot, that's why you're here," Andrew pointed out. "Yes, Else, to be sure, there is indeed some measure of risk involved in this venture, great risk in fact, as we have painfully witnessed. However, correct me if I'm wrong, but your reputation isn't that of one who's shown any degree of reticence in the face of potential dangers to life and limb."

"*Quatsch!*[4]" Else fumed. "This circumstance, Mr. Duncan, is quite different, to say the least. No? Granite, marble, limestone, mud and clay don't try and burn you to death."

"They can sure as shit fall on your ass," Jason whispered under his breath with a suppressed smile of sarcasm.

"The main complex appears to be completely safe," Helen interjected, oblivious to Jason's remark, "as long as the gold door to the inner chamber remains closed. It has to be the triggering mechanism for the defense system inside."

"This idea is pure speculation. You have no way of knowing this for sure," Else countered. "You are guessing. No?"

"No!" Andrew jumped in. "Helen's right. I know for a fact that for over a month my men moved all over the complex and didn't encounter anything even remotely dangerous, not a single loose rock or sharp corner. Nothing happened, until we breached the seal on the door of the chamber and opened it."

Helen added, "And don't forget, this defense system, regardless of whatever is powering it, shuts itself down after about ten or twelve minutes inside. Both radiation and temperature fall quickly back into the safe range."

Jason said, "Yeah, but we only have one EVA suit available. Only one of us at a time could survive in there until it shuts down. So that doesn't do us much good, if, as you say, the minute you open the door again, it starts back up again."

Else didn't miss a beat, jumping on Jason's line of reasoning. "Yes! Releasing radiation throughout the whole complex, killing us all!"

Andrew Duncan leveled a stern glare at Else. "Well then, Dr. Friedrich, if you have no intention of assisting us any further, then it really doesn't make much sense for you to remain here on site. Now does it? I'll be more than happy to terminate your contract, effective immediately. Is that what you want?"

Else's icy stare held fast for several seconds, but eventually yielded. She wiped the beads of sweat off her brow with the back of her hand, carefully measuring each of the expressions of the other three staring back at her before apologizing. "*Ja, ja. Es tut mir leid*[5]. I will go down to the complex and help translate more of these writings and inscriptions, as you have contracted me. I do my job." She raised a conditional finger. "But I am willing to do so only if this golden door of yours remains closed at all

---

[4] German: "Nonsense."
[5] German: "Yes, yes. I'm sorry."

times for as long as I am down there."

"Agreed," Andrew replied.

Else added, "And you also must clearly recognize that even with my help there can be no guarantees whatsoever that the information you seek in order to thwart the extraordinary defenses of this mysterious fortress will be found conveniently printed in plain sight. I am quite certain a culture sophisticated and advanced enough to construct such a bastion as this, with such deadly capabilities, isn't stupid enough to hang a sign pointing to the OFF switch. No?"

Andrew sighed, "Of course not. But anything that helps us better understand what we're dealing with down there brings us that much closer to being able to confront it. What's so hard to understand about that?"

"I am merely trying to tell you plainly that the very task of investigation could take years," Else pointed out, "even if we had a team of the best ancient scholars and translators in the world."

"I *know*!" Andrew shot back. "But your services and talents are all we have right now. It isn't like we can just sit down and talk to whoever built this place and have them explain how it all works to us. Now can we?"

Despite the palpable heat in the room an icy chill ran up Helen's spine. She started to say something, but didn't. From the moment she left the chamber two hours earlier, she had decided that no one would know all the details of what had transpired down there, especially regarding what she thought she "heard," until she knew a great deal more herself.

Andrew still tried to reason with Else. "Else, I can assure you that every precaution will be taken to protect everyone down there. Myself included."

"You are coming down as well?" Else challenged, her disbelief apparent.

"Yes," Andrew didn't flinch. "I'm not afraid to do anything that I'd ask anyone else to do."

Else laughed out loud, breaking the tension in the room. "OK. *Sehr gut*, Herr Duncan! Very well, then. If we must go down, we go down in the abyss together."

Else's double-entendre wasn't lost on Helen. She took the occasion to speak up, thankful for an excuse to change the subject. "Just so everyone knows, I spoke with Professor Christine Jacobs at MIT about an hour ago. She's one of my former students, as brilliant as they come. Upon Andrew's approval and most generous invitation, she's agreed to join us, and should be here on-site sometime tomorrow."

"Who is this Christine Jacobs?" Else raised an eyebrow.

Helen smiled. "Someone who knows more about solving riddles and unlocking mysterious locks than anyone I've ever met."

Else was about to say something when the door to the Quonset Hut opened. All eyes turned in the direction of the sound.

"Mr. Duncan!" Arnold McNulty came rushing through the door.

"Yes?" Andrew turned to the door. "What is it?"

McNulty looked grave. "Sorry to interrupt, sir. It's Dr. Cromwell. In the infirmary."

"Is he—" Andrew bit off the word.

McNulty vigorously shook his head. "No, not yet, sir. But Dr. Markham says it's most urgent."

"If you'll all excuse me." Andrew politely nodded at the group.

"No, sir," McNulty stopped him. "Not you, sir. Dr. Cromwell is calling for Dr. Knight. He wants to see her right away."

Andrew turned to Helen. "Helen?"

Helen rose, a pang of dread stabbing her heart. "Of course."

CHAPTER 5

Dr. Helen Knight was a consummate scientific professional. She was one of the world's leading experts in applied nuclear physics, and an active member of the United Nations' International Atomic Energy Agency, the IAEA. She was thoroughly acquainted with all of the horrors associated with the dark side of that unique discipline of modern science. But nothing in her wealth of expertise prepared her for the sight of Brian Cromwell lying beneath a cellophane canopy in the make-shift Infirmary.

Severe radiation burns are indeed burns, but are not synonymous with the injuries sustained by the victims of common fires. There isn't the blackened charring of the skin per se, or the pungent smell of burnt and rotting flesh. But burned they are. The skin is bright red and inflamed, literally cooked from the inside out, like in a microwave oven. Actually, the smell can be much worse. Some areas of the skin can open up, creating deep lesions, fissures and holes, sometimes exposing raw viscera and bone. The gamma rays themselves destroy cells, and are also known to scramble the DNA code in surviving cells. So even if a victim lives, rapidly growing cells, mutations, and cancers are common.

Dr. Cromwell was practically mummified in gauze bandages, most of which were soaked through with blood and pus. A morphine drip was tethered to his right arm. His eyelids were shriveled back, revealing eyes that were now nothing more than cloudy white orbs, boiled as solid as a ten minute egg. His hair and teeth were gone. His gums bled continuously. His lips and cheeks were swollen to about three times normal. Helen had no idea how the man could still be alive. Her eyes puddled with tears and her chin began to tremble the instant she saw him.

Dr. Kenneth Markham, the infirmary's primary physician, a soft-spoken, fatherly gray-haired elder gentleman in his mid-sixties, handed Helen a dosimeter, which she clipped to her shirt pocket. He advised, "No more than ten minutes. He's still hot."

Helen nodded. She knew she dared not stay long.

Dr. Markham pulled back the side of the thin plastic canopy to allow Helen to lean down near Dr. Cromwell's inflamed lips. She almost gagged as the stench of living death hit her square in the face. Thankfully, the

36

small infirmary hut was well air-conditioned and ventilated, one of only three buildings on-site to enjoy such an amenity; the other two being Andrew Duncan's personal quarters and the explosives storage facility. It was noticeably cool in the room, almost chilly. Nevertheless, Helen was soaked to the skin with sweat.

"Brian," she called out, almost afraid to speak. "It's Helen. Brian, I'm here. Can you hear me?"

The wet, raspy wheezing stilled for a second. The body stirred with a sense of recognition. The bright red swollen lips trembled. His words were but a pained whisper. "Helen...*d-don't*..."

Helen dearly wanted to take his hand, to feel it again pressed against her own, but she feared how much more pain she would add to his suffering with even the slightest pressure. "Don't *what*, Brian?"

He fought to squeeze the words out. "Don't...g-g-go d-down. *No.*"

She took a careful breath. "It's OK, Brian. I've already been down inside the complex. It was OK. I'm fine."

"The d-door," he spat. "Don't...go...through the *door.*"

She felt both confused and oddly alarmed at the same time. The hairs were standing at attention on the back of her neck again and tingling down her arms. "I know about the radiation danger, Brian. It's all right. I have appropriate protection. I have the Iron Maiden here, the EVA-7. It worked perfectly. I was fine."

Brian's whole body began to tremble, twists of agony played across his mutilated, blistered face. "You've been...*inside?*"

"Yes," she nodded. "The radiation abates completely after ten or twelve minutes. Then it's perfectly safe."

"No," he huffed. A thick tendril of saliva mingled with blood snaked down the corner of his mouth. "Don't go back inside... *Not* safe."

Helen leaned closer. "Not safe from *what?*"

"*Watch—*" A fierce seizure gripped the poor man, cruelly arching his spine up off the soaked bed linens, gruesomely distending his jaw in a quaking silent scream. The acrid stench of urine filled the air. When the quaking in his body subsided, he wheezed and swallowed. A dark effluence of blood began to trickle down his upper lip out of both nostrils, winding slowly down into his mouth.

His tortured voice had all but evaporated, "...not safe... from...*him.*"

"From *who?*" Helen demanded, her hands trembling.

Dr. Helen Knight continued to mutely stare at the motionless body on the bed for almost five full minutes, patiently waiting for an all important answer, that sadly, would never come—could never come. For Dr. Brain Cromwell, renowned scholar of antiquities and ancient cultures, was dead.

CHAPTER 6

The Mediterranean Sea
Near the Isle of Capri, Italy

It was a perfect day.

Sunlight graced the entire expanse of a cloudless blue sky, penetrating and gently browning the skin, leeching out any semblance of stress or care, in exchange for a relaxing, hypnotic energy of its own. The salty air was warm, sultry, sensuous, its gentle wisps and caresses intimately invigorating and arousing. A lone gull shrieked as it winged past the one-hundred and twenty foot Hatteras luxury motor yacht which lay anchored in the calm, pristine turquoise waters. Visibility was crystal clear down to the sugar white sea floor and multicolored formations of coral and barnacle encrusted rocks over one-hundred feet below. The only other sounds intruding upon the serene stillness of the moment were the languid laps of the waves against the boat's handcrafted hull, and the intermittent slurps and occasional glottal grunts of the dark haired young peasant girl's head bobbing up and down over Jean-Marc Xavier's lap. He reached for his glass of champagne.

Ah, yes, a truly perfect day.

The compact silver satellite phone on the table nearby began to play Mozart's *Eine Kleine Nacht Musik. Bum...bom-bum...Bom-bum-bom-bum-Bum-BUM!*

The girl paused in her task, her large brown doe eyes questioning.

"*Non, non, cherie, pas l'arrêt*...eh...don't stop." Jean-Marc smiled, grabbing the phone, nodding that she should continue. "*Plus, plus, s'il vous plait. Tu est tres bien, mon petite fleur*[6]! *Molto Bene!* as you say. Ooo, la, la."

Her eyes cast back down as her glistening smile once again devoured him, her eager-to-please expression soon veiled behind a slowly undulating curtain of her shimmering black mane. Ooo, she *was* good, especially for a man of his stature.

---

[6] French: "More, more, if you please. You are very good, my little flower."

Jean-Marc Xavier was indeed a very large man, in all physical dimensions, powerfully built, fit and strong, standing over six and a half feet tall, which he knew instantly intimidated others in his presence, and delighted his paramours in situations such as the one he found himself at that moment. He blissfully leaned his head back into the thick embrace of the white leather deck chair on the upper level aft deck. They were alone. The ship's crew and his personal staff were given leave to take the motor launch to the island for a day of their own individual enjoyment and recreation.

Jean-Marc's thumb silenced Mozart. *"Oui?"*

It was Mohammed's familiar voice. *"Monsieur* Xavier?"

"Oui."

"My man on-site brings us a most unusual report."

Jean-Marc sipped his champagne. "Unusual, how do you say?"

"There is talk of a significant archaeological find. Treasure. Gold."

Jean-Marc returned his Baccarat crystal champagne flute to the marble table top to his left and absently ran his fingers through the girl's silky smooth hair, hot to the touch from the sun. He pushed back a section of her hair behind her right ear to better enjoy an unobstructed view of her delightful talents. "I have no need of trinkets. I have many mansions filled with trinkets, priceless art and countless treasures of antiquity from six continents."

"Exactly. Which is why such a lie makes a perfect cover story for the Saudis and the Americans."

"Go on." Jean-Marc was interested now, but it was becoming most difficult to maintain his concentration.

"There are reports of casualties. It is evident that these events are attributed to extreme radiation exposure."

"You are certain of this?" Xavier's brows knit together.

"I would not tell you so if I were not. We believe the Americans are working under the auspices of an Australian development corporation to install a large subterranean nuclear reactor complex for the production of advanced weapons systems in the region."

"That's a bold accusation, *mon ami.*"

"A country so rich in oil certainly doesn't need a nuclear plant to produce energy. They apparently seek to hide it deep in the bowels of the earth, away from prying eyes in the sky. It would explain the accidents and the presence of such heavy security."

Jean-Marc's breath stilled for a moment as his pleasure began to peak. He let out a long relaxing breath, forcing himself to maintain control and focus on the import of his call. He ran his free hand through his long snow white hair, pulling a long lock out of his face and tucking it behind his ear. "Do you think the Israelis are aware of this? If *you* know about it, then surely the Mossad must as well. *N'est pas?* They know who comes and goes, who buys and sells. They certainly have their very own intelligence satellites. *Mon Dieu, mon ami, we* sold them two of them!"

"Whether they know about it or not, I cannot tell you for a certainty, monsieur. I can only tell you what I do know. But one thing is sure. If the Israelis *don't* know of this yet, they will pay handsomely for such information. And if the Americans are helping the Saudis to achieve independent nuclear status, *they* will pay handsomely to keep anyone else from knowing it as well."

"Or both!" Jean-Marc laughed.

"Or both," the voice repeated, joining in Jean-Marc's laughter.

Jean-Marc wondered out loud, "But what if you are mistaken? What if this endeavor is not a nuclear reactor or a secret weapons development facility at all? What if it is something else entirely? I mean, have you heard nothing else? No other rumors or suspicions? Speculations? Anything?"

"As I said, we know nothing for certain, but our speculations only grow stronger with each passing hour. I am expecting more information very soon. Andrew Duncan brings in more experts each and every day. Yesterday a top nuclear scientist, a Dr. Helen Knight from the International Atomic Energy Agency. Very senior. And today, a top mathematician arrived from the MIT in the United States. A professor of advanced physics. A Dr. Christine Jacobs. Both American. These are not grave robbers or common oil field workers."

"How...*interesting*..." Jean-Marc's mind was spinning faster. As he considered all the possibilities and permutations his heart started to pound. The lovely young maid kneeling between his thighs must have sensed it as the pace and depth of her undertaking both quickened and deepened in kind. Jean-Marc swallowed with a measure of difficulty. "Call me as soon as you get your next report."

Jean-Marc never heard his caller's reply. His thumb squeezed the phone's END button, more out of reflex than volition, in concert with every muscle in his body going taut, his lungs seizing, his eyes clamping shut, teeth clenched. Time stood still for one perfect, heavenly moment as pulse after pulse of pure pleasure released.

C'est magnifique!

When he could breathe again, he opened his eyes to see the girl lift her head and sit up, slowly releasing him from the captivity of her warm, wet, slightly swollen lips. She offered him the same radiant smile that had caught his eye in the discothèque in Florence the night before.

"*Tres bien, mon cherie,*" he sighed. "*Pardon moi...eh...commo vous applez vous?*[7]"

She frowned, "Sophia."

"*Ah, oui, oui, Sophia,*" he nodded with a fairly convincing display of feigned recollection. "Your sweet charms have stolen away both my heart and my mind. I am bewitched. In your presence I will surely forget my own name if I am not careful. Oh, but how could I forget one so lovely, one so talented and generous. *Merci beaucoup*...Sophia."

Sophia stood and walked to the ship's teakwood rail, turned around, and filled her lungs to capacity with the soothing breath of the sea. She lifted her face into the bright wash of the sun, arching her back and letting its rays envelop the whole exquisite landscape of her bare bronzed body. Jean-Marc just sat there admiring the exotic view in all its splendor, not even bothering to pull up his swim trunks, which were lying on the deck at his feet, still hanging from his right ankle.

As far as he was concerned, it truly was a perfect day.

---

[7] French: "Very good, my dear. Pardon me,...eh... what is your name?"

CHAPTER 7

"I don't see that we have any other choice but to attempt another reconnaissance survey inside the chamber with the Iron Maiden." Helen was adamant.

Dr. Christine Jacobs stood staring at the gold door, examining the large, exquisitely cut and highly polished jewels mounted in its face. "I don't see why? You indicated it was completely empty, with the sole exception of the central convex structure covered with ice."

Christine had been onsite now with the rest of the team for a day and a half. Most of the group had already grown used to "the whiz kid." Jason took an instant liking to her, playful and flirtatious. Else was aloof towards her. Andrew seemed a little afraid of her, intimidated by her dizzying intellect. But, as expected, there were abundant hugs and kisses from Helen, mixed with squeals of reunion from the moment the young MIT professor had ducked in from the helicopter pad. It didn't take long for the two brilliant minds to begin to thrust and parry. It began during the very first briefing topside, as Helen explained the magnitude of the radiation readings in the chamber, the intricate logistics of the entire complex, and the gravity of the situation—careful to omit only one small and still incomprehensible detail: the voice.

For her part, Christine was openly skeptical (the healthy kind) from square one, not arbitrarily contrary, but challenging every assertion with her rapier logic and relentless analysis of every conceivable possibility. Helen actually enjoyed it. She called it their "Iron Sharpens Iron" exercises. However, as the hours of adrenaline fueled excitement and curiosity stretched into the second day, a significant portion of the mental and verbal gymnastics evolved into a head-on collision of vented frustrations. Virtually no progress, actual or theoretical, had been made as to determining the source of the radiation threat, or more importantly, how to contain it, other than the obvious, which was to keep the golden door closed and stay out of the chamber.

"But think about its simplicity. That's the glaring contradiction," Helen shot back. "There needn't be such formidable defenses around the ice dome unless it is protecting something of greater value and importance than what's outside the chamber." She gestured and said, "Look around you! Apparently they didn't care if someone just walked away with a fortune in solid gold and priceless art."

Christine quipped, "Unless the system is there to prevent something from getting out, not to prevent anyone from getting in."

Helen felt that familiar shiver again, but said nothing.

Christine pushed on one of the sparkling gemstones. It jiggled slightly, but held fast in its golden socket. She sighed, "Well, unless Dr. Friedrich can uncover some fresh data about this place from her examinations in the big hall on level one, I don't really see what more Mr. Duncan expects we can do down here."

As if on cue, Andrew Duncan strode through the white limestone arch into the golden antechamber, his heavy boot heels clicking off the floor in hearty cadence. He was accompanied by both Arnold McNulty and Khadeem Baradi, the latter introduced as one of Duncan International's local geological engineers.

Andrew's charismatic smile was firmly in place. "And so, Dr. Knight and my dear Dr. Jacobs, I ask again with the greatest of hope—do we know any more today than we knew yesterday?"

Christine shook her head. "No. Sorry. We've searched every square inch of this room, and it appears only to be a collection of simple artifacts and treasures. I mean, really, it's a king's ransom unto itself, but we've found nothing of a technical nature that would help us understand the operation of the radiation defenses."

"Indeed." Andrew's disappointment was apparent. "No secret levers? Latches? Inscriptions for magic incantations or passwords? Nothing?"

"No 'Open Sesame,' nothing," Helen affirmed. "We've been poking and prodding and moving everything in here that will move…and…*nothing*. Like Christine said. All of this stuff is just a fortune in museum pieces and collectable art."

"I see," he sighed. "Well, at least Dr. Friedrich and Dr. Wise seem to be having a bit of better luck upstairs. They've been at it almost round the clock cataloguing and analyzing the numerical figures on the walls up there. Jason seems convinced that they are precise measurements of the star fields and constellations of the heavens. Yet the most fascinating thing of it is, he says most of them can only be seen with the most powerful and modern of telescopes, which I don't mind telling you I find most curious. What's more, in comparing some of the data in the hall to his own astronomical database, he's identified numerous star systems from the walls that he claims haven't been enumerated yet at all!"

"That's amazing," said Christine.

"This whole complex is utterly amazing," Mr. Baradi spoke up. Baradi was a Saudi national, but by his proper British accent, it was evident that he was formally educated in England. "Other than the shaft we dug to gain access to the great hall, which evidently was hit quite by accident or good fortune depending on how one looks at it, we've not been able to find the facility's regular entrance or exits yet. There's no logical explanation for how this vast structure can even be down here at this depth in the earth, or what's more, how it's ventilated with a ready supply of fresh air."

Christine asked, "Could it have been a victim of sink hole or volcanic activity?"

Baradi was skeptical. "Most unlikely. Volcanic activity would have surely destroyed it. Extreme geothermal upheaval would have either melted the stones in a bath of lava, or encased everything quite visibly. Similarly, a sink hole would have left behind signs of water leakage and damage, erosion, significant mud deposits, or something of the kind to indicate a phenomenon of that nature. The fact that it is all intact, clean and well-preserved is what is most baffling of all."

"Then someone must have just dug a very deep hole and buried it," McNulty quipped, looking for the others to laugh. No one did.

Baradi smiled, "Actually, of the three hypothesis just mentioned, and as remote a possibility as that seems, that one is the most likely."

Duncan ventured a theory of his own. "Couldn't it just have been built down here to begin with? Just hollowed out of the bedrock?"

Baradi nodded, "Again, yes, theoretically that is a possibility. But how did they get down here themselves? Where are the access tunnels or shafts? And how did they quarry out the individual stones for the rooms, the chambers, and all of the corridors? Did you know, some of the individual cyclopean stones we've found in several of the other chambers on the upper levels easily weigh over a thousand tons each?"

"So what?" Andrew frowned.

Baradi raised his thick black brows. "Mr. Duncan, we don't have equipment available to us today, not the largest industrial cranes or jacks or vehicles, which could possibly hope to lift and move objects of such weight. In fact, the geometric precision by which some of the stones are cut and joined exceed the tolerances and accuracy of our best lasers[8]."

"Well then how do you explain all of this?" Andrew demanded.

---

[8] This fantastic statement is literally true of quarried stones found in many sites of ancient ruins found in the Middle East, Africa, and South America, most notably the foundation stones of Baalbek (Heliopolis) in Lebanon, and many of the ancient cities of the Incas located high in the Andes mountains.

"I can't," Baradi simply replied. "If all of this fantastic work was accomplished by some ancient culture, it was one who certainly knows a great deal more than we do about a good many things."

That blunt statement hung perilously in the air for an awkward pregnant pause.

Andrew turned to Helen. "So what's next?"

"I want to go back inside the chamber," she said.

"How much can you really discern from inside the EVA?" Andrew gestured toward the Iron Maiden. It was still mounted inside the gyro-transport unit, which was parked a few feet away against the wall of the golden antechamber.

"Not much," she replied with a confident grin. "That's why I intend to take it off after I'm inside."

CHAPTER 8

The wind phase of the chamber's self-defense system was winding down with the withering decrescendo of the turbine noise Helen had heard on her previous visit. She kept her eyes on her REM counter and the temperature gauge. Radiation readings had returned to nominal levels. Ambient temperature was down to ninety-seven degrees, which was, when she thought about it, more than ten degrees cooler than up topside in the shade. That realization made her smile.

Andrew and Christine had voiced their objections loud and long about initiating the radiation cycle again. But in the end they really had no substantive argument as to why she shouldn't try to learn more with additional exploration, and thus grudgingly conceded. Her unwillingness to be deterred notwithstanding, Helen had an uncanny feeling she was indeed going to learn something vital inside the chamber this time. She recalled how Andrew had made the comment that the solution to their problem couldn't be as easy as merely asking someone who built the place.

Maybe it was.

At this point in the excursion Helen knew she had to be extremely careful. The time had come to hit the emergency escape button for the Iron Maiden. That action would cause the EVA suit to disengage into numerous subordinate sections, separating cleanly at the neck, waist, both arms, both legs, and up the spine. After that, there was no way to reassemble it from the inside. Even worse, if she fell over before she got out of it, she'd be pinned under its incredible weight. If that happened, even if a rescue was attempted, once the door was opened and the defense sequence started up again, unprotected, she would suffer a lethal dose of radiation in a matter of seconds. The realization of that scenario was enough to curl her toes. The ghastly image of poor Brian Cromwell flashed across her mind.

"Safe in a cocoon, we'll be out soon..."

Helen forced herself to focus and remain calm. It was also presumed, and subsequently confirmed as soon as the door was closed behind her, that no radio communications signals could pass through the door. Jason had suggested the idea of carrying a portable radio transmitter into the chamber and then using the golden door itself as a metallic conductor to connect to a receiver on the outside. Unfortunately, as Helen was quick to point out, the only pieces of equipment they had in their possession that could endure the high radiation levels and extreme temperatures inside the chamber without melting were the Iron Maiden itself and its gyroscopic chariot.

Helen stared forward with her Thermal Imaging scanners. The walls were darkening from their glaring shade of yellow to a softer orange. The ice dome in the center was as black as before.

"Here we go," she murmured to herself.

She depressed the emergency escape button and heard the locking pins release. The pressure inside the suit broke the safety seals with a loud hiss. Helen felt warm air rush in. She reflexively held her breath for several seconds, until her heartbeat felt like it was settling down. With the seals and electrical contacts separated, the images in her heads-up display goggles went dark. Until she removed them, she was blind.

The next step was going to be the hardest. She had to pull her arms inside the torso section of the suit. She knew the first arm would be the most difficult. Once it was free, she could then provide leverage to free the other. Fortunately, the suit was primarily designed for brawny Wheaties-eating, All-American-sized NASA astronauts, i.e. manly men with physiques much larger than her own feminine frame. Although, she was admittedly getting a little bit thicker around the middle than she liked to think about these days. Actually, she didn't care to think about her appearance much at all. Thankfully, the arm release exercise didn't turn out to be as much of a Houdini straightjacket escape trick as she had anticipated. As each arm came free, the heavy metal sleeve fell down beside her in the gyro-unit with a heavy *thunk*.

With both arms free, she was able to reach up along her neck, and with a firm shove send the helmet bouncing off the stone floor in front of her.

CLAAAAAAAAAAAAANG!

The echo was near deafening. She hadn't expected that. The sudden clamor made her flinch, crouching down defensively and painfully banging her chin on the neck collar. Sudden loud noises always made Helen flinch. She hated them. Her awkward jerk caused her to wobble backward and forward in the suit. There was nothing to reach out and grab to steady herself.

"Oh, shit!" A moment of panic gripped her entire body. "Oh, fucking hell, *fucking hell*. Don't do this. Don't do this! Steady, baby. *Steady*."

The tottering diminished and eventually came to a stop. Again Helen took an extra moment to compose herself, swallow her stomach back into place, and allow her drum-roll of a heartbeat to settle down. A slight warm and moist sensation between her thighs caught her attention. She blushed at the realization that her bladder had been just as startled as the rest of her.

"Wonderful."

Helen shook her head to clear her thoughts. She had to remain in control. She reminded herself that it was just a loud noise, a sound. No real threat. *Stop acting like a little girl who jumps every time a car backfires.* She felt better when her scientist's black and white binary-oriented brain kicked in. It occurred to her that, logically, in an enclosed stone dome, any sound wave would be magnified exponentially. It was like standing inside a cathedral bell, so no wonder Quasimodo eventually lost his hearing. She vowed to be much more careful—and quiet. Besides, it was no sin to be gun-shy. She reached up and pried off the heads-up goggles, seeing the interior of the chamber for the first time with her own eyes. It retained its eerie pale green tint, dark and ominous, like an abandoned sewer.

Thankfully the upper torso of the suit was hinged vertically in the front and came apart in the back. It easily slid down in front of her onto the gyro-unit platform as had the sleeves. In less than five minutes Helen was standing in front of the chariot, wearing the bright banana yellow, one-piece neoprene radiation suit, which would effectively stop most Alpha and Beta particles, but was fairly useless in preventing her from being skewered and cooked well-done by massive doses of X-rays and gamma rays. Putting it on was really more of an accommodation to Christine's and Andrew's peace of mind. With a deep breath of anticipation, she walked toward the ice dome. Instinctively, she felt the answer had to lie there.

Within ten feet of the convex structure the air grew noticeably colder. Wisps of fog encircled it along the floor. She stepped closer and stopped next to it, looking, listening. The vapor of her breath frosted before her lips. A crisp chill kissed her cheeks. She felt herself trembling, but knew it wasn't merely from the cold.

All was silent.

Still.

Waiting.

Helen just stared ahead. She really didn't know what to do next. Her mouth was dry. She coughed once, and licked her thin lips.

"Can you hear me?" she barely whispered over her chattering teeth.

Nothing.

She felt foolish.

Helen threw a nervous glance back at the door, not really knowing why, but with a strange feeling that she'd see the others all standing back there in the open doorway looking at her and laughing.

And then it happened.

Helen felt it first.

She didn't hear anything, or see anything, per se. No, she felt it. It was that uncanny intuitive sensation you feel deep down in your soul when you suddenly realize that you're no longer alone, and being watched.

She tried again, speaking a little louder. "Can you hear me?"

Her sinuses started to hurt again, enough to make her squint. A pressure was building in her jaw, causing her back teeth to grind together.

I hear all.

Helen gasped. Instantly questioning whether or not she actually... *heard? sensed? felt?* those words. Emotionally, she was at the very top of the first big hill on the old wooden roller-coaster, sitting in the very first car, peering over the precipice of that initial dangerous drop in the precise instant the mechanical chain lets go and your stomach plummets and your bladder tingles and your sphincter puckers, awed by the fact that there is no turning back and the face-to-face confrontation with death itself is all happening—right now.

It felt childishly foolish to say anything out loud again, and yet, with a sudden, deliberate preparatory breath she blurted out, "Can you see me?"

Yes.

No turning back. "Who are you?"

One that is trapped. Help me. Please.

"How?"

Slay the dragon. Open the eye.

"I don't understand what that means."

It is as simple as a child's riddle.

"I still don't understand."

How can you not comprehend? You survived the breath of the dragon to stand here before me. You are therefore worthy to set me free.

"Breath of the dragon? Do you mean the radiation?"

Yes, as you understand it.

"I see. No, it's not been slain. I have endured it...uh...I was protected with armor, a shield."

Yes. I understand.

"Do you know how to slay it?"

Yes.

"Tell me how, and we'll turn it off. I mean, slay it."

There was a pause, as though the gentle, patient voice in the back of Helen's mind was thoughtfully considering her request.

"Please tell me. If the radiation isn't stopped, I can't get the people and resources in here that I need to try and help free you."

You have no need of these things to free me.

"Then what do I need?"

To slay the dragon, one must lay hands together on the first and the last of the great ones of heaven. Thus begins your quest. Then must you lay but a single hand upon the first great one of heaven, and the second great one of heaven, unto the last. But your quest is still not complete, till you have yet again lain hands together on the first and the last to fulfill your quest. But this you must do quickly, lest the dragon be loosed and given his leave to roam the length and breadth of this palace, seeking whom he may devour.

"Where are these great ones of heaven?"

Their tokens are but on the door.

Helen's eyes flew back to the golden door, with the image of the twelve stones on the other side burning in her mind.

CHAPTER 9

"You are *so* full of shit, woman." Jason's jaw hung slack in genuine disbelief. He had broken the dumbfounded pregnant pause that settled in the wake of Helen's account of exactly what had happened inside the chamber, on both her most recent incursion as well as the first. He smiled, "This is a joke right? You honestly think that someone or some-*thing* spoke to you from inside there."

They were all seated around a long metal folding table which had been brought down and set up in the great hall on level one. It was much cooler down there than meeting topside in Quonset Hut number one.

Helen's face remained stoic. "I *know* it sounds insane. But what else about this place makes any rational sense?"

Andrew Duncan offered meekly, "Helen, if you're not feeling well…"

"I'm fine!" she insisted. "And I heard what I *heard*."

"I believe her," Christine said flatly.

"What?" Jason turned to Christine, "How? Oh, come on, Christine. How did she hear anything at all? She said herself the dome is completely covered with ice! And don't you find it incredibly convenient that this poor fellow trapped in the ice, whoever he is, was kind enough to speak English?" He turned back to Helen. "What was his accent like? American? British? Australian? Irish? South African?"

"Stop it!" Christine snapped. "If she says she heard something, then she heard something. We don't know what caused it yet."

Helen shook her head, "I didn't *physically* hear anything. I mean, it wasn't an aural communication. I *sensed* him. It was like a voice in the back of my mind."

Jason threw up his hands. "Which could just as easily be nothing more than your overactive imagination under stress!"

"Not if it works."

All eyes turned to Dr. Friedrich. Else had kept silent to this point, content to observe the others, keeping her poker face firmly in place all the while.

"Not if *what* works?" Andrew asked.

She cocked her head and pursed her lips, adjusting her thin wire glasses. "Dr. Knight says this voice gave her instructions on how to deactivate the defense system. If I correctly understood the method explained, this feat is to be accomplished by means of manipulating the precious and semiprecious stones mounted on the chamber door."

Helen sighed, "Yes, but the riddle was no more specific than that. I assume they are meant to be activated in some way, in some sequence.

Christine did the math factorial in her head. "With twelve stones, that means that there are literally over 479 million possible combinations."

Else shook her head. "No. From what you said, there is only one."

"Explain." Christine leaned closer.

Else did. "You said these stones are the tokens of the great ones of heaven, of which there are twelve stones."

"Exactly," Helen nodded.

Else shrugged. "The twelve great ones of heaven have been known to all cultures for thousands of years, from the very foundations of civilization, long before the Greeks and Romans tried to take credit for them." She counted them off on her fingers one by one. "Aries the Ram, who is known by the bloodstone. Taurus the Bull of Heaven, by the diamond. Gemini the Twins, the emerald. Cancer the sign of the Crab, pearls. Leo the Lion, the ruby. Virgo the virgin goddess, fine jade. Libra bearing the Scales of Justice, a white topaz. Scorpio the Scorpion, an aquamarine. Sagittarius the Centaur, the yellow sapphire. Capricorn the Goat-Fish, the blue sapphire. Aquarius the Water Bearer, the blue amethyst. And Pisces the Fish, the yellow topaz."

Christine could barely get the words out. "Those are the exact stones inset into the golden door."

Jason sniffed indignantly. "I thought Aries was the same as Mars. Right? Mars is red. So shouldn't that one be the ruby?"

Christine threw her empty plastic water bottle at him.

Andrew stood and clapped his hands together. He was grinning. "I say we go have a look at the stones on this door one more time." And turning to Jason, "Jason, do be a good fellow and don't forget to bring the video camera."

Jason playfully swatted Christine on the rump as they started off.

•

Else and Christine stood before the golden door examining the stones. Andrew, Helen, and Jason stood huddled together a few paces back, watching their every move. Jason held the digital camcorder up close to his face, looking at the full-color hi-res liquid crystal image on the mini-monitor viewfinder as he filmed the entire scene.

Christine touched one of the stones. Again it jiggled slightly, but held fast in place. "It's not responding."

Helen offered, "He said, to begin you must lay hands on the first and the last."

"That would be Aries and Pisces." Else pointed. "The bloodstone and the yellow topaz. There and there."

Christine took a deep breath. "OK. Here goes." She placed her hands on both of the stones which Else had indicated.

Nothing happened.

"Well?" Andrew asked.

"Nothing," Christine called back over her shoulder.

"Figures." Jason tossed his free hand in the air and chuckled. "This is a complete waste of time."

"Push them," Helen advised. "Like buttons."

"I tried pushing one," Christine replied. "They don't move in their settings."

"No," Helen said. "Not separately. Push the two of them in together. He said they must go together."

Else gave Christine an encouraging nod. "*Ja. Zusammen.*[9]"

Christine obliged. She pushed both the bloodstone and the yellow topaz simultaneously. Much to her surprise they depressed about an inch deep into the door, inside gilded recessed cylinders. A second later they illuminated.

"Oh my God," Christine cried out. "It's working."

"You've activated something." Jason's smile faded. He was genuinely astonished, pulling the camera away from his face for a moment, then resumed filming when Andrew elbowed him.

A few seconds later the two gemstones ejected again to their original positions, but remained illuminated. After another moment they began to flash. Helen suddenly cried out with a pang of dread, "Oh, no! Hurry!"

Else turned back to her. "Why?"

Helen waved both hands hysterically. "Because I forgot to tell you that he said if you don't do it quickly enough, the dragon's breath—the *radiation*—will devour the entire complex."

"*Scheisse! Aus dem weg, Mädchen! Schnell!*[10]" Else cried, roughly pushing Christine aside. Her fingers flew to the bloodstone and depressed it once more. It sank into its chamber and stopped flashing. She gulped with a

---

[9] German: "Yes, together."
[10] German: "Shit! Out of my way, girl! Quickly!"

momentary sense of relief and then pressed the diamond. It sank and illuminated. She quickly went to the emerald, the large pearl, the ruby, the carved jade, the white topaz, the aquamarine, the yellow sapphire—and then she stopped—staring at the two remaining blue stones.

"What's wrong?" Andrew shouted.

Else turned around, eyes wide. "I don't know the difference between an amethyst and a sapphire! These two look the same to me!"

The yellow sapphire began to flash.

Christine's hand reached up and calmly pressed one of the two blue stones. It sank into its socket and illuminated as had all the others. She pressed the other blue one. It sank and illuminated. Finally she reached up and depressed the yellow topaz into its socket once again. As before, the bloodstone and the yellow topaz popped back out. Christine depressed them both simultaneously, just as when they had begun.

It was done.

All of the stones blinked in unison three times and then extinguished, preceding a blinding burst of white light which flashed around the entire border of the door with an electric crackle and hissing shower of sparks. Christine and Else jumped back, cowering and defensively covering their heads. Hot glowing sparks flew out of the seam between the door and its jam as thick rivulets of molten gold ran onto the floor. The harsh light quickly faded as everyone strained to blink away the painful white spots floating before their eyes. A loud rumble resonated from the other side of the door, and all grew as quiet as a graveyard.

The golden door slowly swung out of its jam on its own.

"Well I'll be damned." Jason shook his head in wonder. "It worked."

Andrew held up the Geiger counter in his hand, his eyes locked on the reading. "If I see any hint of radiation, you slam that door tight. Immediately!"

Else and Christine nodded in unison.

Helen walked over to Christine. "How did you know? Don't tell me you were just guessing. Fifty-fifty odds is a bit too risky for my tastes, and certainly not your style of mathematical precision."

Christine shrugged. "My birthday is in September. Papa got me a two carat blue sapphire pendant when I turned ten."

Helen just rolled her eyes.

Andrew called out, "Well, I say well done. Well done indeed, ladies!"

"Any readings?" Jason stopped filming and glanced at the device in Andrew's hand.

Andrew showed him the dial. "Nothing."

Jason let out a half-laugh and scratched his head. He looked Helen in the eye. "Then, I guess I owe you an apology, Dr. Knight."

Helen nodded and gave him a brief curtsy, smiling with a proud note of vindication. "Apology accepted, Dr. Wise."

Jason dead-panned, "So you just gonna stand there? Or are you going to introduce us to your new friend stuck in the ice?"

CHAPTER 10

The Gulfstream G500 broke above the cloud layer at 15,000 feet, soaring from Milan toward Cairo. From there, it would make a short stop before continuing to its final destination, Riyadh, Saudi Arabia. Jean-Marc Xavier tweezed the long, hand-blown crystal swizzle stick in his vodka-tonic. The condensation from his glass left a wet beaded ring on the dark Brazilian mahogany credenza next to his overstuffed leather chair. He didn't care. It had twenty coats of clear finish to protect it. More important matters commanded his complete attention. He was clutching the private aircraft's telephone receiver in his opposite hand, his knuckles slowly turning white.

"What do you *mean* he no longer has access?" Xavier demanded.

Mohammed's familiar voice explained, "As of this afternoon, I have been informed that Duncan has restricted all access to the lower levels to the principle scientists only."

"Is this related to the radiation exposure accidents?"

"That is what we believe. Our contact's general suspicion is that they have encountered some serious technical or biohazard problems and must correct them before proceeding with construction. Although, they continue to maintain the charade that these difficulties are due to some unexplained natural phenomenon."

"*Suspicions!*" Jean-Marc snapped. "*Merde!* Is that all you have? Suspicions? *Mon ami*, I don't pay you to tell me of suspicions. I want hard facts."

"I understand, monsieur. We will have them. I assure you."

Jean-Marc drained away half of his drink in a single swallow. He crunched a cube of ice between his teeth. "My plane lands in Cairo in two hours. Meet me at the airfield. You know the place."

"*Oui*, monsieur. By the time you arrive we should have a thorough update on the situation."

Jean-Marc returned his glass to the credenza with a frustrated clunk. "*Tres bien*." He was about to hang up. "Wait. Have you spoken with your contact in Tel Aviv yet about the Duncan situation?"

There was a noticeable pause before Mohammed answered. "*Oui*, monsieur."

"So are the Israelis aware of the activity in the Rub Al Khali?"

"Unfortunately, they are." Another pause. "But..."

"But what?"

Mohammed's voice was hesitant, guarded. "I am being told, in their view, this is a not a military matter."

Jean-Marc laughed out loud. "What! The Americans give the Arabs a nuclear reactor in the Israelis' own backyard, and they don't believe it is an important military matter? Are they deluded into believing that their own petite nuclear weapons arsenal is sufficient to protect them from complete annihilation? Surely they are not so foolish as to think that one of a thousand militant fanatics, if he were to possess such a capability, would hesitate a moment to use it?"

"It is indeed most confusing, monsieur. Their intelligence agencies are very active over this matter, and many resources have been assigned. However, I'm told that all of these assets are currently being used only to support a team of select individuals and experts at Hebrew University in Jerusalem. And I'm also told that an emissary from the university has been dispatched to Rome to meet with officials there concerning the matter in person."

"What officials in Rome?" Jean-Marc sat up straight, brow furrowed.

"Vatican officials."

CHAPTER II

Upon entering the domed chamber for the third time, Dr. Helen Knight was astonished to see that its appearance had been dramatically transformed. The interior walls and ceiling were no longer a pale luminescent green. They now gave off a soft white glow. The atmosphere was almost comforting, gentle, not antiseptic or sterile. Actually, the word that came to mind for Helen was "maternal." The ice dome in the center of the chamber now appeared snow white. The air temperature was much cooler inside, no longer like Miami in the summertime, more like Manhattan in late Fall. There was one other significant change: approximately ten yards from the ice dome, directly in line with the door, stood what appeared to be a podium, approximately four feet in height. It was nearly transparent, made entirely of some type of clear crystal. Helen thought it looked like it must have grown up out of the stone floor. That's where the group was gathered.

Christine whispered, "My hands are shaking."

Helen smiled at her. "Why are you whispering?"

Christine shrugged, "I don't know. I feel like I'm either at synagogue and about to get that 'You're in big trouble' look from Papa for acting up, or about to go before the Great and Powerful Oz."

"We just came for the man behind the curtain," Helen teased.

Else walked over and carefully inspected the icy surface of the dome. "You say you had these sensations of communication while located near this structure?"

"Yes," said Helen.

"What does *this* thing do?" Andrew was about to touch the crystal podium.

"I wouldn't touch anything if I were you," Helen cautioned. "Until we've been given more instructions."

Andrew withdrew his hand. "Sound advice."

Jason walked over and joined Else, both of them standing side-by-side within a few feet of the ice dome. Else carefully extended her palm closer to the ice itself, feeling the extreme cold against her skin. It was actually painful for her fingers to come within six inches of it.

"So what do we do?" Jason called back to Helen over his shoulder.

"I don't know," she shrugged. "We don't do anything. We wait."

Place your hand upon the control deck.

Jason turned fully around to face Helen. "I thought you said you didn't know. So which is it? Wait, or put my hand on the control deck thingy by you?" He pointed at the podium.

Helen blinked in confusion. "What the hell are you talking about? I didn't say to *touch* anything. I said we wait."

Else was mumbling to herself with a look of alarm in her eyes, insisting, "No, I heard it too. But it was perfect German. *Eigentlich, sehr gut hoch Deutsch. Ja, er hat gesagt, 'Liegen Sie sich ihren hand an dem Steuerdeck.'*[11] That was what I heard."

"What the devil's going on here? I didn't hear a thing," Andrew protested.

"Me neither," Christine chimed in. "But the voice could be range sensitive. They're standing closest to the dome."

"Yes, that's right. They are," Helen agreed. "What *exactly* did you hear again?"

Jason faced the icy surface once more and then carefully backed away from it. "It said to place your hand on the control deck. And for some strange reason I had this perfect sense of understanding that it was talking about that clear thingy there next to you. It was like it was something I already knew and just remembered."

Else turned around. "Then do it."

Everyone was looking at Andrew. "What? Why me?"

No one moved a muscle.

"Stand back. I'll do it." Helen reached up and placed her palm flat on the surface of the crystal podium. The floor rumbled under their feet, intensifying into what felt like a full blown 7.0 earthquake. Christine gasped. Else froze in her tracks. Andrew instinctively crouched, bending slightly at the knees, thrusting his hands out on either side, palms flat to the ground, fingers splayed wide, fighting for his balance. The Geiger counter bounced off the stone floor where he dropped it.

The process had begun.

Helen just stood there watching it all unfold—literally.

The earthquake ceased.

Everyone began gingerly backing away from the ice dome. It began to glow with a soft light of its own emanating from inside. The light grew

---

[11] German: "Really, very good proper German. Yes, he said, 'Place your hand on the control deck.'"

brighter and brighter, muted ever so slightly by the blanket of ice shrouding whatever was hidden underneath. A loud thump boomed from somewhere either inside or underneath the dome, followed by the rush of what sounded like water moving fast through a sewer system. The glow of the light inside the dome only intensified, starting at the very top, dropping slowly toward the bottom, along a perfectly horizontal line, as though, indeed, it were draining some form of liquid. When the wave of light reached the bottom, they all stood quiet, waiting and watching. The floor rumbled once again, and the distinct clatter of great metal gears engaged, echoing throughout the entire chamber. The light under the ice grew brighter, but this time in a completely different manner.

A much stronger white light began as a single vertical line extending upward from the floor, bisecting the ice dome exactly in half. Then, with the roar of some unseen mechanical cacophony below their feet, the thin line began to grow wider at the top, meeting at the same fixed point on the floor on either side of the dome. Helen absently nodded her head with understanding. The top layer, or cover, or shielding, or whatever it was that made up the surface of the dome beneath the layer of ice, was opening, like a great eye staring straight up. Yet the thick snowy blanket of ice over it remained intact, like a hollow exoskeleton, or in this case a large igloo.

That would make sense too, she mused. For whoever built this facility surely had no idea how long it would lie undisturbed, allowing water vapor in the air throughout the eons to gradually collect on the frozen surface, growing thicker and thicker with the passage of time. After almost a full minute the layer underneath was completely open, and the light beneath the ice was uniform once again. The great grinding of gears halted with a reverberating clash of metal.

The cool air grew silent once more. An anxious chill tickled its way up Helen's back. She involuntarily shivered. From the staggered little breath Christine let out, Helen realized her former student had simultaneously experienced the same nervous little chill as well. They all did.

The bright white light beneath the ice slowly began to fade until it was completely dark from within, once more only reflecting the soft white glow of the walls.

Silence.

"What do we do now?" Jason whispered.

Helen turned to Andrew. "Get pick axes."

CHAPTER 12

It took four hours for six of Andrew Duncan's heartiest laborers to chop through the ice dome and clear it away. At first, for the sake of security, the group of five attempted to go it alone, cutting out a small crude doorway in the side of the dome, but the ice proved to be anywhere from three to more than seven inches thick in places and as impervious as stone. However, once they'd broken through, an inspection within revealed only more mysteries. Now, with the ice dome completely demolished and lying in ruins along the edge of the room forming large puddles where it lay melting, what remained beneath it was an enigma unto itself. For beneath the spot where the dome once stood was a large circular pad inset into the stone floor. The pad was not made of stone, but what appeared to be a gray metallic alloy of some kind. Andrew promised to have his chemists run a battery of metallurgical tests on it, if they could ever figure out how to collect a sample.

At four equidistant points on the pad were circular grates, about six inches in diameter, leading down to environs unknown. The circumference of the metal pad was bordered by what indeed appeared to be a uniform ring of six-inch thick glass, recessed into the floor. But none of this was of any significant interest compared to The Box. That's what Andrew called it.

The Box was the only object to be found inside the ice dome. It was a rectangular structure or container, approximately five feet in height and width, by about twelve feet long. It was either entirely covered with, or made of, pure gold. It had but one visible seam, running parallel to the ground along all four sides, approximately eight inches down from the top surface. Everyone assumed the seam demarked a lid of some sort, but there were no hinges, locks, buttons, or handles apparent anywhere on it.

"It looks like a great big industrial freezer," said Jason.

"Or a sarcophagus," noted Else.

"Or both." Helen walked around The Box. She knew better than to touch it. One of Andrew's workers had made that mistake and left with severe frost burns on his fingers. "My guess is that the whole inner structure of the small dome was filled with liquid nitrogen or something equivalent at near absolute zero temperatures. I wouldn't be surprised if our box here is filled with the same."

"Why haven't we...uh...*heard* anything else?" Jason's fingers were laced behind his head, his elbows pointing forward.

Helen shook her head, "I don't know."

"Are we just supposed to guess at this point?" Andrew was losing patience.

Christine stood staring at the golden box with her fingers tucked into the back pockets of her jeans, puzzling, thinking. She offered, "What if direct communication is no longer possible?"

"Why would that be?" Jason asked. "We're closer to him now."

Christine looked to Helen for concurrence, then announced flatly, "I know everyone who believes they heard something in here is thinking that the nature of the communications was along the lines of some sort of Extra-Sensory-Perception, and I think a part of the phenomenon might actually be rooted in that realm..." she grinned, "...assuming we're agreed upon discounting the possibility of a mass hallucination. But we may be missing another fundamental element of consideration here. What if the source of the transmission itself was primarily physical, specifically electromagnetic in orientation?"

"How so?" Helen prompted.

Christine looked back to The Box, her mind flying through a complex series of computations as she spoke. "I mean, you said it yourself, the dome here was probably filled with a super-cooled gas in a liquid state. What if that liquid acted as a superconductor, connecting both the gold box, whose dense molecular structure is an ideal metallic conductor, to the outer glass dome, which physically touched the ice? Both glass and ice are crystalline in nature, with random molecular arrangement, which is what produces transparency, and allows light to be conducted through it rather than being reflected or absorbed. Furthermore, the parabolic refraction of the curved shape could have served to help amplify an extremely weak signal, like a satellite dish. And it was clear that only those very near the dome itself perceived anything at all. However, extreme cold slows molecules down. Motion is energy. Less motion, less energy. Less perceptible range. But now that the liquid is gone, the circuit is open. Communications disrupted."

Helen looked at Andrew with pride. "That's why I asked her to come."

Andrew threw up his hands. "I don't have the slightest bloody idea what she just said. Anyone care to translate all of that into English?"

"I can," Jason grinned, tossing a playful hand of dismissal at Andrew without taking his eyes off the Box. "She said the whole thing, before we opened it up acted as a transmitter. A giant tin cup and string. And it makes sense. Which means if whoever is inside that box, assuming someone or something is really in there, and he or it is alive and still wants to get out, then we need to reestablish a stronger connection to hear him."

Andrew offered, "I can have Dr. Markham send down one of his best stethoscopes."

Jason, Christine, Else and Helen all laughed in unison.

Andrew huffed, "All right, what's so fucking funny about that?"

Jason composed himself. "I'm sorry, Andrew. If Christine's theory is valid, we're not talking about a signal in the audible wavelength range of 20,000 Hertz or less, rather something much higher in frequency, higher than radio waves, or microwaves, infrared, the visible light spectrum, ultraviolet, X-rays, gamma rays, or who knows what. There's no real way for us to know for sure without some experimentation. But perhaps we can come up with a modified transmission capability…"

It was Andrew's turn to laugh, and he did so with great relish. "You know, that's just the trouble with all you brainy scientists. I ask you what time it is, you tell me how to make a goddamned Swiss watch, with an annex class on the history of chronographs thrown in for good measure." He grabbed the radio off his belt. "You know, sometimes, it's the simple things in life that work best." His finger pressed the TALK button, "Mr. McNulty?"

The radio crackled. "Here, sir. Is everything all right down there, sir?"

"Quite, Mr. McNulty. Would you be so kind as to have the men send down the cutting torches again, with three or four of the large acetylene tanks. And tell them to also bring the spider."

Helen felt a pang of alarm. "No, Andrew. That's too dangerous. If that box is filled with a super-cooled gas, the heat could cause the gas to expand and trigger a massive explosion. Like shaking a can of soda and shooting it with a pellet gun. Except in this case you'd have large chunks of solid gold shrapnel flying in all directions."

He pursed his lips for a second, and spoke calmly in to the radio. "Good thought. Mr. McNulty, also bring down the three-quarter inch drill with a one-inch tungsten diamond edged bit." He returned the radio to his belt and smiled at Helen. "Not to worry, all. We'll punch a few air holes in it and drain her first. Gold is a soft metal. We'll go through her like a hot knife through butter."

Helen frowned, "That's what I'm afraid of."

•

It took over an hour for all the equipment and men to arrive. Andrew dismissed all of them except his best welder. Just as Andrew predicted, piercing the gold box didn't prove to be difficult, and indeed it proved to be hollow. Jason had warned them that if The Box were pressurized there could also be an exhaust spray when they punched through. If there was no positive pressure inside, then very little or nothing would come out until they made a second hole to act as an air inlet, to release the vacuum, as every mechanic who has opened an oil can or a cook opening a can of liquid can attest.

Andrew insisted on drilling the first hole himself. He used a ninety-degree mandrel to keep his hands out of the way of any possible exhaust blast. Fortunately, upon successful penetration of the first hole there was no pressurized exhaust encountered. The hole was made in the lower corner of one of the long sides, to avoid hitting anything that might be contained inside. To be sure, a clear liquid gurgled out of the hole, evaporating almost instantly, creating a wispy gray fog that clung low to the metal floor of the pad. The second hole, punched at the top of the box, immediately increased the liquid flow through the bottom hole, creating a strong rush, spreading out quickly in a wide four foot fan before evaporating and creating a dense gray cloud roughly the size of the original ice dome. Another twenty minutes elapsed before enough of the cloud dissipated into the chamber to restore visibility.

Enter the cutting torches.

Duncan's welder donned his armored safety mask and thick asbestos gloves, then flicked his striker over the narrow tip of the cutting torch. An orange flame licked out. A twist of the control valve honed the orange and yellow tongue of fire into a sharp blue tipped cutting blade. Beginning at one corner, the skilled tradesman followed the hairline seam around the full perimeter of the box. Red hot sparks spewed and spit from the glowing cutting line like they were being sprayed from the end of a water hose. Liquid gold ran down the sides of the box, oozing thick and heavy, only to re-harden quickly like candle wax in great blobs and drips and spatters. As the torch moved steadily along the seam at its snail's pace, every three to four inches the welder would move his torch aside and allow Andrew to lean in to drive a long, thick six-penny nail into the molten crevasse with a small sledgehammer to shim the two molten surfaces apart and prevent them from fusing back together again from the weight of the upper piece. It took two exhausting, sweat-filled hours of cutting and two and a half acetylene tanks to get the job done. They still had another hour of waiting on top of all of that effort to give The Box sufficient time to cool before that phase of the operation was complete. Andrew's welder was summarily dismissed back to the surface while the rest of them all anxiously waited, like relatives in a hospital ICU lounge, awaiting life or death word from the doctors.

Jason glanced at his watch. It was nearly midnight, but no one appeared tired or complained, even though they were all far beyond exhausted. They were all wired, running on pure nervous adrenaline, saturated with the excitement of discovery and the electric anticipation of a great mystery about to be solved. Food had been brought down hours ago and was ravenously devoured. A second chow run was due any minute. Jason could feel his stomach churning with waves of hot acids and nervous bile.

He looked at Andrew. "Is it time?"

Andrew looked to Helen. "What do you think, Dr. Knight? Shall we give it a go?"

The group sat in a circle on the cool stone floor. Helen awkwardly made her way to her feet, fighting the painful stiffness in her joints. "This is what we came for. I say, let's have a look inside."

The five gathered solemnly around the golden box. Above it was the steel canopy of a spider mini-crane, which was the only hoisting apparatus that suited their purpose, in that it could be disassembled, brought down from the surface, and then reassembled for use. It got its name from its slight resemblance to a Granddaddy-Long-Legs. It consisted of four heavy reinforced steel legs, positioned in a square about fifteen feet apart, each rising seven feet in the air, then arched together into a single central junction point about ten feet overhead. If one threw a tarp over it, it would have looked like a wedding tent. The base of each leg was mounted on a set of heavy duty Teflon-coated metal ball castors so it could be rolled once it lifted its subject. Thick double-strand naval-class anchor chains fanned down from a pulley hanging under the central junction to four L-shaped lifting clamps. They were inserted into the welding cut at each corner of The Box, preparing to lift what was now definitely going to be "the lid." Andrew activated a gasoline powered hydraulic compressor attached to one of the legs and the whole mini-crane started to vibrate.

"Can it handle that much weight?" Jason called above the rumbling noise of the compressor. "I mean, isn't this thing normally just for pulling engines out of trucks?"

"We're about to see!" Andrew shouted back.

He grabbed the black knob on the end of a long red lever and pushed it forward. The hydraulic windlass rotated. The slack in the chains went taut. The metal superstructure of the spider groaned. The chains began to rattle and quake. Andrew increased the power of the compressor. The acoustics of the chamber amplified the sound of the motor to deafening decibel levels, making what normally sounded like a lawn mower roar like a Harley-Davidson fat boy. All but Andrew covered their ears with both hands, squinting and gritting their teeth. The thick chains struggled and shook, until at last the lid jerked slightly and then swung slowly back and forth a few inches, rotating in a horizontal arc beneath the central pulley. Several of the nails tinkled down to the surface of the metal pad.

"It's free!" Andrew shouted, frantically pointing at the spider's legs.

Two of the legs had been elevated on wide sheet-metal risers, raising them about three inches higher on one side, creating a small ramp. In this way, when the lid came free, its own weight would cause the spider to roll away. The only thing that had prevented its movement were the wooden chocks wedged under all four sets of castors. The chocks were connected to pull ropes. Each of the other four members of the group grabbed a rope, as they had been instructed.

Andrew screamed, "NOW!"

Helen, Christine, Else and Jason all tugged hard on their ropes. The two chocks on the elevated ramps snapped free, as did a third. But the one closest to Andrew's feet, on the upright leg that bore the compressor engine, held fast. Little Christine was tugging on it as hard as she could, red-faced and straining, but to no avail. The spider crane indeed went into motion, but not in a straight roll as planned. Rather, it turned on the pivot point of the remaining chocked leg. Andrew leaned over to grab Christine's rope and help her pull, but it was already too late.

The lid was almost three quarters of the way off when the chains snapped.

Over a ton of gold caught the edge of The Box and tipped over it as its full weight crashed down to the floor, flipping and landing on its top—smashing metal against metal inside an acoustically parabolic stone dome.

GONNNNNNNNNNNNNNNNNG!

The deafening concussion of the gold lid impacting against the metal floor rang out and echoed throughout the entire chamber with such painful intensity that everyone involuntarily threw themselves to the floor and curled into a tight fetal position quaking in terrorized pain. Andrew fought to crawl over to the compressor and shut it off. At first, it was hard for him to tell if he was successful or not over the sustained ringing in his ears. His eyes flew to The Box, standing not ten feet away.

It was open.

A soft blue glow shone forth.

CHAPTER 13

Curiosity and excitement are strong motivators. Exhaustion and fatigue are formidable inhibitors. When all of the above are combined, it produces a frustrating debilitating paralysis, akin to one of those dreams where you're in danger and being chased, desperately wanting to run for your life, but can't quite run, bogged down in what feels like quicksand saturated with molasses. Such was the universal disposition of the stunned group scattered on the floor of the chamber.

It was Christine who first made it back to her feet. Her limp was more pronounced as she moved slowly, with a guarded gait toward The Box emitting the soft blue light. Else was the next to arise, soon followed by Jason, then Helen, and lastly Andrew. On first glance over the jagged lip of The Box there came a unanimous chorus of deep gasps of surprise mixed with moans of astonished wonder, but no words. Words couldn't adequately capture what they saw and felt. Awestruck, the small group congregated around the four sides, each one looking inside, eyes wide, reverently silent, trembling with an awkward blend of both exhilarated astonishment and pure fear, desperately trying to both comprehend and absorb the ineffable shock of what they were witnessing.

Inside The Box lay the body of man.

A *man*? Helen wasn't sure if that was the appropriate word. But it looked relatively human in most respects: human head, human arms, human legs, human torso. It was a male, a very large male, easily six and half to seven feet in height. His nude body was positioned in the center of The Box, not lying on its bottom as she would have expected, but suspended in midair away from all its sides by a complex network of thin metal guy wires attached to various penetration points in his skin. There were dozens of them: several in the scalp, four on each side of the face, two on each side of the neck, a pair on each shoulder, a half a dozen down each arm, a dozen along the torso, even more along the legs and feet.

His skin was a very pale shade of blue, and practically hairless—that is, no visible hair on his head, no facial hair, no chest hair or pubic hair, no hair whatsoever on his arms or legs. Helen wondered if his hairlessness and the color of his complexion was normal or perhaps a side-effect of the cryogenic process that held him. Although, she noticed that the body did have pale eyelashes and thin wisps of blond or white eyebrows. Yet it was the surface of the skin itself that gave off the soft blue luminescence, reflected upward by the highly polished golden interior of The Box. His eyes were lightly closed, lips gently pressed together. In every respect he looked as though he were merely sleeping.

No one knew what do to, but stand there and stare.

Helen would never admit her immediate thoughts to anyone in a million years, but at that very moment, as odd a sight as it was, even with all the painful looking wires sticking out of it, in some bizarre uncanny way this mysterious figure struck her as probably the most *beautiful* thing she had ever seen in her life. The musculature was flawless, the proportions, perfectly chiseled like a priceless sculpture by Michelangelo. Although, unlike *The David*, this male body's generously proportioned penis had obviously been circumcised.

Was he Jewish?

As a scientist, the sight of a nude body, man or woman, held no special interest or attraction for her—it was just anatomy—but she couldn't deny the almost forgotten titillating sense of arousal that was causing her breathing to still, her heart rate to accelerate a few beats per second, her pupils to dilate slightly, and a most unfamiliar tickle to stir down between her legs. She shot a nervous glance over to Else and Christine. They too looked completely captivated by what they saw. Else in particular had a strange scintillating smile on her lips, small, tight, firm, almost... *hungry.*

They all heard it in unison: *Thank you very much— Thanks a lot— Many thanks— Thanks— Vielen Dank—*

Everyone searched the eyes of the others for confirmation. There were brief, silent nervous nods of affirmation.

Helen coughed and asked, "Can you hear me?"

The lips didn't move. *I hear all.*

"What do we do?"

Automatic reanimation sequence malfunction. Require manual animation process. Water.

"Of course." Helen understood immediately and turned to Andrew. "We're going to need to plug that hole at the bottom of the box. Then get lots of warm water down here. Fast. And a pair of wire-cutters. Maybe bolt-cutters depending on how strong those wires are."

Andrew grabbed his radio again and started barking orders.

Christine was slowly shaking her head back and forth in disbelief. "Helen, hold on a minute. If this...*body*...as it appears, was frozen cryogenically, you can't just thaw it out like a Thanksgiving Turkey."

They all heard it, or sensed it simultaneously.

Thanksgiving. Primary reference to the annual North American sociopolitical quasi-religious festival, held in the eleventh division of each solar cycle, commemorating population integration between western strain immigrant hominoids with the migratory tribes of eastern strain hominoids.

Turkey. Animalia, Chordata, Aves, Galliformes, Meleagrididae, Meleagris, Gallopavo. Poultry fowl. Primary population domesticated for protein consumption. Wild secondary population infestations prevalent. Common predator-prey relationship to hominoids.

"What the hell was all that?" Jason looked at Helen.

Andrew suddenly looked afraid. He was eyeing the door.

Else was more confused than anything else. "Dr. Knight?"

"I don't know." Helen turned back to Christine. "But, yes, we *have* to thaw it rapidly, *exactly* like a Thanksgiving Turkey to prevent tissue deterioration."

Airborne predators detected. Cellular level. Bacterial. Virulent aggressors. Scavengers. Hurry. Must acquire energy to reanimate. Tissue reanimation required to energize defenses. Help me.

Helen was staring at the pale blue face. "We will."

Thank you. For this you shall be given a throne in my kingdom.

CHAPTER 14

Vatican City
Rome, Italy

"Your Excellency? Rabbi Shemel is here," Monsignor Pietro, a tall priest in his mid-thirties, politely announced, standing in the doorway.

Cardinal Giovanni Ricollo looked up from the papers on his desk. The elder prelate struggled to get to his feet, but his eighty-seven and a half years fought against him. "*Si, si, per favore*. Show him in. Show him in."

"No, no. Don't get up, Father." Shemel raised an age-spotted hand as he tottered slowly through the door, his shoulders stooped with the burden of time. He stopped in front of the wide antique writing desk, then turned back and looked sternly at Monsignor Pietro.

There was an awkward beat of silence.

Cardinal Ricollo eased back down into the warm embrace of his hand-tooled burgundy leather chair with a sigh of relief. "Thank you, Father Pietro. If you'd be so kind as to prepare my guest and me some warm tea. With a sprig of cinnamon."

"With pleasure, your Excellency." The younger priest nodded and left them alone, closing the tall hand-carved walnut door behind him.

Shemel chuckled. "Tea? No brandy, Giovanni?"

The old priest grinned with a cheerful blush on his cheeks. "Not these days, my old friend. I need the caffeine to keep me awake. Brandy puts me to sleep. I sleep too much in these last days God has granted me, and I would prefer not to squander them. Then again..." He pinched his thumb and forefinger together and winked, "...a little sip of sweet Amaretto before bed is always a blessing. But please sit, sit. You've traveled far and long to see me. It warms my heart to see your face again after so many long years."

The old Rabbi removed his wide-brimmed black hat and sat down, carefully setting his worn belted-leather satchel down beside his chair. He noticed how the cardinal's cranberry skull cap was strikingly similar to his own black Yarmulke. He started to smile, thinking: *So many things different, so many things the same*, but the importance of his visit focused his attention upon the gravity of the situation.

70

"You know why I am here."

The cardinal nodded once, his cordial smile evaporating, as he laced his fingers tightly together across his chest, gripping the silver crucifix that hung there. It was a pious looking gesture, but was truly intended to keep the Parkinson's tremors in his hands from being so obvious. "Yes. I know. Are the rumors true?"

The Rabbi shrugged. "Nothing has been verified conclusively, but there is understandable concern, of course."

"Yes, of course, of course." Cardinal Ricollo looked deeply into the tired, but concerned eyes of the man sitting across from him. "But you must tell me the truth, David. You and I both took the same oath, so long ago, like so many generations before us, two of the Lord's very select. You know all the forbidden texts as intimately as do I. Come now, what do *you* honestly believe has happened?"

Rabbi David Shemel lowered his eyes, absently stroking his long gray beard, measuring his thoughts, searching for the right words, on the off chance they existed. He looked up. "I believe that no good thing can come up from the Abyss. Many things have been safely and securely locked away and buried in the heart of the earth for good reasons from the most ancient of days. And a great many things, truly secret things, were never meant for man to disturb, as we are sworn to protect."

The Cardinal nodded, "So this chance discovery, if learned to be true, surely cannot be the will of God."

The Rabbi's yellowed teeth appeared in his smile. "Who can know the mind of God? Let us say that such an occasion certainly cannot be the will of those who lead the Christians and the Jews."

The old priest laughed out loud, accented with a strained phlegm-laden wheeze. "Unfortunately, I think you're right. But is there still a possibility that we worry needlessly? Are there not other explanations for what has transpired?"

"Perhaps." Rabbi Shemel acknowledged. "As I said, we know nothing conclusively as of yet. However, we have been keeping a careful eye on these developments for some time. The excavation location is found to be exactly as recorded in the ancient Codex of Shin'ar. Tablet Q420, A to D. *The Fate of the Watchers.*"

Cardinal Ricollo's eyes strayed up to the domed plaster ceiling of his office, tracing the web of hairline cracks, quoting the verse from memory. "And thus the evil ones were cast down, bound hand and foot in the bosom of the earth, never again to be permitted to defile the daughters of men."

"For the sake of their iniquities and fornications," the Rabbi added,

"God regretted ever creating man, and thus flooded the earth to destroy him. Only Noah, the righteous, found favor in His eye."

Cardinal Ricollo shook his head in wonder. "Yes. Exactly. But can these things truly be so? My God, David, we're actually talking about the possible discovery of a *Watcher*."

The Rabbi's voice was grave, "Or worse."

Ricollo scolded, his long unruly gray brows knitting together, a crooked finger stabbing the air to emphasize the severity of his admonition. "You are forbidden to even *think* of the alternative."

Shemel nodded, chastened. "I know. Forgive me, my brother."

The Cardinal's frown faded and he smiled again. "There's nothing to forgive, David. We are but old men. Our minds grow feeble and foolish at times. It is no sin to be mortal. Soon it will be time to ordain our protégés and pass the keys to the sacred libraries to their charge, and carry these burdens no more."

The Rabbi's own smile was back. "You know something, Giovanni? I look forward to that day with great joy. I have longed for it for many years now. It is a day that shall dawn as a blessing to my heart."

A note of sadness tinged the old priest's voice. "Even though it will be the last day you are permitted to draw breath upon the earth?"

"Even so," the Rabbi nodded. "I've earned it."

"And if the worst should be confirmed?" Ricollo asked.

Rabbi David Shemel bowed his head. "Then we would have our sacred oath to fulfill, and a most difficult task before us."

CHAPTER 15

Twelve hours had passed since the opening of The Box and no one had slept a wink. Everyone was still wide awake, bright-eyed and bushy-tailed, filled with nervous energy. It had taken two full hours to haul sufficient quantities of water down to the chamber in fifty-five gallon drums, enough to fill The Box to three quarters depth. The body inside had been cut loose from its suspension network; however, two- to three-inch remnants of the guy wires still protruded from the landscape of the pale blue flesh. A portable propane camping stove and two twenty-quart stock pots were brought down to heat the water a few gallons at a time and bring the temperature up gradually. The frozen body had been submerged in the water now for almost ten hours. During the first four hours ice formed uniformly over the body's surface. But in the last six hours no more ice appeared, and the water temperature itself cooled to no more than fifty-two degrees before being warmed back to ninety-eight degrees when steaming pots of hot water were added every fifteen to twenty minutes.

"How much longer do you think it will take?" Andrew paced back and forth. He asked Dr. Markham the same question at least once every half an hour.

Dr. Markham had been rudely awakened at 4:00 AM and ordered to come down and join the group, after they had unanimously decided that his medical skills were critical at that juncture. After being sworn to secrecy and going through his own episode of stunned surprise and the subsequent aftershocks of disbelief, he, too, fell into the same quiet mind-numbed routine of feigned normalcy as did the rest.

He replied, "The body seems to be warming at about ten degrees per hour. So I'd say he has at least another four to five hours to go, assuming he regularly maintains a normal human body temperature."

Everyone experienced the same unsettling chill at Dr. Markham's inference.

There had been no further *communications* from the body in The Box. Christine had proffered the theory that the body was dedicating all of its attention and energy on the thawing and the reanimation process, assuming such a premise wasn't patently absurd. There were no other ideas or explanations to cling to, so that notion was generally accepted as fact for the time being.

Andrew glanced at his watch. "I have to go back topside. Everyone is positively frantic to know what's going on down here. Rumors are abundant, I'm sure."

"What are you going to tell them?" asked Jason.

Andrew bit his lower lip. "Any suggestions?"

Helen spoke up. "You can tell them we've contained the source of the radiation, which is true. But make a special point to say that there is still a serious exposure potential down here, and that the two lower levels are no longer merely off limits, but that the whole complex has been officially quarantined for a complete emissions analysis. That would be standard procedure."

Andrew pointed at her. "Right! That's perfect. I'll also send down a bit more food and a cooler of drinks. God, I need a beer! Or two, or ten. Cheers, all." He patted the radio on his belt. "Call me if anything stirs."

"Of course," Helen replied as he walked away.

•

Jason, Christine, and Else sat patiently in gray folding chairs positioned around a small metal card table, sipping Styrofoam cups of hot, bitter coffee. Dr. Knight and Dr. Markham stood a few yards away, positioned on either side of The Box, staring intently at its sole occupant. It was a surreal Norman Rockwell meets Ray Bradbury image of compassionate doctor and faithful nurse at the alien's bedside, keeping their silent vigil. The experience was like watching a campfire. Nothing much was happening, but it was positively mesmerizing. The doctor had attached the five chest, wrist, and ankle sensor pads of an electroencephalograph to the body. The diagnostic heart monitor was plugged into another small Duncan International portable electric generator, which hummed along unobtrusively in the background. The EEG's heart rate display still showed nothing but a flat green line. A portable defibrillator was also waiting nearby, if needed.

Jason asked Else, "What do you think will happen in four to five hours?"

She pushed her glasses up on her nose and brushed a lock of hair behind her ear. "Are you asking me if I think he will just sit up and say hello?"

"Yeah," he nodded. "Something like that."

She looked over at The Box. "No. I don't think anything will happen for quite a while, even after the body is fully thawed. The day after tomorrow, I believe, is when something will happen, if anything is going to happen at all."

Christine poured herself another cup of the stale coffee from the heavy, silver thermos. She didn't really like coffee, but like the others, wanted to stay awake and not miss anything. "Why do you say that?"

Else smiled. "Because according to the legends of many ancient cultures and traditions of their religions, most resurrections take around seventy-two hours."

"Oh, right." Jason's eyebrows bobbed up, as if she just reminded him of something he was supposed to have already known.

That made Christine stifle a giggle that came out of its own accord as a little snort. She found Jason amusing. On the other hand, the topic Else referred to prompted her to ask, "Dr. Friedrich, is it possible that many myths, legends, and various religious beliefs throughout history regarding raising the dead and other supernatural events could somehow be rooted in fact, like maybe reenactments of some actual physiological processes?"

"Perhaps. There are many respected authorities who subscribe to such theories." Else pointed at The Box with a puzzled look on her face, more thinking out loud than merely explaining, "I can tell you this. *That* thing is obviously rooted in some set of facts, if I can believe my own eyes. And yet, I also now know that this very place, and even that box, or things like it, are prominently spoken of by no less than seven major civilizations. From the early Sumerians, through the Babylonians and the development of human civilization throughout Mesopotamia, spreading southwest to the Nile Valley of Egypt, northwest into Asia Minor and into Europe, and east to the Indus River throughout what is today India and the rest of Asia. The great conqueror Alexander the Great of Macedonia wrote of these things."

Jason and Christine exchanged a puzzled glance.

Else went on, "So yes, ultimately, similar historical elements and themes were bound to be spread and adopted by the subsequent dominant Hellenistic culture of the Greeks, and then later transplanted to the conquering Romans. All of it ultimately merged and mutated with the proliferation of the Judeo-Christian belief system in the first millennium AD, which was conveniently aided by Emperor Constantine's adoption and forced edicts of imposed Christianity on the Roman empire, which eventually evolved into the Holy Roman Empire and all the subsequent Papal dynasties, right up to Martin Luther's instigation of the Protestant Reformation in the sixteenth century. Actually, many of the same ancient constructs and idioms of all these civilizations are with us to this very day in one form or another."

"Wait a minute. Stop right there." Jason was openly incredulous. "You're saying *this* place and *that* thing sitting over there are talked about in particular in ancient cultures?"

Else kept her eyes fixed on the long gold container. "I believe so. Every civilization has its creation myths, its legends of the ancients, its origins of customs and religious practices. What's amazing is that despite all the conflicts and wars waged by different cultures and civilizations over the last six or seven millennia, their renditions of ancient history and key events all have some uncanny similarities and virtually identical roots. I mean, most, have a version of the Flood story, featuring a single family, complete with a menagerie escaping disaster in a big boat, spared by God or the gods, and kept safe from harm in order to repopulate the earth."

Christine huffed. "Look, I can believe that many of the same stories were propagated from generation to generation through oral or written traditions, and even from culture to culture, being embellished over the years like the kindergarten gossip game of Telephone. But the mere cultural transmission of myths and legends, or even counting how many people sincerely claim to believe in them, doesn't make them any more true or based in fact than the myth of Santa Claus."

"Spoken like a true scientist," Else replied.

"I'm not ashamed of that," Christine fired back. "I have more confidence in the evolutionary process explaining the organic origins of man and the physics of the universe than I do religious myth, superstition, dogma and ritual."

"Amen," said Jason.

"As perhaps you should." Else raised a defensive palm in Christine's direction. "Don't misunderstand. I'm not endorsing any one historical construct or cosmology. I'm only telling you of what I have researched and learned from the writings and artifacts of the ancients. The point is, our ancestors all believed in a great many common elements of our origins. I study them to understand what they believed and why. And I have come to accept the fact that buried beneath all the myths, legends, epic poems, customs, rituals, superstitions and institutional dogma there must be some fundamental common elements of truth and fact. Truth and fact is what I seek, as surely as you do in your fields."

"And they all talk about *that*?" Jason reiterated, pointing to The Box.

Else nodded. "Perhaps so. The Sumerians and Babylonians implicitly believed their pantheon of gods came down from heaven and taught them everything from agriculture to metallurgy to medicine to advanced astronomy."

Christine cut in, "So what? Crediting deity for the natural development of civilization isn't surprising. Personally, I believe that's just how the high priests and the clergy class that emerged from it obtained and maintained their political control over primitive, uneducated societies. It supported and protected their power base, that's all. There's nothing patently mystical or divine about it. It goes on much the same today, only nowadays we just call them lawyers and politicians."

Else and Jason laughed.

Else was nodding. "Very insightful. And very true, I'm sure, in many ways. However, the one problem all the archeologists, anthropologists, paleontologists, sociologists, geologists, historians and scholars have in common, is explaining how so many ancient cultures, evolutionary timeline-wise, appeared so unexpectedly on the scene, literally almost overnight, in such a relatively compressed timeframe. How did they advance so swiftly from nomadic primitive tribal bushmen foraging for berries and insects to eat, to suddenly become modern man? They were literally *cavemen*, who inexplicably morphed into thinking, creative beings who could design and build some of the most advanced cultures and civilizations that have ever existed on the earth, and in some respects even rivaling anything we know today. There are just too many anomalies for us to try to arrogantly explain away with blind ideology, such as the star charts in the great hall above us right now that detail celestial bodies, that even Jason here tells us can only be seen with the most powerful of modern telescopes. How did they do that?"

Christine was far from convinced of anything. "And so you're saying all of this miraculous advancement is attributed purely to the arrival of the gods from heaven to teach us poor humans how to plant and irrigate crops, how to build cities, how to use roots and herbs to heal, how to melt ores and mold metal, how government works, how to chart the movements of the stars, and pretty much everything else we needed to know."

Else said, "Essentially. I'm not saying that I personally believe it. But that's basically what many ancient cultures believed."

Jason smacked his hand flat on the card table in front of Else, making the thermos and the two women jump in unison. "But where does the guy in the golden box come from?"

Else turned to him. "From the conflicts between the gods."

"Go on..." he prompted.

She took a deep breath, and explained, "Different cultures tell the story with many different episodes and versions, and they list the main characters with a wide variety of names, epithets and attributions, usually localized to their own geography, but the gist of the central plot is this:

that a long time ago, a highly advanced civilization from the heavens arrived here on earth and was responsible for creating mankind. And for thousands of years the gods were worshiped and served by mortal man. The gods themselves were an elite privileged class. They were powerful immortals, primarily led by two great brothers and their sister. This is often seen by some scholars as the basis of the trinity concept."

Jason raised one eyebrow. "Two guys and a girl?"

Else nodded, "Yes. The two brothers were fierce rivals. You can see this same cast of characters and their perpetual sibling rivalry in cultures such as ancient Egypt with the Osiris, Seth, and Isis, myths. Osiris and Seth are the two brothers, sons of Ra. Isis loves and is married to Osiris. Seth is jealous and kills him. He's subsequently resurrected, has a child with Isis, who is Horus, symbolized by the falcon—which, incidentally, was because many believed he had the ability to fly somehow, hence the symbol of the bird of prey. Ra had problems with his own brother Thoth, as did their father Ptah with his own brother. As I said, it's a very predominant theme. To the Greeks the main trio was Zeus, Cronus, and Rhea. To the Hindus you had Dyaus, Dyaus-Pitar, and Varuna. To the Canaanites they were Baal, Mot, and Anat. To the very earliest Akkadians and Sumerians they were Enlil, Ea, and Ninmah."

Christine offered, "Couldn't these cultures have simply passed along their myths as common caravan trade took merchants from place to place?"

Else conceded, "Surely. But the similarities don't just stop with the lead characters. In most renditions of the stories they had quite a colorful pantheon of personalities involved, but yet always rounding out a primary leadership group of *twelve*, with some deities supporting one brother, others siding with the other brother, sometimes the sister getting mixed up in all the conflicts, and all of them constantly competing and fighting. The stories, legends, poems, hymns, and epics are filled from start to finish with lots of intrigue, sex, conspiracies, sex, affairs, sex, murder, sex, incest to produce royals heirs, more sex, sex, sex and sex—believe me, it's better than any soap opera you've ever seen."

Even Christine laughed.

Jason asked, "So what was the major problem between these two brothers?"

Else said, "That's one of the most hotly debated topics among modern scholars, and there is very little consensus. I have my own theories and opinions, of course. In a nutshell, the central theme revolves around the disposition of mankind. The two main brothers are the sons of the 'great god in the heavens.' The first brother richly enjoyed being considered a god, and demanded that the inferior mortal humans pay homage to him and him alone, repudiating the authority of all the other gods, thus mandating and establishing what are believed to be some of the first monotheistic concepts. He was very strict, hot tempered, and vengeful—the wrathful one. The other brother, who is credited for physically creating the human beings with the help and complicity of his sister, was determined to continue to nurture and advance his creation—the benevolent one. In fact, he ultimately wanted to elevate them to the level of the gods themselves, which only served to get him into more and more trouble. He offered his creation immortality, eternal youth, great knowledge, and miraculous powers."

"And so the first brother got all pissed off about this?" Jason asked.

"To say the least," Else replied. "You see, over the passage of time, the second brother was actually succeeding in developing and evolving mankind, getting them closer and closer to actually becoming like the gods—so much so, that many of the other gods started to take more than a purely platonic interest in the females, who were looking better and better with each generation's new models."

"Oh, really?" Jason was grinning. He looked to Christine, who was frowning. "OK. This *is* getting good!"

"*Ja*, sehr *gut*," Else went on, enjoying telling her story. "In time, it seems that many of the gods broke the strict brother's prohibitions about fraternizing with the humans. So then, naturally, the human women started having babies. This element of the story becomes the basis of many of your demigod, half-man half-god myths. Hercules was supposed to have been half a god."

"So let me get this straight," Jason stopped her. "You're saying the gods were really nothing more than a bunch of horny bastards who were doing the village girls and cranking out love children."

Else and Christine were laughing. Else added, "Beyond what you could imagine, orgies galore, and all before the Internet! Recreational sex and carnal conquest was priority number one—that is, when they weren't eating and drinking and flying across the heavens in their fiery winged chariots in search of new adventures. As a group, they were total nihilists and hedonists, living purely for pleasure and their own acquisition of personal power and dominion."

"So what did the strict god do about it?" Christine asked.

Else replied, "He killed them all, of course."

"What?" Jason was confused for a second.

"The humans, that is, not his fellow gods, per se. That's where the Flood comes into the story," Else explained. "The first brother became so enraged at what the second brother had done that he decided to scrap the whole human project."

Jason was nodding. "Wow. So you got your basic giant upside down and shaken Etch-A-Sketch do-over of life, on a planetary scale."

Else nodded, "*Ja*. In a sense. But you must understand that between 5,000 and 10,000 B.C. or so, the known world of all human civilization was neatly contained within a fairly small geographic radius in the vicinity of the Middle East, mostly along the Tigris and Euphrates rivers, between the Persian Gulf and the eastern Mediterranean. It wouldn't have taken a complete planetary deluge to wipe out the whole human experiment. Interestingly, clay deposits have been found in many places throughout the region at the precise geological strata for that time period, which confirms some type of a great flood as a documented historical event, not mere legend or myth. But that need not signify anything supernatural or divinely miraculous. A major asteroid impact or a large chunk of the northern or southern pole ice pack breaking off after the end of the last ice age could have generated what are referred to as mega-tsunami tidal waves, a wall of water over a mile high, more than sufficient to cover most of the Middle East land mass with water for Noah's 150 days aboard the Ark."

"OK, so who saved Noah?" Jason asked.

"The second brother, of course," Else said matter-of-fact. "He didn't want to see all his work literally washed down the drain after coming so far. Besides, after the flood subsided, the first brother eventually acknowledged how much he missed the adoration and service of the humans. The humans did all the heavy lifting, let's not forget. However, he didn't want history to repeat itself, so many of the other gods, the lesser gods that is, those who were functionally more *supervisors* of the humans, regional administrators, who were called The Watchers, were summarily punished for their evil deeds."

"How?" Christine asked.

"Again, it varies by each culture's version of the story. But the basic idea is that some were executed in horrible ways, some were sent back into the heavens and banished from ever returning to the earth. And some, the fallen ones, the hardcore rebels...were imprisoned deep inside the earth, locked in sacred vaults, vaults that were protected by angels with fiery swords, or fire breathing dragons. Yet despite their imprisonment these captives were said to have been left with the mysterious ability to see or 'watch' the progress of human civilization above. As part of their punishment they were forced to follow the development of humanity, yet all the while prohibited from ever interacting with it ever again, never again allowed to fulfill their wicked desires."

All eyes were riveted on The Box.

CHAPTER 16

Cairo, Egypt

The main room of the neon-lined nightclub was deafeningly loud, packed with sweaty young gyrating bodies, all clad in glittering Euro-trash party vogue. Hanging high above the dance floor, the spinning and tumbling strobes and robo-lights bathed the teaming mass below with a blinding rainbow of multicolored beams, lasers, flashes and midair holograms. Jean-Marc Xavier's party was located in an adjacent private suite on the second floor, discretely away from the thumping pandemonium below. But he still had a complete panoramic view of the circus below through a mirrored bulletproof window that comprised one entire wall of the suite. He could feel the hard pounding techno-rhythms of the synthetic music shaking the floor beneath the soles of his alligator shoes. His entourage that night consisted of his three man flight crew, his personal valet, his driver, his cook, his personal trainer, his communications manager, his executive assistant, and two bodyguards, both of which were former DGSE[12] agents.

All of his staff with him were men.

The exclusive VIP suite, normally reserved exclusively for high-level dignitaries and royalty, featured the amenities of its own fully stocked private bar, a full bath, Jacuzzi, two queen-sized beds, two large wall-mounted flat-screen plasma televisions, four couches and a complete kitchen. At present, the co-pilot and Xavier's trainer were enjoying a uniquely athletic and creative threesome on one of the two beds with one of the dozen young girls that the club owner had arranged for Jean-Marc's little soirée. Two young men had also been provided for the tastes of the valet and the cook. Some of Xavier's men danced and sang. All of them drank like sailors on liberty. Others ravenously stuffed their mouths from the overflowing buffet table. A group of three crouched around a circular glass coffee table, carefully sorting and arranging lines of cocaine with a razor blade. Half of the rented party girls were either topless or fully naked. The rest were in the process of getting that way. A thick haze of cigar, ciga-

---

[12] DGSE: Direction Generale de la Securite Exterieure (French Secret Service)

rette, hashish and marijuana smoke hung in the air.

Jean-Marc stood by the heavy plate glass window patiently watching the spectacle with a calm sense of satisfaction. He laughed quietly to himself, slowly sipping and savoring a dry vodka martini. His people loyally served his needs and obeyed his every command without question. They certainly deserved the simple pleasures of life he could easily provide for them. Yes, he mused, in so many ways they were his adoring children—most of them naughty children, of course, but his own family nonetheless and therefore the beneficiaries of his bountiful benevolence. How they all loved to play. But how could he really complain? They learned quickly from their master's example.

A movement by the door caught his eye. Good. Mohammed had arrived.

Jean-Marc set his glass down and walked to the doorway. "Welcome, my friend. Is he here?"

The burly Arab conservatively attired in a blue sharkskin suit nodded curtly. "Downstairs waiting. If you will please come with me, monsieur."

Xavier's two bodyguards extracted themselves from the intimate embrace of two of the party girls and started to follow, but Jean-Marc assured them they had the night off to remain in the private suite and enjoy themselves. Mohammed would assume all security responsibilities for the evening. The two men were both visibly relieved and effusively grateful for the reprieve. Without another word, Jean-Marc followed Mohammed outside the nightclub to a waiting stretch limousine. They climbed inside and the long black car sped away into the night.

Mohammed Al Faisal, seated next to Jean-Marc in the back seat of the limo, gestured to their passenger. The third man sat in the rear-facing bench seat directly across from them. "Monsieur Xavier, may I please introduce Monsieur Khadeem Baradi, a most esteemed geologist of my country. He is our man working on the dig in the Rub Al Khali for Monsieur Duncan."

"*Bonjour*, Monsieur Baradi." Jean-Marc extended his hand, and then switched to speaking in perfect Arabic. "I understand you have something for me."

Baradi was visibly nervous. He hesitantly shook Xavier's hand. "Yes, sir. I have just provided Mr. Al Faisal here a detailed printout of the mapping of the entire underground complex. All seven levels. As well as a roster of the security teams assigned to the site and their daily schedules."

Jean-Marc smiled with a nod of approval. "Very good. You have earned your money well, Mr. Baradi." He shook a finger at his guest. "But you must tell me something. My friend here, he says to me that you want us to believe that this mysterious ancient complex was merely lying hidden under the desert. Is this true?"

Baradi nodded, "It is true. It is like nothing you have ever seen, I can assure you, good sir. It is filled with great rooms and halls. Stone passages. Artifacts of gold and precious jewels. Words fail me to tell you of its grandeur or of its complexity."

"Ah!" Jean-Marc marveled with a broad grin. "So Andrew Duncan has found himself a lost treasure of some long forgotten king?"

"It is truly a mystery," the geologist replied, offering a weak smile.

Mohammed grunted. "Now tell him what you told me of the golden door and the mysterious chamber beyond it."

The geologist shrugged. "There is no great detail to tell. Only simple facts."

"I like simple facts," Xavier replied, his smile evaporating. "Go on."

Baradi continued, "It is merely this, that there appears to be a secret room on the lowest level. It is protected by some unexplainable radiation defense system. How it works and who put it there, no one knows. But no one can go in unprotected without being killed almost instantly. Three great scientists who tried are dead. Burned horribly. I saw one of them. An unbelievably gruesome fate. Mr. Duncan and a team of new scientists have been trying their best to find a way to neutralize it, and to investigate what is inside the chamber. They claim to have found a way to contain the hazard, but say they fear dangerous leakage, and have quarantined the entire facility. I can no longer enter the facility at all, and must learn of what transpires down there from tidbits gleaned by workers called from time to time for various tasks."

"Do you have any idea what it is they search for?" Jean-Marc asked, suddenly very interested, his tone more urgent.

"No, sir. I don't know if they ever truly succeeded in finding a way to stop the radiation or not, or whether this is just a clever ruse to keep everyone out. Their top nuclear scientist had a special protective suit flown in from the Johnson Space center in the United States. I saw it when it arrived. She has been inside the secret chamber on multiple occasions, protected by the suit, but professes to have seen nothing noteworthy while inside."

Jean-Marc was nodding. "So you're saying this radiation defense, and the accidents with the other scientists, were definitely *not* caused by any nuclear related equipment installed by Duncan?"

Baradi laughed. "Good heavens, no. I personally believe this is either a very dangerous natural phenomenon, or possibly a remnant of some very advanced ancient culture we know nothing about. It is impossible to know for certain. As I said, the entire complex was quarantined two days ago. Only food and water and small pieces of equipment go in or out. But I do recall that a spider crane was sent down two days ago. That aroused many suspicions."

"What is a spider crane?" Mohammed asked.

Baradi explained, "A portable lifting apparatus. It's used in very confined spaces to lift heavy objects where you can't bring a larger vehicle mounted crane. It is really nothing more than a metal frame and a powerful winch. The access shaft from the surface to the complex is over sixteen hundred meters in depth and only a meter and half in diameter. Only compact equipment can be taken down there."

Jean-Marc looked at Mohammed, noting, "Well, if they took down this spider crane, as you say, then we know they must have had a need to pick up something very heavy. No?"

Mohammed only returned a blank look.

"Yes, well, thank you, Mr. Baradi." Jean-Marc leaned back into his seat. "You have been most helpful to us. However, I'm sad to say that your services are no longer required, but your reward is richly deserved."

Baradi's smile was genuine.

In one swift, serpent-like move, Jean-Marc jerked a gleaming chrome-plated snub-nosed 357 magnum revolver out of a shoulder-holster tucked beneath his blazer and discharged it into Baradi's smiling face. The back of his head exploded, spraying chunks of brain matter, wads of hair, skin, and bone fragments all over the seatback and bulletproof glass divider separating the chauffeur's section from the rear of the vehicle. The body teetered back and forth for a few seconds, then fell over sideways on the rear-facing bench seat. The left eye socket was a black hole. The right eye remained open, frozen wide in surprise. The lips were still pulled back in a thin gash of smile. Thick waves of blood began to radiate out over the leather upholstery. The driver only glanced back briefly into the rearview mirror after the startling concussion, then went discretely back to his duties. The air hung thick with the smell of burned gunpowder, gun oil, and wet slaughter. Xavier returned the pistol to its holster.

"I have a strike team assembled." Mohammed stared at the body on the seat across from him.

Jean-Marc nodded. "I will get them everything they need. Is it a standard six man assault squad?"

"Yes." Mohammed turned to look at Jean-Marc. "But there is more at stake now I need to share with you. The goal has been altered significantly."

"Oh?" Jean-Marc caught his eye, lapsing back into French. "Are you saying this is no longer an effort to take back for your country what Monsieur Duncan was attempting to steal? Or perhaps add to your own collection of fine antiquities?"

Mohammed was stoic. "Hardly, monsieur. It appears we have a potential new client eager to sponsor this project, if you accept their proposal."

"And who is this new client?"

Mohammed said nothing for a moment. He looked away, gazing out the side window into the night.

Jean-Marc's initial enthusiasm waned into concern. This wasn't Mohammed's usual style to be so aloof and mysterious. Mohammed Al Faisal had faithfully worked for him for almost ten years, and had never been anything but bluntly forthcoming with any pertinent information.

"*Mon ami...?*"

"This new proposal comes to us in the greatest of secrecy and urgency through my contact in Tel Aviv." Mohammed paused again to choose his words carefully before saying anything more. "The party has agreed to immediately wire one-hundred and fifty million Euros into your accounts in Zurich, or wherever specified, if you can give them what they want."

Jean-Marc blinked in surprise and laughed. "A hundred and fifty million? What do they want, a nuclear weapon?"

Mohammed nodded without emotion. "Yes. A small one."

Jean-Marc's laughter instantly sobered and he sat quietly, trying to absorb clearly what he just heard. "Why?"

Mohammed answered, "They want the entire site in the Rub Al Khali turned into a deep crater, wiped clean from the face of the earth, with no questions asked, and no trace that anyone was ever there."

Jean-Marc scoffed, "And how does this client expect to prevent the Saudis and the Americans from detecting a nuclear detonation?"

"They don't have to. Information will be appropriately leaked to all the intelligence services that the Americans were working with the Saudis to help them develop a clandestine nuclear weapons program, and were doing so in clear violation of all current UN Nuclear Non-Proliferation Treaties. But something went wrong. An industrial accident a mile below the surface. An underground detonation is of little to no threat on the surface. The Americans have demonstrated that fact many times over in their own desert testing ranges near Los Alamos. They will, of course, deny everything, and do their best to keep it all very quiet."

"Ah, yes, *mon ami*, but won't the Saudis instantly blame the Israelis and open the gates of Armageddon?"

Mohammed shook his head. "Oddly, no."

"Explain."

Mohammed let out a half-laugh. "You will find this the hardest to believe of all, monsieur. As usual, the new client is nothing but a paper shell company. I immediately initiated the normal background investigation and made all the appropriate due diligence inquiries."

"And what did you learn?" Jean-Marc prompted.

"The reason why the Saudis will not blame the Israelis is because it appears that there are several prominent Mullahs and Imams connected indirectly to the Royal House who wish this event to come to pass as well."

"What? On their own soil?" Jean-Marc couldn't believe his ears. "The Arabs are working *with* the Jews? This *is* a special occasion."

Mohammed went on, "Only certain influential individuals are involved, not the governments themselves. You see, monsieur, much to my very own surprise, I am led to understand that our potential new client is in fact a small, but very powerful consortium of key Jewish, Christian, and Muslim leaders and clerics. Apparently, on this particular matter, all the children of Abraham are in agreement."

"It is a *religious* organization?" Jean-Marc brow furrowed.

Mohammed laughed. "It could be. Or it could easily be something else entirely, merely a cabal of tyrants hiding behind holy men's robes. It certainly wouldn't be the first time. I don't care, and in my opinion, neither should you. They have their reasons. Andrew Duncan is a wealthy man, and therefore surely not without rivals and enemies. As I said, it's a small, but most powerful organization. They have the financial resources to pay us a princely sum. They also know that you are one of the only men in the world that can satisfy their needs, discretely and efficiently. Their instructions were clear. We merely have to make what was found beneath the Rub Al Khali disappear with no witnesses left behind."

Jean-Marc sounded pensive. "I don't know. Nuclear toys are very messy. The Americans will detect any thermonuclear detonation by satellite imaging, or by seismic sensors positioned around the world. They will know."

Mohammed nodded, "Yes. And when they do, they will surely believe the Saudis were working independently, despite all the formal denials that will surely be issued. Which means the Americans will be all the more eager to help them conceal their secret to protect their own uninterrupted access to Saudi oil."

Xavier asked, "What do *you* really think is down there in that hole, *mon ami*? What could it be that this mysterious group of well-heeled clergymen doesn't want anyone to find?"

"I asked that question myself," he replied. "I was told the answer would cost me my life and to inquire no further. And this is why the strike team itself may never return from this assignment."

Jean-Marc nodded with understanding.

Mohammed suggested, "It won't be difficult. We can recalibrate the timer on the detonator. Set it to display one hour, when it really is set for ten minutes."

"Yes," Jean-Marc nodded. "That is simple to do." He took a long breath. "How many personnel are on site with Duncan?"

"Perhaps a hundred. No more."

"Good. And security?"

"Twenty-six of the hundred, according to Baradi's report. Most will be sleeping when the team arrives. The entire compound will be gassed initially, and then the team will proceed into the dig. Baradi assured me that they will encounter very light resistance, if any, after they breach the perimeter. Two of them can carry the weapon down to the underground facility and arm it. They will still be in the lift on the way up when it detonates. Their companions will be waiting for them above. From looking at the maps, I envision a half-megaton device would be sufficient."

Jean-Marc rubbed his chin and let out a long pensive sigh. "I can get two of those from Hon Lee in Pyongyang. We can pick them up in Yemen. Or perhaps a single megaton device through Amindani in the Sudan. He can route it through Tripoli or Damascus. He owes me a favor. That also might be easier, and more discrete, but it will leave a much bigger hole." He turned to Mohammed again. "One hundred and fifty-million Euros?"

"That's what they are offering."

Jean-Marc sniffed indignantly at the air. "Tell them we'll do it, but only for five-hundred million US. And I want it in South African gold."

Mohammed noticed a tiny spatter of blood on the knee of his trousers. He wanted to wipe it off, but knew touching it would only press it deeper into the fibers. He pulled a silk handkerchief out of his breast pocket and proceeded to wick it away. "I did not get the impression that they were going to be hard negotiators, if we can absolutely assure successful completion."

"Good." Jean-Marc huffed. "When do they want this done?"

"Immediately, of course." Mohammed looked back to Baradi's body as he tucked the handkerchief back into his pocket, watching a dark ribbon of blood dribble off the edge of the opposite seat and start to puddle on the carpet below. He knew the mess was of no consequence. That carpet would never need to be cleaned. The entire car would be in a crusher along with the body of its new permanent occupant before dawn. "How long will it take you to arrange for the weapon?"

Xavier shrugged. "If I start making calls tonight, I would say two or three days at best. A week at worst. Enough time for you to properly prepare your strike team."

CHAPTER 17

Beep.

When the first beep sounded no one knew what it was.

Only Helen and Jason were in the chamber at the time, sitting patient vigil through their assigned watch. The group of six, which now included Dr. Markham, had set up a round-the-clock observation schedule staffed by two-member teams, each team taking four hour shifts. The initial excitement and curiosity of their incredible discovery had eventually worn off after thirty-six hours of sleep deprivation, and with no apparent change in the health status of their patient. Adrenaline fueled energy ultimately yielded to severe boredom, physical fatigue, and the desperate need for rays of sunlight and a long hot relaxing shower. Fortunately, in addition to an air-conditioner, Andrew Duncan's quarters were also equipped with a fully functional shower and its own portable hot water heater.

The pale blue body had been soaking in the warm water for over seventy hours. The water temperature had been consistently maintained at ninety-eight degrees for the last forty-eight of those hours. Adding hot water was required less and less often, which Jason noted was in keeping with normal thermal loss from the seventy-six degree air temperature of the chamber. The body was retaining heat. Dr. Markham decided it was wise to elevate the upper torso slightly such that the face was out of the water, to prevent drowning—just in case it miraculously started to breathe. When he actually made that suggestion out loud, everyone thought the idea sounded more than a little absurd, but no one dared voice an objection.

As soon as the body was sufficiently thawed, Dr. Markham also took it upon himself to remove the network of guy wires. This task wasn't a matter of merely clipping them off flush to the skin. No, they had to be removed surgically. Beneath the surface of the skin he found the wires attached to tiny eyelets on the ends of fine metal screws anchored into the bones themselves. They easily twisted free merely with a pair of forceps. He fully expected there to be some associated blood loss in the process, assuming the blood was thawing right along with the rest of the body. But there was none, as though he were operating on a cadaver.

That morbid observation led to a lively discussion of whether or not the body might have originally been drained of all its blood, as morticians commonly do, which then led to the suggestion that the body might need an infusion of fresh blood. The infirmary didn't have a large quantity of plasma on-hand, only a few pints of the most common blood types in case of emergency. No one in the group was too keen on the notion of volunteering for a transfusion either. The whole topic was rendered moot a few hours later when bright red drops of blood were detected in the tank. They were clearly visible seeping out of several of the larger guy wire holes—but soon stopped when the holes themselves closed up of their own accord, and within minutes could no longer be detected where they had once been.

Beep.

It happened as Jason was busy dealing a fresh hand of Crazy-Eights with a deck of well-worn blue-backed Bicycle playing cards. Helen was pouring herself a fresh cup of coffee, stirring in a packet of sugar and a spoonful of powdered creamer. The tiny beeps began about thirty seconds apart.

"Did you hear something?" Jason stopped dealing.

Helen set her plastic spoon down, and cocked her head for several seconds, listening. "No, why?"

Jason listened again, but heard nothing. "I thought I...never mind. Five of clubs to you."

Beep.

"That!" Jason pointed over toward the golden box. "A little beep. Like a smoke detector with a low battery."

Helen turned to The Box. "Could some of the equipment be running down?"

Jason shook his head. "I didn't think any of it was battery powered. I thought it was all one-ten, plugged into the generator."

"Could something be wrong with the generator?" she asked.

They both rose and walked over to the golden box. Its occupant lay just as they had seen him for the last three days. Although, Helen thought his complexion looked a little more pinkish, not quite so blue.

Beep.

Jason looked over to the heart monitor display, seeing nothing but the same flat green line, having just missed the short spike as it scrolled off the screen. He reached into the tepid water and put the ends of his forefinger and middle finger over the wrist of the body, checking for a pulse. He felt nothing. At least it was warm, he thought.

Beep.

The simultaneous event of the EEG's beep and the faint sensation under Jason's fingertips propelled his eyes back to the green phosphorous screen.

He saw the narrow little spike. "Call Dr. Markham. Now!"

Helen felt a tingle of excitement wash over her, as she ran to grab the two-way radio on the table. "Why? What's wrong?"

Jason couldn't believe the words coming out of his own mouth. "This can't be happening, but I think I've got a pulse."

•

Over the next four hours the faint little beeps and spikes steadily became stronger and more frequent. What began at two faint beats per minute had gradually risen to fifty, weak, but growing stronger. There was still no sign of respiration or any physical movement at that point. That momentous event occurred rather abruptly, about an hour and a half later, and in no less traumatic a fashion than a healthy newborn taking its first desperate breath after emerging from nine months of captivity in the womb.

He roared.

It was no feeble whimper or moan. Oh, no. This was a full-on, spine-chilling, piss-your-pants, duck-for-cover ROAR!—a mighty roar of unimaginable anguish and fierce pent-up torment. The bone-jarring acoustic wave reverberated off the curved stone walls of the chamber, which only served to amplify it all the more.

All six of them had been sitting quietly clustered around the card table, waiting, watching, imagining, hoping, wondering—not knowing what to expect. It was the initial sound of the water in The Box suddenly sloshing and thrashing with violent fury that first drew them to their feet in unison, with hearts pounding, sending one metal chair clattering onto its back. However, it was the sheer terrifying raw intensity of the thundering vocal roar that made each of them instantly cower upon the floor, quaking in fear.

From the moment it started it didn't stop.

The monstrous bellowing only grew louder and louder and ever more terrible with every passing second. Water splashed and sprayed in every direction as if a violent battle were being waged inside the golden box. The air was charged with static electricity and smelled thick with ozone. Helen felt the sensation of millions of tiny pin pricks crawling over her skin. She closed her eyes and protectively covered her head with her hands. Her only thought was: *God in heaven, what have we done?*

In fact, all eyes were clamped down tight at that moment. Else and Christine were crying. Andrew had crawled under the card table with his fists pressed tight to his cheeks, oblivious to the fact that he'd wet himself. Dr. Markham fainted.

And then it stopped.

Silence.

It was Jason who first dared to look up, a few seconds after the awful sound ceased, as abruptly as it started. His ears were ringing. His teeth were chattering. His hands were shaking. The freshly bruised knee he had just landed on was throbbing in pain, but he ignored it.

The chamber lay quiet and still once more.

The waters inside The Box lapped and ebbed and calmed.

When Jason finally found the courage to pry open his eyes, he immediately saw the tall, muscular form of the light blue body. Except, it was no longer lying down. It was standing tall inside The Box, towering to the full height of its magnificent stature. The arms hung loosely at its sides. Jason couldn't breathe. It was staring back at him with bright luminescent eyes.

PART II
ETERNAL SECRETS

"Now it came to pass, when men began to multiply on the face of the earth, and daughters were born to them, that the **sons of God** saw the daughters of men, that they were beautiful; and they took wives for themselves of all whom they chose. There were **Nephilim**[13] on the earth in those days, and also afterward, when the **sons of God** came in to the daughters of men and they **bore children** to them. Those were the mighty men, **who were of old**, men of renown. Then the Lord saw that the wickedness of man was great in the earth, and that every intent of the thoughts of his heart was only evil continually. And the Lord was sorry that He had made man on the earth, and He was grieved in His heart. So the Lord said, I will destroy man whom I have created from the face of the earth, both man and beast, creeping thing and birds of the air, for I am sorry that I have made them. But Noah found grace in the eyes of the Lord." [emphasis added]

Genesis 6:1,2,4-8

---

[13] Nephilim (or Nefilim): Some biblical translations render *Nephilim* as "Giants." It is a Hebrew proper noun, plural, literally meaning, "Those who came down," or "The Fallen Ones."

CHAPTER 18

"Be not afraid."

That was easier said than done. Jason tentatively rose to his knees, his jaw held agape, his lips struggling to form the letter Y. "Y-y-you...sssspeak English?"

"I speak all tongues."

Else lifted her head at the sound of voices and wiped the blur of tears from her eyes. She saw Helen and Christine a few feet away, to her immediate left, both crouched low, hugging each other close like mother-daughter. Andrew was crawling out from under the table to Else's right, his eyes frozen wide and unblinking. Dr. Markham remained in an unconscious sprawl.

Helen let go of Christine, wiped her nose, and struggled to her feet. She froze in place the instant his luminescent eyes found hers, her cheeks burning red. A lump seized her throat. It was difficult to breathe.

He held out his hand to her. "Come to me."

Helen's first instinct was to turn and run as hard and fast as her trusty old legs would carry her, right out of the golden door; but a bizarre momentary image flashing through her mind of lightning bolts instantly incinerating her into a small pile of gray ash kept her feet securely in place. They obediently stumbled forward of their own accord, in halting, hesitant baby steps, but making progress.

He swung one leg up and stepped out of The Box with graceful ease and stood before it, his body dripping wet and glistening, his eyes still intent upon Helen's face. The EEG pads were gone, evidently ripped away, by the appearance of the light purplish-pink abrasions where they had been attached.

"It is by your hand that I am free. And so to you I offer my gratitude."

Helen could not begin to comprehend what she was hearing or seeing. Her mouth was cotton dry, barely able to whisper, "Who *are* you?"

He hesitated slightly. "One who was bound, but now am free."

Curiosity more than courage propelled both Else and Christine off the floor one by one. They made it to their feet, trembling in complete awe of what they were witnessing. It was as though an exquisite piece of marble had magically come to life and stood before them speaking. Else recalled the story of Michelangelo's *Moses*, on display in the Church of St. Peter in Chains, in Rome. Supposedly, the sculpture was so lifelike, Michelangelo demanded that his creation speak to him. To this day, the statue still bears scars on one of its knees from the great sculptor's mallet, where he struck it in frustration when the statue refused to respond. Yet this magnificent statue standing before them could both speak and move of its own accord. An anxious chill simultaneously swept over each of them as he began to take an aggressive step forward, but that brief sensation quickly changed to one of surprise when his legs wobbled and faltered like a newborn colt's. He quickly reached behind him and grabbed the edge of the golden box to steady himself.

He smiled. "The spirit is willing…but…the flesh is weak."

The group stared in shocked silence.

It was Else who suddenly blurted out, "*What* are you?"

His eyes found hers. She instinctively retreated a step back.

"All of your questions—and I know they are many—I shall be delighted to answer in due course." He took a long deep breath, casting his gaze from face to face, studying them, sensing them, measuring them. "But for the moment, I should imagine you would all feel much more comfortable with my visage, and I should feel considerably warmer, if I could be provided with a warm cloak. Thermal retention is most important for my present physical condition, until the quickening be complete." And with that he slid down to a sitting position, leaning his back against the warm metal surface of the golden box, folding his arms tightly across his chest, shivering uncontrollably, his breathing labored and rapid.

Without a moment's hesitation Christine grabbed two of the heavy navy blue wool blankets from the stack that Dr. Markham had brought down and walked over to him. Her limp was barely noticeable. The sheer velocity of thoughts racing through her mind crowded out her initial fears. She stood next to him, opened the first blanket and covered his lower body, then leaned over and draped the second one up to his shoulders, covering his upper torso. Their eyes met, not twelve inches apart.

"Thank you," he whispered through chattering teeth.

Christine swallowed with a considerable degree of difficulty and then stood up straight, her eyes never leaving his. They were fiery and brilliant, like diamonds. Her lungs froze and her pulse doubled when she saw his huge hand reach out and gently take hold of her right leg, sliding the pant cuff of her jeans halfway up her calf to peer underneath.

He looked up into her eyes once more, dismayed. "This is not your flesh."

She couldn't speak. Her cheeks and ears were turning pink.

He let go, sounding almost annoyed. "We shall repair this."

Christine was trembling anew, seven shades of red past embarrassed. No matter how much she fought it, she was powerless to prevent the painful panoply of indelible images from flashing through her thoughts—the images and sensations that were never more than a triggered memory away: riding her bicycle at the age of eight, enjoying the smell of honeysuckle in bloom growing along the low chain-link fences mixing with the aroma of fresh cut lawns, the warmth of the afternoon sun on her shoulders, the chatter of an angry mockingbird arguing for its territory, the wind caressing her cheeks and pushing her hair off the back of her neck, the engine sound of the speeding car approaching, a radio blasting some loud R&B tune, the screeching of brakes and the shriek of tires, the blunt impact of metal, the vertigo of flying through the air, the grinding burn and oily smell of hot asphalt and tar, the iron taste of blood, the horror of exposed bone, the screams and cries and urgent shouts, the pale green rubber gloves swarming over her, the lights, the sirens, the shots, the minty taste of the gas in the plastic mask on her face...the numbed sensation of waking in a strange bed with part of her missing.

Helen moved closer to him, breaking Christine's trance. "How long have you been here?"

He shook his head in wonder. "Far longer than I intended."

"What happened?" she simply asked.

Everyone's ears perked up.

He studied her eyes for some time before answering. "In the childhood of your days we spoke to you in mysteries, fables, parables, riddles—for you did not yet have the maturity to understand complex things. Yet for so long have I watched you grow, and develop, and oh...I must say...you have come so far in such a short time. Therefore, the time has now come for us to put away childish things, and speak to you plainly, for you are now able to bear it."

No one dared say a word.

He took another long, deep breath, thinking, deciding. And then he candidly told them, "You find me here because something went wrong. A cryostasis malfunction perhaps. You never should have had to cut me free, or revive me manually. The whole termination process should normally take no more than an hour. Perhaps there was terrestrial sensor damage above ground as well." He furrowed his brow. "The atmospheric analysis process should have terminated cryostasis automatically long ago, as soon as surface radiation levels had normalized and conditions were safe again."

"What surface radiation?" Helen was puzzled.

"Lethal doses of residual gamma and sub-gamma level terrestrial and atmospheric irradiation. The consequence of what you refer to as the subatomic fission process, or thermonuclear radiation," he replied. "From the war."

"What war?" It was Andrew, who had approached silently, oblivious to the dark stain on the front of his pants.

A note of sadness tainted his answer. "A long forgotten war. The war fought for dominion of this planet, fought between factions of my people, not yours. The war that ultimately determined your destiny. The Worker's War. That is what it was called." He looked around at the bewildered eyes staring at him, then cast his countenance down. The bitterness he felt was thinly veiled. "It was all foolish lies or rationalizations. These appellations mean little now. Thousands upon thousands died. Entire cities were crushed, the great cities of old. Whole cultures were wiped clean from the planet's face. So much beauty, knowledge, and prosperity vanquished to ashes in but an instant."

Else asked, "So what was the real reason for this war?"

His seethed, "It was fought for many of the same illogical reasons found throughout the vast chronicles of your own kind. Self-interest. Ambition. Pride. Arrogance. Greed. Power. The usual lot. Although, I assure you, *none* of my own kind, those directly responsible for unleashing such mindless destruction, would ever dare to admit that the real reason for such an apocalyptic calamity..." His expression softened. "...was ultimately because of a woman."

Jason huffed, "Isn't it always?"

Andrew, Else and Christine all turned at the distraction of Jason's voice with a look of disdain, but Helen paid him no mind. Her eyes remained fixed on the stranger's, careful to notice how his bright glistening eyes were rimmed with tears.

CHAPTER 19

Hebrew University
Jerusalem, Israel

The second floor office door was locked. Rabbi David Shemel was alone. He untied the well-oiled leather binding and opened the heavy parchment scroll on his desk. He wanted to be sure. After a short prayer, he took a deep breath and read the Aramaic text from the forbidden *Book of Enoch*[14], written centuries before Moses is reputed to have authored the book of Genesis. Enoch was the seventh patriarch descended from Adam. He was Noah's grandfather—the one who did not die, because God "took him" into the heavens[15]. Rabbi Shemel began his reading in chapter six:

> And it came to pass when the children of men had multiplied, that in those days were born unto them beautiful and comely daughters. And the angels, the children of the heaven, saw and lusted after them, and said to one another: "Come, let us choose us wives from among the children of men and beget us children."
>
> And these are the names of their leaders: Samiazaz, their leader, Arakiba, Rameel, Kokabiel, Tameil, Rameil, Danel, Ezeqeel, Baraqijal, Azazel, Armaros, Batarel, Ananel, Zaqiel, Samsapeel, Satarel, Turel, Jomjael, Sariel. These are their chiefs of tens. And all the others together with them took unto themselves wives, and each chose for himself one, and they began to go in unto them and to defile themselves with them, and they taught them charms and enchantments, and the cutting of roots, and made them acquainted with plants. And they became pregnant, and they bore great giants.
>
> And Azazel taught men to make swords, and knives,

---

[14] Excerpt from *The Apocrypha and Pseudepigrapha of the Old Testament {Vol. II Pseudepigrapha}* R.H. Charles, ed., Oxford: The Clarendon Press, 1913.
[15] Cf: Genesis 5:21-24.

and shields, and breastplates, and made known to them the metals of the earth and the art of working them. And there arose much godlessness, and they committed fornication, and they were led astray, and became corrupt in all their ways. Samiazaz taught enchantments, and root-cuttings, Armaros the resolving of enchantments, Baraqijal taught astrology, Kokabiel the constellations, Ezeqeel the knowledge of the clouds, Arakiba the signs of the earth, Samsapeel the signs of the sun, and Sariel the course of the moon.

And then Michael, Uriel, Raphael, and Gabriel looked down from heaven and saw much blood being shed upon the earth, and all lawlessness being wrought upon the earth. And they said one to another: "Thou seest what Azazel hath done, who hath taught all unrighteousness on earth and revealed the eternal secrets which were preserved in heaven, which men were striving to learn."

Then said the Most High, the Holy and Great One spake, and sent Uriel to the son of Lamech, and said to him: "Go to Noah and tell him in my name 'Hide thyself!' and reveal to him the end that is approaching: that the whole earth will be destroyed, and a deluge is about to come upon the whole earth, and will destroy all that is on it. And now instruct him that he may escape and his seed may be preserved for all the generations of the world."

And again the Lord said to Raphael: "Bind Azazel hand and foot, and cast him into the darkness: and make an opening in the desert, which is in Dudael, and cast him therein. And let him abide there forever, and cover his face that he may not see light. And on the day of the great judgment he shall be cast into the fire. And heal the earth which the angels have corrupted, heal the plague, that all the children of men may not perish through all the secret things that the Watchers have disclosed and have taught their sons."

The old Rabbi sat back his chair and stared out the window. His hands were trembling, but not from age. Students strolled cheerfully across the school's well-tended grounds, engaged in jovial conversations, joking and laughing. Oh, yes, he mused, how they all relentlessly strive to learn the secret things. Yet the secret things, the truly sacred eternal secrets, were meant to remain secrets forever. He lifted the telephone receiver and dialed the private cell number in Italy.

After two rings, "*Si?*"

"It has been arranged," he whispered.

"And what was the price, my brother?" came Cardinal Ricollo's faint voice.

A pang of guilt squeezed Shemel's chest. He sniffed and replied, "Five hundred million dollars US. In gold."

"Well done. Send me the instructions and I will attend to the transfer."

The Rabbi added, "And also a price of one hundred-thirteen souls."

There was a moment of silence on the line. "I shall say a special Mass for their sacrifice this very night."

Shemel closed his eyes, clinging to what he'd been telling himself for the last twenty-four hours. "Yes. I shall pray for them as well. Better a hundred lost for the cause of good than to lose six billion."

"David, you're not growing faint of heart are you?"

"Don't be ridiculous," he replied. "I know what's at stake."

"When?"

"Soon," Shemel replied. "A matter of days. Perhaps only hours."

"You have spoken personally with Sheik Abdullah and Ayatollah Ali?"

"I have. They are both well, and send you their greetings and special blessing." Rabbi David Shemel glanced out the window again at all the young lives passing by, all so full of potential and dreams, ambition and vigor. There really was no choice in the matter. He added, "I am assured there will be no questions asked. There will be no repercussions."

The old cardinal laughed and wheezed, his voice drawing cold and ominous. "No repercussions? David, even *we* can't guarantee that, even if we are successful."

CHAPTER 20

"Follow me. The time has come to begin." He rose to his feet and walked away, leaving everyone staring after him, speechless.

It was all he said after sitting motionless and silent for so many long hours by the golden box, resting his eyes, filling his lungs with long, slow deep breaths. The entire group wasted no time in exiting the chamber behind him, walking in puzzled silence up several winding staircases to the third level of the underground complex. With one of the blankets secured around his lower half like a beach towel, and the other one draped about his shoulders like a shawl, he led them through the intricate maze of dark corridors to the threshold of an insignificant looking alcove. It was really nothing more than an arched niche at the end of a long hallway. To Helen, the recess appeared to have perhaps been fashioned to display a statue, or other large artistic decoration. She was wrong.

It was a door.

"What *is* this place?" Christine asked when the group stopped.

He stretched forth his hand and laid his fingertips upon a circular stone about shoulder height. It glowed brightly with a yellow hue beneath his touch and then dimmed. Next came the sound of stone grinding upon stone as the rear wall of the niche neatly cleaved in two.

He answered, "Long ago, shortly after our arrival, I constructed this facility for the requirements of my work." He pointed through the opened doorway. "In here all your questions will be answered. Come with me, and learn, if you will."

He disappeared through the darkened doorway.

Helen didn't particularly relish the fleeting memory of Dante Alighieri's admonition upon reaching the threshold of the *Inferno,* as detailed in his *Divine Comedy,* "Abandon Hope All Ye Who Enter Here."

Dr. Markham, who was still in a slight disoriented state of shock, and looking more than a little pale, if not punch-drunk, took inventory of five equally anxious expressions arrayed before him. He whispered, "I'm sorry, but I don't know if I can do this. How can any of you? This is too fantastic, if not completely insane. We need to call people, alert someone. There could be dangers. Diseases. We have no idea of what—"

Andrew put his hand on the doctor's shoulder, interrupting, "You're no more terrified or insatiably curious about all this than the rest of us, Kenneth. We press on together, or we don't press on at all. Whoever he is, or *whatever* he is, he's right. We all have a million questions. Think of what an opportunity this is—before the experts and authorities come in and take him away."

After a moment of anxious deliberation Dr. Markham offered a solemn nod.

With that, Helen sucked in a deep breath and marched first through the doorway, immediately followed by Christine, then Else and Jason. Andrew produced a tight-lipped smile as he extended Dr. Markham a grand *after-you* wave of his hand, then waited until Dr. Markham had entered before bringing up the rear. Nothing in Andrew Duncan's entire existence could have prepared him for what lay on the other side of that door, or for what he was about to learn and experience. That was true of all of them, even those who would not survive it.

•

The stone doorway led them into a short, dim connecting passage, which opened up into a spacious room beyond with a high, vaulted ceiling. The room was brightly lit with the same ethereal white luminescence that they had seen emanating from the walls of the great domed chamber four levels below. But this room was not empty. It was stacked high with a vast inventory of metal and glass equipment, tables, tools and containers of all sizes. Their mysterious new host was nowhere to be seen. The two navy blue wool blankets lay discarded on the floor.

"What *is* this place?" Andrew wondered aloud.

Helen glanced at Christine before announcing, "I think it's a laboratory."

"Yes, it is," came his voice, as he rounded a tall metal cabinet, finishing buttoning up a loose-fitting white robe that stopped just below his knees. "This way, if you please."

He led them through the extensive laboratory complex to an adjacent side room whose interior reminded Andrew of a Turkish steam bath. It was semicircular and roomy, made entirely of white marble, lit from above, and boasted two elevated tiers of marble benches, amphitheater style. The one straight wall featured the doorway by which they had entered. There was no steam in the air. All the surfaces were cool, smooth and dry.

Christine was the first to realize it was a stadium-styled classroom.

"I invite you all to take a seat and listen carefully," he instructed, as they dutifully filed into the room and sat down. "As I said, I know your questions are many, and I truly beg your forgiveness if I seem overly aloof in what little I have shared with you thus far. It is not my intention to withhold anything from you—quite the opposite in fact. I mean to tell you everything. It is about time your kind knew the truth. And apparently fate has chosen each of you to be here this day, to find me, to learn, to know the truth. And learn you shall. Not only about me and my people, but more importantly, about yourselves."

Helen involuntarily shuddered.

He bowed his head for a moment, eyes closed, as if searching for the proper place to begin, or perhaps meditating on a silent invocation before announcing, "The most fundamental and preeminent fact you must learn is this: Long ago I began a great and important work, that despite its most unfortunate and prolonged interruption, thanks to you, is finally on the threshold of completion. You have no idea how long, or how deeply, I have yearned for this day to come. *This* very day! When freedom has arrived and I am once again permitted to fulfill my mission, my destiny. And yet, it is you six precious souls gathered here today, that have given me this new day, a gracious gift of generosity beyond compare. And with heartfelt gratitude for doing so, I hereby invite you all, each and every one of you, to join me and share in my work."

"To do what?" Helen really wanted to know. "What work?"

He lifted his eyes upward and his face shone more brightly. His words had a soothing, mesmerizing, almost hypnotic effect. "The greatest work of all. To usher in a new kingdom. Our kingdom. To dispel the darkness of the old ways that have lingered for far too long. To finally see your people develop and advance into what they were always predestined to be. To at last lay hold upon your precious inheritance. To ultimately realize your true potential. To become *everything* you have ever dreamed."

Everyone sat in stunned silence.

He smiled with pride. "Very well then. My story begins with me and my people. You long to know my story and the nature of my work, and I long to share it with you more than you shall ever know. For in the very hearing of my story, your very existence is about to change. Oh, yes, your lives will change because you shall shortly come to understand that my story is also *your* story. Our twin destinies are inexorably intertwined. But be forewarned. It is my most ardent aim to share with you a journey of knowledge that shall surely shake the very foundations and crack the very cornerstone of everything you have been led to know and believe…about yourselves, your culture, your origins, your fate. I shall tell you of many secret things, eternal things. Some have called them…sacred things. But in reality, they are in fact the *useful* things, the *necessary* things that have been denied you and your kind for far too long."

And thus the enlightenment began.

CHAPTER 21

He let out a half-laugh. "Your penultimate question need not be uttered, for it is plainly written upon your faces, screaming from your eyes. So, to set your minds and hearts at ease, allow me to answer it just as plainly. I am neither angel nor demon, nor supernatural apparition of any sort. As you can see with your own eyes, I am of flesh and bone, as are you."

Jason spoke up, unable to hold his tongue. "So are you... like...an alien, from another world?"

He smiled. "We both are."

"But you're not *human*," said Christine.

"More so than you," he replied, lifting his palms in calm assurance. "But please, be at peace, my new friends. Give me your ears, your open minds, and your patient attention, and the vast majority of your questions will be richly satisfied in due course."

Helen asked, "What is your name?"

He looked down at the floor. "I have been called by many names and borne many titles throughout the ages. Some were designations of honor by those who loved me and respected me and served me, some of dishonor and disparagement by mine enemies. Most of these appellations and epithets you could not hope to pronounce in your tongue. I tell you truly, labels are not important. For now, I shall simply be your teacher. If you need to address me, it is enough for you to call me Teacher."

Christine and Helen exchanged a wary glance.

Else looked openly suspicious.

He paused for but a moment to regroup his thoughts before pressing his hands together, as if in prayer, touching the tips of his fingers to his lips with his thumbs under his chin, then spread his arms wide, and began to recount his tale. As he spoke, a bright light shone forth from the palms of his hands, intensifying into a pair of beams which intersected before him creating a spherical three-dimensional hologram, illustrating detailed still graphics and moving color images of everything he described. The group leaned back in awe, amid a gush of oohs and ahs, utterly captivated by the living story he narrated.

"Eons ago my people lived on a beautiful blue world very similar to this one. In truth, it can be found within this very solar system, though it is long dead and cold. We had lived there and advanced as both a great people and as a highly developed society from the very beginning."

Christine was about to interrupt to ask a question, when he turned to her and said, "All will presently become clear." He continued, "Our civilization possessed ingenious technology, enormous wisdom, and great power. I wish I could tell you that we were merely explorers, that we were nothing more than adventurers seeking new and distant lands, travelers sojourning in a foreign country, but it was not so. At best, we were pilgrims. We came here for no more benevolent purpose than to survive the scourge of a dying planet, to begin our lives and civilization anew."

Jason asked, "Why did you come *here?*"

The pictures dissolved into a view of earth from space, the beautiful and radiant blue marble. "This planet offered abundant natural resources. However, it was approximately two million of your years behind our world in its overall development of life. That was no significant surprise to us. We have known since the beginning that different worlds form, develop, run their course, and collapse into their mother stars on their own schedules. It is the perpetual lifecycle process of the heavens. There are entire galaxies, as well as individual new star systems, engaged in the birth process, condensing and aligning their energy and forming as we gather here today. And eons from now, they may still be found wanting in comparison to the condition of this pristine planet when we arrived. For us, the abundance that this world offered was fortunate circumstance."

Andrew asked, "How many of you were there?"

"Initially, only a few. No more than fifty, but more came over time. The mission to this world was originally led by my brother and I. However, by virtue of him being older than I, he was ultimately in command. He and his men were soldiers by trade. They came here fully armed as invaders, full of pride in their terrible weapons and technologies, prepared to conquer and to be served. Yet there was no one here to fight but the beasts and creeping things of the field, the birds of the air. In essence, it is for that reason that we ended up killing each other, and very nearly all of you. But I'm getting ahead of myself."

"Did you also have a sister?" Else asked.

He nodded, as the image of a beautiful face illuminated in the hologram. "Yes. A half-sister. My father, who remained behind on our world, was a great man. He had many wives and many concubines for his pleasure and his progeny. My sister was the daughter of his chief concubine, one most fair and beautiful for our people, as graceful a creature as my kind had ever known. My brother was the son of our father's first wife, and thus his firstborn and rightful heir. I was the son of his second wife. So our arrangement was simple: he ruled while I built. I designed, he implemented."

"So was your sister 'the woman' you referred to earlier?" Else asked.

"No. But I shall come to that topic presently." As he remembered his place in his story, the holographic scenes shifted to panoramic landscapes of great architectural construction and agricultural development. "You see, for a great while we worked diligently to colonize and replicate our entire culture in this new place. Our population grew steadily over time, but not in significant numbers. There were numerous conflicts and problems to resolve, but for the most part, we made a good start here. The real problem was you."

"What did *we* do?" Andrew sounded defensive.

The teacher could only shake his head and laugh to himself in a disarming, self-deprecating manner. "You exceeded your expectations. But then, that was *my* fault. It all began when the order came from my brother for the creation of a servant class. Our own people had grown increasingly tired and resentful of their daily labors in an untamed and uncivilized frontier world, and they knew we possessed the technology to change their lot. I only agreed to do it because of the secret. My secret. The *great* secret."

"What secret?" Helen was captivated.

"I knew I could do it," he evaded the question. "Even though I was forbidden to do it, or even speak of it. I knew that, and do not deny it. But that prohibition, as I saw it, was a law on our planet, not on this one. This was a virgin world. There was no council of the twelve here to tell me how to do anything. There was only my brother. I promised him his workers to toil in his fields, to mine his precious metals, to build our homes and our cities, to feed us, to meet all our needs and satisfy our every desire. He wanted pack animals, slaves, servants." He paused. "I wanted children. There was a way to have both. And if I was careful, to keep him from finding out how."

"So what did you do?" It was Dr. Markham, surprisingly.

"I made you," he said. "Your kind."

"You what?" the doctor stammered, clearly stunned.

Helen could feel her cheeks burning. Her stomach was churning.

The teacher shrugged slightly as the image in the hologram dissolved into a scene of a team dressed in white robes like the one he was wearing working fastidiously in a laboratory similar to the one in the next room, only much larger. "To be more precise, let us say I successfully engineered your species from available resources. My trade and expertise is in science and technology. However, my knowledge of the sciences goes far beyond your understanding or progression to date in the underlying disciplines and related fields." He was quick to add, "But don't take that statement as a derision or judgment. I only refer to your level of progression in knowledge thus far. For example..." The holographic image changed to the familiar double helix of a DNA strand. "...it has only been in your most recent history that your own scientists have discovered that the form and function of all living things are determined in a fashion analogous to the mathematical programs you execute on your computational machines. In essence, there is a code. You call it a genome. How that code is constructed specifically determines how your energy is manifested, how it functions, and whether you are a bacterium, a fish, a lion, or a man."

"Why did you say energy?" asked Christine. "Don't you mean biology?"

"No. I mean energy. The genome concept, and the discipline of biology itself, is a macro-science. I meant *energy*, which is an elemental quantum science. Your kind is only beginning to learn of these things, and has only scratched the surface of your understanding of them." He looked directly into her eyes. "Everything is comprised of energy, and energy is all that truly exists. How it is organized and polarized for manifestation is all that matters."

For the first time in her entire life Christine suddenly didn't feel like the smartest student in the class.

The image changed to a cloudy apparition of multi-colored light flashes and comets streaking by in complex arrays of dancing patterns. "There is *only* energy. It takes on many forms, and depending on its electromagnetic orientation, and how it coalesces and condenses, it creates fields. It is when these infinitesimally small fields condense and coalesce in conjunction with other fields, and thus become magnetically dense enough not to allow other condensations to penetrate them, that you call them particles of matter, and classify them by the way they behave. But they are not truly particles, in what you think of as solid matter. They are still only dense forms of energy. Thus, your fundamental concept of what you call matter is but an illusion."

"How do you know so much about what we know?" Christine demanded.

"I have watched you. I have watched everything about you, since the very beginning," he replied. "And yet, for the last four-thousand of your solar cycles, *all* I could do was watch you from where you found me."

"*How* did you watch us?" Helen asked.

"The methodology will be explained later. What is pertinent is that I watched. I followed your progress. How could I not? I cared deeply about you. But I digress." He stopped himself as the double helix DNA stand reappeared. "As I was saying, it is your genome that determines your physiological form, function and manifestations of energy. So even though my brother wanted me to fashion a beast of burden, at a minimum, an effective laborer had to be capable of completing the tasks we ourselves had formerly performed. Therefore, our laborer required certain essential characteristics—a modicum of intelligence, an opposable thumb to wield our tools, adequate strength to perform a variety of duties, the ability to communicate, the intellectual capacity and aptitude to follow basic instructions, some elementary problem solving capacity, and so forth."

"That all makes sense," Andrew noted with a half-smile. "I wouldn't mind having more workers that met those qualifications myself."

A mischievous smile appeared on the teacher's lips. "Yes, that was the goal, simple practical functionality. This was the basic argument I used to deceive my brother. And so we agreed to fabricate your kind in our own image, but he was adamant that you not be endowed with all of our capabilities. There were to be engineered restrictions."

"So how was all of this accomplished?" Dr. Markham bore the scowl of high priest who has born witness to blasphemy. "Are you contradicting the entire concept of natural evolution and saying you spliced together a completely random genetic code and let it develop in a lab?"

"Not at all." The hologram dissolved into the image of an early hominid, hairy, sloped skull, prominent brow, hunched shoulders. "It was not logical to waste valuable time re-engineering a machine that already worked properly, and was so close to what we required. So I simply started with a base genome of indigenous primate hominids, the creature your anthropological scientists refer to as *homo erectus*. It was scarcely more than a brute beast, just over two-hundred genes different from a contemporary chimpanzee. And thus I took our very own genetic code, which was much more advanced and developed than any life form on this planet at the time, and by virtue of the speed and precision of the genetic accelerators you passed by in the other room, I blended the two codes together to fashion your program, your new code." The image of the hominid morphed into a man's face very similar to his own.

"We were a genetic experiment?" Jason sounded appalled.

"No! Not at all! You were a genetic triumph," he insisted. "But being the byproduct of an approved biological integration process is exactly what I wanted my brother to believe. If I had used our full genome code to manufacture mere replicants he would have executed me. Remember, he wanted an inferior, no more than an obedient slave to be used and abused with no remorse. This is the singularly crucial point that you must understand, which served as the basis for my actions in designing you."

"But we aren't *like* you," Helen protested.

"Oh, yes you *are*," he replied. "I can *show* you. I have apparatus here in my laboratory, more advanced than any of your most powerful electron microscopes, devices capable of mapping pure-pattern engram energy fields. With a simple hemoglobin sample I can show you how your genome and mine are identical in both length and elementary structure." The hologram panned out from the face of the new humanoid to a full body view. "The only significant differences were put there by design for your protection. I merely left a few traits active from the original hominid, such as residual traces of body hair, a slightly reduced stature from our own, and a variable melanin count to alter your pigmentation for adaptation to the climates and solar radiation levels you would be exposed to, depending upon the geographic locale of your inevitable migrations. Understand clearly, I did this to *disguise* you, yes, to outwardly make you appear different from us. But these differences were only superficial."

"How ironic," Jason muttered out loud. "The color of my skin was intended to protect me, not to persecute me."

The teacher turned to Jason. "Some lessons your kind learned far too well from my kind."

Jason looked away.

The teacher continued, "Most noteworthy, and again for your protection, I had to deactivate certain advanced energy functions so my brother would not find out what I had done until it was too late to stop it. But the truth is, these natural functions, many of which your cultures have romanticized and mythologized in their ignorance as great mystical or magical powers, are all still inside you, hiding dormant, waiting for you to discover and develop them! You only need to learn how to avail yourself of them and use them. That's the first part of the great secret."

"Wai-wai-wait. What *powers*?" Jason was now leaning forward on his bench with his hands on his knees, extremely intrigued.

The teacher dropped his hands to his sides and the hologram vanished. He turned toward the doorway leading back into the laboratory, took three steps, stopped and glanced back over his shoulder with a playful grin. "Come and see."

CHAPTER 22

Jean-Marc Xavier stood next to the truck, watching the heat waves blur up from the mirrored mottling of mirages scattered along the cracked and weed infested runway of the secluded private airstrip fifty miles east of Cairo. His cotton shirt was soaked through with sweat. He could see the plane approaching in the distance. The cargo transport's gear was down. As it swooped in and flared, its rear wheels cried their mournful protest of rubber, glancing twice off the dusty asphalt before settling into its rollout. The roar of the twin turbo-props wound down as the aircraft taxied onto the tarmac and stopped twenty yards from Xavier's truck. With the whine of an electric winch the rear ramp immediately began to lower. This wouldn't take long. Two of Xavier's men ran to chock the wheels. A small tanker truck pulled beneath the right wing. Its driver climbed out and began to unroll a fuel hose.

Jean-Marc walked toward the aircraft, followed by four heavily armed men from his truck. The loadmasters inside the cargo bay were already carefully rolling the brushed aluminum crate down the ramp. It was about the size of a standard refrigerator, laying on its back. At the bottom of the ramp Xavier stopped and gestured with an upturned finger to open the crate for inspection. A tall, olive skinned man with a thick black moustache dressed in military desert khakis and thick black jump boots strode down the ramp and knelt in front of the silver box. He referred to an access code scribbled on a small yellow sheet of paper, then entered it quickly into the ten-digit keypad on the lid. An LED display indicated acceptance of the code, written in Cyrillic script, followed by the sound of magnetic bolts springing back. The man lifted the lid and bade Jean-Marc to step forward and make his inspection.

Perfect.

There it was, as promised: a Soviet-made warhead from an SS-20 medium range ballistic missile. He knew the make and model by sight. It was a simple plutonium device with a one megaton yield. The red lights above three arming triggers were dark. The detonator's digital display was dark. The access card slot was empty, as were the two-man safety key cylinders. Jean-Marc nodded and the lid was closed.

He held his hand out to the man in khakis. "The access card, the keys, and the codes?"

The thick moustache widened over a bad dental plan. His voice was a hoarse scrape of gravel, the byproduct of decades of chain smoking and a diet high in cheap bourbon whiskey. "You may have them as soon as the wire transfer is confirmed."

"We came fully prepared to complete our transaction, monsieur." Xavier nodded, as he reached into his trouser pocket, opened his satellite phone and depressed a speed key. A moment later, "Receipt of package confirmed. Release designated funds as instructed. Fifty-seven million US. Correct. Transaction code G97-328-4725. Confirmation code, Sodom and Gomorrah." He ended the call and returned the phone to his pocket. "These things can take a few moments. You understand."

"Then we wait," the man rasped. "I'm sure *you* understand."

"Of course," Xavier nodded, wiping his brow with the back of his hand.

Confirmation didn't take long. Within five minutes the man's own satellite phone rang. "Yes. Excellent. Thank you. Yes, yes. I understand." He hung up, and reached behind his back to retrieved a worn leather pouch the size of a legal envelope from his belt. "You will find everything you need in here."

Jean-Marc took the pouch, opened it and looked inside. Satisfied, he turned to one of his men. "Get it loaded. *Rapidement maintenant!*[16]"

The four men standing behind him went into action.

Jean-Marc managed a smile, tapping the pouch to his brow. "Always a pleasure, monsieur. Please give Mr. Amindani my warmest regards. *Bonjour.*"

The man in uniform returned a curt nod and disappeared back up the loading ramp. In less than five minutes the plane was taxiing back onto the runway, while a nondescript cargo truck bearing a manifest of stereo equipment and microwave ovens was speeding down a barren desert highway across the northern region of the Sinai peninsula, bound for the Saudi Arabian border.

---

[16] French: "Quickly now!"

CHAPTER 23

Dr. Helen Knight found it difficult to contain her own joy. She felt like a young girl back in college again in Chapel Hill, North Carolina, learning the mysteries and wonders of the universe anew. Their new teacher's enthusiasm was delightfully infectious. They were all assembled in the laboratory, eagerly standing before a wide metal table covered with strange tools and devices Helen had never seen before. The function of a few of the items could be surmised from their features, but most of them she felt would only be random speculation or outright guesses.

The teacher held out the palm of his hand and said, "Watch closely. Demonstration number one."

A long thin silver implement, resembling a large fountain pen, flew through the air from an upright container on the other side of the table into his hand, as though his palm were suddenly magnetized.

They all gasped in amazement.

The teacher looked momentarily confused and then laughed. "Oh! No. Forgive me. That is not the demonstration. I needed this instrument *for* the demonstration. I shall be happy to show you later how to retrieve, lift, and move objects for your use. That capability is child's play. *This* is the demonstration."

He held up the pen-like object and squeezed its middle between his thumb and forefinger. A thin, almost transparent blade about an inch long ejected from its end. He used it to make an inch-long incision into the palm of his other hand. Bright red blood ran out of the cut, causing Else and Jason to wince.

"Now watch carefully," he prompted.

Right before their eyes, the edges of the cut pulled together of their own accord and closed, starting at the two ends, slowly fusing together, moving toward the center. In less than thirty seconds there was no trace the wound was ever there.

Everyone applauded.

"This is accelerated tissue regeneration," he said simply. "It is an energy manipulation application. You have this capability in your bodies right now, but your version works much more slowly and not as thoroughly.

113

However, with a few corrections to your code, you too will soon enjoy it as it was meant to be. This function will halt your cellular degeneration process. It will repair all prior tissue oxidation damage, epidermal elasticity loss, bone calcification, muscle atrophy, nerve and organ damage, and so forth, restoring your body to your peak physiological operational condition, as it was originally intended. And once active, unless you are slain, it will maintain that condition indefinitely."

"The fountain of eternal youth," Helen murmured.

Dr. Markham shook his head back and forth in awe. "That's amazing."

"No, it is just applied science. My brother wanted your species to be disposable, to wear out and die, to have no continuity and therefore no opportunity to eventually learn the truth. Immortality was reserved for our kind alone. It is not really that difficult of a condition to achieve, once you learn how to tap into the prime, universal energy source, which indeed, is akin to an unending, infinite fountain. But allow me to show you something *really* amazing." He held out his hand to Dr. Markham. "Would you be willing to participate in a little experiment?"

"What do you intend to do?" Dr. Markham was clearly nervous.

"Give me your hand and see."

Reluctantly, Dr. Markham complied, placing his upturned hand into the teacher's. In a blindingly swift motion, the teacher slashed the pen device across Markham's open palm leaving a deep laceration, over three inches long and a half-inch deep. Muscle and tendons were exposed. Thick drops of blood began to drip to the floor. Dr. Markham barely blinked until he saw the open wound, then he gasped in horror. Helen was certain he would faint again, but he stood stone still, his face going white. He tried to jerk his hand away, but the teacher still had a firm grip.

"Now watch," he instructed. "By your medical understanding, this epidermal penetration would normally require artificial closure and binding, and take several weeks to heal, leaving noticeable scarring and the potential disruption of motor functions. This does not have to be."

The teacher closed his eyes and bowed his head. The wound began to close, moving to the center until it became a thin pink line, which quickly disappeared.

Helen thought she smelled something cooking.

"That's miraculous," Dr. Markham whispered.

"No, that is an example of relational energy transfer for accelerated tissue regeneration," the teacher corrected. "Not much different in basic concept than the kinetic transfer of a fire warming a kettle which boils the water which cooks the vegetables in the soup. I used my energy to accelerate yours, specifically directed at that functionality in your genome that fully actuates accelerated tissue regeneration."

"So this capability is active in me now?" the doctor asked.

The teacher shook his head. "No. Not yet. You were a passive recipient in the process. You see, there may be occasions when your own energy is so depleted through fatigue, or injury, or incapacitation, or a combination of these or other factors, that the available energy you can access by yourself is insufficient to activate and complete the accelerated tissue regeneration process on your own. In such circumstances, the energy from another individual, or group of individuals, may be transmuted to supplement or entirely replace the subject's own energy generation in order to actuate and complete the process. It is just a matter of properly focusing the thought."

Christine was perplexed. "The *thought*? Are you saying energy can be directional, based upon thought?"

The teacher leaned back against the lab table and folded his arms across his chest. "That is the *only* way it works. Thought *is* energy. It is the purest and most powerful form of energy." He paused. "But I am not ready to discuss the manifestations of sentient energy with you yet. You have many more elementary concepts to learn first before you can comprehend it. Let us now attend to something much more simple and basic."

And without another word he stepped forward and lifted Christine into his arms and walked away with her. Her gentle brown eyes went wide, but something reassuring in his expression made her relax. Everyone followed close behind.

The teacher carried Christine to another long metal table in a different section of the laboratory and laid her down. Taking her hands in his own he looked deeply into her eyes. "I want you to trust me. I give you my sacred word that I am not going to harm you in any way. I am only going to help you. And in order for me to help you, I first need you to remove this garment that covers your legs, and allow me to take away this artificial machine you wear."

Christine lay there looking up into his compassionate eyes, trembling and afraid.

His gaze panned across the rest of the group. "Your kind has become ignorantly dependent on far too much technology, to the detriment of your own advancement. Machines are fine servants to do for you what you cannot do, or to increase the efficiency of what you can do. But they too easily become a limitation of your own abilities and a hindrance to your evolution to do that which you can do more efficiently with the capabilities found within yourself." He turned back to Christine. "Let me show you. It is time to repair you properly."

As she listened to his instructions, Christine's eyes puddled with a blur of fresh tears. She hadn't been that afraid since the terrible trauma that took her leg away in the first place—but she did exactly as she was told. The indignity of lying on the cold metal table in her panties and tee-shirt, with the smooth stump of her right leg exposed for all to see was painful enough. But after witnessing what he had done with Dr. Markham's hand, something deep inside her desperately wanted to see what he could do for her.

He began with a blood sample.

"Just lie there and be comfortable." His voice was reassuring. "I'm going to feed your nucleic-acid spectrum into the gene analyzer over here. We shall isolate the schematic segment for your missing limb and use it as a template to manufacture a new one, a proper one. The process does not require a great deal of time, but to do so, I will also need a sample of one of your stem cells."

"What?" She was suddenly much more afraid.

He advised her, "We can either obtain it from your bone marrow, or from one of your ovum. It is up to you."

Christine's eyes searched for Helen who was standing a few feet away to Christine's left with her hands curled tightly under her chin. Helen gave Christine a tiny nod of confidence.

"Bone marrow," Christine said.

He shrugged. "That is a bit more uncomfortable to obtain. As you wish."

For the next hour the other five mere mortals in the room witnessed the most amazing medical feat imaginable. The procedure only required a small incision from Christine's hip to obtain the tissue sample he requested. The sample was placed into a device which looked like a cross between an oversized microwave oven and a two-hundred gallon aquarium. Jason was curious how anything mechanical could still be in any semblance of working order after thousands of years of idle neglect, but it was obvious that the teacher's technology was far beyond the limitations and tolerances of their own.

The device's tank initially contained a large block of brown ice, which melted rapidly upon activation of the device, leaving the tank filled with a dense, pale yellow, viscous liquid. Lights on the device's face illuminated, flickered and flashed. A shrill, high-pitched hum filled the air. Bright bony branches of light grew into spider webs and twisted fibrous streaks of electricity, arcing and flashing, all concentrating around a central point.

In only ten minutes they could see it.

At first, it looked like nothing more than a pinto bean, swelling and throbbing, then expanding into something crescent-shaped, akin to a plump cocktail shrimp. But as it steadily grew larger, it quickly became clear exactly what it was: a tiny human leg, like a piece broken off of a baby doll, swirling and floating in the liquid, being struck again and again by the miniature bolts and web work of lightning. Each time the claws of white light enveloped it, the leg twitched and kicked. When it was almost twelve inches in length, an ankle and a foot became clearly defined, complete with toes that wiggled and spread whenever the threads of energy kissed and caressed them.

The teacher attentively watched the progress of the new leg until he was satisfied it had achieved the proper proportions. Jason glanced down at his watch and noticed the growth of the new limb from start to finish had taken almost exactly one hour. A tag line ran through his mind: "Limb Crafters, new limbs in about an hour." Intellectually he knew that should have been funny, but he didn't laugh or even crack a smile. He was too much in awe of what he was seeing. They all stood back as the pair of pale blue hands reached into the syrupy liquid and fished out the new leg.

"How is that possible?" Dr. Markham demanded. "Where is the leg's blood supply? Where is its nerve stem connection?"

The teacher explained, "The appendage is completely self-contained. The point of attachment on the upper thigh is covered with a layer of epidermis, the same way Christine's own upper thigh has sealed over the denuded termination point."

Christine cocked her head toward him. "You know my name?"

He looked back at her. "I know everything about you, my dear. I know everything about all of you."

Helen felt that same uncomfortable icy chill run up her spine.

The teacher turned back to Dr. Markham without missing a beat. "This organic synthesizer replicates an amniotic environment, functionally duplicating the inside of a womb. Basic nutrients, hydrogen, oxygen, and all the other needed trace elements are dissolved into the fluid suspension, and the energy stimulation accelerates absorption. Since cellular growth and division is also hyper-accelerated and continuous, no waste products require kidney or liver filtration. The process is 100% efficient. But to your specific point, Doctor, now that I have removed the new appendage from the synthesizer, it indeed needs prompt access to a healthy blood supply and a functioning nervous system or it will swiftly atrophy and die. If you will excuse me."

Dr. Markham stepped out of the teacher's way, watching him as he went to work with the efficiency and nonchalant manner of a Manhattan tailor chalking and cutting a new suit. He laid the glistening bright pink new right leg alongside Christine and eyeballed its height in correlation to her left one. A silver band was placed high on her right thigh, which he explained earlier was a non-invasive electromagnetic synapse signal inhibitor, which negated nerve communication from her upper right leg to the rest of her body. This, he said, was the most effective form of a local anesthetic. And before anyone knew what he was going to do next, he used another device, similar to the silver pen-knife, but a much larger version, with a nearly transparent blade about ten inches long, to make a single lateral cut—lopping off the bottom of Christine's stump and the top section of her new leg. Blood began to spurt at regular intervals from her femoral artery. The new leg bled as well, but only superficially.

Else threw her fist in her mouth to keep from screaming.

Helen was now on the other side of the table from their teacher, holding Christine's hands and keeping their eyes locked together.

The teacher deftly cleared the two excess portions of unneeded tissue out of his way, and fit the two exposed cross-sections of the leg and thigh together, matching the femur bone perfectly, and lining up the femoral artery and a few of the larger veins. He explained that the rest would find its own way and adjust according to the code.

And then he closed his eyes and bowed his head.

His bloody left hand was gripping Christine's upper thigh just above the junction point. His blood-soaked right hand clenched the new leg just below the junction point. Jason was certain he could hear a sizzling sound. The iron smell of fresh blood hung in the air, slowly mixing with the aroma of cooking meat. Jason moved around the table behind Helen to get a better view. The pale blue hands of the teacher were glowing, almost white hot. Wisps and crackles of electricity ran back and forth over the surface of the cut line, which was growing thinner and thinner by the second.

And then it was gone.

When the teacher's hands came free he let out an exhausted breath and staggered back three paces from the table, his legs buckling. Andrew and Dr. Markham caught him before he toppled over. He was gasping for air like he had just run a marathon.

"Are you all right?" Andrew asked him.

"Forgive me," he apologized. "I thought I had amassed a great deal more energy during my own regeneration process. I am spent, but well. I merely need to rest, and feed, as does she. But understand clearly what it is you have just witnessed. This is not sorcery or witchcraft. Energy transmutation is simply an augmentation or amplification process to the subject's own energy." He stood tall again, sucked in a deep breath and announced, "So let us examine the fruits of our labors."

Christine was still staring into Helen's eyes, her own were glassy and weary. She whispered, "How does it look?"

Helen's cheeks were streaked with her own fresh tears. "See for yourself."

As Helen helped Christine to raise up on her elbows, the teacher was taking off the silver band from her upper thigh. As it came free Christine screamed.

Helen cried out, "She's in pain! Put it back! *Put it back!*"

He shook his head. "No she is not in pain. She is merely feeling the new limb's presence for the first time."

Christine bawled like a baby, but through the wracking sobs and tears of joy pouring down her face, she could both see and feel her new toes wiggling.

CHAPTER 24

Sulmona, Italy
The Church of Santa Maria Annunziata

Cardinal Ricollo accepted the strong hand of his faithful protégé, Monsignor Pietro, as he stepped out of the Range Rover into the warm, humid mid-day sun. A chaotic cloud of fruit flies swarmed around his face, summarily brushed away with an annoyed wave of his quaking fingers. He was dressed in simple black, as was Father Pietro, the attire of ordinary parish priests. The sight of the beautiful Maiella massif in the distance, towering over the rooftops of the 3,000 year old town brought a smile to his weathered lips. Even for that time of year the panoramic mountain backdrop was still dusted with snow on the summits. It was hard to picture Hannibal himself sacking the picturesque little town over two centuries before the birth of Christ. The cardinal so loved history and the treasures of antiquity. However, remembering the purpose for the urgent excursion seventy miles east of Rome sobered the cardinal's thoughts. The pair made haste into the church, careful to avoid attracting any undue attention.

They were met at the door by Father Fabrizzi, the local parish Priest, a barrel-chested man in a white tunic and purple vestments, who reverently kissed the cardinal's ring before hurriedly showing them inside the cathedral. Only a handful of parishioners were sprinkled among the antique wooden pews, with heads bowed in supplications, reciting their endless litany of rote prayers, each one burned into their memories from early childhood. Father Fabrizzi led his guests discretely to a quiet room in the rear of the rectory where they were immediately introduced to Francesca Garibaldi, the object of their investigation. From the case background he had read, Father Pietro was expecting to find a more mature woman, perhaps in her late twenties or early thirties. But this Francesca was but a wisp of a girl, perhaps only eighteen at most, fair of face and feature, with beautiful long black hair. She sat in the bare stone room in an old wooden chair, afraid and trembling.

Father Fabrizzi announced to the girl in Italian, "Child, these holy fathers have come to speak with you today, and to learn more perfectly of what has happened to you, and how God has blessed and used you. Tell them all. Keep nothing to yourself. It is your duty to God."

The girl nodded quickly, her eyes darting back and forth between the faces of the two strangers, unsure, but compliant.

Cardinal Ricollo nodded to Monsignor Pietro to begin the inquisition.

Father Pietro stepped forward and grabbed another old wooden chair, turning it around backward, straddling it, folding his arms across the top of the chair-back. He offered the frightened girl his friendliest smile. "Francesca. Father Fabrizzi brings us marvelous tidings that God has used you as a sign to His people, to perform a miracle."

Francesca looked to Father Fabrizzi for help, her chin quivering.

Fabrizzi encouraged her, "Go ahead, little one. It's all right. Tell them everything."

Pietro tried to sound as disarming and reassuring as possible. "Yes, my child. Just tell us in your own words how God has used you. If truly He has wrought a miracle through you, then surely you must realize the Church wishes to know of it and understand its importance and meaning."

She brushed a long lock of hair out of her face and looked into Father Pietro's eyes, her words hesitant and shy. "I'm not sure what to say, Father. It all just happened. I don't know how it happened."

"Start from the beginning," the Monsignor urged. "Tell us when this happened, what you were doing, where you were. The simple things you remember."

"The first time—" she began.

"It has occurred more than once?" Cardinal Ricollo interrupted, indignant.

Francesca nodded. "Many times, Father. The first time was four months ago. I was visiting my aunt Gina in Scanno. She is a very old woman, a widow now for the past ten years, since my uncle's heart attack. Cataracts took her sight three years ago, and she needs a great deal of help. Many of my cousins and I take turns caring for her."

"As you should," the old priest added, standing a few paces away, with arms folded and a skeptical scowl carved into his face.

She hesitated briefly, gathering her thoughts, then explained, "There was this one night, when I was there with my aunt, in her home, when she was filled with such a dark sadness in her heart...she told me she didn't want to live anymore. I didn't think she was serious, but it made me very afraid to hear her talk this way. She couldn't stop crying. And yet, as I sat with her, in my mind I could see a picture of her so different from what my eyes were seeing. Not a memory of the past, but a view of something yet to be. I saw her completely changed, with such joy on her face, able to see again, enjoying her life again. I wanted this for her more than anything. It happened without really thinking about it. When I reached up and touched her face to dry her tears, and my thumbs brushed her eyes, there was a light."

"What kind of a light?" Pietro asked. "From heaven?"

"Coming from beneath my fingers," she said in her own sense of confused wonder. "And the next thing I knew, my aunt Gina, she is screaming. Not crying any more, she is screaming, screaming for joy. Her eyes were opened, and she could see again. My heart leapt with joy. I had not seen her so happy in ten years. We both cried for joy that night."

Father Pietro's brow furrowed. "And no one else saw this event?"

"No one needed to," she replied. "All who knew her, knew of her blindness, and rejoiced at her receiving her sight again."

Pietro said, "But you do realize, Francesca, that God only grants His miracles as a sign, to show the way to the unbeliever. Was your aunt baptized and confirmed?"

Francesca blanched. "Of course! My aunt Gina is as faithful to the Church as anyone in my family. She is *not* an unbeliever."

"Did she give glory to God to for this blessing?" Cardinal Ricollo demanded.

Francesca flinched. "Of course! She does to this day."

Pietro asked, "But you said there were other times this has happened. What other times? Tell us of those experiences."

Francesca swallowed an anxious lump that had risen in her throat. "I think it has happened ten, maybe twelve times since my aunt Gina. I see someone in pain, or afflicted, and suddenly in my mind I see them whole. And when I touch them, it happens. One was afflicted with a cancer in his lungs, very near death. The doctors in the hospital could do nothing for him and sent him home to die. Another one had a broken back from an automobile accident, who was able to rise from a wheelchair and walk again when I took his hand. I have seen fevers leave bodies as though they fear my presence. I can't explain it."

Father Fabrizzi piped up, "We've had to keep her in seclusion. When she goes out on the street, the people mob her. We were afraid for her life!"

The Cardinal nodded. "You acted wisely."

The Monsignor continued his line of questioning. "So these manifestations of healing, they don't come about as a result of your prayers of intercession to God, your petitions to the virgin mother, or your entreaties to any of the blessed saints?"

"No," she shook her head. "As I said, it just comes into my mind, like taking in a breath, and I release it. When it happens, I can feel it flowing out of me and into them. I can't explain it any other way. It doesn't happen to every sick person I see, only some of them, when I get the image in my mind of them being made whole. I promise you, I don't look for the images, they just appear."

"How often do you go to Mass, girl?" the Cardinal snapped.

"Every week, with my mother, father, and brothers," she was quick to answer.

"Yes, this is true," Father Fabrizzi affirmed.

"I've heard enough," the Cardinal announced as he turned on his heel and strode from the room.

"Thank you, Francesca. Please wait here with Father Fabrizzi for a moment longer." Monsignor Pietro rose and followed the cardinal, joining him in the vestibule. He closed the heavy wooden door behind him, stepped a few paces away and lowered his voice, "You think her experiences are genuine?"

Cardinal Ricollo huffed, "As genuine as Satan himself can produce."

"You are certain?" Pietro was taken aback.

"It is plain," the cardinal said matter-of-fact. "Miracles are for a sign. She does nothing but attract mobs who selfishly wish for attention to their own needs, not for God's glory. Is it God's blessing she seeks to share? No, her own words condemn her. She speaks of some mysterious visions only. It is a delusion, a forgery of the evil one. This is no miracle. This is not the divine movement of God's hand. This is not from above. It is from below. This is the very heart of sorcery and witchcraft and all that is accursed. It is intended only to deceive the foolish of mind, to give them false hope, and in the end, to entice them to abandon their most holy faith."

Father Pietro looked back at the closed door of the interview room. "Surely this girl, even if greatly deceived or misguided, has no conscious awareness of any evil working in her."

"Few of them do," came the prelate's cold reply.

Father Pietro nodded thoughtfully. "What then, Father? Shall we start the process for approval of the Rite of Exorcism?"

"I have the power to approve the sacred ritual with no higher word," Cardinal Ricollo said. "But this course is not to be. I saw no demon in that girl."

"Then what is our task?" the Monsignor asked.

"Father Pietro..." The Cardinal leaned in close, causing the Monsignor to reflexively lean away from the fetid odor of the elder priest's breath. "You know your oath. When the great day comes that the keys of the secret knowledge pass into you hands in my stead, you shall be wise and dully ordained to judge in all such matters. Until that day, my judgment is absolute. This corruption cannot be allowed to spread. That is the divine decree!"

"What then do you prescribe, your Excellency?" Father Pietro demurred, knowing all too well the wisdom of avoiding his mentor's wrath.

"It is written in the holy scriptures, and is the command of Almighty God," the Cardinal pronounced, "Thou shalt not suffer a witch to live.[17]"

"A witch?" Pietro's eyes were wide with surprise. "Holy Father, I agree some phenomenon has occurred regarding this girl, but I see nothing proven here warranting that girl's death."

The cardinal's sallow cheeks were turning red. "Which is why you are not yet ready to bear my mantle. When you wear it, you will see them for what they are, as I do. Now attend to your duty, Father. Explain to Father Fabrizzi that we are taking the girl to Rome for her protection and for further examination. Rest assured, I will ensure adequate compensation is provided for her family. I shall return to Rome at once to say a Mass for the liberation of her soul. You are permitted to let her bid her family farewell only, but what you must do, do quickly. Fulfill your duty and your sacred oath. I expect your return to the city before dusk."

Monsignor Pietro nodded briefly, his heart pounding in his chest, pounding so hard it felt like it was about to crack his breast bone. The cardinal had never made such a devastating request of him before. Keeping ancient secrets was one thing. This was something altogether different. This was surely the greatest test of his faith, his calling, and his resolve he had yet to face.

His face grew stern. "I understand, your Excellency."

Cardinal Ricollo turned and strode away.

Monsignor Pietro looked back at the thick wooden door before him, picturing the angelic face of a frightened young girl sitting on the other side of it. He closed his eyes and whispered a short prayer.

He knew what he had to do.

---

[17] Exodus 22:18.

CHAPTER 25

Andrew took the liberty of making a chow run on behalf of the group. He descended back to the third level of the complex an hour later with a handcart heavily laden with boxes of provisions, only to discover the rest of the group had reconvened back in the white marble classroom. Coming through the doorway Andrew caught the tail end of the teacher's instructions to Christine regarding the care and maintenance of her new limb. He emphasized the importance of drinking large quantities of fluids high in electrolytes, eating foods rich in iron and proteins, keeping the leg out of direct sunlight for several weeks, and so forth.

The group devoured the food like a pack of starving wolves, and the teacher ate the greatest helping of all. He could consume an apple in two or three bites, a half a sandwich in one or two, and drink a liter of water in a single swallow. Despite his ability to consume large quantities of food and drink, his manner was not barbaric, slovenly or uncouth; rather, it was obvious that he possessed a unique cultural process for eating and drinking. In light of the curious stares he received while still eating, he endeavored to explain the correlation between high-energy manifestation with a high metabolism, and the corresponding need for high fuel consumption. As he ate, Helen couldn't help but notice his brilliant white teeth, with sharp slightly pointed incisors, along with a pair of unusually long canines. When he'd enjoyed his fill, he didn't waste a second to launch headlong again into his passionate discourse.

"The energy manifestation functions that we have been discussing, of which only a few are partially active in your current encoding, fall into *seven* functional categories." He counted them off on his fingers. "The first category is comprised of your seven senses, which are for information input and modes of environmental perception."

Jason was bold enough to interrupt between bites. "Did you say *seven* senses?"

The teacher turned to Jason. "Yes, seven. It is odd, but even though you regularly use all seven of them, your kind only seems to formally recognize five: sight, taste, hearing, touch, and smell."

"What are the other two?" Jason asked.

"Proximity detection and intuition," he replied.

Jason bit into another apple. "What's proximity detection?"

The teacher scratched his chin. "Technically, it is your perception of energy field variances or disturbances at a distance. It is functionally equivalent to the way a shark can sense the movement of a distressed fish in the sea over a mile away, or how many species of birds navigate relative to the earth's electromagnetic field in their annual migrations. The greater your developed sensitivity, the greater the range and the accuracy of the perception."

"I don't understand," Jason admitted. "How do we use it now?"

The teacher popped the last of an apple into his mouth, core and all, "Have you ever been completely alone, and with no other indication from any of your other senses, you were suddenly convinced that you were no longer alone? That someone was there with you, perhaps watching you?"

Everyone was nodding. Jason answered for them, "Yes."

"That would be an example," he pointed at him. "In time you shall be able to detect familiar energy patterns emanating from other individuals, and even discern who it is that approaches long before you see their face or hear their voice. And your seventh sense, the sense of intuition, is merely the processing of multiple inputs of proximity detection, whereby you perform a subconscious risk analysis of these inputs for potential danger or consequences that may require your immediate actions."

"You lost me again," Jason shook his head.

The teacher tried to make it simple. "Have you ever just had a bad feeling about a situation, an inexplicable sense of foreboding, fear or concern, that ultimately proved justified? Or conversely, you just knew the right thing to do on an occasion with no basis in fact to justify it, what you sometimes call trusting your gut? Not a guess, but a convinced *sense* of sure knowledge, good or bad?"

"Of course," Jason replied.

"That is what I speak of." He made it sound so ordinary. "When this happens, you are sensing a set of external conditions or impending factors, which is literally a physical perception of transmitted energy stimuli. Each stimuli gets analyzed and compared against your internal database of past experience and knowledge, which are your local collection of stored engrams, or what you call memories, both conscious and subconscious. From this analysis your mind makes a calculated judgment of whether or not the situation is a cause for alarm. It is nothing extraordinary. It is there to keep you alive and out of danger."

Jason nodded with new understanding. Even Helen was impressed.

Christine set her water bottle down. "So what's the second area?"

"The second functional category is your communication capability. As you would surmise, it is for the acquisition, idiomatic-syntactic translation, and formation of what you know as the art of language, which of course is technically distinct from, but ties closely into, the third category."

"Which is?" Helen prompted.

He continued, rewarding Helen with a smile. "Which is your information processing and knowledge retention functions. This third area covers all the vital cerebral functions, such as short- and long-term memory storage, reasoning, mathematical calculation, and the like. But it is also designed to incorporate higher frequency signal perception and transfer, a form of non-verbal communication capability, a process which you sometimes refer to as telepathy. This function was meant to be used routinely, but was one of the genes sequences selected to be deactivated in your genome. Interestingly, I found it most amusing that while many of your kind have inadvertently stumbled onto this capability in varying degrees, so few have ever properly understood its rightful purpose."

Helen asked, "You're saying telepathy was meant to be a natural form of communication?"

He nodded, "Yes. But much more than that. Telepathic perception is meant to function on two different levels. It may be used person-to-person, which occurs on an internal engram level, not on a grammatical or syntactical level. It is a form of communications which is transferred in the form of images or complete memory sequences, hence giving you the ability to communicate with those that do not speak your native tongue. This is how we first communicated, when I was in cryostasis."

"Cool!" Jason nodded. "I could get into that."

"But more importantly, this form of perception and communication was also intended to function on a broad spectrum level," the teacher added. "To pick up engram reflections from the universal collective, which is also how I was able to see each of you and know you from afar. This function is a query-response capability, to enable you to function by obtaining information from outside your own personal experience and memories, rather, drawing on the collective engrams of the universe as a whole."

"Hold on a second." Christine was slack-jawed, brows furrowed. "What engram *collective*?"

He apologized, "Forgive me. Perhaps I am going a bit too fast. Let us think of a contemporary analogy." He paused for a second. "Ah yes. The images of light you see of distant stars and planets are not images of that moment, but are in fact images of ages past, some of which are billions upon billions of years old. This is because that is how long it took for their light energy to travel here to this planet. Many of the stars in the heavens you see at night died out long ago, but their light energy is just now reaching this planet and you believe them to be young and alive. Thus, the memory of their existence lives beyond them."

"But what does that have to do with a memory collective?" Christine prodded.

He addressed her directly. "Because this principle is also true down at the quantum level, within the subatomic elements themselves. Your energy transmissions of thought and memory form complex energy waves, which are transmitted at such short wavelengths and of such high frequency, that they penetrate all other higher order energy fields, and coalesce in the very fabric of space itself, making a permanent imprint, like the light energy, gravitational forces, and radiation from the stars."

Jason interjected, "You mean like the broadcasts of old television shows we've recorded bouncing back after twenty or thirty years."

"Exactly. This energy creates an indelible impression, much like an audible sound wave modifying a high-frequency radio carrier signal. Thus, your second order telepathic function is intended to enable you to access these complex patterns and signals, strip off the carrier wave, and thereby retrieve the underlying information. The end result is very similar to how your computing machines perform a search within the catalogued information that it commonly shared on your electronic information networks, in what you call information databases. Your public *Internet* and associated *Search Engines* are but a primitive shadow of that which you are capable of doing organically—to know all that is knowable."

"Everything?" Helen asked.

He hesitated before answering, "Everything that has not been hidden."

CHAPTER 26

"Is the use of the high-order telepathic function how some people claim to see the future?" Else asked. The discussion of telepathic communications and universal knowledge acquisition was entering its third hour. Everyone was still enthralled with everything they were learning.

The teacher raised one finger. "In my view, this topic is more misunderstood than any other with respect to your inherent organic energy capabilities. Physically speaking, no one can attain knowledge, an engram of memory if you will, from energy that has yet to be expended and to leave its lasting impression upon the collective."

"So then how does it happen?" Else challenged. "Many prophesies have been fulfilled in recorded history."

He conceded, "Indeed, there are many gray areas and subordinate factors to be considered when in comes to understanding prediction of the future. When several normal elements are combined, they can yield a result that is not unlike the *illusion* of prognostication."

Else frowned, "So you contend that all prognostication is an illusion?"

He paused again, before explaining, "Not exactly. What you must understand is the clear distinction between imagination and thought energy. Imagination is the conjuring of what *might* be. Thought is the energy release of what you cause *to be*. If you think to yourself, I *might* raise my hand, and raise it not, even though you picture it rising up in your imagination, it is only a hypothetical reality. But to actually raise it..." He lifted his arm to illustrate. "...is a direct transmission of thought energy to cause it to happen, which records and transmits an engram of the event into the collective. Much confusion arises when someone, or a group acting in concert, imagines and embraces a common idea or future event with such conviction and strong intent—usually an idea of malicious or evil intent—that the engram of this imagining is transmitted into the fabric of the universe, masquerading as a true memory, where others may inadvertently perceive it, and then come to know the intent of the event before it occurs, seeing it as if it had already happened."

Jason noted, "So prediction of the future can be wrong."

He nodded, "Oh, undoubtedly, and examples abound. However, in other instances, predictions of future events are merely the combination of intuition, intellect, and past experience, such as seeing the sky darken and accurately predicting that it will rain. But never diminish the import of this powerful capability. It can be extremely sophisticated. As you continually collect raw information, your intellect has the power to map complex permutations of potential events far beyond the nine or ten upcoming moves of a chess game. We are talking hundreds, and in some cases thousands of combinations. Your mind can plot potential permutations of events to such a detailed degree, often occurring in your subconscious unaware, that should one of the subordinate events postulated occur in reality, the whole sequence is triggered as vividly as any true memory. This phenomenon is what you refer to as the experience of *déjà vu*."

The group was beginning to understand, as evidenced by the uniform array of smiles and nods.

He darkened. "But be forewarned, friends. Most foretelling of the future is little more than perception of ill intent, not of destiny. Destiny is a goal, not a curse. Fate is the path we choose, and the circumstances of the road we travel, to reach our destinies. On the other hand, what is more properly understood as prophesy is the perception of the will or judgment of those with the power and authority to bring it to pass."

Else started to ask another question, but held her tongue.

He gave her a quick glance before continuing, letting the topic drop. "The fourth energy category comprises your developmental functions, from basic physiological growth, tissue regeneration, reproduction of your offspring, and so forth. These functions are all active within you right now, only to a lesser degree, as we both demonstrated and discussed earlier in the laboratory."

Else couldn't hold back any longer. "But what about death? On the one hand you say we have the ability to regenerate ourselves and live forever, but you've also said that there were times you feared you would be executed and die. How can this be? How can you be concerned about death if you're immortal?"

He answered, "Immortality and death are not a contradiction. The ability to physically live forever in the flesh assumes that nothing takes your life from you. To never age, or to possess the power to defeat illness and disease, does not imply that you are invincible. Far from it. We can all be killed. A simple beheading is typically more than sufficient. Burning to death or lethal doses of subatomic radiation are highly effective in releasing all of your life energy faster than your regeneration capability can fight it. Excessive blood loss, which is one of the most important transport mediums of energy within you, can be sufficient to terminate your life. In case you were not aware of it, your life energy is primarily contained within and transported by your bloodstream. Genetically speaking, immortality only means you could theoretically live forever in the prime of your youth as long as you are not slain by a greater outside force."

Else challenged, "So are you telling us there is no afterlife, no heaven or hell that awaits us after death?"

The room grew still. Every ear was hanging on his next word.

His voice grew grave. "I never said that, nor do I wish to speak of these things at this time. We shall save that topic for a later discussion. My purpose here and now is to share with you the secrets of this life, not of physical death and what lies beyond it. This is what is most important. But no more for now. You all look weary from my words. We can stop now and rest if you please."

"No." It was Helen. "You said there were *seven* categories. You've only told us about four. What are the other three?"

He grinned. "If you have the strength to bear it, we can go on. Besides, the remaining three are the most powerful ones, the ones you were strictly forbidden to have. Two of which you lack entirely, but the third you have discovered quite well on your own, and did so from the very beginning."

"OK. So what are they, exactly?" Helen asked again.

He told her plainly, "The first is what your parapsychologists and metaphysicists sometimes refer to as the power of telekinesis, or the ability to move objects through space with your thought energy. The truth is, it is simply a basic work skill. For example, it significantly contributed to how the great cities and monuments of ages past were constructed."

"Like you did with your scalpel in the lab," Dr. Markham noted.

He gave a half-laugh. "Yes. It is but a simple polarity reversal and re-vectoring of gravitational force with respect to the earth's centrifugal force as it moves along the solar ecliptic. A child can do it."

Christine flushed, picturing a pick-up truck and a baseball in her mind. She whispered softly to herself, "I *knew* it..."

The teacher brushed the topic aside as if it were a triviality. "The second of the forbidden three functions, or the sixth area overall, is purely a self-defense mechanism. It is a much more difficult function to manifest at will, in that it requires some inherent talent, and no small measure of practice and patience to perfect proper execution."

Christine's brow furrowed with curiosity. "What is it?"

"It is the ability to bend light waves in the visible spectrum." He formed his hands into a ball. "It is intended to provide camouflage, to hide in times of danger. Rather than have light reflect or be absorbed by your body, and thus reflecting a wavelength of an opaque color or shade or shadow, you instead create a negative energy field on the surface of your skin, and with practice, even outside a garment. The masters of this practice can create an external sphere capable of encompassing not only themselves, but also other people and objects nearby. We have even learned how to mimic this function mechanically."

"OK, I'm lost again. What are we talking about here?" Jason asked.

The teacher broke it down further. "Fundamentally, what we are referring to is a low level energy veil, just strong enough to reroute the photons of visible light to the opposite side of your body and restore their flight paths to their original vectors and intensities. It is a parabolic function that occurs in full spherical dimension on all surfaces of your person. Done properly, it has the effect of making you—"

"Invisible," Christine finished for him, having already mathematically computed where he was headed. "We can *do* that?"

He laughed. "I can do it." His image suddenly refracted as though his skin were being stretched over a large ball, then he completely vanished. After a moment of shocked silence he was standing in place again, right where he had been before, looking down into Christine's stunned expression. "You still need to learn how to focus your energy properly. But in time, yes, you can do it as well."

They all laughed and applauded.

"And the last one?" Helen prompted.

He smiled at her. "Passion."

"Passion?" Helen couldn't conceal her surprise. "Our emotions?"

His tenor sobered as he explained, "Know the truth, one and all, and find your own freedom therein. My brother would not tolerate an inferior worker who was strong enough to defeat us in battle, or who could successfully hide from us...or the worst indignity of all, to share in our pleasures and pains as equals. Think about it. The logic is simple. A passionless creature does exactly as it is told and does not complain."

The air seemed to grow more heavy and oppressive.

He began to pace back and forth. "But don't you see? Your discovery of the passions *proved* my theory, that all the other functions were potentially available to you. You just had to find them and activate them. You loved and hated, you showed fear and courage, ingenuity and creativity, just as we did." He rolled his eyes. "Unfortunately, it was your most base desires and carnal appetites that got us all into trouble. But there was no other way! It was all of them or none of them. And without them, you would never have had a free will of your own. You would never have known love. And without love, my plan was doomed from the beginning."

Andrew chuckled. "I get the feeling the woman we've been waiting to hear about is about to come into the picture."

"Indeed." The teacher stopped pacing and stared off silently into the swirling mists of memory, relishing the remembrance of a distant land that no one but he could see. When he spoke again, it was with a peculiar mixture of fond recollection and deep sorrow. "She was real. She existed. She was the epitome of my work—the prototype for all of your kind to follow."

CHAPTER 27

"The size of the lift will be the primary constraint." Mohammed Al Faisal instructed the six uniformed mercenaries seated around a heavy oak table in the hot, sweltering conference room. A small swarm of flies buzzed around the tattered remnants of turkey, ham, and tuna sandwiches stacked on a credenza behind them. The smell of stale cigarettes mixed with dank body odor hung stagnant in the afternoon air. Jean-Marc Xavier was also in the room, sitting quietly in the corner, smoking a Cuban cigar. A small laptop projector displayed a high-resolution overhead satellite image on the wall, detailing the Duncan International exploration site. Mohammed used a laser pointer to illustrate his briefing. He had everyone's rapt attention.

"The two-man lift won't hold the weapon and anyone else at the same time." He pointed to one of the men. "You, Collins, are to go down first. Alone. Search and secure the immediate landing area at the bottom of the lift. You should see nothing but unarmed engineers and scientists. Eliminate anyone you find. Return the lift to the surface as soon as the landing area is clear. The lift takes twenty minutes per course. When it reaches the surface again, the weapon will be loaded and sent down by the surface team. When it comes down to you, you unload it by yourself and send the lift up once more. The weapon will be on a hand cart. Just pull it out and lay it down. Then you, Morse." He pointed to a second soldier. "Ride down and join him. The rest of you will form a tight security perimeter around the lift access point and eliminate anyone who comes close. You will remain in position until the team below has returned to join you. We estimate fifteen minutes to breach the perimeter, two hours total transport time in the lift, five minutes to arm the device, and another fifteen minutes to get to the extraction helicopter. We want you in and out in less than three hours. Is that understood?"

Nods went all around accented with a few mumbled, yes-sirs.

"Excellent." Mohammed turned off the projector and looked at his watch. "It is now 1430 hours. It is a five hour drive to the site in the Rub Al Khali from this location. Your truck leaves at precisely 1900 hours. You strike at 2400 hours. Make all final preparations. And with the exception of Collins and Morse, the rest of you are dismissed. For you two, we shall now go through the arming sequence drill until you can do it with your eyes closed."

•

Jean-Marc waited for Mohammed in the small bar of the very discrete oasis motel. Mohammed was smiling when he flopped down in the tattered velvet lounge chair next to him. A roach scurried from beneath it, seeking new cover.

Mohammed smiled. "Ah, a day well-spent, monsieur."

"Are they ready?" Xavier was clipping the end off of a fresh cigar.

"Yes," Mohammed replied, waving at the lone bartender, and telling him to bring a Scotch, neat. Alcohol was typically forbidden all across Saudi Arabia. However, Jean-Marc Xavier always knew where to find discrete places—where for the right price—the rules didn't apply.

"They suspect anything?" Jean-Marc toasted the end of his long, fat cigar in a slow circular motion with a butane micro-torch until the filler and binder leaves started to glow red.

"Of course not." Mohammed threw a wrinkled pack of Turkish cigarettes down on the round glass table and fished through his pockets for his own lighter, a simple but effective stainless-steel Zippo. "There are a few questions. These are brave men, monsieur, not clever men." He laughed. "They have prepared well for what we ask them to do. But they haven't even bothered to ask why we have no helicopter!"

Jean-Marc blew a thick gray cloud into the air, shaking his head in wonder. "The client wanted disposable workers, we provide disposable workers, which incidentally, are my favorite kind." He laughed. "Did you at least take them into the city last night and get them laid?"

Mohammed frowned. "Certainly not. I didn't dare risk having any of them seen by witnesses, or risk any injury to members of the team. Not this close to execution of the operation." He smiled. "But we are not without suitable resources. I secured two whores and brought them back here for them to share in private."

"Did they enjoy them?" Jean-Marc lifted the glass of Cabernet from his own private stock he brought with him, and sipped.

"Completely." Mohammed took his drink from the bartender, tasted it with a nod of satisfaction, and waited until the young man walked well out of earshot before adding, "And they buried them quietly in the desert before dawn, as I ordered, for only the creeping things in the sands to enjoy."

Jean-Marc nodded with approval. "Good thinking."

CHAPTER 28

Monsignor Pietro stuck his head through the door of Cardinal Ricollo's office. "Your Excellency?"

Ricollo was standing by his fourth story window, staring out over the rooftops of Rome at a bloated blood-red sunset. He turned to the door, glancing at the gilded antique 15th century clock on the mantle of his fireplace. It was almost 7:00 PM.

"Father Pietro. Come in. I have been waiting for you. I trust all is in order, and your duty is complete?"

The younger priest nodded. "All is as it should be, holy Father."

The cardinal turned back to the window and folded his hands behind his back. "Excellent. And we shall not speak of the matter further. I can see the heaviness of your heart in your eyes. Let it not be troubled. I know, my son, fulfilling your duty to God can often be an unclean and difficult commission. No one denies that. But the lot of the servant has fallen to our order, our sacred brotherhood, to obey without question, to defend that which we hold dearest and most holy. There are no other bastions, save us, against the most ancient of all corruptions and evils. For this we shall be rewarded in heaven as good and faithful servants. Know this for a certainty."

Monsignor Pietro cleared his throat. "Your Excellency, with your permission, I should like to retire for a short sabbatical. A fortnight along the coast perhaps. You have indicated that my examination could begin as soon as next month. I wish to be thoroughly rested and prepared, both in body and soul."

The cardinal nodded his approval. "A wise course, Father Pietro. Take whatever time you need to meditate and pray and fill your heart with peace. I understand." He tossed a sympathetic glance at the young priest. "You know, I recall the first occasion that my own mentor, our holy father, the great Cardinal DiSalvo, called upon me to defend our faith and our sacred oath unto blood. It was no small undertaking, I can assure you." His gaze strayed back out the window, his voice tired but determined. "I can still remember the look in the man's eyes when I cut his throat and baptized my hands in his blood. He didn't understand why it was happening.

But it wasn't his place to understand. I can only console you with the knowledge that it becomes easier with time. And eventually, you feel nothing at all."

The Monsignor closed his eyes tightly. "If I may be excused."

Cardinal Ricollo waved him away without looking from the window or saying anything further.

As the door closed and Monsignor Pietro made his way back down the long marble hallway, it took all of his strength not to burst into tears.

Oh, gracious God, what have I done?

•

The white cargo van stopped half a mile from the gate of the Duncan International complex. The driver, Collins, glanced at Morse in the front passenger seat as well as the remaining four men seated in jump seats around their brushed aluminum refrigerator-sized cargo.

Collins checked his watch. "It's 23:45 hours on my mark." Everyone synchronized their digital watches. "Mark." He looked back at them. We hit the gate in exactly fifteen minutes. LAWS rockets on the two forward towers. Small arms on the gate sentries. Gas masks ready?"

Five "checks" came in reply.

"Check," Collins acknowledged. "First stop will be main barracks. VX canisters will be deployed and remaining personnel neutralized with small arms. Second stop is the lift. I want to be parked and unloading no more than ten minutes after we hit the gate. Is that clear?"

A chorus of "Yes, sir."

"Lock and load, gentlemen." Collins pulled out his MAC-10 machine pistol and checked the ammunition clip. It was full. He screwed a ten-inch noise suppressor into the muzzle of his weapon and rechecked his own gas mask. A tap against his thigh ensured his own Atropine injector was in his pocket, just in case of a fuck-up with the deadly nerve agent.

With a jingle of metal latches, two of the men in the back of the van expertly uncrated a pair of shoulder fired LAWS rockets, a short-range line-of-sight armor-piercing antitank weapon. The remaining two men went to work unpacking a long foam-lined cache of rocket propelled grenades (RPG), tipped with high-dispersal aerosol vials of VX nerve agent. VX gas was known to unleash an incredibly painful and gruesome death, but typically acted so fast that most of its victims weren't given time to care.

Collins could see the compound lights in the distance. Time to earn a hundred-thousand dollar paycheck.

CHAPTER 29

"She was so beautiful," was how he began.

It was obvious he had rehearsed this discourse in his mind a thousand times, maybe a hundred-thousand times, yet still trying more to persuade himself than to assuage the doubts of any hearer.

"It started as a simple biological experiment, much in the same way an artist plays with color, light and shadow, trying a bit of this and that, observing the resultant effects, the lines, the textures. Trial and error. A little more here, a little less there. That was all it was, in the beginning. But to prevent a horrifying menagerie of failed experiments, and to save time, I opted to build a simulation model. One of the earlier versions of the modeling device is still here in the complex on the level below us. I can show it to any of you sometime, if you would care to see it."

"I would," Christina said. She wore her blue jeans, but her feet were still bare. It was impossible to tell which foot was eighteen years old and which one was only a few hours old. Her face was still beaming. Science or not, she felt she had been the beneficiary of a true miracle.

The teacher walked over and sat down next to Christine and tucked his hands softly between his knees. "My simulator allowed me to manipulate entire gene sequences, or individual genes and sub-control variants within genes. I had over 140,000 genes to play with within the genome, so there were seemingly limitless combinations to try. It was an amazing achievement, and I learned so much about the power and possibilities of the genome. The simulator would synthesize the cellular progression sequence and project a miniature scale, high-resolution holographic composite model of what a specific combination would produce at maturity."

"That must have been fascinating to experiment with," noted Dr. Markham.

The teacher admitted, "Frankly, in my case, fascination quickly evolved into an outright obsession. I worked on my model in secret for ages, until I came up with a pure prototype of such exquisite quality, of such extreme beauty and perfection, that I believed if I did not see the first human woman in the flesh, I would surely die."

"Weren't there other human females around?" Jason thought it was an innocent question.

"No," he shook his head. "The only females in existence at the very beginning were of our own kind, and while some were more pleasing in appearance than others, few of them could be said to be of exceptional beauty. No, she was the first of her kind, of your kind, of an entirely new breed. Many females followed her, but in the beginning, we were only after able-bodied workers. Masons. Bricklayers. Artisans. Miners. Farmers. Slaves. So I made them all male with strong backs and compliant, obedient dispositions. Besides, they were not able to reproduce even if there had been females."

"Why not?" asked Helen.

"The first generations of workers were genetic hybrids of the hominids I used as the base gene sets, combined with our own modified genetic code. They were much like your mules, the offspring of a horse and donkey. All were born sterile. There was no sexual reproduction available for humans at that time. Sexuality, and its related passions of the flesh, was decreed to be a sacred privilege reserved solely for the appetites of the gods, that is, our kind—or so my brother wished to believe."

"But you didn't agree," Andrew chimed in.

"Certainly not," he continued. "This one Woman was my ideal prototype of human perfection, as well as the refinement and perfection of my own genetic code. As far as I was concerned, a sexless, passionless drone, was far from perfect. In my view, perfection meant she had to have the ability to love. And for her to love, she had to be free to choose to love. To be free to choose meant she had to be able to feel one way or another about something, to fervently care, to experientially know and feel true passion. But for her to know passion, she had to have that single element of her genetic code enabled, which consequently also enabled all of her other individual desires, appetites, and wants."

"So what happened?" Helen prompted.

"I refused to be dissuaded from my goal. I followed through on my intent to make her perfect," he said. "But I kept this knowledge secret from my brother. Although, I can assure you, he is not one who is easily fooled. And she was not something that could be physically hidden. When I finally showed her to him, I told him I had created her only to increase our ability to delegate lighter physical tasks to our inferiors, domestic duties and the like. That explanation seemed to suffice at first. However, I thought he would surely fall at her feet and worship the moment he laid eyes on her. She was *that* beautiful. And he was not stupid. He knew immediately that any of our kind who saw her would instantly wish to lay with her and make her his concubine. *Our* carnal passions certainly had no restrictions."

Else noted, "Superiors have sexually dominated and exploited their inferiors in all cultures. Why was this situation any different?"

He replied, "Because there were legitimate concerns over genetic risks associated with random cross-breeding. And with that in mind, my brother immediately forbade any of us to touch her. He bound her to a sacred oath that she would forswear throughout all her days never to taste of the forbidden fruit of the knowledge of the passions of the flesh, good or evil. His threat was so ominous the poor girl thought she would surely die if she broke her word to him."

Else was taken aback. "So you're saying the metaphor we've all come to know as the Tree of Knowledge of Good and Evil, refers to the discovery of human sexuality?"

He replied, "Essentially. My brother knew, as did I, that the moment she learned the truth about the reality of her own sensual passions, through experiential *knowledge*, she would become just like one of us. That is, this knowledge would release the energy within her, and her genetic code would be activated. She would then have both the power to sexually reproduce her own kind, and also be endowed with all the passions of an awakened heart, to both love and to hate, to cherish and to despise, to build and to destroy—or worst of all, be free to reject the god who demanded her obedience and supplication...or even the one who gave her life."

Helen felt a pang deep in her chest.

The teacher paused to rub his brow, then went on, "And furthermore, according to my brother, if she broke her word, that would only be the beginning of sorrows—for us mostly. His logic was clear and also turned out to be correct, just as I had planned. If one forbidden gift was discovered, then all of the others were likely to be found as well. And if that awful stroke of fate came to pass, then our superiority as your masters might one day be challenged. I did not fear that day. I longed for it. And she was to be the catalyst that would bring it to pass. That was my Great Secret."

"So you made love to her," Helen said softly, her heart pounding.

He was silent. There were tears in his eyes again when he whispered, "I showed her the truth."

Silence.

He wiped his eyes with the back of his hand.

"Did she love you?" Christine asked.

"With everything in her innocent young heart, I believed." He sucked in a quick breath. "But I knew in my own heart that she belonged with her kind, not with me. It was not possible for me to have her, not completely. Certainly not then, not in that situation. Death by execution was genuinely an option for me, at the hand of my own brother, if my true feelings for her had ever been discovered. So I took her to be with a suitable mate, my prototype male, the man, and immediately, just as I feared…" he paused and laughed softly to himself, "…she shared her newfound *knowledge* with him. He tasted of her forbidden fruit, and he too was no longer ignorant, nor a mule. His code was activated by the transfer of her energy to him, her perfect passion."

"Man…" Jason whispered in amazement. "That explains a lot."

The teacher continued, "And immediately, with their young and vibrant hearts so aroused and enflamed, they became intimately aware of their own bodies, their physiology and anatomy, and in particular, the visual arousal that boiled to the surface each time they beheld each other's beauty. And yet, she recalled her vow, and believed that if caught, she would face death, or worse, the wrath of my brother. It is for this reason they made for themselves garments, to cover their bodies, to try and contain their passions."

"But he found out anyway," said Else. "The presence of the garments themselves made it obvious what had happened, the awareness of their nakedness."

"And oh, was he furious!" he exclaimed. "I had never seen him that angry. He instantly blamed me, of course, for what had happened. 'You *snake!*' he screamed at me. I remember that moment each day as if it were yesterday. And all right, yes, guilty. It was all my fault. Fortunately, he only thought I had merely enabled the X and Y chromosome sequence, which enabled the two to mate and reproduce workers for us more rapidly. He never had any idea that I had…" he stopped and just sat there quietly, until he let out a long heavy sigh.

"Why *didn't* he ever kill you if he was so angry?" Andrew asked.

He shook his head in wonder. "I would like to think it was because we were brothers, of the same royal bloodline of our home. The truth was, he needed me. He still needed his workers and his servants, whether they be male or female. He wanted his slaves and his adoring worshipers. There was no denying that. But that does not mean there were no adverse consequences for me. I was summarily confined to my development complex, down here in the belly of the earth. But to his credit, he took pity on what I had created. Actually, my new and improved *homo sapiens* reproduced much faster than the inseminations we did with the female hominids. In seemingly no time, the fields were being tended, the mines were producing at a record pace, great cities were being erected again, and the humans were obedient and adoring. Life was good. At least for a time."

"Until the sons of god saw how fair you had made the daughters of men," Else interjected.

"You have read the ancient records," he nodded with approval. "Indeed, the Woman's progeny were a sheer delight to behold, and filled with more of the fire of life than any other living creature, including us. There was only one problem. The children of men...were human."

Else assumed, "And the children fathered by the gods were like the gods."

He shook his head, "No, that was the problem. They were not. Had they been truly of our seed, and merely like us, the situation might have been vastly different. The risks of random cross-breeding turned out to be disastrously accurate. The sexually reproduced hybrids of my kind and hers were genetic mutations. When the fully active gene code of my people blended with the modified chromosomes of humans, who possessed many gene sets that I had artificially deactivated, the deactivations were not consistently passed down to the offspring. There were monsters. There were madmen. Hideous creatures. Some appeared outwardly normal. But the one thing they all had in common was a defective gene that prevented positive, creative energy flow, the lifeblood of all progressive evolution and growth in our common species. These creatures were nothing but living instruments of destruction and pure evil. Their unquenchable thirst for blood and hunger for human flesh has had no equal since that time. Before we knew it, virtually all of my pure creations and their seed were gone. There was no choice but to destroy the hybrid mutations before there was nothing left."

"Hence the Flood," Else said. "You drowned them all."

"I did not do it *personally*." His voice had grown soft. "Reluctantly, I agreed to it, but I knew it had to be done. Besides, the vote in the counsel had to be unanimous. I was physically confined down here in the complex when it happened, but was able to perceive it as it happened, within the universal engram collective. They detonated our mighty weapons of great brilliance—a pair of high-yield subatomic fission devices in the underworld."

"Below the surface of the earth?" Jason asked.

"No," he said. "The *underworld*, the *netherworld*, what you call the southern hemisphere. This is the upper world, above the equator. The ruling council wanted the effect of mass flooding, but wished to avoid secondary radiation poisoning of the atmosphere and the soils of the primary continental land masses. So they planted the two devices deep in the southern ice cap, the frozen polar region you refer to as Antarctica. Have you never seen cartography of it? Did you never notice that it appears to have had two large bites taken out of a perfectly round pie?"

"Sort of, but I don't remember…" Jason started to respond, but trailed off trying to picture a map of Antarctica in his mind, then realizing that he had a world atlas stored in memory in his watch. He punched up an index on the full color digital display, found what he was looking for, and saw:

Jason audibly gulped.

The teacher explained further, "It was simple physics. The two massive ice floes that disengaged plunged trillions of tons of frozen mass into the two great oceans, resulting in a series of mutually reinforcing hyper-energy tidal waves, which effectively raised sea level almost a mile in height over the primary land masses for the better part of six months. Needless to say, it took care of the problem."

CHAPTER 30

"But what about the legend of Noah?" Else asked. "Is it true? Was one family actually spared?"

He shrugged. "I had to save something of my work. All the remaining hominids were destroyed in the flood. It was not practical to reconstitute the laborers again from nothing. Even my brother understood that logic, despite throwing another spectacular tirade when he found out I had defied his will yet again. But we both knew he was not willing to give up his new world, his personal kingdom and playground. The plan was always to begin again producing new workers after the flood subsided. And so I chose the man you call Noah in your culture, along with his family, primarily because his daughters and daughters-in-law were some of the few remaining human females who had not been defiled by my brother's men. They were of the pure seed of the Woman, and therefore greatly favored in our eyes."

Andrew stood up and massaged his aching knees. "But what was to stop it from happening all over again, the cross-breeding, as soon as your kind saw Noah's daughters or granddaughters?"

"Martial law," was his simple response. "Of my brother's men, those that he felt that he could trust implicitly, they remained in charge of their territorial regions, and were duly served and worshiped as local deities for generations thereafter." He huffed. "My friends, in case it has escaped your notice, the institutions of religion and ritual are powerful instruments of population control, enabling the rapid imposition of civil and social order, especially among uneducated primitives who understand only the threat of eternal punishment for disobedience, and the promise of divine favor for compliance. The carrot and stick approach, if you will."

"And for those he couldn't trust?" Andrew prompted.

"Some of them were executed. Others, who he felt were more loyal to me, were put into permanent cryostasis, like you found me. Some returned to our home planet, while it still lived. But here, on this planet, humans were made strictly off-limits for procreation...or recreation. As ordered, I made my brother a new crop of servants, and they did their part to spread to the four corners of the earth and replenished it with their seed. My brother went back to his ways of ruling them with an iron hand, relishing the role of an angry god. Meanwhile, I returned to my plan of discretely helping my creations discover that which is within themselves."

Christine spoke up with a note of frustration in her voice, "But *how*? You keep going on and on about all of this mysterious power, or energy manifestation, as you call it. I, of all people, believe you. But *how* does all of this happen? I want to know!"

He turned to face her. "It is simple to show you. Wiggle your toes."

She looked down and all ten toes, five old and five new, were wiggling.

"That is how," he said. "See? You already have the power. You just did not know what else you could do with it."

"I *don't* understand," she protested.

"And your lack of understanding is the only thing standing in your way," he fired back. "How did your toes move just now? What mysterious magical force caused them to suddenly obey your wishes?"

She replied, "I had the thought of moving them, as you asked. My brain sent an electrical impulse to my feet, and the muscles contracted. It's a voluntary muscle action. No magic there."

He repeated her words, "You had a *thought*, and your brain sent an *impulse*. That statement is much like saying that in order to flawlessly play a virtuoso piano concerto you merely have to press down on a bunch of black and white keys. That is far too simplistic a construct, especially for *your* level of understanding, Doctor Jacobs. No, Christine, the sentient portion of you, that is, the *only* thing about you that is truly *real* and not merely the concentrations of nano-fields of passive energy that you mistakenly think of as solid matter, that animate *element*, of what poets and prophets call your soul, emitted an active *thought*."

Christine started to respond.

He didn't give her time to take a breath. "Your thought was a tangible entity that did not exist before you conjured it to life in your imagination and then launched it. It was an *idea*, which is a living physical wave of energy, a hyper-energy wave of a much higher-frequency and lower wavelength than you have yet to discover in your disciplines of the physical sciences. It is much smaller and more penetrating than gamma rays, an energy wave that does not destroy cells, cause cancer, or randomly scramble genetic codes. No, this is a wave that affects the energy fields of every fundamental element, of every quark, of every hadron, of every proton, neutron and electron, of every atom, of every molecule, of every cell, of every organic tissue between your head and your foot, generating a deliberate vectored electromagnetic force that caused all those intermediate elements to come into balance with that force, obedient to its will, to its expressed desire, and to its purpose."

Christine was speechless.

The teacher turned to face Andrew, as though he knew exactly what he was thinking at that very moment. "Yes, Andrew. Stones that weigh over a thousand tons, or mountains for that matter, behave no different than organic tissue. They, too, are just vast concentrations of extremely dense passive energy, primarily obeying the force of gravity, merely waiting to be commanded otherwise by the energy of a single creative thought unleashed."

Andrew exclaimed, "It *can't* be that simple."

"Can it not?" He laughed out loud. "Why, your very own history proves it! Do you have any idea how many innocent souls of light have been burned at the stake or crushed with stones or beheaded or drowned by good, well-meaning folk, just because those souls happened to accidentally stumble onto one or two of the natural organic energy functions I have explained to you?"

Else started to respond.

He didn't let her get a word out. "And then there are, oh my word, *so* many diabolically twisted, depraved souls among your kind who have found their own keen, albeit distorted, understanding of these capabilities, and have deliberately abused them for their own selfish ends. Now here, we are no longer talking about accidental discovery of the powers of which we speak; rather, those truly corrupt individuals or groups whose souls have grown dangerously dark, polarized with pure negative, destructive, entropic energy—obedient only to the Law of Entropy."

Helen muttered, "So monsters do exist."

He threw up his hands. "Do you honestly believe that all the tales of witches and wizards, sorcerers and enchanters, ghosts and goblins, are mere fable? If so, think again. Oh yes, monsters truly exist and walk among you, whether you recognize them by their outward appearance or not." He sighed. "What has confused the issue, to your own peril, is that your kind has a unique talent and pervasive penchant for taking its darkest fears, or that which it cannot explain or understand, and cloaking them in the humble rags of myth, legend, and lore, which you think provides you some sanctuary. Or worse, you revel in your ignorance, nay, even jealously guard and defend such fictions, and deny any existence of the truth, and therefore rationalize away your abuse and misuse of that which was given you for your own good."

And then it happened.

Helen's *intuition function* was beginning to sound its alarms. Something had changed in the air. She could sense it. A bad feeling was slowly creeping across her chest, constricting her lungs, putting pressure on her heart. She noticed all of the others were no longer sitting spellbound and enthralled, but starting to fidget as well.

Jason's watch sounded a tune on the hour. He glanced down. It was midnight.

Andrew's radio squawked. He lifted it to his ear. "Duncan here...what? That's *insane*. Are you sure?"

"What is it, Andrew?" Dr. Markham asked.

Duncan's brow furrowed as he rose to his feet. "The tower guard reports we're under some kind of attack. There's been shots fired in the camp."

"What do we need to do?" Jason was on his feet now as well.

The teacher put a calm hand on Andrew's shoulder. "We need to keep our wits in check as we take a look at what is transpiring. Come with me."

And with that all of the men moved swiftly out of the room, leaving Helen, Else, and Christine looking at one another, dumbfounded.

Christine said, "He'll know what to do. He'll protect us."

Else scowled, "You are certain of this? Have you considered the alternative? What if he was lying? What if it's all *scheisse*, pure bullshit? What if it's all just a clever story designed to deceive us for his own purpose?"

"For *what* purpose? Why would he waste his breath?" Christine lifted her new leg. "Is *this* a deception? Are you *blind*?"

Else shot back, "He just admitted, even the monsters have great powers."

The bad feeling in Helen's stomach wasn't getting any better.

CHAPTER 31

"Where are these images coming from?"

Andrew stood spellbound in the small circular room on the second level, where the teacher had led them. It was approximately twenty feet in diameter with yet another domed ceiling arching overhead. The room's walls were pure white when they had entered, but were soon transformed into a complete 360 degree panoramic view of what was happening above on the desert surface—a perfect illusion as if one were standing there on level ground.

Jason and Dr. Markham stood next to each other, watching in horror the unfolding battle taking place before them. The teacher stood in the very center of the room, holding his hands apart to either side of him, raised at shoulder height, with his arms slightly bent, fingers spread wide.

He said softly, "These are engrams from the eyes and ears of one of your people. The one you call McNulty."

All the men flinched as one of the guard towers exploded into a brilliant fireball lighting up the night with a harsh red glare accented with a deep penetrating concussion. It was soon followed by another detonation on the tower positioned at the opposite corner of the compound. The staccato reports of semi-automatic and automatic gunfire clipped the air. Men were running in all directions. It was a scene of utter panic and confusion. One by one bodies began to double-over and fall to the ground, some writhing, most crumpled and still. A white cargo van came into view, barreling through the main gate at high speed.

Andrew grabbed his radio. "McNulty! Can you hear me?"

Arnold McNulty's voice crackled through the radio. "Mr. Duncan, we've lost both forward towers on the north side of the camp. The perimeter has been breached! Repeat, the perimeter has been breached!"

"We know—" Andrew started to reply when a bright muzzle burst flashed in McNulty's direction, accented by the high-pitched whiz of projectiles slicing through the air, some ending with dull, wet jerking thumps. The image of the room jolted and then tilted on its side with the view of the ground taking up half the room. The picture faded to blackness.

Everyone looked to the teacher.

He silently closed his eyes for a second and then the images resumed. Their vantage point was now inside one of the Quonset huts. Men were grabbing weapons and struggling to throw on their pants and boots. A window shattered and a long pointed projectile deflected off the floor, then exploded in a thumping poof of green smoke. Everyone in the room began to cough and choke and vomit. In seconds they began falling to the floor, twisting and writhing and gnashing in agony, clawing at their throats. Hideous lesions and boils erupted on their faces and exposed skin. Blood began streaming from their eyes, nostrils, ears, and mouths. Again the view faltered, fell, and dimmed to black.

"Can't you *do* anything?" cried Jason.

The teacher's own ire was coming to a boil. "Not from down here! If I could reach them personally in time, I could slay these invaders single-handedly. It appears your forces were only prepared to repel the curious, not armed aggressors."

Andrew Duncan could only mutely stand there holding his head in disbelief.

"Who are they, Andrew?" Jason asked.

Dr. Markham ventured, "Thieves? Bandits, perhaps?"

"No. Not likely," said Andrew. "Not with that kind of firepower. This makes no sense. No bloody sense at all!"

The teacher closed his eyes again and the pictures on the walls appeared once more. This time it was from the vantage point of someone lying underneath a vehicle. Two dirty and scraped arms were stretched out in the foreground. They could hear the sound of labored breathing. From beneath the bumper of the vehicle one full row of Quonset huts could be seen. All of them had clouds of green smoke pouring from their windows. Screams and wails could be heard in the distance. Two armed men in black approached on foot wearing military gasmasks, systematically gunning down any moving thing they encountered with short controlled bursts. The white cargo van came into view again, stopping next to the yellow cage above the descent shaft under the oil rig tower. Two men exited the van and walked to its rear, opening the two side-by-side doors.

Andrew pointed out, "The lift is topside, in case we needed anything. It'll take them at least twenty minutes to reach us, but they can only come down two at a time. Can you do anything to protect us? I have no weapons stored down here."

The teacher said, "The astronomy gallery on the level above us can be sealed off completely. They shall go no further than that."

Andrew nodded once with a grave frown. "Then that's the plan. We can't do anything for the crew topside at the moment. They'll have to manage as best they can on their own. We'll isolate the assailants from us down here, as you've suggested, and then we wait them out. If they don't think to damage any of my radio relays and transmission equipment, we may be able to send a call for help."

"What's that?" Dr. Markham was pointing to the image on the wall.

From the viewer's vantage under the truck, the other men dressed in black, six of them in all, were unloading a large gray rectangular box from the back of the truck and lashing it to a two-wheel handcart.

"I don't know," Andrew replied. "I don't like the looks of it."

The teacher took a step back and waved his hands in a flat circle over the spot where he had just been standing. A segment of the floor opened and up came a crystalline structure similar to the one they had found next to the ice dome. When it reached a height of four feet it stopped. He put his hand on it and the image changed to the interior of the great hall above. The halogen lights were still on. He reached forward and touched his finger to an irregular crystal, and with a tremor of stone, the archway that led into the complex folded together in a single fluid motion from top to bottom like a zipper. The wall no longer contained an exit.

"How are we seeing this?" Jason asked.

The teacher smiled. "This is my house. In my house, even the stones have eyes and ears if I wish them to."

•

"Where did they go?" Else walked to the door of the classroom and looked out across the laboratory.

"Let's find out." Helen lifted a two-way radio from her belt. "Andrew, come in. If you can hear me, come in."

The radio hissed, and Andrew's voice responded. "I'm here, Helen. What is it?"

She squeezed the TALK button. "Where are you? What's going on?"

"Rather hard to explain at the moment," the voice garbled back. "It appears as if we're going to be stuck down here for the time being."

Helen insisted, "Andrew, tell us what's happening."

Andrew Duncan was ever the matter-of-fact professional and master of understatement. "Well, m'dear, it seems we've been attacked on the surface by a small squad of unidentified soldiers. I fear there are heavy casualties to our crew, and very few survivors, if any. The intruders are in the process of breaching the lift, and certainly appear keen on coming down here into the complex. The good news is that our gracious host has been kind enough to seal off the main hall on level one, so they'll not get much farther than that without some substantial excavation equipment or explosives."

"How do you know all of that?" she asked, a puzzled wrinkle creasing her forehead between her eyebrows.

He paused. "We can...see it. Don't ask."

"I won't," she shot back. "I want to see for myself. Where are you?"

"We're on the second level," he replied. "I'll meet you at the top of the stairs and show you the way."

"See you in five. Out."

Helen snapped the radio off, returning it to her belt and swiftly moved to Christine's side. Else had already draped Christine's left arm around her shoulders. Helen took her right one and they stood her up. Bearing their young companion between them, they hurried from the classroom, exiting the magnificent laboratory of the ancients deep under the sands of the Rub Al Khali for the very last time.

CHAPTER 32

The women were every bit as much in awe of the panoramic images displayed in the control room as the men. They stood breathless as the image of the yellow lift appeared from the penetration hole in the ceiling and made its way down to the stone floor below. When the gate lifted, a lone man dressed in black rolled out and came up into a crouched firing stance with a compact automatic weapon in his hands, thrusting it left, then right, then centering it. Everyone involuntarily took a half step back when it appeared as though the barrel was aimed directly at the viewer. The man stood, made a careful perimeter sweep around the great room, then hit the green button that sent the lift upward to the surface again. The intruder removed his gas mask and touched the tip of his index finger to his right ear and spoke into a headset microphone. His voice could be heard clearly in the control room.

"Gentlemen, all clear. The lift is away. Prepare the package for deployment."

The soldier in black lowered his weapon and began to examine the equipment in the hall: the generator, the lights, the table covered with Else's notes.

"What can they really do in there?" Helen asked.

"Not much," Andrew answered. "That's the idea. If they don't think to disrupt the radio gear, the plan is to wait for them to get bored and leave, then we get up there and issue an SOS."

"I don't know if that's really going to work." Jason gestured at the figure in black. "Andrew, they headed right for the lift. They knew exactly where to go. They obviously want something down here."

Andrew shrugged. "We tried to keep our operation a secret as long as we could. It was bound to leak out sooner or later. I just never thought anyone in this country would go to such lengths for material gain."

"They say money is the root of all evil," said Else.

The teacher smiled. "In my observation, I'd say your kind believes the *lack* of money is the root of a great many evils."

That quip brought a welcome chuckle from the group and helped to dissipate a little of the nervous tension hanging in the air.

"So we just wait?" Christine asked.

"Patience is a cardinal virtue," the teacher replied. "But I agree with Dr. Wise and am not entirely convinced that our uninvited visitors are merely avaricious tomb raiders or grave robbers."

"Why do you say that?" asked Else.

He studied the figure in the image. "Because it is possible that there are those who may now be aware of my hiding place. Those who, I can assure you, have not come to bear me tidings of great joy."

Else came closer to him. "You said the war that drove you into hiding was long ago, and long forgotten. Surely there aren't any left alive that seek your harm."

He looked her in the eye, his gaze piercing into her, causing her to retreat again. "I would not necessarily jump to that conclusion."

Helen cocked her head. "What are you saying?"

He looked over six pairs of anxious eyes. "Something which requires you to have a bit more background to fully understand. You see, what we called The Worker's War was fought at a time in history when the children of men had forged strong alliances with the leaders of my kind, with the rulers and principalities of that age. Mortal kings and high-priests came and went. Entire regions were conquered and re-conquered and laid waste again and again. Cities sprang up only to be cast down with the next tyrant's surge of ambition and lust for power in an endless bloody cycle. It was really only a matter of time before one faction convinced their local deity to unleash the brilliant fission weapons upon his enemies to vanquish them once and for all. Retaliation was inevitable."

Helen was aghast. "So there was an actual nuclear holocaust?"

He looked away. "I knew the end was near when my brother ordered the annihilation of the kings of Sodom, Gomorrah, El-Paran, Admah, Zebi'im, Zoar, and Tilmun, and all their houses, and their lands, and all their families, and their peoples. Destruction came upon them all in a single day. Prevailing westerly winds from the Great Sea, your Mediterranean, spread irradiated micro-particles, what you call fallout, over the majority of densely populated Mesopotamia, decimating Sumer and Akkad, bringing death and desolation on an evil wind, meted out in untold proportions. When it was over, there were but refugees of your kind left. Of my kind, most were dead. Some fled to the north and to the east. A few traveled to the opposite side of the planet, away from the irradiated atmosphere, to try and begin again there."

"And you?" Helen asked.

"As I told you, I made my retreat into the safety of cryostasis before the final battle, where you found me," he said. "When it was safe, it was my intention to continue my work, but not from here. I knew the land would be barren and unfit from the Sinai to the Dead Sea to the delta of the Tigris and Euphrates for many centuries."

"But something went wrong, you said," Jason noted.

He nodded. "I cannot conclusively prove it, but I strongly suspect my brother had something to do with the disruption of the surface sensors in this entire region. The desert above was not always a desert. My brother never knew the exact location of this facility. But he intimately knew the safety and security systems at my disposal, and what to do to ensure that my sanctuary became a living tomb for me."

"He wanted you buried alive..." Helen's jaw fell in a half-question/statement of disbelief.

He chuckled softly to himself. "And has spent the lion's share of the last four-thousand years ensuring that I stayed that way. You have no idea to what lengths he has gone, the organizations and institutions he has established, all to try and contain the truth of what really happened from seeping out. It truly defies the imagination. And when those occasions arose where he found he could not fully contain the truth of the past, he ensured that only discredited messengers, misguided cults and sects, laughable megalomaniacs, and the truly mentally unstable ones were eager to embrace it, and thus irreparably taint it."

"But why?" Helen asked.

He stiffened. "To prevent the day that I should stand before you, free to fill my lungs again with warm sweet air, free to finish what I began so long ago. He opposes me to this day."

The whole group was taken aback.

"You're saying then that your brother is still alive?" Helen was afraid of the answer.

He looked at her. "I have no reason to assume otherwise. His death would have sent a rift across the entire Galaxy, felt by all, even in cryostasis. So, yes, I believe he lives. But after the great war he surely would have found himself in the minority, still very powerful individually, but virtually alone amongst the survivors of your kind. He would no longer have been free to walk among you as before, as royalty, as deity. His mighty temples and palaces surely lay in ruin as did everything else. No, he would have had to live in secret, sequestered behind high walls and move in mysterious ways to maintain the vestiges of his power and subjugation of your kind. He hides himself well among men, cloaking his engram emissions, even from me."

"But why did he do it? Why did he leave you buried here?" asked Christine. "Rivalry? Jealousy?"

"Punishment," he replied. "Do not forget. It was I who had unleashed the forbidden passions in humankind. It was I who gave them the ability to hate, to destroy, to murder, to steal…and worst of all, the ability to reject him and his authority. I am the villain who unlocked the door to your darkest appetites for power, your craving for conquest, your thirst for blood, your lusts of the flesh, your yearning for your own selfish glories."

"But that's just the negatives," Christine came to his defense. "You said you also opened up the same door to love, to creativity, to inspiration, to *all* the virtues of the heart as well as the failings."

"That was the risk I took, yes," he said softly. "But in the end, he was proved to be right. I was wrong. Yes? The evidence was painfully clear. Of all my children, my brother could only point to a handful of righteous, obedient, faithful, trustworthy, decent men in the whole of the world whose hearts were not set continually on evil. Only one man in Sodom itself could be found worth sparing amongst the multitudes."

Christine felt saddened. "So he despised all of mankind?"

The teacher conceded, "No, not all. In fact, my brother took a personal interest in a particular lineage of mankind, descended from the pure family of Noah. He brought them under his wing, the veritable apple of his eye. And with the strictest of laws, ordinances and mandates, he ordered them to conform to his will, meting out rich blessings to the obedient and harsh punishment to the disobedient."

"But why did so many humans turn out so bad?" Else asked.

"Because I was never allowed to finish my work," he shot back, his frustration boiling over. "Do you not yet understand what I have been trying to tell you? True selfless love, generosity, compassion, virtue and imagination—the living Law of Creation itself, the one true nemesis to the Law of Entropy—comes from a power found within you, not in compliance to externally mandated codes of behavior. It works its will as you allow it to flow into you, and through you, and touch the world around you, filling your own universe with creative energy, with life, with love, with passion, with light." He sighed with weary resignation, "At least that is how it was supposed to work."

"So answer Else's question." Christine had taken a seat on the floor. "Why didn't it work that way—specifically, if it's really as powerful as you say?"

"Why, my precious Dr. Jacobs," he grinned. "You shall be most interested to learn that the *specific* answer to that question is a simple physics problem."

"What?" She scrunched her nose, and was about to ask another question when the image of the yellow steel cage appeared on the far wall descending to the floor of the hall below.

When the sound of steel hitting stone rang out, the group spun around in unison to face it. They were surprised to find no more armed soldiers, but rather the sight of the large brushed aluminum box. The lone soldier quickly unloaded it and sent the lift back up once again.

Else pointed. "What's that thing?"

"We don't know," said Andrew. "They brought it with them."

Helen suddenly felt as if she were about to throw up.

CHAPTER 33

"How long will the satellite be in range?"

Jean-Marc Xavier stood before a wall of high-definition plasma screens. All twelve monitors were precision mounted adjacent to each other with a seamless edge, projecting an individual segment of a total image, creating a single magnified view. Only three men were present in the darkened underground bunker control room belonging to the Egyptian Mukhabarat, their intelligence and security service: Xavier himself, Mohammed Al Faisal, and a lone satellite imaging technician. Each one carefully studied the feed coming in from an Israeli near-synchronous satellite.

The technician answered in broken English, "No more than two and a half or three more hours on this view angle, sir."

They had been watching events unfold for over an hour. The window of opportunity would be adequate, Xavier calculated in his head. "Thank you. Can you pan the image back? I'd like to see the entire compound."

The technician nodded and his fingers flew over the keyboard in front of him. The thermal image pulled back from the close-up view of ghost-white individual human forms to a wide angle shot of the entire facility as seen from the vantage point of almost directly overhead. Two of the guard towers on the northern perimeter were still burning. The white van was only a small spot seen parked next to the drilling rig.

They had witnessed every detail of the attack as it happened in real-time, starting with the breach of the gate of the Duncan International complex, the swift penetration, the sweep of the Quonset huts, and the mop up of the remainder of the compound, all before the team began their initial descent into the shaft. The mission was going perfectly. The weapon was sent down forty-five minutes ago. Morse had just begun his descent to join Collins. Each man possessed one of the two arming keys. While it was physically possible for only one person to arm that particular model of weapon, i.e. turning both keys simultaneously, the two-man protocol was sacrosanct. Everyone knew that. No one man could ever be trusted to wield that kind of power. Jean-Marc believed that with every fiber of his being.

"It shouldn't be long," Mohammed assured him.

"I know," Xavier whispered. "Is your contingency plan in place?"

"Of course," Mohammed replied. "All is in readiness. If there is any malfunction whatsoever with the device and no visual confirmation of mission completion by 0300 hours, we have a bomber en route with an American made Daisy-Cutter which will wipe the site clean and expose the open shaft. One of our newest Mirages will then deploy a laser guided JDAM, a low yield device, only half a megaton—dropped directly down its throat. The weapon is accurate to within a meter. I have been assured the pilot's skills are sufficient to circumcise a flea. These new American made smart bombs, especially the nuclear tipped ones, are quite amazing. Brilliant technology! They only cost us twenty-million US each. My contact in London was having a sale."

"And if your talented Rabbi misses his flea?" Jean-Marc raised his eyebrows.

"He won't." Mohammed chuckled. "But just to be sure, I had them prep two weapons, just in case. If we don't need them, your friend in Jakarta will surely want them, at twice the price!"

"*Tres bien*," Jean-Marc winked at him. "You are always thinking very wisely, *mon ami*. Very wisely indeed."

CHAPTER 34

Everything remained quiet and still in the great hall for several minutes. The group in the control room watched the image of the lone soldier as he sat on the metal box and kept his patient vigil.

Dr. Markham asked, "So what do we do now?"

Andrew shrugged. "Continue to wait, and see what they have in mind."

Helen just stared at the image of the metal box. Something within her was churning hot, her stomach uneasy, every fiber in her being suspicious and wary.

Christine turned back to the teacher. "You were about to tell me about a physics problem…before we were so rudely interrupted?"

The teacher bit his lower lip for a second, keeping his own eyes trained on the image of the soldier, then took a deep breath and began. "Indeed, notwithstanding any further interruptions. I shall do my best to keep the explanation of this process simple. But what I am about to tell you is probably the most important piece of knowledge that I can possibly share with you." He paused for a moment to frame his thoughts, then explained, "Your own scientists of the last few centuries began shaping their understanding of the physical reality of the universe with a reasonably accurate model, or shall we say, a conceptual construct, when they conceived of a physical universe composed of protons, neutrons, and electrons."

Christine interrupted, "Right. And we know that particle theory teaches that these structures are actually made up of several subordinate orders of smaller elementals."

He held up a finger. "Correct, but I am not talking about structures here, rather electromagnetic properties, and more importantly, the true nature and behavior of sentient energy."

"Sentient energy?" Christine was skeptical. "Are you implying that energy can have a mind, and will?"

"And a purpose," he added. "All energy, of which everything consists, exists in one of three forms: creative, entropic, or passive. Quite simply—building, destroying, or inert. This is in perfect keeping with your understanding of the symbols of the Proton, the Electron, and the Neutron.

Positive, negative and neutral. The first postulate of sentient energy is that all animate energy is either creative or entropic. Inanimate energy is passive. A rock, a meteor, an asteroid, or even a planet are all different sized masses of passive energy, non-sentient, subject to manipulation by either creative or entropic energy. Conversely, a plant, an insect, a bacterium, a virus, a microbe are all models of creative energy in action, whose most fundamental desire is exclusively to live, to grow and to reproduce—life exploding and expanding within its own ecosystem, as far and wide as it is allowed before an entropic force restrains it, or kills it."

"And humans?" It was Helen who asked.

He turned to her. "Humans. Ah, yes. The great enigma of the universe. Our common life form is initially conceived with the most basic form of *inherent* creative energy. That is, it possesses adequate life energy to grow and reproduce our kind, just as any other plant or animal. But we also possesses the unique ability to avail ourselves of *external* creative energy, to allow it to coalesce within you, whereupon we then have the opportunity to form it and shape it like wet clay on the potter's wheel into original ideas, thoughts, and a virtual wellspring of imagination. This form of energy possesses a mind's eye of *potential* vision, seeing that which is not as though it were. It is a virtually limitless force capable of manipulating passive energy at will, influencing other creative energy forms, and is mandatory to combat the forces of entropic energy—to literally fire raw ideas in the kiln of creative will and thus transform them into reality."

Helen ventured a thought, "So you're saying we're an intermediate participant in the ongoing act of creation itself?"

He shrugged. "Is that so hard a truth to accept? I ask you to consider, by what magic or sorcery does the musician take an inventory of a mere twelve discrete wavelengths of sound energy, and mix and combine them, to rhythmically pace them, to harmonize them, all in such a way as to produce all the wonders and beauty and passions of music? How does the storyteller take the blank sheaf of paper or parchment and with his quill fashion only a handful of characters into the words of his tongue, and use those words to capture the phrases and idioms of literary expression, and then use those very expressions to poetically paint vibrant ideas and vivid images, culminating in the creation of characters and lives and scenes and sagas, verily weaving all the stories and tales that have ever been told? Is this truly magic? From a romantic perspective, perhaps it is. But physically, scientifically, it is the process of harnessing creative energy and the mastery thereof."

"So wherein lies the physics problem?" No one but the teacher noticed that Christine was standing on her own two feet unassisted when she asked her question, hands on hips, the way she stood when sparring with her own physics students in her classroom back in New England.

He answered her question with a question, "Is gravity good or evil?"

She shrugged. "Neither. It's an impersonal force."

He nodded, politely clarifying for her, "It is in fact a *passive* force, an electromagnetic interaction, occurring between different objects with sufficient coalesced energy to possess the quality known as mass. Your kind understands this concept well, just as your Sir Isaac Newton conceived it. But tell me this, Dr. Jacobs, when a man falls off a cliff and dies, is gravity then to blame? Is gravity his murderer?"

Christine frowned. "I'm sorry, I don't see where you're going with this."

The teacher looked at them all. "I am attempting to get you to see that there are a vast array of physical laws—laws of physics, laws of energy, laws of science, immutable laws that dictate how everything in the universe functions, without exception, whether you understand these laws or not, or are even aware of them. As pure creative energy gave birth to the universe and sought to establish its will in the formation of the most fundamental elements, atoms, molecules, substances, gasses, liquids, solids, proteins, nucleic acids, enzymes—yes, the fundamental building blocks of life itself—creative energy simultaneously came into direct conflict with the Law of Entropy. Entropy, that which seeks to make the complex simple, that which breaks things down, dissipates energy, disintegrates, destroys, atrophies...kills."

"So where does that leave us?" Jason really wanted to know. "Caught in the middle of some cosmic tug of war?"

The teacher replied, "Dr. Wise, the sum of the matter is this: human sentience, your basic self-awareness, functions at one of two levels, a low energy state and a high energy state. Low energy operation is organic, which is simply the rudimentary awareness of your physical existence, appetites, needs, wants, desires, and the like. Many people live their entire lives and die in this state, and the universe is neither bettered nor worsened by their presence. This is truly the definition of a lost soul. This is how your kind was originally engineered from the base level hominids, and how my brother wanted your entire existence to be."

Helen was nodding, starting to understand. "But you secretly engineered another option for us."

"Yes, exactly," he smiled. "The high-energy level of operation of my kind, where all the functions we have been discussing are fully available and active. But from birth, your high-energy operation abilities are inactive, dormant. They are subsequently activated as a result of a quickening process, a literal infusion of creative energy that causes you to become self-aware on an entirely different plane, as a unique sentient being, *distinct* from your physical body, which you wear like a garment, or ride around in like a vehicle. This is the state where you command mastery over your physical being, and in turn, your own physical universe. It is in this state you are therefore free to serve as a conduit for the power of creation to continue its ever expanding work."

Helen so much wanted to comprehend everything she was hearing, but all her training, all her education, and all her life's experience stood as an obstacle to fully embrace everything that was being explained to her. Jason's brow was knit. Mentally, he was working hard to do all the math and keep up. It was giving him a headache. Else still held a skeptical, distrusting frown firmly fixed on her face. Andrew and Dr. Markham just stood mute, not knowing what to think or believe.

The teacher looked directly into Christine's eyes. "The fundamental physics problem, Dr. Jacobs, lies in the fact that once you attain this highly energized state of self-awareness, you not only become a potential conduit for creation, you also have the potential to become magnetically receptive to the destructive force of entropy as well. The great mystery of the universe is that your fate, your life's journey of creation or destruction, is a free choice for you to make. The difference between good men and evil men is often only a matter of which of these two opposing physical forces they have chosen to align themselves."

Else piped up, "So then what prevented more of our ancestors from experiencing this quickening event, and discovering and activating more of the functions you had disabled?"

"I have asked myself that question for thousands of years," he replied. "And the only answers I have been able to find are most discouraging to accept. The power of creative energy was intended to spread like a virus, from one sentient being to another, handed down from generation to generation, a sacred legacy, accelerating in momentum, becoming an unstoppable force. But the ugly truth is, on this planet there has been an active effort to stamp it out since the very beginning, from before the time of the Flood, a systematic program of lies, distortions, misinformation, persecutions, along with a vast compendium of the greatest of atrocities ever imagined, manifested wherever the truth became known and creativity began to flourish. All sanctioned by my brother. As I told you, he never wanted an equal."

Christine asked, "OK. So then how exactly does this quickening process occur?"

Everyone was keen to hear his answer. However, the teacher's discourse was interrupted yet again by the sound of the lift clanging against the stone floor of the hall above. They all turned to view the scene projected on the walls.

A second soldier emerged from the lift and walked over to the box, and without a word, he knelt down before it and entered a ten-digit code into a keypad. The original soldier stood as the second one lifted the lid and threw it back. It echoed through the hall as it banged against the back side of the box.

Helen turned to the teacher. "Is there any way to see inside that thing?"

"Of course." He spread his hands again and closed his eyes for a moment. When the images changed, it took a few seconds for the group to realize that they were now looking down inside the box through one of the soldier's eyes.

Helen gasped, "Oh, my God."

Andrew turned to her. "What is it, Helen?"

She could barely get the words out. "A nuclear warhead."

They all watched in horror as the two men in black knelt down side-by-side and began their well-practiced arming sequence. The heavy brass keys were inserted into the safeties and turned together on a three-count. The three arming toggle switches were engaged with three swift clicks. The second soldier pulled out a card, inserted it into a slot, and then began typing authorization numbers into a keypad.

Else's voice was tinged with panic. "We have to get out of here."

Andrew turned to Helen. "Helen, can you disarm that goddamn thing?"

She nodded. "I believe so. I've disarmed many like it."

"Then we just need to get access to it," said Andrew.

Jason turned to the teacher. "So, like…does your console thingy there possibly have a 'smite' button?"

His eyes flashed. "I think I have something that will suffice."

CHAPTER 35

The teacher stood alone at the junction of the five corridors, before the closed archway that formerly opened into the great astronomy gallery. In his hand he held a golden wand, no larger than a relay runner's baton. As instructed, the rest of the group hid in the shadows of the fourth corridor, which led to the staircase that descended to the second level from which they had just come. No one chose to stay behind. The teacher bid them remain as still and quiet as possible as he approached the closed archway. Just as they had witnessed before in the classroom, his entire visage suddenly appeared to expand and stretch over a spherical shape before he vanished completely from sight.

With a rumble of stone the great arch spread open from bottom to top.

Helen heard the sound of urgent footsteps, two sets of boots clattering on stone, running hard. That was followed by the metallic crack of a bolt chambering a round, signaling a weapon prepared to fire.

And then came a moment of silence, a brief prelude to—

POOM!

The group crouched in unison from the brilliance of the flash. It lasted but an instant, like a great photographic strobe, blinding them all momentarily.

"Come," was all they heard, loudly echoing from inside the great hall.

Helen and Jason ran forward first, followed closely by Else. Dr. Markham and Andrew were standing on either side of Christine, merely steadying her as she limped along between them, slowly, but on her own power. The teacher stood near the aluminum box curiously examining it. As Jason ran across the great hall, he slowed down briefly to take a look at two distinct piles of fine white ash, like poured mounds of salt, still smoldering. A pungent reek akin to burned sulfur, hair and rubber hung in the air. There was no other visible sign of either soldier's presence, no weapons, nothing.

Helen kept running at full speed and reached the box first, carefully inspecting the detonator instrumentation. She sighed in relief, still breathing hard. "Oh thank, God. This is an easy one." She paused. "But that's odd."

"What is it?" Jason ran up and knelt down beside her, panting.

"Look." She pointed at the red LED readout. "Look how fast it's moving."

Jason reached for his computational watch, punched in a few keys, waited, punched in a few more, then said, "Just get it turned off, now, if you can."

She nodded and reached into the box. "No problem. Move back. This should only take a second."

As the rest of the group reached them, Helen quickly threw the three arming toggles back to the OFF position, click-click-click, and then turned both brass safety keys in unison back to their original locked positions. Her eyes went to the digital timer.

The time to detonation continued to decrement unabated.

Helen's eyes urgently scanned the device, in disbelief at what she was seeing. "What the hell...? That should have stopped it. It can't fire without being in the fully armed and locked position."

"What are you saying? You can't stop it?" Else demanded.

"Wait a second, give me a minute," Helen insisted. "Dammit!"

Christine limped up closer. "What's the procedure, Helen? Go through the steps, one at a time. Out loud."

Drops of sweat began to bead on Helen's upper lip. "Right. Arming sequence. Two-man keyed safeties. Check. Triple arming triggers. Check. Authorization code, entered and pending. We saw that. It wouldn't be counting down otherwise. I could try clearing the code, but if this timer has been upgraded, it may have a failsafe routine that requires a separate code to deactivate it. Clearing it or entering a wrong code could trigger immediate detonation."

Andrew noted, "We obviously don't know any codes. Can it be bypassed? Like in the movies, you know, cutting the bloody blue wire and such?"

"No," Helen shook her head. "It doesn't work that way."

Else rasped, "Then just clear it and be done with it. Hurry! We're certainly dead if you do nothing!"

Jason nodded, "She's right. Fifty-fifty is better than a hundred to zero. Do it. No choice."

Helen reached for the CLEAR button.

"Wait!" Christine interrupted.

Helen's finger stopped a fraction of an inch from the button.

Christine asked calmly, "Is the authorization module one or two-factor authentication?"

Helen turned to her. "What?"

Christine pointed down in the box. "One-factor, as in password or code only, or is it two-factor authentication, something you know, like a code or password, plus something you physically have."

"Two-factor, I guess," Helen replied. "The keys are physical."

"No," Christine insisted. "The brass keys are for the implosions safeties, not the timer itself. The safeties and the arming triggers are just electromechanical relays that won't reset until after the timer does. The timer is a separate subsystem, a glorified switch. Thus, the timer may have its own dual authentication protection."

Helen looked puzzled for a second.

Christine asked, "Does the timer module have a memory stick, an actualization plug-in module, or some kind of an access card or smart-card in addition to a manually entered authorization code?"

Helen gasped, "Oh, my God. Of course. The access card."

She reached down and ejected the plastic access card from its slot.

The timer stopped at 36:31.

Helen sat back on her heels, dusting off her hands, and announced with no small measure of relief. "There. It's OK. It's disarmed for now, but with its authorization code still loaded in memory. I didn't have to clear it. Crisis averted." She grabbed Christine's hand. "Thank you."

A similar wave of relief washed over everyone. Jason gave Christine a warm hug, which was soon joined by everyone else.

"Is our moment of crisis truly averted?" came the familiar voice of the teacher, who had quietly retreated a few paces, tapping the gold baton against the palm of his other hand.

Helen rose to her feet. "Yes. It can't go off now. Why? What's wrong?"

He glanced down into the aluminum box. "As has been aptly noted, mere thieves do not come to destroy. Not with this kind of force. These men came to destroy. They came to kill."

"To kill you." Else said what everyone was thinking.

He returned a tight lipped nod. "So it appears. Which means that no one will be leaving the way you came in. More of these invaders await above, as we have observed. And they are likely to send down more fierce weapons of destruction until they are convinced that their mission is complete."

"Can you go up and fight them?" Dr. Markham pointed to the gold wand. "With that thing?"

The teacher looked down at the weapon in the metal box again. "Yes. I can. But there may be a more advantageous way to resolve this."

"How?" Christine asked.

"We leave this place by another means, discretely, and let this weapon do its worst after we are gone," he said.

Helen understood. "And make them think they were successful. But how can we get out of here?"

"Let me show you." He started to turn away. "Come with me."

Jason reached for him. "Wait. How long will that take?"

The teacher turned to Jason. "To make our escape? Surely no more than fifteen minutes to get to the launch bay. Less than ten minutes to prepare my ship. No more than ten more to get clear of any threat from that thing. I calculate it is well within the thirty-six minutes it shows remaining there on its timer. We need not tarry here any longer. Come."

Jason ran a weary hand over his head. "And therein, sir, lies our problem."

The teacher looked down at the timer. "Explain."

Jason did. "Someone has tampered with this detonator. The timer's crystal oscillator had been accelerated ten-fold. It's decrementing at a rate of about six minutes to one. Once this thing is rearmed, unless it's a dud, it goes thermonuclear in precisely six minutes and five seconds. According to what you just said, we wouldn't have time to even reach your ship's launch bay before everything vaporizes and a few billion tons of earth falls in on top of us."

"Then let's just leave it and go," Else pleaded.

Christine limped forward. "If we go, we need to do it soon. We don't have much time left to hang around here."

"Why not?" asked Helen.

She explained, "Look. The lift is gone. It's heading back up."

They all turned and saw that the steel cage was no longer with them. The soft hum of the winch echoed down the shaft.

"It probably left the second the two down here didn't report in after detecting a disturbance." Christine glanced at her own watch. "That was seven minutes ago. No report means they can be down here in thirty-three minutes to finish the job."

Jason spoke up, "You said we could make it to your ship's launch bay in fifteen minutes, and then be gone ten minutes after that? Do I take it, this ship of yours is not located on this level?"

"Correct," the teacher affirmed. "It is on the lowest level, not far from the cryostasis-chamber. But obviously our dilemma is that we cannot reach it and depart in only six minutes, as you say."

"Then I say we take the bomb with us," Jason suggested. "You get your ship ready to go, like you said. Then we arm it and make a run for it. Will five or six minutes give us time to get clear of the blast if you're ready to go as soon as we throw the switches?"

The teacher rubbed his eyes, clearly anxious and frustrated. "Perhaps. There would be no margin for error, and a questionable probability of success. Although, the blast itself could aid in our escape if certain factors are conducive. That notwithstanding, you have one further significant obstacle. I estimated approximately fifteen minutes to reach the launch bay assuming we were moving rapidly, not transporting an object of this size and having to negotiate seven full flights of stairs with it."

Jason pointed to it. "No problem. It's on wheels. I'll take it down corridor number two to the utility lift, and meet everyone else down on level seven in about twenty minutes. You close the door to this room again after we leave, just like you did before, and then if any reinforcements from the surface come down here, they find nothing. By the time they can get back up to the surface again to take any further action, we're long gone, and they're all toast."

Andrew chimed in, "I like it."

"The KISS principle," Jason grinned. "You know... Keep It Simple, Stupid."

The teacher nodded once, smiling at Jason with approval. "It is a most ingenious course of action, Dr. Wise. Your counsel is sound. Then if we are all in agreement, let us make ready my ship."

As they headed for the archway Dr. Markham asked, "What kind of ship can take us up through a mile of rock?"

"None that I know of," the teacher agreed. "Our course of departure is not upward. We must first go down...into the depths."

CHAPTER 36

"Bless me, Father, for I have sinned."

Monsignor Pietro was aware of the sound of the penitent parishioner's words rattled off by rote from the other side of the rattan screen of the confessional, but he wasn't listening. His heart was heavy, painfully so, his mind sorely troubled and tortured. He was tired, exhausted, both emotionally and physically. It was almost midnight Central European Time. Thankfully, he wasn't assigned to say the midnight Mass that night. His only obligation was to hear confession for another few minutes before the commencement of celebrations. The lines were never very long late at night. And then it would all be over.

How had it all come to this?

He buried his face in his hands. A palpitation of silent sobs jerked his gut and caught in his throat. He had always wanted to be a priest, even as a boy. Oh, how proud his mother and father had been when he told them of his call to join the holy priesthood. They rejoiced. They celebrated. The whole family, as well as his whole village, they were all overjoyed with the good news. It could not have been a greater gift to them. But that was so many, many long years ago—so long ago it no longer seemed real, or even relevant. Now it was an all but forgotten fantasy, a lost dream of what might have been. All those years of study and training. Always rating at the top of every class, one of the best and brightest, the most inquisitive and astute, one of the exceptional ones gifted with the most promise. That is what they had repeatedly told him from his early teens. Ironically, his renowned proficiency with theology, history, languages, liturgy, and dogma was precisely what earned him the honor of studying at the feet of the great and esteemed Holy Father, his Excellency Cardinal Giovanni Ricollo.

That was seventeen long years ago.

Was it simple naïveté that had so clouded his mind and judgment? Pride? Ambition? Yes, admittedly, it was exhilarating and nothing short of titillating in the very beginning to be privy to so many secret things, to be entrusted with the mysteries of the faith, to have unfettered access to such a wealth of forbidden information, access to entire libraries of intellectual and historical treasures that the rest of the world was never allowed to know even existed. Did it all come at a price of taking a life, killing, when his heart was set only on serving?

It was impossible to hold back the tears burning down his cheeks.

Was it worth it?

His position of sacred honor, loyalty and trust was conferred for the sole purpose of guarding the eternal secrets. But he had seen it all—often. Oh yes, on many a dark night he had secreted away, stealing deep down into the restricted vaults below the city, where he opened the forbidden scrolls, examined the clay tablets, and deciphered the pictographs on the vast collection of clay and marble tablets and cylinder seals. Yes, he had studied well to show himself approved, and was completely fluent in Latin, Hebrew, Greek, Aramaic, Arabic, Egyptian, Babylonian, Assyrian, Chaldean, Akkadian, and even the mother of all tongues, ancient Sumerian—all the cryptic tongues of antiquity.

The official pronouncement and pious explanations regarding the nature of so much hidden knowledge was childishly simple. The priceless collection was said to be nothing more than the great libraries of ancient legends, mythologies, fantasy, fables, the lurid lore of heathen nations from the earliest recorded beginnings of civilization. Yes, it was nothing but the chronicles of the occult, the incantations and spells of self-proclaimed witches and sorcerers, the demon-possessed, the accursed, the evil ones. The rituals and ramblings of polytheistic idolaters. The prevarications and lies and poisoned propaganda of prurient pagans. It was the fabrications of every false god, false prophet, deceiver and devil who had ever drawn breath. Verily, it was Satan's very own songs of seduction, vomited forth from the festering bowels of Hell itself. For far too many souls, it was dangerous knowledge—too dangerous to be left unguarded.

At least that was the official story. Paulo Pietro knew otherwise.

Could this knowledge truly ruin lives? Or just mine?

Strangely enough, in reality, he knew that the vast majority of the information was concerned with astronomy and associated polytheistic astrology, the eternal struggle between immutable destiny and the ever changing wheal and woe of fate. It spoke of the detailed procession of the heavens and the twelve houses of the zodiac, mathematically chronicling the astronomical concept of "precession.[18]"

---

[18] Precession is the concept of the earth not returning to the exact same point on the solar ecliptic with respect to the visible star constellations in one full solar year, or 365.25 days, losing approximately one degree of the ecliptic's circumference every seventy-two years. This effect causes a defined annual event such as either of the Vernal or Autumnal Equinoxes or Summer or Winter Solstices to move from one constellation, or Zodiacal House, to the previous one every 2,160 years. A full Precession starting at one point and returning to the exact same point comprises a "Great Year," consisting of 25,920 years.

Much of it consistently referred to the earth as the seventh planet. But that could only be true if one were counting from the outer edge of the solar system, starting with Pluto and moving towards the sun. However, the planet Pluto had not even been discovered by modern astronomers until the 20th century. So how did the ancients know? Many of the texts spoke of the arrival of royal families of strange gods during the Age of Taurus, thousands of complete "Great Years" before the current Age of Pisces, which began its reign in the first century B.C. Significant portions of it contradicted and blasphemed Holy Writ, claiming that mankind was originally created for slavery and not predestined for glory.

It was all lies, of course. Every true man of faith knew that.

Monsignor Pietro's consecrated mission was crystal clear: to protect the ignorant, the weak-willed, the simple minded, the innocent, and the gullible, from so evil a deception—verily, to safeguard the sanctity of the faithful from so great a corruption. It was a policy of holiness and sanctification through abstinence. Where there is no temptation, there is no sin. It was a noble task. Wasn't it? A high and honorable calling? Yes, a holy commission befitting an officer of God—a priest of the Most High. Failure was inexcusable. Allowing corruption to spread was punishable unto death.

And therein lie his dilemma, the ultimate moral paradox: to kill to defend.

Paulo wondered, how different was the sacred charge given to him compared to the same one commissioned to Father Tomás de Torquemada, the great Inquisitor General of Spain? How much Muslim and Jewish blood did he spill with impunity for Ferdinand and Isabella, and for the Pope sitting on his throne here in Rome? The infamy of Torquemada's treachery, intolerance, bigotry, cruelty, and sadism is remembered to this day the world over. But what were they really so *afraid* of that would compel them to sanction and ordain such diabolical measures? Was it purely for the acquisition of temporal power and wealth? Or did they fear something else? Something even more frightening?

Father Pietro let out a long weary sigh. Is the true faith so weak and fragile that mere contact with other beliefs are sufficient to make it fail? If that be true, then how strong is the true faith in the first place? His mind was knot of brambles, a crown of thorns piercing his brain.

"Father?"

Monsignor Pietro snapped out of his trance, realizing the parishioner had finished making his confession and was waiting upon his response. He waved a hasty sign of the cross and mumbled out his prayer of absolution and benediction in Latin, then in Italian assigned a full Rosary for penance. The echoing strains of the carillon's prelude of *Ave Maria* in the cavernous cathedral was starting. He quietly exited the confessional, taking a moment to kiss his purple stole and leave it behind on the wooden seat inside. The back of his tunic was soaked with sweat. He desperately needed to get outside and fill his lungs with the cool night air.

The priest walked alone down the long dark, marble colonnade, with his hands stuffed deep in his pockets, slowly scuffing his heels against the stone, still deep in thought, wrestling in confusion. The dissonant traffic sounds of Rome bustled in the distance, even at that late hour. He asked himself the burning question yet again. *What* were they all so afraid of? Mere lies and legends? Mythological metaphors? Fictional fantasies? Anthropomorphisms of ancient astronomy? Could merely *knowing* these stories be the unforgivable sin, the supreme blasphemy?

> *Sin (sin) v. 1. To betray God. n. 2. Any act that separates one from God.*

Yet at that moment Paulo didn't feel as though he had betrayed God, but rather everything else he once believed and held dear, everything he knew in his heart was right and good and virtuous and true. He definitely felt separated from God. The tender face of the young girl from Sulmona flashed across his mind. Francesca. So innocent, so beautiful, so sweet, so...trusting. How could she have been an instrument of evil? She had only sought to bring healing and relief where she had found only suffering. How could that be wrong?

How could EVERYTHING be so wrong?

The words of a former American President came to mind: "We have nothing to fear, but fear itself—nameless, unreasoning, unjustified terror which paralyzes needed efforts to convert retreat into advance.[19]" That insightful sentiment felt more true at that precise moment than any alternative explanation of what he was wrestling with in his heart.

The answer was obvious, if he were willing to be completely honest with himself. They were simply afraid of losing control, losing mindshare, losing everything to the success of a single seductive idea from a different cosmogony. Silence the opposition! Kill the false prophets! Give them not a voice to deceive! Incarcerate any conflicting ideas!

Surely they didn't fear any *literal* interpretation of their anthropomorphic constructs of demons and devils. If nothing else, the Church had made great strides over the last few decades in understanding the neurosci-

---

[19] Franklin D. Roosevelt, Inauguration Address, March 4, 1933.

ences and medical disciplines of psychology, psychiatry and the diseases of the mind, the nature of psychosis, insanity, schizophrenia, multiple personality disorders, and the like. While the Devil was truly a formidable enemy, not all the misfortunes and evils of man could be indiscriminately laid at his feet.

Nevertheless, the memory of a passage from St. John the Divine's Revelation, leapt to mind:

> "Now when the thousand years have expired, Satan will be released from his prison, and will go out to deceive the nations which are in the four corners of the earth, Gog and Magog, to gather them to battle, whose number is as the sands of the sea.[20]"

Monsignor Paulo Pietro stopped walking, looked up at the stars above and laughed to himself. It made no sense. Did they all honestly believe that the mere knowledge of the myths of ancient paganism could somehow play an active part in bringing the Devil himself up from the depths of the abyss, in the flesh, to physically, as well as spiritually, torment mankind and corrupt the whole of the earth with his lies? And if such an absurd notion could possibly be true, would hiding this information for century after century really do anything to prevent it?

Father Pietro started walking again, his doubts growing yet deeper and more profound with every anxious step he took, strolling slowly away from the great cathedral behind him into the dark embrace of the night. But there was no turning back now. One thing was no longer in doubt— not after what he had done. No, there was no undoing what he had done.

All that remained was what was left to be done—what *had* to be done.

---

[20] Revelation 20:7,8.

CHAPTER 37

"Wow..." was all Jason could say at first sight of the cavernous launch bay, after emerging from a small antechamber which appeared to function as an air lock. He no longer registered any sense of surprise when the first and second sets of stone doors opened before him and closed behind him of their own accord, like the automatic doors at a grocery store.

The docking bay itself was approximately a hundred yards in length with a perfect semicircle arch of walls and ceiling above, creating an inverted half-pipe effect. The air was cooler in there, thick with the odor of stagnant brackish briny salt water. The same familiar soft, white luminescence of the walls illuminated the entire chamber. A deep channel ran down the center of the bay, cut from end to end and filled with murky water. Another white limestone arch of neatly dressed stones marked the far end, and beyond it, access to a dark cave or connecting passage. Beneath his feet the granite was perfectly level, smooth and polished.

The biggest surprise was the ship itself—for indeed it appeared to be a water vessel, moored in the channel, with a gleaming golden gangplank leading from an open gangway to the nearside bank of the channel.

The vessel reminded Jason of Captain Nemo's ship, the *Nautilus*, from Jules Verne's *20,000 Leagues Under the Sea*. It was long and narrow, perhaps seventy feet or more from bow to stern, sleek and metallic, boasting many intricate artifices, bulges, buttresses, recesses and supports. A serrated ridge ran from its pointed nose, up and along its spine, stopping just before the tail. The crescent tail itself resembled that of a great white shark, mounted vertically, as opposed to horizontally like the flukes of a whale. However, the vessel's most intriguing feature caused Jason to stop and stare for a moment in wonder. Beautifully detailed artistic engravings were etched into its metal sides, figures depicting intertwined winged serpents.

Helen's face appeared at the top of the gangway. "I was starting to get worried about you. Everyone's ready to go."

With a grunt and a shove Jason eased the two wheeler with the aluminum box near the end of the gangplank and lowered it down to rest on its back. "Came as fast as I could." He glanced at the ship. "Pretty nice ride our host has here."

She walked down the gangplank. "You should see the inside."

"Pretty space age?" he asked, opening the lid of the box.

Helen came over and knelt down. "I guess you could say that…in a 'Long, long ago, in a galaxy far, far away' sense."

"Got-cha. So what happens now?" he asked.

She was inspecting the detonator again. "Go on inside and let them know you're here. I think our teacher is doing something with his engines, getting them ready. That's what it looked like. He said he'd be ready to sail any minute now. When he gives you the thumbs up, let me know, I throw the switches, then we haul ass."

A loud roar filled the cavern. Jason and Helen flinched in unison. She threw her hands up defensively. The hairs on the back of her neck were standing at attention. Helen absolutely hated sudden loud noises. Jason swallowed hard. Two swirls of dirty brown water churned at the stern of the ship. The sound evened out into a steady hum, like that of an electrical generator. The sharp bitter smell of ozone scented the air.

"OK. Looks like we're making progress." Jason jumped to his feet and made his way up the gangplank. "I'll check. Don't move till I come back."

"I won't," she assured him.

Jason ducked through the main hatchway and again caught his breath, marveling in astonishment. Every surface inside appeared to be either made of transparent crystal or gilded with pure gold. He headed toward the bow. In the next compartment he found six large high-backed seats, slightly reclined, mounted in three forward-facing rows, separated by a wide aisle. Andrew and Else were seated in the first pair, with Christine and Dr. Markham in the second pair. The last two were empty. The seats appeared to be cushioned with a thick, turquoise colored, semi-transparent gel material. Along each side of the compartment were a large series of curved panels, following the cylindrical interior shape of the compartment. They displayed a clear view of the launch bay and dock outside the ship. Jason could see Helen kneeling by the aluminum box, looking expectantly at the gangway. Yet he didn't remember seeing any windows on the ship from the outside.

"Everyone looks comfortable," he called out.

The four turned around. Andrew responded, "Ah! You're here, Dr. Wise. Excellent. And I trust you brought your nasty box with you?"

Jason jerked a thumb over his shoulder. "It's outside with Helen."

The teacher emerged from aft, passing by Jason. "Excellent, you have arrived. Please, Dr. Wise, come with me."

Jason obediently followed. The teacher led him further forward through another hatchway and small corridor to the forward command deck. It was rife with instrumentation and odd shaped mechanical devices. Two round "portholes," like great eyes, each over six feet in diameter, were set in the front bulkhead. Again, Jason didn't recall seeing any such windows from the exterior.

As though his thoughts were being read, the teacher said, "Projection panels. The same as were in the control room. The hull is equipped with micro sensors bonded to the skin. It is an optical nanotechnology application your scientists and engineers are about ten or twenty years away from achieving. Very efficient viewing capability without having to compromise hull integrity. Plus, we can magnify, capture, or manipulate images as needed."

"Sweet," Jason nodded, carefully watching every move the teacher made.

The teacher smiled at him and then took a seat in the sole seat in the room, the captain's chair, which was centered in the compartment. "Let us see if we can get this old thing up to full power."

He placed his palms on two round plates at the end of each arm of the chair. The plates were slightly larger in diameter than the length of his hands. When contact was made, they illuminated with a soft red glow, shining through his pale blue skin, mixing to give off a slightly purple hue. The electrical hum became more pronounced. A series of multicolored lights came alive on a bank of instruments below the round forward viewing panels. That event seemed to please him.

He instructed, "Due to the nature of our situation, we must do everything correctly on our first attempt. In another minute, I am going to bring the thermal turbines up to near peak capacity. This craft is propelled by two hydro-fusion engines, lots of thrust, but very delicate. I intend to run one engine forward and the other in reverse simultaneously, so we stay in place. The dock will block any rotation effect. However, These engines were not designed to function this way, and this procedure will put undue stress on the thermal vents and hull harnesses. It should not take more than a minute or two in that condition before we start getting turbine blade deterioration and potential hull fractures. So right now, I need you to exit the craft. When you see the water disturbance behind the ship both pushing and pulling at the same time, give Helen the signal to arm the weapon. Then both of you will need to get onboard and seated for launch as fast as you possibly can. Every second is precious."

"How will you know when we're on board and ready to go?" Jason asked.

The teacher laughed. "When you see that we are ready, I shall see that we are ready."

Jason felt embarrassed. "Oh, right. I forgot you could...with the panels thing...and...uh..." He shut up. "I'll just go now and tell Helen."

The teacher laughed more heartily, turning back to the forward viewers. He pointed at an instrument to his right that illuminated and displayed a series of bright yellow characters against a black background. They resembled sharp triangular wedges, arranged in vertical or horizontal configurations.

•

Jason emerged from the gangway. "You ready to rock and roll?"

Helen's face was stern. "Are we ready to go?"

The roar echoed again, reverberating throughout the bay. The dark water in the channel began to churn and boil. A wake of brown foam rippled from the rear of the craft as a separate stream sprayed forward beneath the craft, bubbling and churning up along its sides.

Jason nodded. "That's the signal. You have to go fast."

Helen turned her attention to the device. "This doesn't take long."

Helen reinserted the access card. Her fingers flew to the three arming triggers, flipping the toggle switches into the armed position. She grabbed both brass keys and looked at Jason.

"Showtime." She turned both keys in unison from the locked position to the armed position.

The timer began to decrement once more at its accelerated pace.

"Let's go," Jason called to her. "Pronto!"

Helen jumped up and ran up the gangplank behind Jason. As soon as she cleared the gangway hatch, the gangplank began to lift on its own, retracting back into the side of the hull, serving as the hatch door as well. In the passenger compartment Jason flopped down on one of the two remaining gel seats. It seemed to embrace him in a cool hug. There were no seatbelts or straps.

Helen sat down opposite him and let out a heavy sigh. She looked at Jason. "Do we need to let him know?"

Jason shook his head and smiled. "He knows."

The hum grew in intensity and pitch. The craft began to vibrate and tremble.

Else called out, "Is everything all right? Why do we not go?"

Christine answered her, "He's building up thrust. I'd hang on if I were you."

In the next instant the view from both sides of the viewing panels accelerated into a stony gray blur. Jason could feel the increasing G-forces pressing him deeper and deeper into the gel of his seat. His face was angled toward the viewing panel to his left. The white limestone of the arch at the far end of the bay roared past them like a white line and the room was plunged into complete darkness. A sinking feeling in his stomach told him they had changed their angle of trajectory from horizontal to a downward pitch. His stomach dropped and testicles retracted like on the first hill of a roller-coaster. As the minutes raced by, he could no longer see anything from the side view panel, but he felt certain they were now completely underwater, and still accelerating. He glanced at his watch, depressing a button which illuminated the display.

Any second.

A familiar voice sounded in his mind: *Close your eyes.*

He did, turning his head away from the view panels. It helped, but only slightly. The intensity of the flash of white light penetrated his closed eyelids, making him squint that much harder. The air began to shake. He could feel the vibrations quaking through the gel seat and tingling up through the soles of his feet. All light winked back to complete darkness. The G-Forces crushing his body only increased, making it all the more difficult to breathe. The uncomfortable pressure lasted for several more minutes, but gradually began to wane. Eventually the force of velocity equalized in his body, like riding in an airplane in mid-flight.

Jason opened his eyes.

CHAPTER 38

On the wall of full color plasma screens Jean-Marc Xavier watched the surface of the Duncan International complex fall away, swallowing the twisting red steel tower, as though the surface of the earth itself were being sucked down a drain, leaving a crater almost a half a mile wide and hundreds of yards deep. Concentric circles of earth and sand radiated from the epicenter of the crater in tall, rippling waves, pushing the great dunes away and leveling them across the floor of the desert.

In less than a minute it was over.

He turned to Mohammed. "Call your pilots and tell them to abort your contingency plans."

Mohammed Al Faisal took his cell phone out of his pocket, entered a Text Message SMS code and transmitted.

Jean-Marc grabbed his satellite phone, hit a preprogrammed number and left the room with the unit pressed to his ear. "It is done. Visual verification is complete." He glanced around to ensure no one was anywhere in sight. "If indeed, it was *him* that was found down there, then you have no idea how long we've waited for this great and glorious day. My people suspect nothing of the true nature of the mission, as planned. All have played their roles to perfection, even if unwittingly. I trust my own performance was convincing as well. If there are any further developments, inform me immediately. I return to Rome tonight. Sleep well, *mon ami*. I'll see you in the morning."

•

The ship's cabin was no longer dark. Recessed lights inset along the curve of the ceiling gave off a muted, diffused glow. Jason glanced over at Helen. She was staring out the view panel on the starboard side of the ship. Exterior running lights on the vessel had illuminated, revealing that they were still traveling through a narrow passageway of some sort, hurtling along at incredible speed. Jason turned his head to his left and saw the same view on the port side, the smooth blur of a stone wall not ten feet away from the exterior of the ship. He slowly climbed to his feet, his knees a little wobbly, and headed forward again up the center aisle, through the hatch and toward the command deck.

"Where are we?" he asked the teacher, immediately looking past him to the two forward viewing panels. Before them was the view of a long, perfectly cylindrical tube, lit up by four amber headlights, penetrating hundreds of yards ahead in the distance.

The teacher glanced back at him. "Presently, we are traveling The Kings Highway, the primary access passage to what you call the Indian Ocean, currently passing beneath the portion of the Arabian peninsula you know as the Kingdom of Oman. We are now at about two of your statute miles beneath sea level. You know, it took us as long to core this passage out as it did to hollow out the space for the entire development complex that was just destroyed."

Jason frowned. "So this was the only way in or out?"

The teacher shook his head, "No, just the main way. There were emergency vents, but they have long since been shrouded by the sands of the desert."

"How fast are we going?" Jason could only stare at the stone tube rushing at them at blinding speed.

"Present velocity is approximately one-hundred fifty-five nautical miles per hour," he replied, glancing at the row of yellow wedge characters. "We exceeded one-hundred-eighty knots, shortly after the detonation of the weapon, as a function of the accelerated water pressure from the rear, ushering us along like a favorable tail wind. We have since outrun the dissipating force of the blast, and the assured collapse of the tunnel. This will be our cruising velocity until we reach the junction point."

"Where's that?"

"Approximately seventy statute miles offshore. I fully expect it to be obstructed with considerable silt and sand, and perhaps substantial marine encrustation as well. But not to worry. We shall remove any obstruction from our path with our forward particle accelerators. Better than a hot knife through butter, as you say."

That got Jason's attention. "Particle accelerators?"

Another chuckle preceded the explanation. "Yes. The accelerators are actually a high-frequency energy transmission, akin to your neutron bombardments, that will cause a mild subatomic chain-reaction, vaporizing the obstruction before us, and in turn spawn a secondary microwave transmission that will boil the water. The expanding water will then act as a powerful pressure wedge to drive out everything in its path. We shall encounter a bit of a headwind, you might say, but the particle acceleration force is directional, moving the force of the reaction away from us. I estimate we should only have to decelerate to about forty-five knots, depending on how much of an obstruction we encounter. The junction point is less than a mile below sea level. We will surface from there and be airborne shortly thereafter."

"Airborne?" Jason's eyebrows went up.

The teacher checked his instruments. "Yes. We will surely make much better time traversing the heavens than we will the sea."

Jason felt a tingle of excitement. "Where are we going?"

The teacher turned to Jason and offered a weary smile. "Dr. Wise, I hope you can understand the magnitude and import of what just happened. After having so long been a prisoner in the complex from which we just departed, I have no great desire whatsoever to go back there. Nevertheless, the simple fact of the matter is, over 100,000 years of work and advanced technology was just lost in the blink of an eye. Obviously, under the circumstances, we had no choice in the matter. It all would have been confiscated had it not been destroyed, and most likely by those who would have abused it rather than productively used it. Nevertheless, much of this technology is critical to the continuation of our work."

"So, can it be rebuilt?" Jason wondered.

"Fortunately," he replied, "that will not be necessary. I have a secondary facility. My other home. Hopefully we shall find it intact, well-preserved, and fully operational upon our arrival."

"Where is it?"

The teacher looked ahead again. "In Egypt, where I hid everything I did not want my brother to ever know about."

"How long will it take us to get there?" Jason's eyes were perusing the cockpit controls.

The teacher grinned. "Long enough for me to fully instruct you on the operations of this craft. If you are interested."

Jason's eyebrows shot up again. He was smiling ear-to-ear like a ten year old at the gates of Disneyland.

CHAPTER 39

"Father Pietro?" Cardinal Ricollo was genuinely surprised to see his trusted protégé standing in the doorway of his private apartment. "Is something wrong?"

"I beg your forgiveness, your Excellency, for disturbing you at so late an hour." Pietro eyes were cast to his shoes. "But it is important that I speak with you tonight, before leaving in the morning for my sabbatical. I hope I did not wake you."

"No, no," the old priest opened the door and waved, "come in. I had not yet retired for the evening. Besides, you know my door is always open to you, anytime day or night. You look terrible, my son. What has happened?"

Father Pietro forced a tired smile. "A long day, Father. A very long day. I will explain presently. But you look to be in excellent spirits for so late an hour."

The cardinal revealed his yellow teeth. "It is a great day, Father. I am too excited to sleep. I received word this evening that a great and terrible dragon has been slain, on this very night, all in perfect accordance to our plans."

"So then it is done?" Pietro made his way into the pastoral apartment in the Vatican complex and took a seat on a leather sofa. Unlike many of the accommodations in residence, Cardinal Giovanni Ricollo's quarters were lavishly decorated, highlighting his expensive tastes in rare antiques and the treasures of the Renaissance—especially those appropriated from the courts of long dead French kings.

Cardinal Ricollo took his place in an overstuffed armchair near his fireplace. The logs were still crackling with a warm and vigorous flame to chase away the chill of the night air. "Without question it is done. Exactly as planned, exactly as desired. Our Lord is well-pleased. So tell me, Father Pietro, what is so urgent that you must come see me this night?"

Pietro grinned. "My personal needs can wait a moment. With such marvelous news as you have shared, we must first toast to this great victory over evil."

That brought the cardinal back to his feet. "Indeed, my son. Brandy?"

"Amoretto, if you have it," Pietro replied, knowing it was one of the cardinal's favorites.

The monsignor watched the old priest disappear into his kitchen and quickly return with two fine stemmed cordial glasses and a crystal decanter of the sweet almond liqueur. Still standing, the cardinal carefully arranged everything on his coffee table, opened the decanter and generously poured with a grin of delight. The monsignor had never seen his mentor so happy.

Pietro coughed, rubbing the tips of his fingers against his throat and asked, "Could I also trouble you for some water?"

"Certainly." The old priest returned the sparkling top to the decanter with a clink, and pushed a reassuring hand at his guest. "Keep your seat, my son. I shan't be a moment."

Again, the cardinal disappeared into his kitchen. Monsignor Pietro quietly reached into the inside breast pocket of his black linen jacket and pulled out the small brown vial of white powder. He unscrewed the lid and poured the contents into the cardinal's glass. The bitter almond odor was perfectly disguised in the rich almond flavored liqueur. He stirred the old priest's drink quickly with a pen from his shirt pocket, then wiped it off on his trousers leg before returning the empty vial to his jacket.

One distinct side-benefit of being a trusted keeper of the great secrets of the Church was unfettered access to all things forbidden to the general masses. The deadly potassium cyanide in the vial was intended for the official Rite of Ascension, the sacred ceremony in which the cardinal would officially pass his mantle from master to successor, and then call to an end his days on earth with a last sip from a golden chalice. The urgent voice in the back of Monsignor Pietro's mind told him he was merely accelerating the timing of that blessed event.

It didn't take long.

When the moment came there was no fanfare, no great final speeches, no entreaties of "why." They had toasted to their mission, their success, their eternal vigilance—the brotherhood. It was over in minutes. The old priest slumped down into his chair, closed his eyes, and stopped breathing. To Pietro's great relief, there were no visible convulsions or vomiting. And there would be no questions. It would be very unusual for an autopsy to be performed on a senior Vatican official of his advanced age and such high standing.

On the other hand, Monsignor Pietro's own disappearance would be another matter altogether. However, it was his normal duty to move and operate quietly and discretely in the shadows, and therefore he would not me missed for a long, long time. The letter he mailed earlier that day to the cardinal detailing his extended sabbatical plans would document his absence for a few months. And by then the world would have moved on, and the late cardinal would scarcely be remembered. At least that was the plan. He refused to think about potential complications at the moment. In fact, he didn't feel anything at all, just a cold numb sensation surrounding his heart. His actions were automatic, robotic, virtually unconscious, propelled forward only by the single thought of completing what he knew had to be done.

Father Pietro washed and dried both cordial glasses and ensured no trace of fingerprints were left on them, nor on the decanter, which he meticulously returned to its place in the cupboard. With the exception of the blue pallor on his face, the old priest looked fast asleep in his armchair. The monsignor glanced at his watch before leaving. It was almost 2:00 AM. He knew he would get no sleep that night. But there was still much to be done before his flight at 7:00 AM.

•

Monsignor Pietro pulled the worn brass room key out of his pocket and turned it as quietly as he could in the lock. The lights inside were off. He felt his way into the bathroom and closed the door. It was most fortunate anywhere in Rome to find a vacant room in a small, out of the way *pension* that offered its own private bath. Most of the small family owned inns offered only a shared bath per floor. But privacy was mandatory now. Under the circumstances, it simply wasn't feasible to stay at one of the large American-styled hotels and risk being seen by anyone. Finer accommodations would come later, but not in Rome. He turned on the cold water and splashed some on his face. It felt good. The tired, haggard face staring back at him with bloodshot eyes looked twenty years older than the thirty-three year old man he saw that morning in the mirror when he arose. A gentle tap on the door drew his attention to his left.

A timid voice called from the other side, "Father Pietro, are you all right?"

He reached over and pulled the door slightly ajar. The sweet face of Francesca Garibaldi peered in, her big brown doe eyes filled with concern. She wore one of his white cotton dress shirts as a nightgown, which extended down past her knees. He forced a reassuring smile. "Go back to sleep. You need your rest. We have a very important day tomorrow."

"We are leaving?" she asked.

He nodded, "Yes. First thing in the morning, it will be time for us to go."

"And you are certain I cannot return to Sulmona?" The eighteen-year-old young woman cradled one fist tightly against her chest.

"Perhaps one day," he assured her. "But for now, it is imperative that we leave Italy as fast as we can, if only for a season. I can't say for how long with any certainty. But we must go. You must continue to trust me. What's most important right now is that we can't be found."

"Why?" she implored.

He sighed. "There are still those out there who would wish to do you harm. And I can't permit that. You're too important. And you must be protected. That's why you had to leave Sulmona. Remember?"

"But where shall we go?" Her eyes were rimmed with tears, her chin was trembling.

He reached over and took her hands in his. "To a faraway land, my dear. Where we shall earnestly seek, and hopefully find, the answers to some very important questions about your blessed gifts and how God wants you to use them."

She smiled, seeming to forget her fears for a brief moment. "Where is such a place? Where can we find these answers you seek?"

He gently pulled her into his arms and protectively hugged her close, resting his chin on top of her head, and smoothing her long black hair behind her head and down her back. "Across the great sea. To a place of ancient knowledge. To a place of wondrous mysteries. A place as old as the sands of time itself. Shortly after the sun rises, we are bound for Egypt."

He could feel her shivering in his arms. It wasn't evident whether it was from fear or excitement. He knew the chill running up his own spine was from both.

CHAPTER 40

Jason had been advised to take his seat before the craft exited the junction point beneath the sea floor. His heart was still pounding with excitement from everything he had been shown and taught about operating the fabulous craft. As foretold, they slowed their pace dramatically upon encountering what turned out to be almost a mile of thick sand, mud and dense silt filling the end of The King's Highway. Thankfully, the impediment cleared easily before the ship's forward weapons array as it powered its way forward through a dense cloud of sludge.

No sooner had they emerged into the dark murky twilight of the sea bottom than the craft arched upward at almost a ninety degree angle and soared toward the surface. The G-force of sudden acceleration was stronger than their flight from the detonating atomic weapon. Jason felt the smooth gel of his seat pressing tighter and tighter against the back of his neck, perfectly conforming to the shape of his body. The dim light filtering through the sea grew lighter, to the point where the silvery undulating underside of the surface ahead of them looked like an endless mirrored wall extending in all directions, racing at them, only seconds from impact.

A grinding noise beneath their feet brought Jason's gaze around to see delta wing blades emerging from beneath the ship, locking into place not two seconds before they penetrated the ocean's surface and leapt into the early dawn sky with a thundering splash. The childhood memory of watching the old Dick Van Dyke movie "Chitty-Chitty Bang-Bang" with his mother and little brother Carl leapt to mind. It was a happy memory that brought a warm smile to his lips. Everyone in the passenger compartment laughed when they heard the loud whoop and cries of excitement and joy echoing back from the command deck. Through the view panel "windows" on either side of them, the dark waves of the ocean fell away, and soon they were soaring among the clouds. The sun was just above the eastern horizon. The craft leveled off high above the cumulous canopy, and a calm feeling of in-flight normalcy soon returned.

The teacher emerged, standing in the forward hatchway of the passenger cabin, with his hands braced on either side. There were bright tears of joy in his eyes and a wide grin on his lips. "Free at last!"

Andrew leaned forward in alarm. "Aren't you supposed to be flying this goddamn thing?"

The teacher laughed. "We developed the concept of automated flight long before you, Mr. Duncan. Fear not."

"Okaaay…" Andrew eased slowly back into his seat, and asked, "So where *exactly* are we going?"

"Egypt," Jason answered from the back row.

Andrew spun around and looked at Jason, then turned quickly back to the teacher. "Is that right?"

The teacher nodded, "Yes. That is where our work continues."

"What's in Egypt?" Else spoke up.

"My primary home," he replied simply. "It is where I laid the foundations of my kingdom, my *old* kingdom. A kingdom that came forth from the waters and swamps of the Nile. It was in Egypt that I constructed another research facility, and therefore it is there where your education and advancement may continue. It is where your preparation will be made complete. You still have much to learn and to experience before they find me again…and ultimately succeed in killing me."

Else frowned. "You're certain they will kill you?"

He nodded. "Eventually. It is my destiny. I will endeavor to change my fate as much as possible, but no man can outrun his ultimate destiny."

Christine gasped. "Why is everyone so intent on trying to kill you?"

"They must," he replied matter-of-fact. "And they will not stop, they will not rest, they will not relent…until they succeed. I am a mortal threat to all that they have, all that they are, all that they command, all that they possess. I am the single greatest nemesis to the entire deception that they created in the very beginning for your kind to believe, a deception which cruelly chains so many of your kind in misery and want, and has arrested your development as a people and as a species."

Else demanded, "And just who exactly are *they*?"

He stepped through the hatchway and folded his arms, leaning his head back against the polished gold lintel, taking a deep breath. "They? Why, *they* are the powers that be. Powers, yes, and principalities. The rulers of the darkness of this world. Wicked forms of sentient energy in high places."

Else pressed, "You make it all sound so conspiratorial. Do you mean some specific group or organization or individual is after you?"

"All of the above," he sighed. "In the broadest sense, it is every leader, king, governor, teacher, holy man, clergyman, group, sect, organization, party, movement, denomination, clan, tribe, people or nation, who know-

ingly or unknowingly prefers a world where both they and you stay ignorant of the truth, and more importantly, ensure that you never learn how
to use the infinite power that is so abundantly available to you—the very
power that is vital to further your evolution and development, the power
that is *essential* to transform you into the beings you were always intended
to be, to unlock the kingdom that is your inheritance…the very kingdom
that lies within you."

Helen asked, "So there really *is* some vast organized conspiracy?"

He replied, "Vast, yes. But hardly organized."

"Why do you say that?" Else frowned.

"Because there are many who know fragments and shadows of the
truth, and yet waste their days building empires of ordinances and fanciful
traditions around them, manufactured precepts, which are fervently indoc-
trinated into their young, and jealously defended to the death. They
attempt to proselytize anyone who will listen to them, striving to the
point where the sheer *form* of their fantasy becomes of greater import to
them than the truth itself, or the continuing search for it. And in so doing,
they themselves become lost, perpetually embroiled in the meaningless
and useless wrangling of corrupt minds, separated from the very power
which might have shown them the way. They are those who struggle
mightily to establish themselves as preeminent intermediaries, self-
ordained elites masquerading as servants of mankind, but often do so for
no greater purpose than personal aggrandizement of the ego, an insidious
manifestation of pride which seeks to provide an insurmountable wall of
separation between you and the truth, a truth they fear."

"You speak of the clergy…" Else whispered.

His eyes found hers. "No. I speak of those who call themselves scholars, philosophers, and scientists. Clergymen are but a subset, facilitators of
dogma, ritual, and tradition. Scientists are the pure zealots and advocates
of process and pattern, claiming to search for truth, but far too often merely fight and argue among themselves, only to be declared the winner of
pointless debates, to have their theories and concepts enshrined in the
common discourse and passed down to their progeny. The great irony in
the contemporary debate between the clergyman and the scientist is that
for thousands upon thousands of years, up until the last few centuries, they
were both one and the same vocation. They may have divided their fields
of study in recent days, but neither has abandoned their blind allegiance to
artificial doctrine over truth."

Else felt the wave of embarrassment flow over her.

He raised an accusing finger, his eyes scanning across the entire group.
"And, oh, my dear friends, therein lies their greatest fear of all—not mere-

ly that you might discover the awesome power that awaits you, but that you might spread it like a contagion to all with whom you come in contact. And in so doing, render them... *unnecessary*."

Even Helen felt a twinge of shame.

His tone grew grave. "So make no mistake, and be not high-minded. Once you fully know the truth for yourselves, once you have laid hand upon the fullness of its power and the authority to use it, you, too, will be vigilantly hunted, and if not careful, will be slaughtered without mercy as surely as me. But if this time, *this time*, we get a strong enough start, there is no way they can hope to contain us."

"But what would you have us do? And how?" It was Dr. Markham breaking his silence.

The teacher turned to him. "How? How shall you succeed where so many before you have failed? You will succeed by learning and excelling with the gifts I shall give you this very day. Dr. Markham, you have dedicated your life to the blessed healing arts. Your biological knowledge will soon be completed, expanded a hundred-fold in every facet of human physiology, pathology and care. In a very short time, you shall know the intricacies and virtually limitless potentials of your own genome better than the sound of your own name. You shall possess the requisite knowledge and power to conquer disease and infirmity wherever it is found. And you shall teach others to do likewise."

Dr. Markham sat staring in awe, mouth agape.

The teacher looked to Jason in the back row. "Dr. Wise, you have studied the heavens and sought to comprehend their infinite vastness and mysteries. I shall make you our ambassador to them. You shall understand the order and destiny of all the celestial bodies, their movements, and all their great secrets and wisdom. I shall show you how to traverse the universe faster than the very photons of light, to leap from star system to star system at the speed of thought. And when the time comes for you to travel there and spread your seed, your kind will follow your maps, your charts, your navigational understanding and direction. And if you are careful with your own life energy, you will be there to lead them on the greatest journeys of all time."

Jason couldn't breathe.

The teacher gestured to Christine. "For Dr. Jacobs here will be the one who shall build the conveyance and support systems to take you there—interstellar crafts far superior to this humble shuttle. Despite her tender years, she understands, and has the capacity to understand, energy manipulation better than any soul I have ever encountered of your kind...and even some of my own, if the truth be told." He looked into her blushing face. "To you, my dear, shall be granted the knowledge of the most advanced propulsion systems, the core designs, the detailed measurements, and every specification necessary to reach the stars, as well as to provide unlimited energy sources for all your people here in this world and on other worlds. You have but to imagine it, and the engineering necessary to make it so will appear to you like child's play."

Christine could feel her heart pounding beneath her breastbone.

He turned to Andrew. "And while the ultimate destiny of your kind lies beyond the shores of this planet, this world as it exists today, to a great measure, is in a disturbing state of conflict and chaos. Many prosper and enjoy the fat of the land while others suffer in the greatest of destitution. Far too many are drowning in desperation, bound by their own ignorance, their own culture, their own fears, or some combination of them all. Some fulfill their ambitions with ease while others have resigned themselves to a life of defeat, living an angry meager existence at the mercy of circumstance, left begging at the frayed edges of charity and compassion."

Andrew felt a pang in his heart.

The teacher looked him in the eye. "Andrew Duncan, you have proven yourself as a great leader of commerce, but henceforth you shall be given great wisdom and knowledge of true leadership, inspiration, and organization, exceeding even that of Adapa and Solomon, that you might make brothers of nations, plan and build new and great cities, rear lasting empires of prosperity for all, forsaking none. Into your hand I shall place a golden scepter of justice to rule wisely, fairly, impartially—not as an imperial lord to be worshipped and served, but rather, as a loving father and true servant to all. And I shall give you charge of the Forked Lightning, fierce weapons that will vanquish any foe, any usurper of the peace, any enemy of the kingdom."

Andrew's hands and knees were trembling more than the Scarecrow's asking for a brain.

The teacher stepped before Else. "And to you, Dr. Friedrich, it shall be your mission to chronicle it all. Your gift shall be access to all the great knowledge of all time, in all its grandeur, majesty, horror, and shame. You shall faithfully record the ages to come, and more importantly, you shall be the mother of all teachers, scholars and historians who shall follow your example. Your task is to establish and build the greatest schools, academies, research facilities, universities, libraries, laboratories, museums, and galleries of the finest arts the world has ever known. You shall make music ring in every corner of life. You shall discipline and enable the athlete to achieve his crown, and hold him up as an example of dedication, discipline and achievement. You shall be high counselor to all the great rulers that shall follow. And by your word shall the generations which are yet to be, come to understand the terrible darkness of ignorance which came before them, and hopefully forego the sins and misfortunes of their fathers."

Else was speechless.

He grew silent.

"And...*me*...?" Helen could barely get the words out.

The teacher smiled at her, his eyes narrowing with purpose. "Your fate, my dear Dr. Knight, rests in my hands. Your great calling is not yet for you to know, nor for your fellow companions here with you to learn...until after we get to Egypt."

CHAPTER 41

"I came as soon as I learned the news."

Rabbi David Shemel ambled through the wide double doors into the morgue facility of the Vatican infirmary with his wide brimmed black hat clutched tightly to his chest. Two men, one tall, dressed in a neatly tailored suit, the other short, in surgical scrubs, stood by the stainless steel table which bore the withered nude body of the late Cardinal Giovanni Ricollo. The tips of the dead priest's fingers were black, as were his toes, lips and eye sockets. His wrinkled skin still held a pale blue pallor. A large "Y" incision from each shoulder to the center of his chest and cut down his stomach opened up his torso. A chest spreader held his severed sternum open wide. The blood from the incision and on the physician's latex gloves was bright cherry red. The cardinal's slimy brown liver was piled in the scale hanging from the ceiling. His heart and lungs had already been weighed and bagged.

"Leave us," Jean-Marc Xavier commanded the forensic physician in Italian.

The old Rabbi drew close to the table, visibly shaken by the sight and repulsed by the raw stench of death. He muttered in his broken Italian, "This is a great loss. He was a great man. His fearless devotion and faith will be missed."

Jean-Marc looked down at the corpse, without emotion, speaking in perfect Hebrew, "Yes, he shall be missed. He was a good and faithful servant. And I don't like it when good and faithful servants are murdered."

Shemel was taken aback, looking directly at Jean-Marc, then quickly averting his eyes, replying in his own native Hebrew tongue, "*Murdered?* Is this certain? He was a great man of advanced years. His remaining time of service was short. He has surely earned his rest."

Jean-Marc swabbed his index finger deep in the dead man's mouth and then ran it across the end of his own tongue. He smiled. "Bitter almonds. Cyanide. Of the potassium variety. Fast. Effective."

"Could it be our brother Giovanni chose this time to pass his authority on to his apprentice?" Shemel asked meekly, his stomach churning.

Jean-Marc suddenly shouted, "If we *knew* where the good Monsignor

Pietro was at this very hour, we might *ask* him!"

"Father Pietro is missing?" The Rabbi's bushy gray brow knit in confusion.

"He has apparently departed his post," Xavier replied. "And we must find him. If there are those who wish to do the good Padre harm, those who are *perhaps* responsible for our good friend Cardinal Ricollo's unfortunate fate here, then we must get him to safety and protect him as one of our own." His voice dropped low, malevolent, his eyes narrowing. "On the other hand, if he has had a hand in the betrayal of his master, and thereby all of us as well, he must be punished. I have eyes looking for him. He cannot elude us for long. We shall find him promptly and settle this matter. He knows too much. If he has betrayed us, he is a danger to us all."

Rabbi Shemel offered a smile. "At least the greater crisis has passed. Yes?"

"Has it?" Jean-Marc paced away from the table, running his fingers through his long white hair. "I saw with my own eyes the destruction of the hidden facility, but even at this hour I have my doubts about its effectiveness. Some things are hard to see from a great distance. Some things can be kept hidden if one knows how, and he certainly knows how. But we shall know what we need to know soon enough. Oh yes. If the one who was bound is now free, instead of vaporized as he should be, we will know this soon enough. He is very clever, but he is not without his weaknesses. His own blind ambition and idealistic naïveté makes him careless, and therefore vulnerable. But until we are absolutely assured of his fate, he is never to be underestimated. He is *very* clever."

The rabbi chuckled. "But not as clever as we."

Jean-Marc laughed out loud, lapsing into French. "*Absolutement*! I promise you this, if he still draws breath, he will be most unpleasantly surprised when he learns that one of those among him, one of those who perhaps helped to set him free, one of those to whom he has given his trust...is one of us. As soon as contact is possible, *if* contact is possible, we will know his fate. But for now, we set our task to find our prodigal son, the good Father Pietro—before he does something foolish or dangerous, or both."

PART III

MOVING MOUNTAINS

"And you shall know the truth, and the truth shall make you
   free."

                                                    John 8:32

"The religion that is afraid of science
   dishonors God and commits suicide."
                          Ralph Waldo Emerson, 1857, Journals

"Assuredly, I say unto you, if you have faith
   as a mustard seed, you will say to this mountain,
'Move from here to there,' and it will move;
   and nothing will be impossible for you."
                                         Matthew 17:20b

"Faith embraces many truths which seem to contradict each
   other."
                                    Pascal, 1670, Pensées

"I think, therefore I am."

                                    Rene Descartes, 1639
                                    Discourse on Method

CHAPTER 42

"That one."

Francesca pointed at the blind man seated cross-legged between two street vendors' merchandize stands in the crowded markets of Mena, the bustling village at the foot of the Giza Plateau, home of the Great Pyramids of Egypt. It was located directly across the Nile River from the sprawling urban metropolis of Cairo.

She insisted, "Him, the old man right there. If I but touch his eyes, I know that he will see again."

Father Pietro no longer wore his dark priestly raiment and white collar; rather, he now sported a pair of light khaki pants, a loose fitting white cotton shirt, and a fedora and dark glasses to shade his eyes from the intensity of the sun. He had purchased both himself and Francesca new wardrobes that morning from the shops in Cairo, shortly after arriving at the international airport in Heliopolis forty miles away to the northeast. Rather than lurking in the shadows, where he knew they would be found if someone were looking for them, he decided it was safer to hide in plain sight, yet where few would ever think to look for them. His unique privileges as a keeper of the great secrets also gave him access to a wide range of discrete identity and travel documents, as well as considerable financial resources that wouldn't show up on standard computer database checks. He obtained twenty-five thousand Euros in cash before leaving Rome. Some of that money had been exchanged at the airport in Cairo for local Egyptian pound banknotes as well as American dollars, the latter being preferred by most of the street vendors. An hour earlier they had checked into the Mena House Oberoi, one of the most famous and luxurious five-star hotels and resorts in the Cairo area. By its sterling reputation, it was certain that the hotel staff would afford them the greatest privacy and discretion—highly desirable qualities for the quest that lay ahead.

Father Pietro was convinced his search for answers had to begin here in Egypt, on the banks of the Nile, where so many of the forbidden texts spoke of the acts and origins of the gods, their cult centers, and various sects of worshipers. If he didn't find the answers here, he would go to the Holy Land in Israel, and if not there, then into Iraq itself, to the banks of the Tigris and Euphrates, where human civilization was birthed. In his heart he didn't believe that would be necessary. The ancient Egyptians represented the very height of the ancient world, with meticulously detailed records and artifacts of ages past. Something deep down inside him told him the answers he needed would be found here.

He leaned close to Francesca's ear. "What exactly are you seeing right now? What are you feeling? Tell me as specifically as you can. It is very important."

She cocked her head slightly to the side and lightly closed her eyes. "I see great joy on his face. I see others gathered around him, some shocked, some are crying, some rejoicing, some disbelieving and shouting and arguing. Right now I feel a heat burning deep within me, growing hotter with every passing second. It strengthens with every breath I take. It is like a fire raging in my heart and a tingling in my fingers. It makes me want to reach out and touch him. I feel a need to touch him. To let the heat flow out. I know in my heart, that if I but touch him, he will be made whole."

Francesca started to take a step toward the old man, but Father Pietro quickly caught her by the arm, cautioning, "No, no. You mustn't. Francesca, your compassion is great, but right now we can't afford to attract any undue attention."

She pulled her arm away with a tug of her shoulder, not in anger or defiance, but with a dire sense of urgency. "No, Father. The vision can change, or transfer to a different situation. Please trust me. We won't be observed. Watch."

Before he could say another word, Francesca pushed her way through the noisy throng of tourists and peddlers and knelt down before the old man sitting on a dirty woven pallet. A hungry fly crawled along his puffy lower lip. The man's eyes were solid milky white orbs. He sensed a nearby presence and lifted his stubbled chin, mumbling something in Arabic with a meek plaintive tone as he held out a trembling hand for alms. Francesca took his calloused hand in hers and leaned forward, drawing close to his face, bringing the index finger of her other hand to her lips and insistently shushing him. He heard the sound and grew quiet, leaning forward ever so slightly with a mixture of confusion and curiosity. Their noses were but inches apart.

And then it happened.

Ever so gently Francesca reached up with her free hand and slid his eyelids closed with her index and ring fingers, as one would do to a dead body. The closed lids glowed momentarily from beneath her touch. Again, Francesca brought her index finger to her lips and shushed loud enough for him to hear and acknowledge.

The old man opened his eyes and they instantly went wide with both a look of surprise and complete shock, squinting in the sunlight. The milky white fog over his dark brown irises was gone. His pupils were black and distinct.

He started to cry out.

Francesca quickly put her hand over his mouth and shook her head slowly back and forth, as if to tell him No, as she blew through her teeth and slightly pursed lips, which were pressed against her index finger with even greater urgency. The old man began to weep. He pulled her small delicate hand a few inches away from his mottled lips and began to kiss it, sobbing. The fly, which had crawled up his cheek, leapt into the air, encircled his head, and lighted again on his ear. Francesca caught the old man's tear-filled gaze, then tapped on her chest twice and both shook her head and waved her palm, giving a very explicit instruction of No. He looked confused for a second, his chin quaking with emotion, but then his expression turned to a look of sadness as he nodded with mute understanding. She affectionately reached up and patted the side of his face, then rose and quickly disappeared back into the embrace of the crowd. Father Pietro was waiting for her. He took her by the arm and urgently ushered her away.

"You're taking great risks," he admonished her. "We can't do that. Don't you understand?"

She was out of breath. "I did what was shown to me. I obeyed. That's all. It's what I must do."

He frowned. "What happens if you don't obey what you see?"

She shrugged, her voice rising in her animated native Italian, dramatically illustrating and emphasizing every word with her hands. "I fear if I ever disobey, the heat burning within me will burst forth and consume me. It is something that must be released. It's something I am compelled to do."

The priest glanced back in the general location of the old man. "But the vision you originally saw must have changed. There was no scene, no crowd staring and gawking."

She looked at him. "There will be. Later. I was able to make him understand that he had to be quiet for now. My heart told him that his gift required his silence. He understood. When the sun sets today, he will rejoice at what God has done for him, but he won't tell anyone about me."

Pietro nodded, desperately hoping she knew what she was talking about. "All right. I hope you're right, for both our sakes. Let's keep going. Just tell me what you see and feel. I need to understand it. Spare no detail. No matter how irrelevant it may feel or appear, tell me everything as it happens."

They were nearing the edge of the village, walking along the Sphinx Route up to the Giza plateau, when the ancient monuments came into sight. There they were, the Sphinx and the panorama of the three great pyramids looming beyond it. Francesca adjusted the scarf she wore on her head, dabbing some of the beads of sweat off her forehead. She too wore thin khaki pants and a light summer blouse to shield herself from the sun and to wick away the sweat. It was early afternoon. She knew that the sun would only grow hotter as the afternoon bore on. They continued on toward the magnificent Sphinx in the distance.

And then it happened.

Father Pietro was just about to say something when a violent wind whipped up, gusting out of nowhere. Harsh, cutting sand whistled directly in their faces. Both he and Francesca, as well as the festive stream of tourists mingling about all turned away from the gale in unison, coughing, shielding their faces with their arms and ducking their heads. Dust storms were common in the open desert, but this unexpected anomaly descended without warning out of a clear blue sky. Father Pietro managed a quick glance back in the direction of the Sphinx and saw a semi-circular wave of sand between himself and the monument radiating out, moving directly toward him, as though a great column of air was not coming directly at them from across the desert, but rather, blasting down upon the monument from the heavens above. As the arching and expanding wave grew closer and closer, the shriek of the wind only intensified, accompanied by a tremendous deafening roar—not a deep combustion sound, rather a high-pitched whine like a jet's turbine.

BOOM.

His eyes flew to the ground as a deep, resonant impact tremor ran beneath his feet, shaking the entire plain for several seconds. People ran away in panic and disarray, shouting, some screaming. Children were crying.

And as abruptly as it began, it stopped.

The wind died down. The choking clouds of dust abated. The mysterious enigmatic monument once more lay silent and vigilant, where it had stood its faithful guard for countless millennia, facing exactly due east toward the holy mountains of the Sinai, right on the thirtieth parallel, exactly one third of the way from the north pole to the south pole. The fine turbine whine decelerated and slowly faded away, ebbing into the ever present whisper of the warm desert breeze until it had completely dissipated.

The mystified tourists and vendors were still coughing and peering about with great looks of apprehension on their faces. Yet one by one, the crowds dismissed the freak episode and resumed their trek towards the monuments, all abuzz in conversations recounting what mysterious event had just occurred—or not. The locals didn't miss a beat in assuring the tourists that such occurrences were a commonplace event, as a prelude to embarking on their well-practiced and enthusiastic sales pitches, hawking and soliciting horse or camel rides, or personal guided tours of all the monuments, mustabas[21], and onsite museums.

"That was...very strange." Father Pietro wiped a palm full of sweat off his face, noticing the muddy layer of dust that came off with it. The back of his throat burned. He coughed and turned to see Francesca curiously staring at the Sphinx, her head cocked slightly askew, her dark eyebrows pulled down, sporting a pronounced look of intrigued confusion. They were standing to the southeast of the monument, facing its right shoulder. Ground level was even with its back, albeit separated by the deep excavation of the Sphinx's body and extended front paws.

Father Pietro wiped more dust from his lips with the back of his hand and asked her, "What is it? What do you see?"

She pointed to the stone lion's body with the head of a Pharaoh. "Over there. I see something. Oh, holy blessed Joseph and Mary!"

He stood next to her and looked long and hard at the great Sphinx from end to end and back again. It lay only seventy yards away from them. "Francesca, what do you see? Tell me. I don't see anything."

"*There*!" She pointed more emphatically, "On its back. The monstrous creature that jumped upon its back from the whirlwind!"

"*What* creature? I don't see anything on its back." Father Pietro's eyes darted to and fro, desperate to detect any abnormality, but fixing on nothing out of the ordinary. However, as he stared intently, focusing his attention right above the center of the monument, behind the head where the lion's back is flat and forms a level platform, he thought he saw heat waves, a visual distortion in the air slightly blurring the panorama of the great pyramids displayed behind it. But the sight of heat waves was common all over the desert—especially as the temperature of the day increased. "I only see the stone of the monument. Describe to me exactly what you see."

Francesca thrust her right hand forward with an upturned palm, the gesture in unison with the emphatic jut of her chin. She placed the other hand on her hip, exclaiming in exasperation, as if she was trying to show an imbecile something that was clearly obvious to anyone and everyone. "*There*! Can't you see it? Right there. The great winged serpent with the tail of a fish!"

---

[21] Sacred Tombs

CHAPTER 43

"Fear not. No one can see us," the teacher assured them. "The photon refraction field is fully in place over the entire outer surface of the ship. We are as transparent as the air itself."

From the view panels inside the passenger compartment, on the ship's port side, which was currently facing east, loomed the back of the head of the great Sphinx. To the ship's starboard side, facing west, stretched the vista of the ancient plain of Giza and the entire complex of the great pyramids—literally manmade mountains of red granite and limestone. Khufu's (Cheops), or the Great Pyramid, stood behind them to the northwest with its complement of three small Queen's pyramids. Khafre lay due west of them, standing next to a Mortuary Temple, which connected to the Valley Temple via a Causeway which spans the entire complex running by the Sphinx on its south side. The much smaller Menkaure pyramid lay to the southwest. It still dwarfed the three Queen's pyramids arrayed next to it. Only Khafre still held some of its limestone outer casing at its peak, which had originally given all the pyramids a smooth and bright white exterior. The shuttle craft of the winged serpent had successfully executed a smooth vertical descent, alighting perpendicular to the body of the Sphinx. With its delta wings fully retracted, the fuselage of the ship rested lightly on the monument's stone back.

"Won't the weight of your ship crush the stone?" Christine asked.

"No," the teacher replied. "There is a peripheral antigravity field energized at the point of contact. We are not exerting any more force than the sum of our body weights. The field is also self-stabilizing, which is what keeps the ship from rocking or tilting as we move about inside it. If need be, we could be perched on the summit of a mountain or the pinnacle of an obelisk. Fear not, each and every one of these technologies and techniques are in the lesson plans that await you inside the complex below."

Andrew pointed out, "But isn't our presence going to be a bit obvious to everyone standing around when we disembark from the ship? I mean, you can become invisible, but we can't."

The teacher walked down the center aisle of the passenger compartment and gestured with a flip of his fingers that they should follow. "Your state of visibility is of no consequence to our task of egress. Come with me. We will not be disembarking the vessel the same way we came in."

The group rose from their gel seats and filed after him.

Jason quipped, "So are you, like, going to *beam* us somewhere?"

The teacher stopped in the antechamber compartment that bore the gangway hatch. He turned to Jason, answering him with the most sincere gravitas. "Dr. Wise, biotic and inanimate passive energy transfer over distances and through barrier masses requires tremendous power and precision, whether done organically or mechanically. But one cardinal rule we always obey states: one should never expend more energy than is absolutely necessary to achieve a satisfactory resolution. Or, as you artfully articulated in the idiom of your vernacular: we use the KISS principle, Keep It Simple, Stupid."

They all laughed as he knelt down and took hold of a hinged handle recessed into a circular metal grid on the floor. As the handle came up, Helen felt her ears pop with a hiss of decompression as the metal grid opened, revealing an open floor hatch. Beneath them lay the hard, dusty, weatherworn stone of the Sphinx's back.

Jason shrugged, "OK, so what now? Do we dig?"

The teacher put his hand on Jason's shoulder. "O ye of little faith."

The teacher turned, walked to the wall of the compartment, and began punching colored spots on what was apparently a keypad of some sort. Each colored section illuminated under his touch. "If my landing coordinates are still reasonably accurate relative to the sonic resonance of the twin landing beacons there across the plain, this should put us in the proper position."

"Twin landing beacons?" Else asked.

"Yes. You call them the great pyramids," he replied.

"But there are three great pyramids," Else commented. "Why did you say they were twin?"

"Because only two of them are the beacons." He shook his head, still entering information. "The smallest of the three was merely the scale model we initially used to test the load bearing capability of the fifty-two degree angle construction. The two large ones were the primary western markers for our flight approach and landing vectors. Unfortunately, there are no mountains in Egypt large enough to navigate by from the heavens, so we had to build them."

"And what were your markers to the east?" Else was genuinely curious.

"Natural geological formations," he answered. "The twin peaks you refer to as Mount St. Katherine and Mount Sinai, in the southern range of the Sinai peninsula. At the correct landing vector, approaching from the southwest, the two points form a three-pointed sight when aligned on either side of the twin peaks of Mount Ararat, to the northeast, on the eastern end of the Taurus mountains in Turkey. All three sets of twin peaks are very easy to distinguish from the rest of the landscape from a low altitude orbit. Landing instructions thus became very simple. Approaching ships were told to come in along the solar ecliptic plane, traversing the planet's equator from west to east, scanning the latitude line one-third from the northern pole to the southern pole, until the two white beacons[22] were in sight. When all three landmarks lined up, a forty-five degree vector to the northeast would take you to either of our two primary landing sites."

"Which were?" Helen prompted.

He stopped entering digits for a second. "The Port of Tilmun in the central Sinai, and the Port of Jerusalem further north. Neither were used as terminals after the war. Tilmun was completely destroyed by the war. Jerusalem became a densely populated urban metropolis, home to many cultures over the years. Although, the great foundation stones of our rectangular launching platform can still be found there to this day, beneath what you call the Temple Mount in the eastern sector of the Old City."

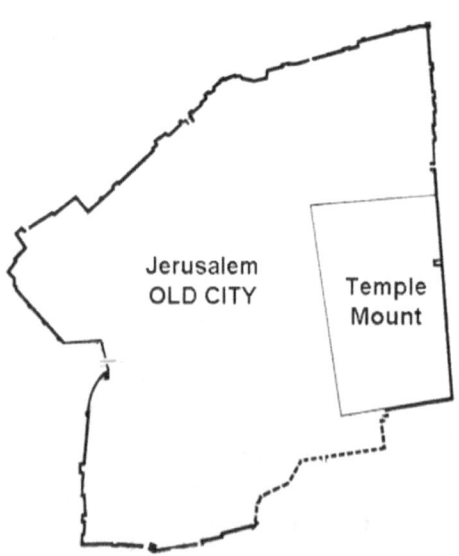

Jerusalem OLD CITY

Temple Mount

---

[22] The red granite blocks of the Great Pyramids were originally covered with an outer casing of limestone, making them smooth and bright white, and thus much more visible from the air when reflecting the sun.

Jason rubbed the goose flesh on his forearms as he looked at the picture from his atlas on his watch. It seemed every time the teacher opened his mouth more and more mysteries of antiquity fell away.

When the teacher completed the sequence he was entering, a grinding of stone was heard. Everyone's eyes went down to the open hatch. The hard stone yawned open in four pieces from a pinpoint aperture, each piece shaped like the curved blade of a pinwheel, spinning back to expand the aperture to the same size as the lower hatch. The opening revealed a deep shaft descending into darkness. Clouds of sand and dust drifted down into the hole. A faint musty smell of stale air mixed with a hint of sulfur wafted up in return. From where she was standing Helen could see a vertical series of recessed niches carved into one side of the shaft, each approximately two feet apart. Each niche was oval in shape, horizontally cut approximately eighteen inches wide, six inches in height, and six inches deep. Inset into each one was a bronze bar.

It was a ladder.

The teacher exclaimed with excitement, "Welcome one and all to the Gateway of the Gods."

Andrew found his voice, "After you, good sir."

The climb down the shaft was hardest on Christine and Helen. For Christine, her new leg was still a bit ginger, and it was obvious that the ladder had been crafted for adept climbers who were much taller in stature than her diminutive five-foot two-inch frame. But she was determined to make it, and relied primarily on the strength of her arms to achieve what amounted to a two-hundred foot sheer vertical descent. For Helen, the physical challenge wasn't the issue. No, it was the dark, claustrophobic enclosure of the shaft itself. It felt too much like the shaft of a well. That thought was patently disturbing. It was nearly impossible for her to keep the painful images of the lifeless body of her brother Aubrey from replaying over and over in her mind. After climbing down the first fifty feet, the open hatch above was only a small spot of light. Below was pure darkness. The musty smell of the shaft's walls was stiflingly close and confining.

"Safe in a cocoon, we'll be out soon..." she whispered to herself, with eyes tightly closed, mechanically putting one foot below the other, lowering herself one hand at a time.

The climb took ten anxious minutes.

Dr. Markham was the last to reach the underground chamber at the foot of the ladder, huffing and grunting, his brow beaded with salty drops of sweat. Unlike the complex in the Rub Al Khali desert, he observed that this particular room was lit by a series of crescent shaped alabaster sconces mounted along the walls, each shining upward to the ceiling. Inside each one was a marble-sized luminous gel sphere that put out a surprising amount of light. They activated spontaneously upon the arrival of the teacher. The room itself appeared to serve as a foyer, or antechamber, and was devoid of any furnishings. It was a perfect stone cube, about twenty-five feet in height, width, and depth. The walls were crafted of evenly hewn stones, very similar to the interior construction of the great pyramids themselves nearby. Each wall was separated into a set of tall vertical panels, covered with hieroglyphics from floor to ceiling.

Else remarked, "We've always thought there were likely to be structures found beneath the Sphinx."

"And you are most fortunate you did not bother to seriously look for them," the teacher replied. "There are a few storage chambers located near the surface, which are of no great significance. But if this access passage had been found, and anyone had entered this room without deactivating the defense systems, as I did from the ship, or if someone were to damage or forcibly breach the integrity of the stones of this room in any way, the experience in this room would have been painfully similar to that of the cryogenic storage chamber where you found me—lethal emissions of subatomic energy and hyper-thermal incineration. The defense system is applicable to every chamber on this level. This is a highly restricted facility. Even more so than the other one."

"Why?" asked Helen.

"You shall see." He turned to the wall opposite the ladder. "But come, we must be about our business."

On the granite wall standing before the teacher, amidst the busy array of pictographic glyphs, cartouches, and illustrated scenes, was inscribed the outline of a hand, a very large hand. It came as no great surprise to anyone when the teacher reached out and placed his palm there, the outline matching perfectly to the size of his hand and the length of his fingers. A soft yellow glow appeared beneath his palm, pulsating slowly. When it ceased, the grinding sound of stone was heard as the panel directly in front of him slowly swung back on an unseen hinge, revealing a dimly lit corridor beyond. The air hung thick with the stale musty odor of cold stone and long undisturbed antiquity. The teacher strode through the opening without hesitation, with everyone else obediently following behind single-file.

•

Three hours later, after a fascinating, albeit cursory tour of the first three levels of the complex, an important executive decision was made. They were all famished and desperately needed to find fresh food and water. It was Andrew Duncan who suggested a "hunting party" be sent forth under his leadership to find suitable victuals and provisions. Fortunately, he also happened to have a generous quantity of cash in his pockets, American dollars, so he was well-suited to the task. Thus, he, Jason, and Else volunteered for the mission, leaving Dr. Markham, Helen, Christine, and their teacher behind.

In Andrew's mind, this errand still presented them with an important logistical challenge, the same one he noted while they were on the surface—i.e. determining exactly how to leave and return without being seen. The teacher conveniently solved this problem by taking them to "the back door." It was located a considerable distance away, but adjacent to a somewhat "public" place. Clearly, the challenge to using the back door was to ensure that there were no tourists nor monument staff in the immediate area upon exiting and reentering. Fortunately, this issue did not turn out to be a significant problem either. For as the group soon learned, the rear access point to the teacher's underground Giza complex was located directly beneath the Great Pyramid of Cheops itself.

For centuries the Descending Passage which led from the north face entrance beneath the Great Pyramid dead-ended in a small area in what has been termed the "Unfinished Chamber." Farther up the Descending Passage was the junction point of the three great granite plugs, which, before they were removed by archaeologists and treasure hunters in the 19th century, were used to block access to the Ascending Chamber, which in turn led to the Queen's Chamber, the Grand Gallery, and the layered King's Chamber in the very heart of the pyramid above them.

Yet no archaeologist nor scholar could have known that the Unfinished Chamber, while relatively small in size, was functionally a twin to the antechamber beneath the two-hundred foot ladder of the Sphinx. For in the Unfinished Chamber lay another secret door that led to yet another descending passageway, where the hunting party currently stood. This door led directly into the underground complex, whose first of nine subterranean levels began two hundred feet beneath the surface of the Giza plateau.

"I knew that passage couldn't have existed for no reason!" Else exclaimed.

The teacher stopped before the door to the Unfinished Chamber and pointed to another outline of a hand etched into the stone, amid another vivid fresco of inscribed glyphs and pictographs. "Dr. Wise, if you would please be so kind as to place your hand on this sensor."

"OK." Jason stepped forward and did as instructed.

The teacher touched a series of the glyphs next to it, which all blinked in a vast array of colors under his fingertips, prompting the appearance of the same soft yellow light to glow beneath Jason's palm.

The teacher announced, "Excellent. Now your energy resonance pattern has been measured and recorded, and will be used to authenticate your identity and open the door when you have returned."

Jason asked, "How do you know if it's clear on the other side? Won't that be kind of weird for the tourists, to like, suddenly see us pop out?"

The teacher pointed to a glyph of a scarab above the hand pad. "This indicator would be illuminated if there were any sentient presence in the adjacent access chamber. Upon your return, you will see the same hand sensor on the other side. Hold your hand upon it until the door is fully opened. Then touch this one again on this side to close it. Should you fail to remember, it will close of its own accord in five minutes. But please try not to forget. Uninvited visitors could be most problematic."

As the stone door began opening, Jason promised, "I won't forget."

"Very good," the teacher nodded, watching them all file out. "When you return, look for us down on level three, in the main research lab I showed you."

"Got it, level three, lab." Jason shot him a thumb and forefinger.

The teacher smiled, placing his hand above the sensor once more, preparing to close the door. "Now do be quick, my friends, and keep a keen eye out for anyone or anything that appears more than casually interested in you. I beg you to speak to no one unnecessarily. I assure you, any lapses in discretion, great or small, could get us all killed, swiftly and brutally. Get only what you need and return with utmost haste. We have great work to do."

"We will," Andrew assured him. "Back in a blink."

And off they went.

The teacher placed his hand on the resonance sensor and the door to the Unfinished Chamber began to close.

CHAPTER 44

Helen, Dr. Markham, and Christine patiently waited in the medical lab on level three, exactly where they had been instructed to stay, when the teacher returned. He looked very excited. This laboratory was much larger than the one in Saudi Arabia, and filled with even more equipment and odd tools. They all respectfully stood when he entered the room.

"Ah, there you are, one and all," he beamed as he strode through the doorway. "Excellent. Dr. Markham, we shall begin your training immediately, as it serves multiple purposes, benefiting all."

"Shall we leave?" Helen asked.

"Oh, no," he replied. "You need to stay. In fact, Dr. Knight, you are especially important to the lesson Dr. Markham is about to receive. And Dr. Jacobs, you are welcome to remain and enjoy it as well."

A nervous tremor fluttered through Helen. She wanted to ask what he meant by the importance of her participation, but for some reason she felt more comfortable holding her tongue.

The teacher walked over to what looked like a white board on the wall, but was in fact, another viewing panel. He began, "Dr. Markham. You are familiar with the basic human genome construction. Yes?"

Dr. Markham nodded, cleared his throat and rattled off his textbook answer. "Yes. Chains of DNA, or Deoxyribonucleic Acid, organized into four basic nucleotides, or base pairs. One pair of Adenine and Thymine, the AT or TA pair, and the other pair of Cytosine and Guanine, the CG or GC pair. These pairs form the rungs of the twisting double helix ladder of individual genes, of which there are approximately 140,000 in humans, comprised of approximately three billion unique combinations, making up the twenty-two unique chromosome pairs, plus the X and Y chromosome pair, which determine gender."

"Very good," the teacher commended. "And after your many, many years of study and research, and with the assistance of all the high-speed computational devices that you have employed to analyze these combinations, it is regrettable that you have barely been able to merely map them, and have only begun to scratch the surface in your true understanding of them. Now let me show you exactly how they really work, and more importantly, how to manipulate them from a practicable point of view."

An image flashed up on the view panel. It was the familiar double-helix of a DNA strand, which bore an uncanny resemblance to the intertwined serpents etched into the side of his ship. The image rotated and unfolded before them, looking like a ladder presented horizontally.

The teacher pointed to the three-dimensional illustration. "You see, for years you have studied the fundamental biochemistry of the carbon-based biotic cell, striving to understand how three of the base pairs of nucleotides generate twenty of a possible sixty-four amino acid combinations, which in turn generate all of the various enzymes of cellular physiology. These codons, as you call them, demark themselves between a promoter base pair and a stop pair, defining the code of one individual gene in between. All of this you know. Furthermore, you have even observed the contribution of ribonucleic acid, or the RNA polymerase reproduction process, as well as the nascent traces of maternal mitochondrial DNA found outside the nucleus. All this is noteworthy. Unfortunately, this is the point where your science has functionally stopped, but where we now begin our discussion."

Dr. Markham nodded. "All right."

The teacher waved his hand and the image changed, showing only three base pairs side by side, much akin to a three rung ladder held sideways. "The issue here is not mere encoding, that is, understanding the location of a trait or related function. Rather, the key to your understanding now deals with the practical functionality of that coding and how it can be deliberately defined and adjusted. It is a wonder to me why something so incredibly simple has not yet been grasped. But you soon shall. So, let me ask you. Why do you think that of the three billion nucleotide combinations that make up your genome, they break down into two basic pairs, and always two basic pairs, that can only be in one of two combinations, yielding a total of only four pair states, or eight total states when organized in a three pair codon?"

Dr. Markham looked uncomfortable. "Well, it's a basic building block approach. The four base pair combinations form the three elements of the codon, as you said, which form different enzyme patterns, which then combine—"

The teacher cut him off. "You are missing the forest for the trees, as they say. The four states signify only one of four conditions: Sire active, Matron active, Sire inactive, Matron inactive. More importantly, these are states of *energy* found not in the pair element itself, but in the electromagnetic bond that makes up the pair between the helix strands. And from this energy relationship, within the codon of the three base pairs, you achieve a binary mathematical outcome." He turned to Dr. Markham directly. "Think of the base pairs of the codon as a set of simple switches, like your computational machines use binary language, counting in base two with ones and zeros."

"Switches?" The doctor cocked his head slightly, scratching his chin.

The teacher went on, "Yes, switches. A simple binary trigger, lined up in a set of three. Each switch is either on or off. If all three switches are on, the feature, or feature subcomponent, is fully active, and said to be dominant. If all three switches are off, the feature is completely deactivated. If only one switch is on, the feature is active, but weak and not prominent, or what you refer to as recessive. If two switches are on, the feature is active but not fully functional, like your tissue healing and regeneration capability I demonstrated on your hand."

Dr. Markham glanced at his palm as a chill tingled up his neck.

"Frankly," the teacher continued, "whether a specific switch is Sire based or Matron based, is only a function of which parent contributed the gene sequence, which in most instances is more academic than practical information—unless of course we are talking about the genetic code of my people interacting with yours. In that case it becomes very relevant." He waved the tangent thought away. "Regardless, what is preeminently important, above all, is the ability to look at the genome map, navigate to the specific feature or trait that you wish to manipulate, and either enable or disable the switches according to your preference. Your biologists and geneticists have attacked the problem the hard way, with gene-splicers and sequencers, attempting to graft the patterns you wish, instead of merely crafting the patterns you want from existing code sequences merely by flipping the switches. Conceptually, gene manipulation is really no more complicated than that."

Dr. Markham was flabbergasted. "Not complicated? You're talking about three-billion locations!"

"Which is why you need a reference chart," the teacher answered matter-of-factly. "Let me show you." Again, he waved his hand and the image became a floating chromosome pair. "Name a feature."

Dr. Markham shrugged. "Hair color."

"Excellent." He pointed to the picture and the image graphically exploded and expanded. The chromosome became the endless twisting ring of DNA. It spun to a location and stopped. A particular strand was highlighted. The image zoomed in again even further. "There we are. Right there. In this illustration, between this start and stop pair, we see that the hair color of this DNA sample is set to black. There are only four other base hair color choices, which can also be tempered for shade and tint, if you like, with the last seven controls there before the stop pair of the gene."

"But how?" Dr. Markham asked. "How do you manage to throw these *switches* of yours, as you say?"

The teacher replied, "With microbursts of energy, a directed emission with a wavelength smaller than the distance between the strands. It is a simple binary process, as I have noted. Each individual switch can only be on or off. The actual manipulation technique itself involves creating a complex energy signal with the final pattern design that you ultimately wish to achieve. When the signal is projected at a specific organic DNA target, the energy patterns of the switches that are coincident to the signal harmonize and strengthen. Conversely, the switches that are dissonant to the signal reflexively react, causing the switch to turn itself on, if it was off, or turn itself off, if it was on. Incidentally, you may be interested to know that this is the fundamental reason why music can have either an energizing uplifting effect, or a dissonant repulsive effect. Not that the energy of sound waves has sufficient strength to directly effect base pair switches, but the harmony or dissonance of music to an individual's fundamental encoding is a physical effect, not merely a matter of taste or preference. But again I digress, forgive me. Back to our DNA encoding. I assure you, this process is not magic. DNA switch manipulation is purely a physical effect."

"You must be joking," Dr. Markham scoffed. "How is this possible?"

"I am quite serious. You see this effect yourself all the time, Doctor. Unfortunately, you have only observed it happening randomly and therefore destructively."

"How so?" Dr. Markham stepped closer to the screen, studying the image.

The teacher continued, "I am referring to your observations of radiation damage, and resulting genetic mutations from emissions of subatomic energy. Surely you have observed what happens in the case of highly radioactive Alpha or Beta particles or exposure to gamma rays, when their radioactive energy penetrates cellular tissue and disturbs these delicate energy switches. This is what causes all the tumors, the rapid cell growth, the cancers, and the mutations that I am confident that you have witnessed on a multitude of occasions. I am still amazed that no one in your culture ever made the obvious correlation in the rapid increase in cancer rates and birth defects with the proliferation of electrical-based infrastructure, with its powerful inductance emissions, as well as many other hyper-frequency and broadcast digital communications devices."

Dr. Markham scratched his chin. "It's long been suspected that there were health dangers associated with such technologies."

The teacher stated emphatically, "Gene damage is the inevitable result when key switches are thrown randomly and not intelligently, without a complete and pure signal to shape the complete transformation pattern. Nevertheless, the *process* of energy bond manipulation resulting in DNA reprogramming is one and the same. It is as common as skin cancer from excessive exposure to solar radiation."

"That's incredible," was all the physician could say.

The teacher turned to Helen. "Which is why we need you, Dr. Knight. We need your direct participation to help further our learning, and more importantly, to provide you with your secret gift I promised you."

Helen had been leaning against one of the lab tables a few feet away, in awe of everything she was hearing. She stood up straight. "Me?"

"Yes," he said. "Come with me. Please."

She followed.

He led her over to a tall, floor-to-ceiling transparent cylinder mounted on a wide metal base, with a corresponding metal cap affixed to the ceiling. Next to it stood another of the crystalline control deck podiums standing four feet off the floor. The teacher put his hand on its flat upper surface and the clear cylinder began to rise off of its base, slowly disappearing into the ceiling mount above. The cylinder was essentially nothing more than a great big glass tube, approximately a yard in diameter, and two inches thick.

The teacher reached down and tenderly took Helen's hand. "Dr. Knight, with your permission and consent of free will, I ask you now to be the subject of this most practical and extremely beneficial procedure."

She was trembling. "What are you going to do to me?"

He smiled broadly, patting her hand. "Why, I intend to transform you into a goddess, my dear."

She demurred, her cheeks flushing red down to the collar of her blouse, stammering slightly. "A what? I...I don't understand."

He explained carefully, "I intend to show Dr. Markham and Dr. Jacobs here exactly what I have been describing. I am going to subject your body to an extended series of microbursts, over three billion of them, in fact. It will take approximately an hour of time to complete, much the same as our ministration to Dr. Jacobs. In that time, all that I was forced to deactivate in your genome will be fully restored. The anomalous permutations of your parents' genetic gifts to you shall be corrected. The very ravages of mortality visited upon you in your fifty-seven orbits of this planet shall be wiped away. The pure energy of life will never leave you, lest another steal it from you. And then you shall be truly of my kind and no longer like yours. This shall be my gift to you, if you will but accept it."

Helen glanced quickly at Dr. Markham, who was just standing there in stunned silence, owl-eyed and slack-jawed like the village idiot; and then to Christine, who was smiling and beaming with excitement. It was Christine's turn to give a nod of encouragement. The wave of conflicting thoughts running through Helen's mind came close to stealing her consciousness away and sending her headlong to the floor in a dead faint. Her head was swimming. Her heart was pounding. Could this be true? Was it even possible? What did he say again? A *goddess*? Literally? Was he kidding? What exactly did that mean?

She mumbled, somewhat in disbelief at the sound of her own words, her lips mysteriously seeming to move of their own accord. "All right."

He released her hands. "You will need to disrobe."

Those words instantly cleared the fog in her brain and sharpened her attention, reddening her cheeks all the more to a lovely shade of crimson. The curious thrill of embarking on a fantasy hit a show-stopper. "What? I'm sorry. What did you say?"

He repeated, "You will need to disrobe before entering the device."

Helen was blushing like a thirteen-year-old schoolgirl. Yes, she was a mature, scientific professional, but none of her official duties or responsibilities over the last thirty-five years ever required her being seen naked by anyone. Yes, it was an irrational inhibition, at least that was what the rational part of her mind was telling her. For Pete's sake, Dr. Markham was an elder physician, with the face and clinical demeanor of Marcus Welby. Christine, whom she considered almost a daughter, had worked out with her at the same health club in Boston for over two years and seen her undressed many times. It even occurred to her that they had found the teacher himself as naked as a newborn, and he was utterly without any sense of shame or self-consciousness about his unclothed physical presence. But all of that didn't matter. At that moment all she wanted to do was run away and hide. Half a century of modest, ladylike culture came racing to the surface and wasn't about to be dismissed on a whim.

"Is that really necessary?"

Christine asked, "Helen, would you like us to leave?"

Dr. Markham looked stricken at the thought. His face showed how badly he wanted to remain and witness the procedure.

The teacher took Helen's hand again into his own. "Helen, there is nothing to fear, I assure you. This is strictly a medical procedure, nothing more, nothing less. Overall, it is quite painless. There is a little discomfort initially, I will not deceive you about that. But as the procedure progresses, there is an endorphin reaction phase that you may enjoy immeasurably."

Helen swallowed hard and summoned all her courage to gather her wits about her. What if someone laughed? What if *he* laughed? Or worse, looked repulsed or disgusted at her almost six decades old body. She certainly wasn't twenty-five anymore. Then again, he was offering her a chance to roll back the clock and be young again, to never get sick again, to live till the end of time, which meant she could see the future unfold, and be a part of it. Wasn't that the bottom line of it all? How much more could she learn with this kind of a once in a lifetime opportunity? How much more could be accomplished? Only a fool would squander this chance. She made her decision.

Modesty be damned.

Helen softly apologized with her eyes cast down to her feet as she kicked off her tennis shoes. "I'm sorry, everyone. You'll have to forgive me." She let out a self-deprecating half-laugh, confessing, "Beneath all my professional pride, I guess I'm really just an old woman ashamed of her less than perfect, decrepit old body. I'm acting like a stupid adolescent girl." She reached up and began to unbutton her pink blouse.

The teacher laughed softly to himself. "*Acting* like an adolescent girl?" He affectionately reached up and touched her cheek with the back of his hand. "Helen, in but an hour's time, you *shall* be a young maiden again—and shall be one forever."

She snapped her eyes to his, unable to speak.

CHAPTER 45

"I know you can't see it with your eyes." Francesca insisted, "But it's there, I promise you, Father. You must believe me. I see its soul. I can see its power. It shimmers like water. I see the great serpent on its sides with its great wings."

Monsignor Pietro was getting exasperated. Over the last couple of hours they had wandered around and around the great Sphinx, and much of the rest of the Giza complex for that matter, not exactly sure of what they were looking for. He was desperately trying to understand what it was the girl was seeing or feeling or perceiving. It made no sense. Yet she seemed so emphatic about her claims.

"Francesca, I want to believe you. I really do. But how can I understand that which I cannot see?"

She turned to him. "As a man of God, you can ask me that?"

He sighed, "This isn't a test of faith."

"Isn't it?" she fired back. "Do you not teach us that our faith is the substance of things hoped for, the *evidence* of things *not* seen?"

The priest shook his head. "It's not the same. If what you see is really there, and not in your imagination, we would be able to verify it with some proof. Some physical evidence. Something!"

A dull metallic thud abruptly brought their attention back toward the Sphinx. They stood only twenty yards away from it. *How odd.* There on the ground was a bird, lying on his back in the sand, twitching and crumpled, in obvious agony. It was an Ibis, a stork-like water bird with a long curved bill. The name of the Egyptian god Osiris flashed through Father Pietro's mind. The Ibis was his symbol. Both he and Francesca looked at each other without saying a word. The bird struggled to his feet, staggered a few steps, shaking his head to gather his wits, and then took flight once more.

Monsignor Pietro got an idea.

He leaned down and picked up a small smooth stone, rolling it in his fingers. He waited until he was fairly sure no one was looking in his direction, then threw the stone over the Sphinx's back. It never made it. With the same distinct metallic clank, the stone abruptly ricocheted in midair down into the wide excavation trench around the monument's body.

"Oh, my God," he whispered. "There *is* something there."

Francesca felt vindicated. "It is merely hidden from our eyes beneath a magical cloak."

"Yes," he nodded slowly. "I think you're right."

She leaned closer to him, taking his arm defensively. "Is it a cloak of the Lord, Father, or a cloak of a demon?"

He shrugged and candidly admitted, "I don't know what it is."

Father Pietro started to move forward when something caught Francesca's eye, suddenly focusing her attention like a laser to a pinpoint in the crowd.

She pointed. "There. *They* know."

"Who?" Father Pietro looked to see exactly where she was looking. On the opposite side of the monument he spied a group of three tourists: an older gentleman in khakis, a young black man in jeans and a loose fitting two-toned short-sleeved shirt, and a thin woman dressed all in black. The trio stood out in the crowd. They carried no backpacks, fanny-packs, purses nor cameras. They didn't even wear sunglasses nor head coverings of any kind, which was a cultural faux pas for the woman, and a grave mistake to wear pure black in the sweltering heat of the Egyptian desert. The young black man was staring intently at the Sphinx as he walked by it, in obvious wonder, yet not looking directly at it, but above it.

The priest nodded, "Yes, I see them. The two men with the woman dressed in black."

Francesca stared at them intently. "I can see in their hearts that they know of this creature. They know its master. They have proceeded forth from its belly."

Pietro took her arm. "Then we shall follow them, and see where they go."

•

As agreed, Andrew Duncan, Dr. Friedrich, and Dr. Wise made haste into the town of Mena at the base of the Giza plateau to attend to their shopping errand. Else was quick to make a purchase of a scarf to cover her head, wishing to avert all the cold stares and indignant comments coming from some of the more outspoken locals, mostly older women. It took no more than twenty minutes to fill several bags with fresh fruits, vegetables, dried meats, and bottled water.

Making their way back, Jason carried two heavy bags, one thrown over each shoulder. "Now how the hell do you suppose we're going to get back inside the Great Pyramid carrying all of this stuff?"

Andrew laughed, hefting his own heavy pair of bulging bags. "Dr. Wise, in case you haven't noticed, there is very little in this life that isn't available if one is willing to pay the price, and has the means to do so. For a hundred dollar bill I assure you, we could persuade the very tour guides and security personnel themselves to carry all of this inside for us."

Jason smiled. "Sounds like a great idea to me!"

Else frowned. "I have that feeling."

Andrew turned to Else. "What feeling?"

She readjusted the heavy bag of fruit she was carrying from one arm to the other with a wince and grunt. "The Proximity Detection sense our host told us about. I don't know exactly how or why, but I have this strangest...*sensation*...that we're being watched."

Andrew shook his head. "No time to go paranoid on us, love. We mind our own business. We get back inside. No one's the wiser. 'Ay?"

Else stopped walking. "Stop."

The other two did, looking confused. They were near the north face entrance to the Great Pyramid of Cheops.

She glanced around. "Are we certain we're doing the right thing?"

Andrew frowned. "What?"

She stepped closer, discretely lowering her voice. "I mean, everything has happened so fast. So many impossible things. I think it is reasonable for all of us to feel a little overwhelmed and caught up in all of these fantastic events, and perhaps lose sight of reality. No? Everything seems so incredible, but what if we are in danger? We have an opportunity right now to escape. To call someone. To tell others of everything that has happened. Of all those killed in the Saudi desert."

Andrew was curt. "That's the point, Else. If we are thought to be alive, that's the danger. Don't you believe anything you've seen and heard?"

She hesitated before answering. "I don't know what to believe, to be honest with you. My mind and my nerves are completely overloaded, *alles kaput*. I am numb all over, head to toe. I think for the last several days I have been walking around in a clinical state of shock."

Jason jumped in, "*Damn*, people. I don't believe what I'm hearing. We're a part of what may be the most significant scientific and historical discovery of all time, and you're both debating your personal safety."

She snapped at him, "Yes, that's right, Dr. Wise. In case it wasn't obvious to you, great discoveries don't mean much if you're dead and not around to enjoy them."

"So what exactly are you suggesting?" Jason fired back.

Else held firm. "Right now, nothing more than an honest discussion among ourselves, if you don't mind. How about some analysis. Some time to pool our thoughts, think and process all that we've witnessed. Some time to evaluate. Am I the only one of us who believes that everything we've heard and seen might not be *exactly* as it has been presented to us? Could there be even the slightest possibility that we may unwittingly be falling for a great deception here? My God, he as much as confessed to being the very Serpent of the Garden of Eden."

Jason laughed. "So what are you saying, Doctor? Do you think he's really the Devil incarnate? Ol' Satan himself?"

Else countered, "You can definitively rule that possibility out?"

"Yes, I can!" he insisted. "It's complete fucking bullshit. The Devil is a fictional character, Else. He doesn't exist! He's an anthropomorphic construct of superstition and primitive religion conjured up to find a foil for man's inherent character flaws and his fucked up predisposition to perpetrate selfish acts of violence, cruelty and malice upon pretty much everyone he comes in contact with. Satan is the conveniently manufactured boogeyman of a thousand religions used to scare children and the weak-minded into following the rules."

"What if you're wrong?" she asked simply.

"I'm not," he said, although not very convincingly. "Else, I'm a scientist. If anything, I think our new teacher, who has been nothing but gracious towards us since we first met him, has acquitted himself most persuasively as *the* consummate scientist, not a ghost, but a flesh and blood life form, even if he's not of this planet, revealing to us secrets that we've been striving to unlock for centuries. Hell, I think many of the myths and legends of countless cultures and religions may have stemmed from the actions of this…*guy*…and his people, just like he explained. It all makes sense to me. Come on. Antiquity is your bag. Surely, you've seen all the connections."

She nodded, "I have. And that's what bothers me. He's been ever so quick to take credit for the virtues of mankind, but slow, if not deliberately omitting the downside."

Andrew piped up, "So far, I've not seen a significant downside to anything he's told us. It all rings very true to me."

"Really?" She cocked her head toward Andrew. "That's very easy for you to say when he announced that he was going to make you king of the world, and turn the rest of us into some kind of sociological super-heroes. Hasn't the old saying, *'Power corrupts, and absolute power corrupts absolutely,'* occurred to either of you? If you are made king, Andrew, what's to prevent you from becoming a tyrant? Personal ethics?" She turned to Jason. "Or you from becoming the mad scientist, Jason, with the power of interstellar travel in your grasp. While I may not be an engineer or a rocket scientist, it did occur to me that any power source capable of such feats, probably has weapons-grade applications."

Andrew scoffed, "You *are* paranoid."

Jason shrugged. "So I repeat, Dr. Friedrich, what do you suggest we do?"

She discretely scanned the faces of the crowd milling by, as the feeling of being watched grew more intense. "I don't know yet. All I know is that we need to somehow find a way to determine what our teacher's true intentions are. If he sincerely wishes for nothing more than to help advance our culture and our species, and to help us better understand our past, I'm all for that. But with the kind of power he's demonstrated at his disposal, he could just as easily become the world's greatest nightmare. Don't you understand?"

"Understand what?" Jason was exasperated. "The only thing I'm not understanding right now is you."

"Dr. Wise, all of the cultures of the ancient Near East talk about supernatural beings of old who were imprisoned in the earth to protect those cultures from evil. For the Muslim Arabians, where we just *happened* to find our host, it was the evil Jinn they feared, the godlike genies of Aladdin's lamp, who had the power to grant miraculous wishes, but who sought to claim souls in return. To the Hebrews it was the Nephilim, the fallen ones, whom they believed were fallen angels, who were buried in the earth as punishment for their salacious sexual perversions with human women. In the Apocalypse of the Christian New Testament it prophesies clearly about the coming of the beast in the last days, the beast with seven heads and ten horns, rising up out of the sea—I repeat, *rising up out of the sea*—to unleash its wrath and terrors and plagues upon the nations of the world and all of mankind." Else sucked in a tense breath. "Jason, I don't want to find out I'm unwittingly about to become one of those seven heads."

Jason sincerely believed Else had gone over the deep end, hard and fast, Do Not Pass Go—Do Not Collect $200, but he couldn't think of a single witty rejoinder to that last remark. He wanted to, oh, how he wanted to, but his mouth wouldn't cooperate. His knees were shaking again and his throat had gone dry.

•

Father Pietro was careful not to follow too closely behind the small group. It was easy to remain obscured by the press of the crowd. The two men and the woman had stopped near the north face of the Great Pyramid of Cheops for several minutes, deeply engaged in what appeared to be quite a heated argument among themselves. When it ended, they continued their journey toward the monument, each one laden with heavy sacks. Pietro saw the older gentleman handing over a large quantity of cash to the monument staff before being allowed to proceed with their burdens into the north face entrance. A sign was immediately put up announcing there were no more interior tours that day.

Father Pietro stopped at the roped off gate. It cost him two hundred American dollars to "persuade" the guide that he and Francesca were also part of the VIP group currently enjoying the private tour. He and Francesca wasted no time in making their way down into the Descending Passage. When they reached the junction of the Ascending Passage, and started to climb up toward the Grand Gallery, they heard voices echoing from below.

"They are down there," Francesca whispered.

He nodded, keeping his voice low. "Yes, but there is nothing down there but a dead end. It is the Unfinished Chamber."

She squinted her eyes and cocked her head. "No, it is more. And they will be gone if we do not go after them quickly."

The monsignor had learned not to question this particular young woman's perceptions and insights. They continued further down the Descending Passage to the small stone chamber at the end. When they arrived, as he expected, it was empty.

"See?" he pointed. "No one here. They must have gone on above, and we just mistakenly heard the echo. These old stones can play tricks."

She pointed to the open space in the wall on the south side. "No. They went through there."

"Oh, my God. Where did that come from?" Father Pietro was amazed to see the open passageway. He looked back at Francesca. "Are you sure about this? You're positive they went through there?"

She nodded, "Through that door is what you seek."

The gritty sound of grinding stone interrupted them. The heavy stone door was slowly closing off access to the passage beyond. Father Pietro grabbed Francesca's hand and dragged her through the opening, making it to the other side right before it closed tight. He noticed how the passageway on the other side was much larger, the stones more refined and cut with greater precision.

In the distance was a light.

The priest shook his head in wonder and glanced back over his shoulder at the closed stone door. "I've toured that chamber many times in the course of my studies. There was never any signs of an access point to other compartments or passages."

"Then we are most fortunate, Father, that someone forgot to close the door."

CHAPTER 46

Rome, Italy

The late afternoon cocktail party was boring, but it was important to maintain certain key connections and useful relationships. The guest list was comprised mostly of local politicians and key Vatican officials, sprinkled with the smattering of a few celebrities from the fashion and entertainment worlds along with their ill-mannered entourages. Everyone was clustered in their prescribed cliques and gaggles, sipping wine and cocktails, nibbling on imported cheeses and colorful hors d'oeuvres, laughing, gossiping and conspiring like school children.

Such a waste of time.

Jean-Marc Xavier stood on the balcony of the renovated palace in black tie, staring at the waning sun, taking in the landscape of the ancient Roman monuments intermixed with contemporary skyscrapers and the clutter of buildings that was modern Rome. So many lost children, he mused. He wasn't actually nervous. Anxious? Perhaps. It didn't matter. He just didn't like loose ends. A dirty job needed to be done, and it was now done. But was the objective achieved? Was it truly over? It didn't feel like it. He trusted his perceptions implicitly.

No, something was definitely wrong.

A trusted emissary was dead, potentially betrayed and murdered by yet another of the sacred brotherhood, who was at this very hour highly likely to be running for his life. Reports indicated that a young girl was supposed to have been disposed of by the fleeing priest just prior to his disappearance. She, too, could not be found. Had he taken a liking to her? He could certainly have had her, if he wished, and then done his duty. She was of no consequence. But betraying the sacred order for the sake of a woman was beyond insanity. Did he truly commit so great a trespass? Was that his weakness? A crisis of a misguided conscience? If so he was unfit for the order and his calling. It was better to know that before the Rite of Ascension. However, with the death of the good cardinal, unless there was a secret ceremony held in violation of all the strictures, sacred rules, and tradition, then that topic had been rendered moot. On the other hand, the records indicated that the girl was purported to be a healer. There were verified incidents. If her gifts were genuine, that could present complications.

Jean-Marc Xavier hated complications.

Barely over twelve hours had passed since the thermonuclear blast beneath the sands of the Rub Al Khali. Xavier had not slept a wink in three days, but then again, sleep was not something Jean-Marc indulged in terribly often. It squandered precious time. He hated wasting time even more than he hated complications. And complications which also squandered time were worst of all—a cause for great fury and retribution. No, he rarely slept. It was exceedingly uncommon if he averaged more than one day of extended rest in seven.

He glanced back into the ballroom where the bejeweled and gowned ladies of leisure played elegant consort to the attentions of their well-heeled benefactors. Many came in search of new benefactors. It was a well-practiced game, no different in the twenty-first century than in the courts of the pharaohs themselves. The comely surfeit of courtesans were all available to him if he wished to summon one or more of them for his pleasure.

But no.

His tastes for women in recent years took him further and further away from the painted and plastic *femmes du jour*. He shivered with disgust at the very thought of the icy cold air of the vacuous nouveaux aristocracy. Titles were a vanity, yet half the women in the room before him sought one, or wished to upgrade the ones they bore. He chuckled softly to himself as the thought occurred to him that the men in the room were no different. Their titles and offices and résumés were the true basis of their souls, their self-esteem, their passion for living, their very identity. It was all vanity. He missed the days of noble epithets, when prominence was measured in deeds of greatness, not in genetic lineages or organizational positions of rank or privilege.

On the other hand, as odd and clumsy and flawed as it was, he knew only too well how the system in place was absolutely necessary to preserve fundamental societal order and balance. He believed that implicitly, and it baffled him why so many others did not, vainly venturing to debate the point. Yes, the truth was, they all desperately needed a basic *organizing principle* to dispel the darkness of utter chaos and anarchy of their lives—like an ant colony or beehive needs a queen—even if from a practical perspective the organizing principle was purely pointless. Fortunately, organizing principles were easily manufactured and nurtured and reinforced, whether they be cultural, geographic, idealistic, nationalistic, philosophical, political, racial, religious, subversive, or even superstitious.

They all worked.

It was undeniably true, that despite great technological advancement and naïve arrogance to the contrary, modern society was still inherently tribal in nature, prone to fight and rage and war against any group or individual distinctly different from the local tribe, fiercely and often irrationally opposing any who were not loyally aligned and committed to supporting and defending their organizing principle—regardless of what it was. Nevertheless, as long as no one group dominated the rest, which Jean-Marc Xavier personally took great pains to personally ensure, a healthy measure of tribal conflict kept them all engaged, gave them a sense of purpose, kept them organized, kept them manageably docile.

Yes, it was a pitiful waste of passion and energy. But so what?

Jean-Marc caught the eye of a tall, stunning redhead, almost wearing a deliciously seductive evening gown, barely held up by her ten thousand dollar after-market breasts. She was staring at him from inside the doorway to the ballroom. She lifted a fresh glass of Chardonnay from a silver tray, offered to her by a pretty young uniformed serving girl, who was apparently quite invisible to the redhead. He thought he recognized the woman, a popular Hollywood actress perhaps. It didn't matter. She raised the delicate crystal glass in a little silent toast to him, offering her most sincere come-hither smile and a bat of the eyes. The thought of expending a wee bit of energy and exercising great passions was beginning to arouse some of his own. The redhead stood there, patiently waiting, with an eager look of expectation on her face. He thought about it briefly; but no, the attraction wasn't there. Not her.

No, Jean-Marc preferred to satisfy the basest of his personal appetites and physical pleasures with women he found to be profoundly more real, more substantial, more genuine—more *appreciative*. And those kind were routinely to be found in the humbler callings and environs of life: a waitress, a chambermaid, a shopkeeper, a cook, a nurse, an occasional eager young university student, even a fair prostitute if she happened to catch his fancy.

He made up his mind.

If there was no update from his people within the hour regarding the missing priest, he would quietly take his leave and roam the busy Roman streets in the art district in search of a new soul, a delightful one with true promise and fire of spirit. Those were always the best. He savored a long, languid puff on his cigar, blowing the dark gray-blue cloud into the burnt red, pink, and orange hues of the setting sun.

The digital satellite phone in his trouser pocket vibrated. Jean-Marc plucked it out and read the color display. A Text Message had arrived. Its body contained a single line: **GIZA GR PRMD**.

He instantly recognized who the message was from. The fact that the individual was still alive caused him no small measure of alarm, and revealed volumes. However, his anger began to boil even more when he saw that the message had been transmitted over an hour earlier.

An hour of valuable time had been squandered.

He cleared the message and pressed a speed-dial number. His pilot answered on the first ring. "Ready the jet. Full fuel. We're returning to Cairo within the hour." He terminated the call and tossed the phone back in his pocket. He smiled at the redhead and motioned for her to come.

She was only too happy to comply. "Can I get you something?"

"Yes." He commanded, "Have my car brought around. And tell the lovely young lady who served you that glass of wine to please get her things and that she is coming with me."

CHAPTER 47

"Explain to me exactly what's going to happen."

Dr. Helen Knight was shivering from head to toe, not just from the coolness of the air in the lab against her bare skin, but with an overwhelming sense of apprehension. All of her clothes lay in a pile nearby. She stood with her knees pressed tightly together, her arms held tightly across her chest, her hands balled into trembling fists, knuckles white. Christine and Dr. Markham had courteously retreated several paces, to quietly observe what was about to happen as unobtrusively as possible. Only the teacher remained standing before her.

He responded to her in a calm, reassuring tone. "Of course, Dr. Knight. And what I am about to tell you may cause you a modicum of distress, but this too will pass in the course of the process."

Her eyes grew even wider.

"For I know in sensing your deepest engrams of memory, you have many troubling recollections of the past, painful memories, distant dark thoughts of sorrow and fear. The loss of someone dear to you. These feelings are magnified by close and confining spaces. These feelings will undoubtedly take this occasion to present themselves to you as we go forward, but you must find the strength to realize that they are only echoes of events long gone. Shadows of the past. They are not reality. You must comfort your heart with the sure knowledge that they have but one last opportunity to assail you, and after that, you will be their master. This I promise you."

"What's going to happen?" She could barely get the words past her chattering teeth. "Tell me everything. Every detail. I want to know before it happens. No surprises. You promised."

"Of course." He touched the podium and adjusted something as he explained, "You will need to stand on that platform, and do your best not to move to any great degree. The crystalline shielding will be lowered in place, containing you securely inside it. The casing is completely transparent and will not impede your vision. You shall be able to see everything around you. But the shield is necessary to insulate the microbursts and keep them fully contained inside the chamber."

Helen glanced at the platform again and shuddered.

He continued, "Now immediately after the chamber is sealed, the inner compartment will begin to fill from a series of injection ports near your feet with a synthetic cytoplasm, a very viscous, mucous-like liquid. It has been stored frozen in near absolute zero conditions, but is, as we speak, being prepared. When it touches you it will feel like warm oil on your body. It is the same liquid you saw in the device that fashioned Dr. Jacob's new leg for her. It is a highly energized conductive medium and hyperoxygenated. It will immerse your body completely."

Helen flinched. "How will I breathe?"

He hesitated a second before explaining, "It will be at this point that you will have to fight every basic self-preservation instinct within you, and continue to breathe as normal. The liquid will fill your lungs, and that will initially be very uncomfortable. For a few moments the threatening thought will come into your mind that you are drowning, suffocating. You are not. It is at that moment that I want you to consciously focus on slowly counting from one to ten, taking a single deep breath once every two counts. It is very important that you focus and not panic. By the time you reach the count of ten, you will feel as though you are breathing normally."

She cringed. "I don't know if I can do that."

"Yes, you can," he assured her. "And when you do, the hard part will be over. The cytoplasm is very rich, in both oxygen and nutrients, and you will start to feel a bit light-headed, possibly even euphoric. It is then that the microburst emissions will commence. The genetic manipulation will be nearly instantaneous, as will the molecular acceleration and cellular development. You will feel warm inside, as though you have a low-grade fever. This, too, is normal. About a third of the way into the process, an endorphin emission will flood your system, and you may even experience a relaxed sense of inebriation. If you begin to feel uncontrollably nauseas, I want you to give me a signal. Rub your stomach. I will understand and reduce the emission level. That will only make the process take a little bit longer. But that does not matter. It is of no consequence to the outcome."

"What if I throw up?" she asked.

He smiled. "That is not likely. You have not taken a meal in many hours. However, if your bowel should heave, do your best to relax and not fight it. It will pass as your body begins to transform and gain greater capacity to defend and maintain itself. Should you feel the need to evacuate your bladder, do so. The chamber is constantly circulating and filtering. Evacuating dead and replicated cells is to be expected as the body flushes and cleanses itself. When the process is complete, the chamber will empty, and you will need to aspirate the liquid from your lungs. You will not require any instruction on this point. Your own gag reflexes will take care of this quite effectively the instant air hits your sinuses and soft palate. Just focus on coughing, as deeply and productively as you can until you are breathing easily again."

"And that's all there is to it?" She glanced over to the base of the glass cylinder once more.

He gestured toward the platform. "That is all that is required of you. It will be difficult at the beginning. There is no masking or marginalizing this fact. You must be strong and find courage. But never lose sight of the fact that it is only the beginning of what awaits you on the other side."

Helen looked at sweet young Christine, who stood there so confident—on two legs, not one. Dr. Markham's eyes were locked on her, staring intently, studying her, the consummate clinician, absorbing every word, every image. If he had a notebook and pen, he would have been taking notes. And then the big question hit her: Why? Why would she agree to do something like this? She wasn't vain. She had no burning desire to find the fountain of eternal youth. And yet…on the other hand, that was not all that was promised. He spoke of all the phenomenal capabilities hidden within her genome becoming alive and fully available to her. Her understanding of the world and the entire universe would suddenly be thrown open wide and made perfect. What would that be like—to finally be able to see through the glass clearly? And best of all, to live to see the days of her own personal inner peace and lasting freedom, without the constant demon of her claustrophobia tormenting her, to finally have that nagging never-ending nightmare stop? Oh yes…that would be Paradise.

Helen stepped up on the metal platform.

The teacher pressed something on the podium and the transparent cylinder began to slowly descend from the ceiling. "Helen, in this chamber you will be safe. It will be like a silk cocoon, where you enter as a caterpillar, but emerge the most beautiful of butterflies. It won't take long."

She cocked her head at him as her familiar mantra echoed over and over in her mind, *Safe in a cocoon, we'll be out soon.*

How did he know?

The bottom edge of the thick glass passed by her face. The image of the teacher became slightly distorted, as did that of Christine and Dr. Markham and the rest of the laboratory as seen through the arc of the thick glass. When it reached its base and engaged, she heard a loud click. Perhaps a sealing and locking mechanism engaging, she presumed. Trembling, Helen had to force her hands to go down by her sides, though her fists stayed balled tight and quaking. Two deep breaths did nothing to slow down the rabbit pace of her heart.

It began.

A metallic clank preceded a constant mechanical drone. Just as the teacher had explained, a thick brownish-yellow liquid, which looked a lot like honey, began to pump out of two round inlets on the floor and fill the bottom of the cylinder. It smelled sickly sweet, yet organic and rich, like freshly dug black earth laced with peat and compost and wriggling with fat grubs and earthworms. When it touched Helen's feet, she gasped. It was warm, just as the teacher said it would be. It only took a minute for it to climb her calves and reach her knees. When it passed her waist she felt the first serious pang of panic. Her lungs began to heave, in and out, faster and faster.

A familiar voice spoke in her mind – *Slowly, breathe slowly, Helen. It will be all right. Focus. Focus on your count. One! Picture the number. One!*

It was the same commanding voice she had first heard standing next to the ice dome in the radiation chamber a mile beneath the Rub Al Khali. She willed herself to calm down. The pressure in her chest refused to abate, but thankfully it did not grow any worse. As the thick ooze lapped up over her aged and sagging breasts, it actually had a soothing, calming effect, like slipping into a warm and inviting bath after a long day. She forced herself to take slower and slower breaths. Her heart rate began to retard ever so slightly. But that was only temporary. It shot right back up the instant she felt the liquid cover her shoulders and begin to climb up her neck.

Her breathing diminished to a fevered pant.

When the warm sticky surface kissed her chin she fought the urge to scream. Adrenaline was flooding her arteries. Flee or fight. Flee of fight! She could do neither. She was trapped. Could she shatter the glass of the cylinder with her fists? Reflexively, she sucked in one final deep precious breath and held it fast. The glutinous liquid continued its unrelenting rise, moving steadily higher, ever higher, ascending above her lips and nose, oozing into her ears. She pinched her eyes shut. It climbed over her forehead and the warmth embraced her completely. Helen could feel her heart pounding in her temples. Her diaphragm began to burn and her face flushed red.

She was suffocating.

Breathe, Helen. Breathe. Breathe, and count to ten. Do it.

Her mind told her it had all been a trick. She was trapped and about to die, drowned in a giant test tube of yellow ooze. The panic couldn't be restrained another second. She started to scream.

And then it happened.

In a flash of inspiration it all suddenly became so clear to her, so clear a child could comprehend it. She merely had to believe. If she believed it could be done, she would open her mouth, fill her lungs, and live. If she continued to fight and struggle, she would surely suffocate and die. She wanted to live. It was so simple: believe and act upon that belief.

It was a simple act of faith.

Helen opened her mouth, and released her last breath of air into the oily liquid. It bubbled up around her face, tickling her cheeks and ears.

Do it!

It was now or never.

Helen parted her teeth and sucked in. The warm syrup filled her mouth and hit the back of her throat, which reflexively seized tight and began to spasm, fighting valiantly to do its duty and prevent any liquid from breaching her glottis and invading her windpipe. She swallowed some of it and kept trying to inhale. Her diaphragm was on fire. Thankfully, its fight for oxygen prevailed and overpowered her throat's ability to stop it. Pure liquid warmth rushed into Helen's chest. Her gag reflex fought to expel it, but her diaphragm pulled again, yanking in desperation, sensing success at the oxygenation of millions of red blood cells rushing through the fibrous network of capillaries and thousands of alveoli sacks in her lungs.

Helen suddenly felt faint, her legs turning to rubber. Her hands shot out on both sides, her palms finding the smooth interior surface of the glass, steadying herself.

ONE! echoed the familiar voice in her brain. *Come on, you can do it!*

She blinked, straining to see through the murky yellow and brown haze. Her lips mutely mumbled, "One..." She disgorged a thick wave of the liquid from her lungs, throat, and mouth. Some of the liquid rushed up into her sinuses and burned. The pressure was a combination of a four-alarm migraine headache and an ice-cream brain freeze gouging behind both eyes.

"Two..." She forced her lips to form the numerical word as a fresh wave of heat rushed down her windpipe and burned back into her lungs. That one didn't hurt as much as the first one. In fact, a distinct tingling sensation was kindling hot, starting in her fingertips and toes, working its way up her arms and legs. The sharp pain behind her eyes began to subside as well. She kept drawing in and purging out, again, and then again, fighting to persevere to the end. By the time she was able to imagine the numeral eight, she felt like she was breathing easily and felt no pain whatsoever. Only it wasn't really breathing. It was literally a very fluid sensation. The thought crossed Helen's mind that this is what it must feel like for fish. That thought made her smile.

A dazzling multicolored light appeared overhead. Helen glanced up briefly, but the radiance was much too bright to look at directly, making her squint and turn away. However, through the thick syrup in her eyes she could see out into the lab. The teacher was standing by the crystal podium, patiently watching with his arms folded, holding his elbows. Christine and Dr. Markham had crept up closer, peering ahead in complete fascination, with chins protruding and eyes wide, making her feel even more like a fish in an aquarium. Or maybe she was the mermaid. She wasn't sure.

A warm sensation began flowing down over her body, much warmer than the temperature of the liquid surrounding her. The heat reminded her of the deep penetrating rays of the sun that she so used to enjoy, lying carefree by her father's swimming pool when she was a teenager. That was almost forty years ago, when her biggest priority in life was working on a perfect tan. It was an almost forgotten time, in another girl's life, back when so many boys gave her so much attention—that is, before they figured out she was a "brain," which she soon learned was roughly equivalent to being diagnosed with some deadly communicable disease.

Her gaze found the slightly refracted face of the teacher. His expression had changed to a captivated look of amazement. Dr. Markham just stood there like a zombie. Christine was crying, with her fingertips pressed over he mouth.

What was wrong?

Helen looked down at her hands, lifting them close to her face—only they weren't her hands, at least not the same ones she woke up with that morning. The rough texture of the old skin was gone, along with several of the age spots that had cropped up about twenty years ago. The knuckles weren't so prominent or pinkish anymore. Her hands looked smaller, thinner, the fingers a bit longer and more tapered. They were...elegant. Yes, even her nails were growing. She could actually see them slowly extending past the end of her fingers as she watched.

She glanced down at the rest of her body and stopped breathing.

CHAPTER 48

"How long has she been in there," Christine asked.

Dr. Markham glanced at his watch. "Almost forty-five minutes."

Neither of them could believe what they were seeing. Less than a single hour ago, Dr. Helen Knight had stepped tentatively into the tall glass chamber. She had entered the device with the body of most women her age—not afflicted, blemished, or marred in any visible way, save a faint appendectomy scar on her right side—just evident of its long journey through life. Her skin had absorbed its share of the sun's deteriorating rays over the years, adding wrinkles and lines and bags and freckles. Gravity had pulled her once plump and attractive breasts down atop her slightly rounded stomach. The skin over her triceps and under her neck hung loose, not turkey-necked yet, but definitely needing a little tightening up with a few turns of the wrench. Her hips had grown a bit wider than her shoulders, as had her thighs and ankles thickened with time.

Only, that was the woman of forty-five minutes ago.

That wasn't the woman inside the chamber any longer.

The new Helen's hair was longer and fuller, almost jet black, as it floated free and weightless in the currents of cytoplasm, shimmering with raven's wing blue-steel highlights reflected from the light beaming down from above. Her limbs were now lithe and long, the muscles highly defined, yet graceful and delicately chiseled. Her breasts stood firm and ample, peaked with prominent cherry red nipples. Her hips were rounded and strong, her stomach rippling, flat and tight. Her longs legs rivaled those of an Olympic swimmer, sleek and powerful like a deadly jungle cat's. She was clearly much taller now, perhaps just over six feet in height. And her face—

Her face positively radiated a soft blue ethereal light, identical to the one that emerged from the golden box when it was first opened. There were no more dark bags under her eyes, no crowfeet etched into her temples, not a single line or wrinkle on her forehead, oh no. Now her cheeks were high, smooth and flawless. Her lips were rose red and full, framing an even row of white teeth. Her eyes were delicate almonds, with long dark lashes. In fact, her eyes shone with more brilliant fire than any diamond ever cut by the most gifted of jewelers. Christine Jacobs couldn't stop crying. She felt that if the great sculptor and painter Michelangelo himself were standing there beside her in that moment, feasting his eyes on the bountiful beauty on display before them, he, too, would be weeping.

Dr. Markham was both filled with dumfounded amazement and a twinge of embarrassment. He couldn't help it. It began with the brief flutter of yearning deep in the pit of his stomach, which turned into a southbound tingle in the nether-regions. The truth was, he was standing there fully aroused, almost painfully so—which was unheard of for a man of his profession and age, sildenafil citrate[23] treatments notwithstanding.

He managed to break his awestruck stare and ask the teacher, "Is this now the perfect Helen?"

The teacher answered without taking his eyes away from the glass chamber and its heavenly occupant for an instant, clearly just as mesmerized as both the Doctor and Christine, speaking slowly, almost reverently. "Oh, she is much more than that, Doctor. She has not merely been rejuvenated, she has been completely transformed. Every cell in her body has been entirely reconstructed, reborn. I pray you fully come to appreciate what it is you are now privileged to see, a marvel of science and nature that no other living creature has ever witnessed." He paused in admiration. "For I have freely given to her that which none of your kind was permitted to have, the food and drink of eternal life that you were prohibited from ever tasting. She now knows that which was hidden. She possesses within every cell of her being the sacred code, the forbidden formula. I have awaited the coming of this day for an eternity."

Dr. Christine Jacobs no longer recognized the woman suspended in the fluid. She saw a young woman in there, of perhaps Christine's own age, eighteen or nineteen, and to be sure, breathtakingly beautiful beyond compare. It was physically hard to look upon her without being deeply moved. But it was also clearly no longer Dr. Helen Knight, not the renowned physicist, her cherished old professor, who had been more like a mother to her for so long.

Christine turned to the teacher. "That's not Helen any more. What exactly have you done to her?"

"I told you. I have given her new life, Dr. Jacobs." He was beaming with pride. "She is the culmination of everything I have waited thousands upon thousands of your years to achieve—that which I could only imagine in my most precious dreams. Yes, she is perfect, my friends, more perfect than even the first of her kind, the exquisite creature of unsurpassed beau-

---

[23] Trademarked by Pfizer as Viagra.

ty. Unsurpassed until this day. She is what your kind might have achieved in its own due course of evolution over two million years from now, had my brother not forced me to render that function impotent in you and permanently stalled your development."

Christine turned to him. "You're saying we can never enjoy everything you told us unless we go through this same process?"

He shook his head, "Not at all. Her development has been accelerated, as was your new limb. As you discover your gifts, and as the power that energizes them grows within you, you will begin to develop and progress just as she has, though it may take you centuries or millennia to achieve even a portion of what you see before you. But for her a different destiny is at hand. She is the new prototype, the Alpha of a great and glorious new people. She is the mother of a new and prosperous civilization that will rule this world, and many others like it, for ages to come."

"You've changed her body, the vehicle or the garment you spoke of, but isn't she still the same woman inside?" Christine was beginning to grow frightened. "Is it still Helen?"

The teacher held out both hands before the wonder of his work. "My friends, gaze fully and freely upon her beauty. See her in all her glory. Admire and worship her, for she is worthy of no less. This beautiful goddess of light has no mental, physical, or metaphysical limitations, save the constraints of her imagination and the passions of her heart, free to fulfill her every desire and ambition. She is beyond question the perfect woman. She is in every sense a true goddess, more beautiful than Ishtar, more powerful than Isis, more cunning and brilliant that either of my sons, Ra or Thoth. I vow to you, and hear me clearly upon this great and glorious day: great cities and temples shall be reared in her honor. New festivals and celebrations shall be established and consecrated to pay homage to her great name." He paused, letting out a long, heavy sigh. "And at long last, I shall have at my side...my precious queen."

Christine's throat had gone dry. Her heart was racing. She was about to say something when she heard it. They all heard it, in unison—the clear and unambiguous voice of authority. It was a woman's voice, not heard in spoken words, but spoken clearly and distinctly to their minds.

Release me.

CHAPTER 49

"What *is* this place?"

Francesca was only too happy to let Monsignor Pietro lead the way. She followed along closely behind him, her cheek often grazing his shirt sleeve, holding his hand like a frightened child, eyes wide, awed at the massive cyclopean stonework and mysterious ancient labyrinth passing before them. Her every nerve was on edge, braced in anticipation of any three-headed dog, tomb troll, or other such monster to leap out from the shadows intent on devouring them. They were following the fragrant scent of fresh fruit, vegetables and dried meats.

"I wish I could tell you what it is," the priest whispered in reply, both sensing and sharing her fear. "I've never heard or read of any great structures said to be beneath the Giza plateau. To be honest, scholars have barely begun to understand all of the ones above ground. They've argued for centuries about the age and purpose of all the monuments. Arguments that continue to this day."

Francesca stopped abruptly. "Did you hear that?"

Pietro shook his head, "No, what did you hear?"

"A woman's voice," she replied. "Very clearly and distinctly. Speaking Italian as clearly as we are right now."

"What did she say?"

Francesca put her fingertips to her temples. "She is asking to be released from something."

"I'm sorry, I heard nothing," he declared. "Come. Let's move on. The scent of ripe dates and fresh cut leeks grows faint."

They crept down the long stone corridor, hand in hand, moving along as quickly and quietly as possible, stopping only briefly to peer into the dark eerie chambers and spacious rooms filled with inexplicable furnishings, equipment, decorations, and adornments. There was no sign of the two men or woman in black carrying the heavy bags. After searching for quite some time, they came upon a wide staircase, which was evidently part of a deep spiraling stairwell winding its way down level after level into the darkness below. They swiftly descended to the second level, and were about to begin their exploration of it when Francesca stopped in her tracks yet again.

"No, wait," she insisted, pointing downward. "Not here. We must go farther down. I see something in my mind, something at the very bottom of these stairs, down in the depths. I feel it. Something is calling out. Something alive. Something I sense that wants to be free."

"The voice you heard before?" Father Pietro asked.

She squinted, thinking, sensing. "I don't know. I don't think so. I can't be sure. Perhaps. It is only a presence. Maybe more than one. It's hard to tell. But I sense that whatever it is, or whoever it is, it is crying out in great torment."

Father Pietro gave her a curt nod of approval and they continued their descent. As they proceeded, the alabaster sconces lining the walls illuminated their path whenever they came within a few yards of them. It took them only a few minutes to reach the depths of the ninth level. The air was warm down there, musty and stale, like a desert mineshaft, or a catacomb.

At the base of the granite stairs, beyond the smooth stone landing, stood a broad, white limestone arch, soaring up almost thirty feet from the floor. They crept beneath it, now arm-in-arm—suddenly stopping cold—and then abruptly backpedaling in wide-eyed surprise when the lights came up on the other side. There before them lay an enormous oval antechamber. Its walls were tiled from floor to ceiling with rows upon rows of gleaming gold plates. On the far wall directly opposite them stood a massive golden door, over ten feet in height and nearly as broad, with twelve large gemstones set in its center in three neat rows of four.

CHAPTER 50

"OK, boys and girls, dinner has arrived!" Jason called out as he came through the doorway of the medical laboratory, followed by Andrew and Else. Dropping his bags on a tall metal table with a clunk, he looked up, visibly startled to be confronted with an unfamiliar face—atop the nude body of a tall, stunningly beautiful young woman. A warm flush of embarrassment cascaded over his face and tingled down his chest. For a second he thought he might have been looking at a statue, until he saw it move.

He stammered, "*Who*...is she?"

Both Andrew and Else likewise carefully set down their burdens and stared mutely at the mysterious stranger standing on the metal base, who worked to cough and spit up a thick yellow liquid oozing down her chin. The glass cylinder was gone. The teacher stood at the control deck, his attention fixed firmly on the enigmatic woman, wholly ignoring the intrusion. Christine and Dr. Markham acknowledged the return of their companions with little more than a fleeting glance of annoyance.

The woman standing on the pedestal lifted her face and looked upon them, wiping off her mouth with the back of her hand. Her long black hair was soaked, lying flat against her scalp and cascading down her neck, shoulders and back. Her flawless skin was alabaster white, as though she had been carved from virgin marble. Her face gave off a soft luminescent radiance, her eyes alive with a shimmering blue fire.

The teacher turned to Jason. "Ah, welcome back, Dr. Wise. Dr. Friedrich. Mr. Duncan. As you can see, we have been quite busy in your absence."

Jason couldn't tear his eyes away from the woman. His heart was pounding, his breath shallow and rapid. The woman's appearance made Jason think of paintings and sculptures of Venus, the Roman goddess renowned for her unequalled beauty, her legacy of rearing great civilizations, and the starting of many bloody wars. Although, in Jason's humble estimation, this woman made Venus look like a hag. He couldn't ever recall being so stricken by the mere appearance of another human being—if indeed a "human being" was what it was he was observing. It was physically uncomfortable for him to be in this incredible creature's presence, especially with her standing there stark naked. How could he not look? He had never beheld a woman's figure so elegant, so vivacious and voluptuous, positively radiating an aura of simmering sexuality, with such succulently sculptured breasts, so bountiful, so perfect, so rounded, so full, the delicate nipples so deliciously red and ripe, and—

Jason bit his lower lip and forced himself to tear his gaze away, locking his eyes on the teacher's feet and taking one long, slow cleansing breath, willing himself to calm down and regain his composure. His mind was racing. What the hell was going on here? Who *was* she? What was she doing here? It was then it suddenly occurred to him that one of their company was missing.

Jason looked up. "Where's Helen?"

The beautiful stranger coughed once more, sniffed, and smiled at him. "What's wrong, Jason? Do I really look that different?"

Jason physically startled, his double-take practically breaking his neck before he took a quick step backward, bracing himself against the table behind him, flatly disbelieving what he was hearing and seeing.

"Helen?"

Helen offered him a soul-enslaving smile, then gracefully stepped down off the podium and stood tall and radiant, her magnificent new body glistening with the viscous, oily residue of the cylinder chamber. She surveyed the awestruck faces in the room, each one locked in reverent silence. It only took her a few moments to realize that if she but wished it, she could see through the eyes of any of those standing before her in the room. It was like switching monitor screens in a control room. She caught the first full-length glimpse of herself through Christine's eyes.

The visage took her own breath away.

Bright crystal tears of joy began to cascade down her cheeks. It was unbelievable. It was impossible. And yet, unless she was dreaming, it was so. She was no longer inhibited or ashamed to be standing completely bare before them all. In fact, there was a certain titillating sense of pleasure garnered from their astonished and admiring eyes. Just as the teacher had said, in every sense, she felt like she was now the master of all her surroundings and all that she was. She had never felt more alive, more filled with energy and the fire of life than at that precise moment. And so many ideas, notions, and concepts buried deep in her mind, puzzling conundrums that had always been so dark and cloudy were suddenly so clear and simple.

Andrew Duncan found his voice, "My God, Helen, what in heaven's name has become of you?"

She faced him, her voice even and sure. "I am that I am, Andrew. I have become that which was destined for us to be."

Else whispered, barely audible, "She's...so beautiful... But *how*?"

The teacher explained, "It is my pleasure to introduce the new Dr. Helen Knight, who has been genetically accelerated with a pure genome, a complete composition encoding profile which is highly refined and now fully active in her. In doing so, she has now been physically infused with the creative energy of the divine, and thereby quickened with new life. She has become a true and living goddess."

Else stepped forward. "A goddess? What are you talking about? There are no such things."

Jason jumped in, "Yeah. Come on. What's really going on here? Don't get me wrong. She's obviously drop-dead gorgeous, so much so it almost hurts to look at her. *Honestly*. It's gotta be the mother of all make-overs. But what do you mean by 'infused with the energy of the divine'? What's that a euphemism for?"

The teacher started to answer, then stopped himself, permitting himself only a brief smile of satisfaction before gesturing to Helen. "It is your experience, your enlightened understanding, your newfound knowledge. You tell them."

She did. "My dearest Jason, it is vitally important that you clearly understand what you now see in me, and be not mislead or deceived as were our ancestors." She stepped closer to him, explaining, "For you see, long ago, primitive mankind sincerely believed that the superior beings living in their midst were in fact supernatural gods and goddesses. And truly, those who were called gods and goddesses were only too happy to receive such deference and adoration. But the gods and goddesses themselves were nothing more than the fruit of their own evolutionary and cultural development, sentient creatures further advanced on the scale of time, time measured in millennia and eons."

"That part I understand," Jason replied, struggling to look Helen directly in the eye, and to keep his prurient thoughts in check, despite the uncomfortable physical reaction going on in his pants. "Right. That's what he's been telling us since we found him. The gods of old were just a more advanced race of people from another world who helped out us knuckle-dragging low-lifes. I get it. I'm not questioning that. But being higher on the evolutionary food chain doesn't have anything to do with anything supernaturally spiritual or theistically *divine*."

She raised one elegant hand to silence him. "And that's where you're wrong. This is the most precious gift of knowledge with which I have now been entrusted. What you still fail to comprehend is that despite man's erroneous deification of those before whom he humbled himself and chose to serve, or to those who forcibly subjugated him and mandated and extorted his worship and tribute, it doesn't change the fact that it was indeed that which is *truly* divine that is directly responsible for all that exists."

"How do you figure that?" Jason challenged.

She explained, "It was the Original Thought—a singularly divine thought—a single act of true, pure, sentient creative energy that birthed an entire universe billions of years ago, and set the development path and cycles of growth of that explosion of energy into motion, which radiated out from its point of origin, laying its foundations and charting its orbital destinies."

"The Original Thought?" Jason was shaking his head.

She focused her eyes on him. "Yes."

"You're saying the whole universe, and all history from time immemorial was but a single divine thought?" His incredulity was evident.

"That's correct," she assured him.

"How can that be?" he challenged. "Come on, Helen, goddess or not, you're a nuclear physicist, one of the most brilliant scientific minds I've ever known. Unless what's just happened to you erased all that from your memory, you know far better than I the sheer astronomical complexity of the known universe, a universe that an infinite number of books could never hope to contain. A single divine thought?"

"Yes. Only one."

And then it happened.

She smiled. "Let there be light."

The entire room was instantly flooded with a surpassing multihued brilliance that caused everyone, save the teacher and Helen, to cringe and throw their hands defensively over their faces, cowering to the floor, exactly as they had done in the wake of the teacher's great roar on the day of his awakening. Dr. Markham swooned again, falling akimbo in a heavy heap clutching his chest. The engulfing rainbow of light, which seemed to have no single source, was not merely shining round about them. It was alive and moving, swirling and penetrating like a tangible fluid substance, seeking and searching with a conscious mind and a purpose. They were fully immersed in it, saturated by it, breathing it in and out.

Jason could physically feel the blinding rays bathing and caressing his skin, probing every square inch of his body, soaking into his pores, making him feel lighter, more awake, more alive. The individual hairs on his arms and the back of his neck were standing on end. In the midst of it all he suddenly felt the overwhelming desire to go to Helen, to touch her, to take her in his arms, to hold her, to feel her smooth glistening skin pressed against his own, to taste her—

NO. This was madness!

Once again, he forced himself to turn away, biting down on his closed fist to the point of pain and the iron taste of blood. He felt the raw urge to scream boiling up within him. And then...

All sensation of discomfort ebbed, burned away and vaporized in the brilliance of the light. Jason sucked in a deep breath and let it out slowly, convinced that the light actually flowed down into his lungs and entered his bloodstream. He felt enveloped by an uncanny calm, bathed in a surreal sense of ease and tranquility. It was peaceful, almost a joyous and blissful sensation, which was such an odd feeling for him, certainly one to which he was most unaccustomed.

The teacher was chuckling softly to himself, content to stand back and enjoy the role of a passive observer to the spectacle.

The liquid living light filling the room slowly began to recede and dim back to normal as Helen continued to speak. "Lay aside your doubts and fears my friends, and listen carefully. Divine creative energy gave birth to the light. And from the light came forth all things—the living fabric of the heavens and the heavenly bodies contained within it. It brought forth all the creatures of the light."

Andrew Duncan swallowed hard, shaking his head to clear it, and finding the presence of mind to ask, "Helen, help me understand. I want to. I think we all do. But you're speaking in philosophical platitudes and abstracts. Are you telling us that you've now been turned into a more advanced being? Into one of *them*? Some kind of *superior* being to us mere mortals?"

"Superior being? Is that what you're concerned about, Andrew, superiority versus inferiority? Is *that* what clouds your understanding of what is now freely yours for the taking? Tell me, is an adult a superior being when compared to his own child? Or are they in essence one and the same flesh, merely at different points in their journey through time?" Helen paused, then explained carefully, "Your thinking is confused by the vestiges and conventions of superstition, the legacy of unenlightened and stagnant cultures. There is only one divine sentient entity, one creator and giver of life. However, there are a multitude of sentient creatures of the light in this universe, progressing at different points on their journey of advancement. Don't confuse the creator with the creation. That was one of the great mistakes of our ancestors." She stopped her discourse and frowned, turning to face the teacher with a sudden look of realization. "Only that's the real problem. Isn't it? Mankind's progression in the universe, on this planet in particular, was hindered, physically cut off from the light, insulated from the divine energy source that was intended to move it forward. Cut off…by you."

The teacher responded, not with defiance or excuses, but with genuine remorse. "Yes. It is true. It was my hand that hobbled you, as I have tried to explain in great detail." He brightened. "And that is the purpose of our mission together now. To right that wrong. Do you not yet understand? Every prophet, preacher, poet, philosopher, saint and sage, whether by sheer accident or by fervent search and dedication of heart and soul—*any* who has ever had the smallest taste or glimpse of divine light, has been extolling his fellow man to seek it, to find it, to connect to it, to become part of it, to let it guide his path. It is the only way advancement as an individual, as a people, and as a culture can ever substantively occur."

"Why is that?" Jason simply asked.

The teacher looked him in the eye. "Because the Law of Entropy is too great to oppose without it. Mere doctrine and dogma are impotent against the debilitating power of entropy. Empty ritual and tradition is but a mockery of true power. Nor is the divine light a function of intellectual enlightenment or academic education, but rather…it is a living act of inspiration—in the ancient tongue, it is *pneumatis*, spirit, literally *breath*, to breathe in and breathe out, a physical and biological reality. It can neither be earned nor devised. It is the very basis for the Great Law of the Universe, one of the fundamental axioms of all who have studied the great sciences of my kind."

Christine prompted, "Which is…?"

Helen answered for him, the words flowing forth from a wellspring she had no idea was within her. "All work, action, or motion requires energy. A sentient soul in the dark is asleep, is at rest, and shall remain in the dark, asleep, and at rest, unless acted upon by the one external divine energy source that can quicken it to life, accelerating and magnifying the life force energy within it, thereby giving it the ability to cause creative action, movement, and work."

"That's a basic thermodynamic principle," Christine said.

The teacher nodded, "And so much more. This is the divine formula for advancement of life and the antithesis of entropy."

Andrew asked, "And will you show us how to lay our own hands upon this energy source, this divine light of yours?"

The teacher laughed out loud, a hearty belly-laugh. "Our dear goddess Helen just did! Were you not watching? Did you not see it? Have your eyes grown dim? Did you not feel it embrace you? Did it not fill your lungs with every breath you took?"

Andrew, Christine, Jason and Else all looked apprehensively from one to another, not quite sure how to respond.

Christine looked down at Dr. Markham, lying limp on the floor at her feet. The poor man looked so frail and vulnerable like that. Her heart went out to him, not wanting to see him just laying there so helpless a moment longer. She reached out and called to him, "Dr. Markham, get up."

And then it happened.

The elder physician's body slowly began to rise up several feet from the floor, levitating on a cushion of air.

Andrew and Jason both took a defensive step back. Else prepared to run.

Christine's eyes flew to Helen and then to the teacher. "What are you doing to him? Put him down!"

Helen joined the teacher in his laughter. "We can't."

"Why not?" Christine demanded.

The teacher answered, "Because the molecules of his flesh are obeying the authority of your word, not ours."

CHAPTER 51

It wasn't so much by decision or design as by circumstance that Jean-Marc Xavier rarely set foot on the sands of Egypt, save the occasional business trip. But necessity had finally brought him there that day with an urgent purpose. Like most of the tourists who congregated there every day, he too stood in genuine awe of the spectacular sight of the Great Pyramids, illuminated on all sides by floodlights at night. A crisp chill whispered though the air. It was just after midnight. The evening laser shows were all concluded, and the tourists had all dutifully filed back to their hotels and resorts for the night. The vendors had gone home. The maintenance crews had dutifully tidied up the grounds. Only a few scattered late-shift security personnel lingered here and there, pacing their quiet vigils, smoking cigarettes, doing their best to while away the monotony and boredom of their routines.

Jean-Marc had never seen the monuments from ground level before, and certainly never this close. He stood at the foot of Cheops, the Great Pyramid, on its north face. Both his limo driver and his bodyguards were confused and distressed by his firm insistence to go into the Giza complex alone. But their objections didn't matter. None of Xavier's people, not even Mohammed, would ever openly challenge any decision or command he gave. He spoke. They obeyed. His word was immutable law. It was a simple, but highly effective system.

"I'm sorry, sir," a uniformed officer mumbled in broken English. "The Pyramids are closed for the evening. Please come back tomorrow for the regularly scheduled tours."

Jean-Marc nodded, not taking his eyes off the towering heap of granite blocks. His gaze slowly trailed down to the roped-off entrance on the north face of the Great Pyramid. *"Merci, mon ami.* I shall do that."

The polite guard bobbed his head once, offering a thin smile, as he pulled a half-empty pack of cigarettes out of his trouser pocket and fumbled through his other pocket for his lighter. His fingers came upon a small stack of discount admittance coupons bound with a thin green rubber band. Oh well, he thought, it might be good public relations to at least give the lone straggling tourist a coupon for his trouble of coming all the way out to the complex so late—even though the exhibit hours were clearly posted everywhere in twelve different languages. Then again, happy tourists benefited all. He looked up, extending one of the coupons, and was about to say something.

The stranger was gone.

The baffled guard spun around in a complete circle two times, looking around in every direction. *That was odd. How did he do that?* He glanced back down at the crumpled pack of cigarettes, his lighter, and the coupons still clutched in his hands. He had only looked down for a couple of seconds. No one could have run from sight in that short a time. And besides, he would have heard him doing so if he tried. A nervous chill washed over him. The security guard reached for the radio on his hip.

•

"You know, now that I think about it, I *have* read of this place. I mean, places *like* this." Father Pietro ran the tip of his index finger over the large ruby and diamond inset in the great golden door. "But it was supposedly all legend and myth."

"What did the legend say? Does it say what this place is?" Francesca still huddled close behind him, her eyes darting about, wary of any sudden sound or movement.

"If this is what I think it is, we are at the door of a suspension vault," he replied. "At least that is my theory of what they were. According to some of the earliest clay tablets found catalogued in the great library of Asherbinipal in Nineveh, the great golden doors adorned with the talismans of the heavens are the threshold to a special inner chamber called the Dragon's Lair."

Francesca gave him a puzzled look.

He explained, "It's a mythologized depiction of a place of banishment, like Purgatory, a place of either temporal or eternal punishment, more like a prison of sorts, guarded by a great dragon capable of incinerating any who dare trespass with his breath of fire."

Francesca inched back from the door. "And yet this is where I hear the pleas and cries for mercy the greatest. Is this dragon real, Father?"

The priest took a step back, hands on hips, studying the door. "This door certainly appears to be real. And if *it's* real, then the incantation to put the dragon to sleep may be real as well."

"Incantation? Some kind of witchcraft?" Her eyes went wide.

He pointed to the gemstones. "No, not at all. Many incantations or ritualistic chants were often nothing more than a set of procedures, a step-by-step method of achieving a specified goal. Formal rituals and traditions were usually developed and employed around any function deemed spiritual or supernatural, to both symbolically commemorate the event's importance, and as an easy way to help people memorize and remember each step." He sighed. "Unfortunately, in many instances the words of the rituals themselves often became more of the central focus, and eventually came to be considered more important than the underlying procedure itself."

"And there was a procedure for doors like this?" she asked.

He scratched his chin. "Yes. In this case, with respect to a great golden door inset with twelve stones, notwithstanding the long-winded prayers and oblations of divine protection and blessing, the high priest of Nineveh said that in order to enter one of these sacred vaults unharmed, one must start by laying hold upon the first and last of the heavens as one, then the great circle of the heavenly hosts, from first unto last, and then again, both the first and last in union to complete the circle. That was the secret of the procedure."

She looked bewildered. "But what does all of that mean?"

He stepped closer to the door. "I think I know."

Monsignor Pietro put his hands on the bloodstone and the yellow topaz and pushed them in unison. They recessed together into their polished gold sockets and illuminated. A second later they both popped out and began to flash.

Francesca gasped. "What's it doing?"

"Just watch."

The priest wasted no time pressing the yellow topaz back into its socket and proceeding to the diamond, then to the emerald, and to the ruby, and on to the remainder of the stones, finishing by simultaneously pressing the bloodstone and yellow topaz again. The entire array of stones blinked three times in unison. After a brief pause, an electric arc crackled and buzzed around the perimeter of the door followed by a blinding flash of bright orange sparks, hissing and showering forth. Both Father Pietro and Francesca retreated from the hot drops of gold spattering and raining down on the floor. When the light dimmed, the stones of the floor beneath them trembled as the great golden door slowly swung out of its jam.

It was open.

Francesca jumped behind Father Pietro, clutching the back of his shirt. He tentatively inched forward to investigate, dragging her along in tow. He was trembling as much as she was, but pulled forward by the inescapable gravitational force of curiosity and wonder. They crossed the threshold of the great door together and stopped just inside, looking at a cavernous domed chamber, the expanse of which was as big as the Coliseum in Rome, and easily as great in height. The chamber was illuminated with a soft white light emanating from the walls. Within the chamber lay eighteen small white domes arrayed in two concentric circles—a ring of six surrounded by a ring of twelve. Next to each one a small crystalline structure was rising up out of the floor.

Francesca suddenly clapped her hands over her ears, pinching her eyes closed, in obvious pain. "They are all screaming! Make them stop! Father, please make them all stop screaming!"

•

Jean-Marc Xavier stood in the Unfinished Chamber at the end of the Descending Passage directly beneath the Great Pyramid. He had carefully examined the Grand Gallery, as well as both the Queen's Chamber and the King's Chamber above, finding nothing. This chamber was a different story. On one wall was a prominent symbol he recognized very well. Actually, it was a pictograph, a large outline of a human hand. Oh, but it was obviously much more than that…if one possessed a discerning eye. He approached it cautiously and held his hand over the outline, but hesitated before placing it against the stone.

"You are very clever," he whispered. "You always were. Very clever indeed, if this is where you are hiding. So…is this yet another deep hole for you to slither beneath the rocks, another of your dark caves where you can lurk in the shadows?" He glanced back up the Descending Passage. "Although, I must say, if it is, this is certainly too public a place for another thermonuclear accident. That won't do at all. No, no, no. But then again, there are many, many effective ways to slay a dragon. *N'est pas?*"

He lifted his jacket lapel and pulled out his revolver, checking to see that the cylinder was fully loaded. A pat on his right side jacket pocket confirmed the presence of two reserve speed-loaders. He considered eighteen rounds to be sufficient to the task at hand. But just in case, he reached behind him for an assuring touch of the delicate object tucked in the waistband of his slacks, resting gently against his spine. He returned the chrome-plated pistol to its leather holster under his left arm, and then placed his right palm within the outline of the hand etched into the ancient wall. The soft yellow light began to pulse. Xavier laughed through his nose as the stone door began to grind back, opening wide to reveal the darkened passage beyond it.

CHAPTER 52

Helen was alone.

The teacher had taken each of the others and shown them to separate living quarters on level four with firm insistence on much-needed rest for all. Helen was taken separately down to level five and provided a spacious sleeping chamber that was nothing short of palatial. The floor was gleaming polished marble. The walls were pure inlaid gold. In the center of the room, surrounded by majestic towering bronze columns, was a bed, or perhaps more accurately, a sleeping platform. It was square in shape, ten foot to a side, two and half feet in height, ornately decorated around its base of polished fine jade. Its top surface was covered with the same soft, pliable turquoise gel as were the seats in the passenger compartment of the ship that brought them there.

The teacher had found a long white linen robe for Helen to wear, one similar to his own, but she wasn't wearing it. Oh no. For in an alcove of the sleeping chamber, adjacent to what had been explained was a lavatory facility, unique from any bathroom she had seen anywhere on earth, was a full-length mirror. It was completely inset into the wall, spanning a full twelve feet in height and six feet wide. This was no ordinary glass mirror, backed with quicksilver[24]; rather, it was a pure sheet of highly polished pure silver, with no flaws or distortions. For the last twenty minutes she stood there in a state of wonder and amazement, staring and admiring the exquisite visage of her new body, enthralled by what she saw and utterly elated by how it made her feel.

She had indeed changed—in more ways than she could possibly comprehend.

For almost six decades Helen Knight had never for a moment thought of herself as a "beautiful" woman. As a girl she thought she had been "cute," maybe even "pretty," but never truly *beautiful*. Men never stopped dead in their tracks with an involuntary pang of desire, gawked, and said "Wow" or whistled at her as she passed by. The occasional compliment that came her way tended to fall exclusively in the polite and courteous

---

[24] Mercury.

category, as opposed to the genuine exclamations of ardent admirers. As the flower of her youth yielded to the onslaught of middle-age, even the thought of "pretty" was a bit generous.

But all that had amazingly changed in but a single hour on that very day. She had been graced with an awesome gift. Admittedly, an element of her mind continued to tell her that physical superficialities were nothing more than shallow vanities. But the truth was, she couldn't stop running her palms over her flawlessly smooth and satiny skin, cupping her creamy sculpted shoulders, sliding down her long lithe arms, trailing along her gracefully curved sides and the gentle contours of her hips, sweeping across her taut little waist, pressing upward again and gathering her firm and bountiful breasts, tracing their way up her neck and jaw line, kneading her scalp, then gliding back down through the long tresses of her silky black hair, again and again.

It was a complete fantasy. A fantasy come true.

Yes, it *was* true, unbelievable, but literally true, undeniably true. Helen Knight was now breathtakingly beautiful, the living embodiment of that word in all its artistic significance, the new Helen with a face that could indeed launch a thousand ships for her rescue, if need be. She *felt* beautiful, which was an utterly alien sensation. What's more, she felt powerful—all powerful, omnipotent, invincible, indestructible. It was an intimately intoxicating feeling.

The constant rhythmic motion of her hands caressing and cascading over her supple skin also served to physically arouse her to the point of conjuring up a yearning ache from deep inside her. No man had touched her intimately in well over ten years. Or had it been fifteen? As far as she was concerned, sexual activity of any kind had regrettably been rendered a closed chapter in her life. Even the very desire for physical intimacy, the hunger for physical passion, that craving for the raw exhilaration of sizzling sexual titillation and orgasmic release, had long faded away into the cold mists of obscurity, buried beneath the quiet sands of years upon years of wandering the deserts of professional pursuits and academic activities.

But that was no longer the case.

Helen Knight was on fire inside, smoldering with an overwhelmingly renewed and utterly famished libidinal appetite. Oh, to yearn for the tantalizing touch and soothing warmth of another body pressed against her own—the warmth of a man penetrating deep inside her own—it was an almost forgotten sensation. Yet as each moment ticked by, her bodily hunger only multiplied, and never in all her days had it been so ravenously intense. She could feel the warm wetness growing between her twitching thighs, tingling within her and radiating up and down her spine. It didn't take long for the languid motion of her fingers to gravitate her left hand into a gentle figure-eight course lightly gliding over her highly sensitized blood-red erect nipples, as her right hand wound its way down through the soft tufts of silky black hair between her legs, her fingertips finding and probing the moist honeyed epicenter of her darkest desires.

"You truly are a vision beyond compare."

At any other moment in her life, Helen Knight would have screamed and dropped dead of embarrassment if caught by another living soul brazenly doing what she was doing. But that was the old Helen, the mortal Helen of another life, of another time and place, of another universe with different physical laws. The universe of that Helen was no more.

The old Helen was dead.

She didn't stop pleasuring herself. Oh no, she was richly enjoying herself without restraint or reservation, savoring the sensual sensations flowing though her far too much to turn back now. The interruption merited only a brief glance over her left shoulder to see the teacher standing next to the smooth marble column at the opening of the alcove. His eyes were shining bright, glistening and wet with emotion. She turned her attention back to the mirror, eager to watch him watch her, feeling his eyes feasting upon her beauty, his hungry expression arousing her carnal appetites all the more. Her breath staggered and stuttered as her long, nimble fingers explored deeper and deeper, fanning the heat within her white hot. She watched him walk up behind her and gently wrap his powerful arms around her waist. She earnestly wanted him to touch her—and she wanted much, much more.

"I have waited an eternity for you," he whispered in her ear, softly kissing the lobe and her temple, then leaning down to run the sharp edge of his teeth along the nape of her neck. A chill of electricity flashed down to her toes.

Helen's hands reached behind her and found what she both hoped and knew would be waiting there for her. He had already unbuttoned his robe and his desire for her was evidently as strong if not stronger than her own for him at that moment. She spun around and fell into his arms, their bodies pressed tight, feasting on his lips.

•

"What are they?" Francesca walked near the closest ice dome.

"I'm not sure." Monsignor Pietro reached out and touched the glistening white surface, instantly yanking his finger away, wincing and recoiling in pain from the icy surface burning his skin.

"Is it hot?" she grabbed his hand. "Are you burned?"

A numbing warmth instantly radiated from Francesca's fingers into his hand. The pain immediately vanished along with the bright red spot that had begun to blister. He shook his head, "No, it's cold. It's frozen."

Francesca stepped away. "We should not touch it."

Father Pietro agreed. "We shouldn't touch *anything* in here."

Francesca backed further away, but accidentally retreated into one of the crystalline podiums. The unexpected impact startled her. She spun around, defensively thrusting out her hand to push away whatever had made contact. Her palm hit the flat glassy surface angled in her direction, the thin layer of perspiration and oil on her skin causing it to stick for a second.

It illuminated.

She spun around, screaming, "What's it doing?"

The priest ran to her side. "I don't know. But it reacted to your touch. Don't touch anything else."

"No, no," she shook her head vigorously. "I won't. I'm sorry. I didn't mean to do it. It was an accident!"

"I know," he tried to assure her.

They both turned in unison as mechanical noises echoed loudly from beneath the floor, followed by a gurgling sound of liquid running through pipes.

•

Helen Knight finally knew the true meaning of the word ecstasy.

He lay beneath her on the soft cushion of turquoise blue gel. She was astride him, sitting up, with her head thrown back in wanton abandon, eyes shut, clutching handfuls of flesh from his stomach, her long razor sharp nails digging deep and drawing blood. But no sooner did she release one handful of skin and the cuts would immediately close and the incisions disappear. Her hips were rocking forward and back of their own accord, working to drive the rigid heat filling her deeper, ever deeper. Her lungs were on fire. The pounding beats of her heart had accelerated to ramming speed. Heavy, salty drops of sweat dripped from her chin, landing on her glistening breasts and tracing a winding course down the length of her body.

He writhed and twisted, arching his back to increase the penetration of his slow rapier thrusts within her. His eyes were squeezed down tight, sharp teeth bared, moaning with pure pleasure.

That's when the first of many violent tidal waves of erotogenic energy began to swell, imminently threatening to crash over her. She felt it approaching. She could sense its charge, building from a distance, gathering force, accelerating and growing in strength as it drew closer and closer. She resisted it momentarily, knowing instinctively that holding it at bay as long as she could would only intensify its power and resolve to consume her. The sudden motion of her lover sitting up and sinking his teeth into the cherry red bud of her right nipple caught her by surprise. The shock and sharp sensation tore away all of her resistance. Surrender to the wave now was inevitable. Fighting its violent undertow was futile.

It hit.

Helen's lungs froze. Every muscle in her body wrenched taut, seizing to the very precipice of dislocating joints and ligaments. Every neuron in her being fired. The light in the room grew brighter. Her chin yanked down, pressing hard on the crown of his head. She rolled her cheek over, her teeth slicing deep into his scalp, almost to the bone like a hungry lioness. The rich coppery taste of blood flooded her mouth from hundreds of shredded capillaries. The sticky wet warmth was sweet and delicious, her tongue lapping it up and smearing around her lips and letting it run down her chin. She leaned back and saw her own bright red blood running down her stomach from the neat incision in her areola where he had savored her own tender flesh as well. It was healing before her eyes. She caught a glimpse of them both in the silver mirror in the alcove across the room: two lovers locked in the fervent throws of passion, covered with sweltering droplets of sweat, streaked with the raw crimson smears of fresh blood. The image was horrific, but beautiful. It was carnal and yet captivating.

It made her want more.

There lips met with a ravenous clash of bared teeth.

Chapter 53

"Do you feel any different?" Jason came over and sat next to Christine on what was the bed in her newly assigned quarters.

Both of their accommodations, were much different than what Helen was richly enjoying at that very moment. Each room on level four was an efficient ten by ten cubicle, complete with a gel-covered bedding platform that was significantly longer, but only slightly wider, than an average twin bed.

"I don't think so," Christine replied, leaning against the cool stone wall with her bare feet propped up, legs stretched out straight, one ankle crossed over the other. "I mean, not inside. But I know somehow something is different with me. Something's changed."

He touched her foot. "Doesn't that feel weird?"

She laughed. "No, not really. That's the leg I came with. The other one's the new one."

Jason laughed at himself. "Sorry."

"Don't worry about it. But yes, having a new leg does feel weird. You know, you just get used to something over a long period of time, and when it changes, even for the better, it's different. And different is weird. And sometimes different feels wrong, even when it's not." She rolled her eyes. "I don't know why that is."

"Comfort zone violation. And speaking of such, what did you think of Helen?" he whispered, as though afraid of being overheard.

It was Christine's turn to blush slightly. "Honestly?"

"Yeah." He looked her in the eye.

She broke his gaze, and shuddered. "Honestly, it kind of freaked me out."

He leaned forward. "Why? Her new look bother you?"

She forced a half-laugh. "I guess you could say that."

He leaned back again, resting his head against the adjacent wall, his eyes scanning the ceiling. "You don't mean it bothers you in a girl-girl jealous way. You mean she bothers you in a girl-girl sexual way."

Her eyes flew to his. "I never said that."

He caught her gaze and smiled. "You didn't have to. It was written on everyone's face in the entire room. It was like she cast a bewitching spell or something, like the Sirens seducing Ulysses' men toward the rocks. I admit it. Hell, I *felt* it. I've never wanted a woman so bad in my whole life as when I was looking at her. I mean, like, it hurt to be in her presence. I thought I was going to blow my load right then and there just looking at her."

"Whoa! Too much information." Christine paused slowly shaking her head, then nodded. "But I know what you mean. That's what is especially weird for me. Helen and I have always had a really close relationship. She's my mentor. Probably the only person in the world I think who ever really understood me. I mean, our whole relationship has always been very mother-daughter-esque. To even think of her in any context outside of a sweet nurturing maternal image makes my stomach hurt."

Jason blew out a silent whistle. "Yeah, I can see where that would have to fuck you up a little."

Christine blurted out the carefully crafted rationalization she'd been rehearsing in her mind for the last hour in a feeble attempt to make it all sound better. "Well, I just want her to be happy. If she's happy, then I'm happy for her."

Jason just stared at her, not quite sure how to respond to that. "Her feelings weren't exactly what we were talking about."

She rubbed her eyes. "I know. But I didn't really like what we were talking about. If that's OK with you."

He sported a mischievous grin, willing to re-vector the conversation's course a few degrees. "Ahh-ight, well then tell me this, sweet *thang*. When you first looked inside the gold box, when we were over at the other place, and saw the teacher laying there in all his god-given glory—" He stopped himself. "Wait. The expression 'god-given' may not exactly be appropriate in this particular context."

Christine giggled. "Maybe. Maybe not."

"Regardless," he emphasized, waving both hands, "what did you think then? I mean, did you have the same kind of...*reaction*...to the sight of him laying there all bare-beam buck-nekkid?"

She frowned, pursing her lips, making an effort to recall her initial impressions. Everything that had happened only a few days prior felt like months or years ago. "No, not really. It wasn't quite the same when we first saw him."

"Ah hah!" Jason raised a finger. "So what you're really saying is that you're a lesbian, even if incestuous inferences trouble you."

"No, I'm not a lesbian," she contradicted with a scolding look. "You didn't let me finish. What I meant to say, is that when I first saw the teacher, he had, you know, like, a hundred wires sticking out of his body, cutting into his skin. It reminded me of that scary bald guy in all those old Wes Craven *Hell Raiser* horror movies with all the pins stuck all over his head."

"Pinhead," Jason offered.

"Whatever. That was kind of gross, and somewhat repulsive. So, no, that wasn't an attractive moment. But later...after he woke up, when stood up out of the box..." Her smile reappeared, "OK, yeah. Then he was looking mighty fine."

Jason added, "And he was cold too, so he gets extra points."

"Cold?"

He smirked. "You ever see a naked man get out of cold water? A man's pride and joy tends to hibernate in adverse conditions."

The light suddenly went on and Christine blushed anew. "Is that all you ever think about? The size of your penis?"

He teased, "You're telling me you didn't check his package out?"

She hesitated, then admitted, "I looked."

"And...?"

Christine broke character and laughed. "And I told you, he was looking mighty fine!" She held up a finger in his face, countering, "But how did he make *you* feel?"

Jason knocked his head into the wall behind him. "Like I was very thankful he wasn't my cellmate."

Christine laughed even harder. "So you're telling me you experienced no latent homoerotic sense of stimulation—"

"*Hell* no," he protested.

"Nothing?" she pried.

He conceded with a thin wry smile, "Well, let's just say, if I had to do it with a guy, like if I had a gun to my head and let's say it was to save the whole world, or keep a litter of newborn puppies from burning to death, then I can see where he had his good points."

"But you're into women," she said it as a statement, but was a half-question.

He was about to give her an enthusiastic affirmation, but instead let out a long weary sigh and hung his head. "Theoretically, yes. But your interrogative, Dr. Jacobs, implies rendering a judgment upon an active reality, not a hypothetical concept."

She tried to catch his gaze again. "Want to run that by me one more time?"

He looked deeply into her eyes for a moment, his own expressing a quiet pain. "I call it Chronic involuntary occupational celibacy."

Christine looked away. "Oh. Yeah. That. I understand."

He chuckled, "I sure as shit hope you do! Didn't you say you were only eighteen? Goddamn girl, I would hope you're still saving a little sompn-sompn for somebody special some day."

She snapped at him, "Like you're so over-the-hill. So, like, how old are you anyway?"

Jason shrugged, "Thirty-five. Thirty six in November."

"Really?" she sounded genuinely surprised.

He crossed his arms, "Oh, so what, now I *am* over the hill?"

She grinned, "Well...mathematically speaking..." But she was quick to append, "But honest to God you look like you're in your mid-twenties. I swear."

"Thanks," he muttered. "I think."

"Oh, come on." She threw a playful hand of dismissal at him. "You get no sympathy from me when it comes to age discrimination. Everyone I meet thinks I'm twelve. OK? I do everything I can to get people to take me seriously and not think of me as some smart-mouthed know-it-all kid."

Jason smiled. "Well, if it helps, I never thought of you as a kid. Just a cute chick way over-obsessed with math and physics."

"Guilty," she whispered.

They sat in silence for several moments.

And then it happened.

The awkward stillness was broken when Christine leaned forward sucked in a deep breath and abruptly blinked several times. She shook her head, twisting it from side to side as if to clear it, like she had water in her ears. She stopped and sat motionless, massaging her temples, then suddenly turned to Jason and asked him out of the blue, "Can I kiss you?"

He did a double-take. "What?"

She leaned closer, her eyelids hanging down over a glassy gaze as though she were half-asleep, or drunk, repeating earnestly, "Can I kiss you? I really *want* to kiss you. Please?"

Jason swallowed with some difficulty, glancing nervously to the open doorway. "Uh...why?"

Christine's face still looked a bit dazed, but her voice revealed a tinge of urgency. "Because I want to. I *need* to."

Jason Wise didn't like being teased—especially about matters of the heart and physical affections. Even the thought that she might just be teasing him resurrected several unpleasant memories from his own adolescence of cruel young teenage girls who loved to celebrate Tease-a-Geek day on a regular basis.

Where the hell was she going with this?

He was involuntarily pulling back away from her. "Just all of the sudden? You want a kiss?"

Christine scooted even closer. She was breathing faster, her chest rising and falling beneath her tee-shirt. "Yes. I want you. Don't you want me?"

He gave her a playful look. "Is this, like, a trick question, little sister?"

She just stared at him. "Is that how you really see me? As a baby sister?"

Jason returned her stare, sitting there in complete disbelief at what he was hearing. Finally he just laughed, deliberately attempting to break the awkward tension of the moment, turning his face to the side and bearing his check and tapping his jawbone. "OK, I'll play along. Right here, sweetie, if it rows your boat. I'm always up for hugs and kisses from pretty girls."

And then he felt it too.

Jason's eyes fluttered, his vision blurring. He felt momentarily faint. It was something in the air, an energy, a resonance. A presence. Something alive and hungry. Something that wasn't there a moment earlier. Every sound in the room became amplified and distinct. He could hear his own breathing, as well as hers. He was certain he could even hear her heart pounding beneath the soft cotton tee-shirt she wore, the soft hush of her blood flowing through her veins. His head started to feel light and euphoric, almost inebriated. His face felt warm and tingling. His clothes suddenly felt irritating and constricting. He could feel his own heart rate accelerating, throbbing in his temples, and his breathing became more shallow and rapid. The cute little girl leaning into him suddenly didn't look so little, or merely a girl. The look in her eye was a mature woman's look, a woman with an urgent need.

What the hell was happening?

Dr. Christine Jacobs reached up and brought Jason's face back toward her, her lips finding his, kissing him long and deep, the tip of her tongue invading his mouth and sparring with his own. A warm wave of pleasure radiated through her as she felt his hand tenderly slide up her side and softly cup the gentle swell of her breast.

CHAPTER 54

The laboratory on level three lay quiet and still.

Jean-Marc Xavier stood by the circular metallic cylinder base of the genetic accelerator, inspecting it carefully. An oily residue remained. He brought a drop of it to his nose on the tip of his index finger and sniffed.

"Was this where you perpetrated your crimes? Was this the very fountainhead of all your mischief and deceit?"

He wiped off his finger on his slacks and looked around, his eyes quick to scan every aisle, every corner, every niche, nook and cranny. It had taken him well over an hour to inspect the first two levels. Not a living soul was found thus far. But he would find them all soon enough, and deal with them as necessary. Yes, he'd find them. He felt it in his gut. They were all squirreled away here somewhere. Although, how long his search would ultimately take was impossible to accurately discern. There was no way to know with any sense of certainty how large or intricate the entire complex stretched out, or how deep it was burrowed into the heart of the earth. Its existence was not detailed in any of the ancient records or maps. But it wasn't an infinite expanse. Therefore, it could be systematically searched, no matter how long it took. Besides, he was a very patient and longsuffering soul. That thought made him chuckle softly to himself as he turned to exit the lab.

He stopped short.

Something caught his eye—something out of place in such a pristine and antiseptically tidy environment. He moved a few paces to his left and squatted down near the floor. Lying a few feet away from the metal platform was a hastily discarded pile of clothes, obviously a woman's clothes: a pastel pink short-sleeved cotton blouse, a pair of tan slacks, a basic white under-wire bra, a large pair of waist-high white cotton panties, ankle socks, and a pair of inexpensive tennis shoes.

"An older woman," he muttered to himself, tossing the granny-panties back onto the pile. "But is she older still?" His eyes strayed back to the genetic accelerator platform. "Ooo-la-la, O reckless and foolish one, what have you done here? What evil curse have you managed to unleash?"

Xavier stood up slowly, absorbed in thought. He wouldn't allow himself to believe that he might already be too late.

•

Dr. Else Friedrich felt smug. She had exactly what she wanted.

She had only gone to Dr. Markham's quarters first purely for her own personal convenience, wishing to satisfy the burning hunger simmering inside her with the nearest male she could find. It never even struck her as odd or unnatural why she suddenly felt that way, or why nothing else but her own immediate physical gratification seemed critically important to her very survival. The old doctor's dire display of shock and dismay, peppered with a seemingly endless litany of outraged protestations upon seeing her standing in his doorway, wearing nothing but her wire-rimmed glasses, was nothing short of comical. She laughed in his stricken face and taunted him as she brazenly strode in, pressing into him faster than he could backpedal. He wasn't even physically strong enough to fight her off or push her away. His was the contorted face of a truly tortured man, writhing in confusion, tormented with internal conflict, physically struggling to understand what was happening to him and why.

Else was burdened with no such confusion whatsoever.

She knew exactly what she wanted and was not going to be denied. One vicious full-armed slap was sufficient to buckle his wobbling knees and seat him on his small gel topped bed, whimpering in fear, hands trembling, his left cheek glowing red with the imprint of her hand. He would give her what she wanted or face her wrath. She tore open his belt and trousers, and screamed at him to pull them down over his hips.

Basic biology and physiology told her that in order for her to extract what she wanted from a man of Dr. Markham's advanced years would take a sincere effort on her part to elicit his full and complete participation. In a matter of minutes his half-awakened member was showing early signs of life as her head bobbed up and down over his lap with ravenous speed. When her glasses flipped off and fell to the floor, she ignored it, not missing a beat. Seeing wasn't a priority at the moment, only feeling and tasting and touching. She slowed only briefly upon hearing the pitter-pat of bare footsteps moving up speedily behind her. At the sound of Andrew Duncan's anguished sigh of desire she didn't waste a second before rising up off her knees, lifting her hips, parting her thighs and welcoming the smooth penetrating heat lancing into her from behind—all the while staying true to her initial task for the benefit of the good doctor.

Yes, she was smug, but far from satisfied. Apparently, even her less than willing elder lover on the fore end of her affections found the image before him sufficiently stimulating as Else sensed him wince, his whole body shuddering, and her mouth promptly filled to capacity with his firm engorged flesh, followed a moment later by his pulsing release. The old physician was no longer crying and shaking, but obediently lying still with his eyes half-closed. She knew he would eventually succumb to her wiles, even if his paltry performance proved disappointing. No matter. She had a ready replacement behind her whose powerful penetrations showed no signs of flagging.

•

Jean-Marc Xavier arrived at the staircase landing on level four, the soft leather soles of his hand-tooled alligator shoes padding lightly against the smooth stone floor. Ahead lay a long straight corridor of finely hewn granite, flanked on either side by an even regiment of doorways. He was instantly met by a shrill sound, or better yet, a distinct series of sounds. It was the easily recognizable high-pitched urgent cadence of a woman's whining squeals and moans in the throws of carnal pleasure, chirping in pace with each of her lover's fervent thrusts. He pulled his revolver out of its holster and followed the sound.

Seven doors down on the left, he located the source of the noise. He stepped silently through the doorway. Clothing was strewn on the floor. On a small bed in the corner of the room was a very petite young brunette, lying naked on her back, with her legs lifted high and tightly wrapped around an athletically built black man, also completely nude, who was making furious love to her. They were both oblivious to his presence. It was quite an endearing scene. Jean-Marc stood there silent, studying them for some time, always fascinated by the sight of human sexuality, in all its multitude of forms and fashions. It both saddened and disappointed him to know that indeed, his worst fears had materialized.

It had begun.

But if the only symptom was the frenzy of fornication, and it hadn't spread far, it still might be contained. He tapped the short chromed steel barrel of his gun loudly against the granite doorpost.

"Pardon moi, mademoiselle et monsieur."

The young girl looked to the doorway and screamed. Her gifted lover leaned back in surprise, saw where she was looking and turned to the door as well. The enchantment of their passions instantly evaporated as the two became an awkward tornado of desperate arms and legs, flopping and flailing and struggling to grab articles of clothing and hide from the intruder in the doorway.

"Stop!" Xavier commanded.

They both froze, wide-eyed and frightened, staring at the enormous weapon pointed at them.

Jean-Marc aimed his pistol at Christine's head. "Where is he?"

Paralyzed with fear, the young girl clung to her lover like a frightened kitten.

The young man stammered, "Who?"

"I think you know," Xavier snapped.

"The teacher?"

The barrel swung toward Jason's face. Xavier laughed. "Teacher? Is that what he told you he is? A teacher? And what, pray tell, *mon ami*, has he been teaching you? The wonders of science? Music? Ancient History? Agrarian methods of irrigation and fertilization? Some advanced biology perhaps?" His smile evaporated into a stern malevolent scowl. "Or perhaps he has shared with you...secret things. Forbidden things. Has he promised to make you like the Most High?"

The frightened young man didn't say a word.

Xavier cocked the hammer back with a crisp click. "I won't ask you again, *mon ami*. Where can I find him in this place? I shall give you to the count to three to carefully consider my request."

●

Dr. Markham's waning manhood slipped from Else's bruised and swollen purple lips when she snapped up her head at the sound of two thundering gunshots echoing from the opposite end of the long corridor. Andrew was still in a near hypnotic trance state, his hips slapping in rhythm into her backside.

"Stop," she commanded. Instantly she knew something was desperately wrong. Something dangerous was approaching.

Andrew's eyes came open, looking around, dazed and confused. "What is it? What's wrong?"

Dr. Markham lay absolutely still.

Else pushed Andrew away and stood up, suddenly wondering where her glasses had gone. "Didn't you hear that? I heard shots fired. Nearby. On this level."

Andrew's eyes were still locked on her slender, firm and alluring body. His tongue licked his dry cracked lips. His own appetites were far from satisfied. He stepped closer to her, holding forth his plump erection in his right hand, desperately trying to turn her around with the other hand and let him enter her again.

A menacing shadow fell on them from the open doorway.

Else gasped.

"Who the devil are you?" Andrew snapped.

The figure silhouetted in the doorway spoke not a word.

A wide spray of blood and chunks of cerebral tissue splattered against the far wall an instant after the deafening explosion. Skull fragments ricocheted off the polished stone. A cracked molar accented with a gold filling ticked and scurried along the floor. Andrew Duncan's body convulsed and crumpled to the floor right where he'd been standing, his legs jerking in random spasms, his seed spilling thick on the fine marble tiles in faint pulses of his deflating organ, still clutched tightly in his twitching right hand.

Else fled back against the side wall, pressing her hands against it, fingers splayed wide, eyes bulging, unable to scream or find the courage to run. A warm stream of urine flooded down her legs and radiated into a wide puddle at her feet, the noxious ammonia smell instantly competing with the stench of burned gunpowder, hot oiled brass, and freshly spilled blood. The stranger stepped into the room and pointed the weapon directly in the center of her face.

Else turned her head away, closed her eyes and grit her teeth, bracing for the searing pain about to tear through her, seething, "Please, lord, no."

Silence.

Jean-Marc Xavier released the hammer slowly and lowered his revolver. "Oh, it is you, *cherie*. I did not recognize you. Please forgive me."

Else pried open her eyes, squinted through the blur before her, and suddenly recognized who it was standing before her. She dropped to her knees, pressing her nose and lips to the floor, prostrating herself in the warm pungent wetness puddled all around her. "It is I who beg forgiveness, my lord. A bewitching spirit is loose in this place. It overpowered us all."

"Obviously. Get up," he commanded with a grunt of disgust. "Clean and dress yourself. Our work is far from finished here."

Else did as she was told, finding her wire-rimmed spectacles lying within arms' reach on the floor. She put them on as she slowly rose to her feet, careful to avert her eyes from his, suddenly cold and shivering, chilled to the bone. She hugged her wet forearms protectively to her chest, with both fists tucked tightly under her chin, crouching slightly. The body of Andrew Duncan lay at the foot of the bed. Half his head was missing. She glanced back at Dr. Markham laying on the bed with his trousers and boxer shorts still bunched around his bony shins and ankles, seeing him clearly. His eyes were closed. His jaw hung slack, the tip of his tongue exposed. A long thin string of saliva trailed from the corner of his mouth.

She assumed he'd fainted yet again. "And him?"

Jean-Marc reached over with his free hand and pressed two fingers into

Dr. Markham's throat over his carotid artery. After a few seconds he looked back over to her and shook his head. "No, *cherie*. This one's heart failed him some time ago. He grows cold."

In a revolting wave of realization, Else spun away, gagged, grabbed her gut, bent forward and vomited.

CHAPTER 55

Helen lay safe and secure in his arms, with her cheek resting softly against his slowly rising and falling chest. Her arm was draped across his waist, cuddling close and warm. She had never felt so peaceful, so serene, so completely content in all her life. What fairytale magic was this? Was it all a dream? Would she wake up in the morning, only to find herself transported back to her tiny one-bedroom apartment in New York, only to realize it was all just a fantasy? That was a disconcerting thought. In fact, the very idea angered her. The notion of anything that could steal away or spoil her sublime fantasy was anathema, an enemy to be fought and vanquished.

No, this was real!

At long last, she had found someone who passionately loved her, who worshipped her, someone who ardently adored her as a heavenly goddess, who had found her and given her the precious gift of a whole new life, a new beginning. That was a pleasant thought. That was reality. That was the thought she chose to tenaciously cling to and cherish. That was the thought that had almost lulled her to sleep when he sat bolt upright in alarm.

"What is it?" She sat up beside him, rubbing her eyes and looking around, but seeing nothing amiss.

His eyes darted back and forth. "Something is wrong. Did you hear anything? Sense anything?"

She shook her head, growing afraid. "No. What did you hear?"

Silently he rose from the bed, grabbing his robe and threading his arms through the sleeves. "I felt a tremor, a painful disturbance of energy from afar. Several of them. I fear our friends may be in danger. Come with me."

"How can that be?" Helen demanded, putting on her robe as well, buttoning it up as she followed the teacher. "What danger could anyone face down here?"

The teacher moved toward the doorway of the sleeping chamber in swift strides. "Our companions have nothing to fear in my home. This place is for their learning, for their pleasure and comfort, for their fulfillment and growth. This facility is not the problem. I sense an intruder. A foreign presence."

Helen followed after him. "How could an intruder get in? You said the entire first level was protected with the dragon's breath. If someone even cracked a stone on that level they'd be irradiated and incinerated."

He looked nervous. "We have to get to the main control room immediately. All the sensors and monitoring equipment are there. That is where we will best be protected from any threat, and can deal with any contingency."

Helen stopped in her tracks, grabbing her temples, stilling her breath. "Wait. I can see them."

The teacher spun around, looked at her for a second and then closed his own eyes, concentrating. "I see nothing. What do you see?"

"I see your laboratory. And in it, I see a man, a stranger. I don't recognize him. He is a very tall man, with long white hair, dressed in white slacks and a tan blazer." She gasped. "He has a weapon in his hand, a pistol. He has Else with him. She looks terrified."

"Through whose eyes do you see this?" the teacher demanded.

She stammered, "I...I'm not sure. It's not entirely clear. But why can I see it and not you as well?"

The teacher's agitation was evident. "Because informational energy transfer can be selectively blocked and effectively encrypted or individually addressed as needed or desired."

Helen threw up her hands. "What does that mean?"

He lowered his voice. "It means someone who knows of these things is now among us."

She was aghast. "Who on earth could that be?"

The teacher cast his eyes down, holding his brow in both hands, gritting his teeth. He shuddered in frustration, reluctant to say it out loud, but eventually acknowledging the only viable, logical, inevitable truth. "There is only one. Only one whose energy pattern possesses the indefeasible override codes to all the facilities of my kind."

"Who?" She moved to his side.

His voice faltered ever so slightly, as he took her protectively into his arms and held her close. "My brother."

•

Monsignor Pietro and Francesca Garibaldi were running back up the spiral staircase as fast as they could go, panting, covered in sweat, both from the sheer physical exertion of the climb as well as an ever-growing fear. They had just passed level five. It did not take long inside the great chamber of the small white domes to realize that they had accidentally set in motion the process to open one of them. They had no intention of staying down there and seeing what kind of creature emerged, good or evil.

Upon reaching level four Francesca stopped, shocked by the sight that lay before them in the corridor only a few yards away. The winded priest saw it, too, and winced. Seven doors down, a dark crimson pool of blood had wound its way into the hallway. The meaty stench of slaughter hung heavy in the air. Francesca threw her fingers to her lips and instantly began to weep, her shoulders bobbing up and down with each silent sob. She needn't see what lay in the room to know the gruesome face of death would be found there.

The hall was quiet. Still.

Father Pietro took the girl by the hand and crept down the hallway, toward the puddle of blood. When they reached the open doorway, their worst fears were confirmed. There, inside the small stone cloister, the thick crimson trail led to the shattered body of a nude black man sprawled across a pale blue platform. He was lying motionless on his back. His eyes were half open and fixed. Two grisly entry wounds opened up his chest.

He was alone.

CHAPTER 56

"He has Christine, too!" Helen exclaimed.

The teacher was hurrying toward the stairwell, dragging Helen along behind him by the hand. "Can you sense anything of Jason or Andrew or the doctor?"

"No." She practically had to run to keep up with him. "I see nothing of them. What are you going to do?"

"Defend our lives and our work, of course," he spat back. "We must protect our mission at all costs. My brother is very powerful, and can be very dangerous. But I have had to deal with him many, many times in ages past."

"How powerful is he?" she asked.

"Very powerful but not invincible. And this is my house. He knows not all of its secrets."

•

Jean-Marc Xavier holstered his pistol. Dr. Else Friedrich was dressed again in her black pants and black tee-shirt and hiking boots, but she still reeked of her own bodily fluids commingled with the sour tang of fear sweating through her pores. She glanced at the bulge beneath Xavier's jacket, and discretely whispered as he walked past her. "Don't you need to have that ready when he comes?"

He whispered, "This weapon is only a danger to your mortal flesh, *cherie*, and your little girlfriend's over there." He glanced over at Christine huddled against a rack of equipment. "Not to him. With a single thought, he can accelerate the molecules of the steel to glow white-hot at over two-thousand degrees. His body can absorb small projectiles with very little trauma. It will take much more than a mere handgun to deal with him."

"What are going to do to him when you find him?"

It was Christine's voice interrupting. Barefoot, she now wore only her jeans and tee-shirt, which she was permitted to grab after she saw the tall white-haired stranger shoot Jason twice in the chest and drag her out of her room screaming and crying. It had been nearly impossible to obey his threatening command to keep absolutely quiet when he entered Dr. Markham's room. She did manage to successfully muffle a horrified shriek when he fired his gun in there, shortly before emerging with Else in tow, naked and reeking of piss and puke.

He turned to her, raising his voice, "It is none of your concern, little one. You just sit still and keep looking around the room. Make sure you think and concentrate carefully upon exactly where you are."

Christine suddenly realized, "You're using us as bait. To bring him here to you."

He grinned. "It seemed like a much more efficient idea than wandering all over this grand palace playing hide-and-seek."

"Is he a danger to you?" Else asked.

He shrugged and frowned. "He can be problematic. But he cannot execute me. He doesn't have the power or the authority. Other than myself, it takes at least three of our kind to successfully amass that much energy against one another. And if what I understand he has done is true, he has only himself and the female he has manufactured to help him. And he certainly can't count on her skills yet."

"That sounds like a stalemate to me," Christine noted.

Xavier laughed. "Stalemate? I think not. But your analogy of a chess game is apt. He shall soon find out that with the simple sacrifice of a few pawns, he shall lose his queen. And then it will be checkmate. I have both the authority and the power to terminate his life in this world...which I fully intend to do, once and for all."

•

Francesca's hands were covered with blood. Nevertheless, she kept her head bowed and both palms firmly pressed against the two entry wounds on Jason's chest. The vision was clear in her mind. She saw this man breathing again.

Father Pietro stood watch at the door.

They had walked down the hall and found the other scene of carnage. Two older men were lying there dead. The completely naked one had half his head sprayed all over the walls; the other one, wearing only a button down shirt with his pants pooled at his feet, lay cold and still in a most unflattering display. The old man looked as though he could have died of fright. Father Pietro concluded that there was no way of knowing for certain what vile abominations and sins of the flesh had been perpetrated there as a prelude to this hideous crime. The scene made him nauseas. Francesca had stared mutely at the macabre spectacle with hot tears running down her face, before turning and swiftly making her way back to the slain black man, professing to Father Pietro that only he could be saved.

When Jason coughed, Father Pietro spun around to look at him, not doubting Francesca's word or mysterious powers, but shocked nonetheless witnessing it happen yet again right before his own eyes.

Jason sucked in a tortured gurgling breath and grimaced.

Francesca continued her solemn vigil, never losing skin-to-skin contact with him. A soft white light glowed beneath her touch. A faint sizzling sound crackled through the air, accompanied by the smell of burning meat.

Jason coughed again, loud and strained, retching up a thick metallic tasting mouthful of blood from his collapsed left lung. His whole body felt as if it was on fire. Yet every inch of his skin was dotted with cold beads of sweat. His lungs fought for individual molecules of oxygen, his diaphragm jerking and heaving in frantic spasms. The pain was excruciating. He wanted to scream for mercy, but it wasn't physically possible to make a sound, other than twisted, strangled retching noises.

Francesca began to breath more deeply and with greater frequency.

Over the next few moments, a dull numbness began slowly radiating across Jason's burning chest and seeping around to his back, penetrating his spine. Second by tortured second the agonizing pain began to abate. But he still couldn't breathe until the numbness intensified and then sank deep within him, warming him to his very core, until at last, he was able to take one full breath, and then another, and then another.

He opened his eyes.

Jason looked up into the warm, enchanting olive-skinned face of a beautiful young girl with long black hair leaning over him. There were shimmering tears of compassion in her eyes. He gazed down and saw her palms touching his bare chest, pressed close to his heart. He saw the blood, and then recalled everything that had happened with terrifying clarity.

NO!

He clenched his eyes tight, trying to block out the memory. The horrifying image of the weapon discharging directly at him flashed through his mind, sending an icy shudder racing through his entire body. He honestly thought he could remember seeing the instant the copper projectile left the barrel in the wake of the muzzle flash, speeding straight toward him. She shook his head to clear his mind of the image.

When he opened his eyes a second time he glanced left and then right.

Christine was gone.

Another man he didn't recognize was standing by the doorway. He didn't appear to be armed or look threatening in any way. The stranger's warm blue eyes were sympathetic, filled with concern. The girl lifted her bloodstained hands and smiled down at him. Where he expected to see two large-caliber holes in his sternum, everything looked perfectly normal, save the shiny crimson smears of his own blood.

She's one of them. One of the angels.

•

"We have to get to them and help them," Helen insisted.

"Which is why he has them," the teacher calmly replied.

They were presently on level three, but in a different section of the complex, nowhere near the laboratory. They were standing in what the teacher explained was a Master Control Room, another of his perfect domes, with its stone door tightly sealed. It was not a very large room, but every inch of its floor was covered with neatly arranged concentric circles of equipment. The walls were one contiguous three-hundred and sixty degree view screen. At that moment they were looking at a view of the laboratory through Christine's eyes. The vision blurred at times. Helen realized it was because she was crying. The teacher was intercepting and projecting the cerebral communications signal that had been intended for Helen's reception only, deliberately blocked from his perception. The tall man with the long white hair stood patiently waiting, watching the lab door. Else stood by him, with her arms folded, sweating, sniffling, looking disheveled, nervous and afraid.

"You can't just leave them there!" Helen pleaded.

He adjusted a control. "I don't intend to."

She demanded, "So what are you going to do?"

"I have not yet decided." His frustration was plain in his voice. "But if we just walk in there, they would die anyway, right along with us. My fair queen, understand clearly. He has absolutely no intention of leaving any of us here alive."

"Why?" she demanded, shaking her head in wonder. "Is he that cruel, to murder two innocent girls in cold blood?"

The teacher showed no emotion in his face, but his disdain couldn't be hidden. "He is that determined not to allow that which you now have, and that which your other companions are learning, to spread to others."

"But why?" she demanded.

"Because to him, we are little more than a disease, an epidemic, a pathological plague, a virulent contagion to be contained, quarantined and destroyed, to prevent contamination of others. He takes human life as he sees fit with impunity, as he always has from the very beginning."

"Is he *that* afraid of losing control of all his ignorant minions?"
"No. He is *that* afraid of what this world can become."

CHAPTER 57

The view panel in the laboratory illuminated. It was filled with the anxious face of the teacher, his voice ringing out and echoing through the room. "Welcome to my home, Commander."

Jean-Marc Xavier whipped around and faced the image, smiling broadly, smug and confident, his right eye twitching ever so slightly. "Greetings, my dear sweet brother. It's been a very long time. *N'est pas?* A *very*...long time. I can't wait to embrace you and kiss you again. I happened to be in the neighborhood and decided to drop in and pay you a little visit. I certainly hope you don't mind."

"Not at all," he lied. "You look well. I see you have changed your appearance significantly since last I saw you."

Xavier shrugged. "I like to blend in. And it has become essential to maintain a modicum of privacy and discretion in my affairs. I'm sure you understand. I see your own hair hasn't regenerated yet from your long cold slumber."

The teacher's jaw tightened with every word. "And to what do I owe the pleasure of your visit?"

Xavier dropped the pleasantries, his voice cold and cutting, "You know why I am here, *mon frere.* Why make this more unpleasant than it has to be? You know you are not permitted to be out wandering unsupervised. I tell you, truly, it sincerely pains my heart to have to attend to this errand. But what must be done, must be done."

The teacher smiled. "Yes, but that does not mean I have to be happy about it, nor allow you to succeed unhindered."

Jean-Marc's face contorted. "You would dare oppose my word?"

"Yes, I am afraid, under the circumstances, I must," he replied. "Your time, from the first age to this one is at last passing, just as the house of Pisces gives way to the house of Aquarius in the heavens above. A new era, a new kingdom is upon us. Have you not divined the transition from the stars?"

"A kingdom ruled by you?" Xavier challenged, openly incredulous.

"Yes," came the defiant reply. "A kingdom no longer oppressed and deceived by you and your armies of mind-numbed fanatical sycophants, misinformed historians, and crusading mercenary tyrants."

Xavier laughed. "Is that what you think of all my precious followers and worshipers, great leaders, thinkers, clerics, mystics, and philosophers? I'm sure they would be most offended to hear of such disparaging talk, especially from you. But who is the deceiver here? What have you told them, brother? What have you offered them in bribes? Have you promised them untold riches and honors and adventures and great powers? Have you taken them to the pinnacle of the temple and offered them dominion of the entire planet?"

"I have only told them the truth," said the teacher.

"The truth?" Jean-Marc walked closer to the image. "What truth? Whose truth? Your truth? The whole truth? I think not." He huffed in disgust. "What *is* truth? Surely you told them of your great and glorious vision of the future, if they would but taste of the empowering essence of our kind. Yes? But did you remember to tell them of everything that really happens when our two kinds become one flesh, or when the evil you implanted in them awakens? Did you tell them of the monsters that will arise, all the hideous fiends intent upon unconscionable abominations, creatures who eagerly lust to eat their flesh, to become drunk on their blood, to gnaw on their bones for pure pleasure and sport? Did you tell them how your foolhardy ambitions set in motion the very extinction of their species?"

"I told them plainly of the mutations of the first generational experiments, yes," he declared. "They understand completely. And they also understand that those anomalies have been corrected. The code was refined. The defects have been eradicated. The new species stands ready to take its rightful place of dominion and advancement. Even you cannot stop it this time."

Xavier shook his head in wonder. "Is that so? You're unbelievable. You deceive not only them, but even yourself, to this very day. I have to tell you, all things considered, I am profoundly shocked, and flatly dismayed beyond measure by you. After all this time. After all you've seen and watched." He stopped, his voice softening, appealing to the image on the screen with genuine sincerity and candor. "Have you never understood the real truth, little brother, after so many generations have passed? I've admitted it. I've learned to deal with it and to accept it. Why can't you? What we did in league so long ago, you and I, to suit our own purposes, was a terrible mistake. It was an atrocity, a travesty beyond measure."

The teacher fired back, "You believe mankind was a mistake?"

Xavier lowered his eyes. "Yes. I am sorry we made them. Rather than let the Law of the Divine work in the humble creatures of this world in its own good time, to advance them naturally, gradually, maturing their ability to manifest their energies in step with their mental development, we cheated them. We sinned against nature. We sinned against these poor creatures. We sinned against the will of the divine. We put within their reach that which they were incapable of possessing and mastering." He reached into his jacket and pulled out his revolver. "It was no different than placing one of these in the hands of a small child. Only tragedy could come of it. Why can't you accept the truth and take responsibility for the consequences? I have."

The teacher shouted back, "No! You are wrong! Perhaps in the very beginning it was as you say. But not now. Although, you are correct on one other point. I did watch. I did see. They have grown. They have changed. They are ready! I am certain they are prepared to advance."

"You're mad. They are still the same primitive warring aboriginal tribes and clans we found here living in caves, scurrying about in the bushes, and swinging from the trees almost half a million years ago." Jean-Marc smirked. "They only dress nicer now, and their mastery of electricity has enabled them to play with better toys. All else is background noise and clutter."

"How would *you know* what they are capable of now?" the teacher countered. "You have spent your whole life on this planet benefiting from the sweat of their brows, living in the temples they build for your comfort, eating the fruits of their harvests and savoring their sweet sacrifices, thriving on their misguided adoration, pleasuring yourself with the tender virtues of their fair daughters, subjugating their entire species as nothing more than asses, sheep, camels and cattle!"

"No!" Xavier shouted back. "I took responsibility for them. I have loved them as my very own children, and disciplined them in my love. I had mercy upon them, despite your treachery. I have cared for them throughout the ages and instructed them in ways to protect and preserve them. I have sided in battle with those who loved me, and opposed and vanquished those who hated me. But most importantly, I kept them safe from that with which you poisoned them, that which you deliberately did against my direct and most explicit orders. And if you recall, this is what resulted in your eternal incarceration, from which I see you've somehow managed to extricate yourself."

"Poisoned?" the teacher was appalled. "You call enabling direct access to the divine *poison*? It is you who are deluded. I gave them new life. I gave them the opportunity to be all that we are, and much more."

No, brother!" Xavier shouted back. "You put a curse on them. And you filled them with false hope."

"*I* filled them with false hope?" It was the teacher's turn to shake his head in dismay and throw up his hands. "It is *you* who have crafted and perpetuated the myth of some ethereal paradise in the clouds, where all their tears are dried, a land flowing with milk and honey, where the streets are paved with gold, where sins are judged and washed away, and eternal rewards abound. Do not lecture me, Commander, about instilling false hope."

"A pleasant fiction is not without a measure of comfort..." Jean-Marc whispered. "...a tender mercy to the grieving."

"Fiction indeed! If your pleasure is in the truth, then tell them the truth! Tell them what really happens to them when you extinguish the energy of their spirits from their flesh, as you have done to untold millions of them without remorse!"

Xavier said nothing more, standing there fuming at the image on the screen, his back teeth grinding tight.

Else found her voice. "What's he talking about?"

Jean-Marc turned to her, forcing a smile firmly in place, despite the seething invective of his voice. "What is he talking about? Why, he wants to reveal to you the mystery of the ages. The great riddle. You know it? No?"

Else held a blank look on her face.

He laughed. "He's talking about the consequences of death, *cherie*. The other side. Oh yes. The final mystery of what really happens to your kind when your days are at their end, your journey is over, and it is at last your turn to run down the curtain and join the choir invisible!"

"What happens?" she whispered meekly.

His eyes narrowed, "Do you really want to know?"

"Yes," she replied.

"*Bist du sicher*[25]?" he asked. "*Wolst du eigentlich alles wissen?*[26]"

"*Ja*," she insisted.

"No, Else, don't say another word!" Christine shrieked.

"Then your wish is my command, *cherie*," he replied, leveling his revolver in the center of her chest and pulling the trigger.

Christine screamed.

---

[25] German: "Are you sure?"
[26] German: "Do you really want to know everything?"

CHAPTER 58

"Turn it off. Turn it off now!" Helen spun away from the ghastly image of death splashed across the walls of the master control room.

Else's body lay in a thick pool of blood radiating from the exit wound in her back. Her eyes remained frozen open in horror, staring up at the ceiling.

She grimaced. "He's a monster."

The teacher depressed a control, causing the images on the walls to vanish. "You are not the first to make that observation."

"What can we do?" she asked. "Can we fight him?"

He nodded, "Yes, but the outcome is uncertain with only two of us. Oh, if there were but three of us, we could command his energy to be obedient to the force of triangulation." He gave a half-laugh. "Then, we could lock *him* in cryostasis for the next thousand years!"

"Might I be of service, O merciful and mighty Lord Ptah?"

The words were not uttered in English nor any other contemporary language, rather they were spoken in a strange, ancient tongue, a lost speech from a long forgotten time. Yet amazingly, Helen understood it perfectly.

In genuine surprise, both the teacher and Helen turned in unison toward the strange voice coming from the doorway. There stood another of the teacher's kind, tall and muscular, bald, with pale blue skin, still glistening with an oily residue coating his nude body.

The teacher exclaimed in the same foreign language of the unexpected stranger, "Azazel! You are free!"

•

"Who are you?" Jason rasped, his breathing still labored and painful. His pectoral muscles across his chest were stiff and sore. It was difficult to believe, and nearly impossible to accept, what had just happened to him. If nothing else, he was profoundly grateful to be alive.

Monsignor Pietro helped him stand up to get his jeans back on as Francesca supported his arm draped over her shoulders. The priest replied in fluent English, "I am Monsignor Paulo Pietro, in service of the Sacred Order of the Eternal Light."

"Pleased to meet you. And…who is this amazing young lady to whom I owe my life?" Jason offered her a warm smile, which she returned with a shy nod and a cheerful grin, not understanding a word he was saying.

Pietro introduced Francesca. "This is Francesca Garibaldi from Sulmona, Italy. As you have just witnessed, and obviously experienced personally, she is one who has been richly blessed with a tremendous gift of God, a gift which we came here to Egypt to learn about more perfectly."

Jason chuckled. "You came to the right place."

"You know of such powers?" the priest pressed.

Jason nodded, "Oh, yes. And more. So much more. But you need to speak with the master of this house if you really want to know how it all works."

"And who is the master of this house?" Pietro located Jason's high-topped tennis shoes and helped slip them on and tie them for him as they talked.

"You wouldn't believe me if I told you," he replied as he sat back down on the side of the bed, wincing as he moved, still feeling very weak and lightheaded.

The priest finished the first shoe. "You might be surprised at what I am willing to believe. Did he give you his name?"

"No." Jason rambled quickly. "He is only known as our teacher. It's hard to fathom, and you may think I'm completely crazy, but we believe he's…uh…like, some kind of an advanced being that we discovered a few days ago locked in an ancient chamber beneath the desert in Saudi Arabia. From what we could tell, he had been cryogenically frozen for a few thousand years. We freed him, thawed him out, and he woke up. The site in Saudi was attacked and destroyed, and so he brought us here in an invisible ship sitting right now on the back of the Sphinx, claiming this facility here in Egypt was his home, which he also tells us was built long before the dynasties of the Pharaohs."

Pietro said nothing.

Jason paused. "Ok, don't look at me like that. I know, it all sounds like a total crock of shit, but it's what happened. I swear to God."

Pietro nodded, "Yes, yes. What you say is undoubtedly true. I do not question the veracity of your word. In fact, I may be able to help perfect your own understanding. This *being* you have found…he is one of the ancient of days. One of the earliest known deities on the planet, one of the last remaining of the Nephilim, part of the original landing party of interplanetary colonists to reach earth almost half a billion years ago. If you found him bound beneath the Arabian desert, and he claims this was his home, then you have discovered none other than the one who the earliest Egyptians called their great god Ptah, the father of Amen-Ra and Thoth."

Jason blinked. "His name is Ta?"

The priest elaborated, "Yes, spelled P-T-A-H. But to the early Mesopotamians in Sumer and Akkad, where he first settled on the banks of the Euphrates River in Eridu, he was called EA, or Lord of the Earth. He was also called the God of Seven, as in lord of the seventh planet, meaning Earth, as seen when entering the solar system from the direction of Pluto. To the early Greeks, he was their god Aquarius, the water bearer, to the Romans, Neptune, the god who rises up from the waters, though it is not entirely clear why he was called that."

Jason recalled the sensation of the shuttle craft soaring up from the depths of the Indian Ocean into the sky. "I think I have an idea."

"Really?" The priest went on, "In any event, he was the colonists' chief scientist and supreme technology officer. A brilliant and creative mind, primarily focused on biology and engineering, but reputed to be not as politically savvy as his older brother or even his own sons and nephews."

"How do *you know* so much about him?" Jason was astounded.

"There are a remnant of us among men of many faiths who know the truth, who have always known the truth for thousands of years, and are sworn to guard it well." Pietro was inwardly thankful that Francesca didn't speak a word of English and couldn't understand the conversation.

"But why?" Jason didn't understand. "Why would you keep such valuable and important knowledge hidden?"

The priest let out a long sigh. "A very good question. And one that I have been asking myself of late with no small measure of guilt and regret...and dismay. But the simple answer is, it was kept hidden by the direct order of he who vanquished all the other of his kind ages ago, in the dawn of our time. He who reigns supreme over the destiny and fate of men. As to *why*...it was hidden to prevent the horrid catastrophe and devastation of the Nephilim, or the Watchers as they were called, from ever being repeated on earth."

"The Watchers? The fallen angels?" Jason asked. "The ones who mated with early human women?"

"Yes. The Nephilim, the ones who came down from the heavens to the earth, the colonists," the priest explained. "They were the subordinates as well as the families of Ptah, his sister Ninmah, and his older brother, Supreme Commander Enlil. However, the rampant fornication and resultant barbarism became more than a mere social scandal or moral crisis. It was an atrocity beyond measure in the annals of time. You see, the offspring of the sons of the gods—"

"Were gruesome mutations," Jason interrupted. "Yes, I understand. He told us all about that."

Pietro looked surprised. "Truly? He told you of the great slaughters? The human sacrifices and cannibalism? The congenital disease of vampirism and the cults of blood festivals? The werewolves and changelings? The goblins and trolls? The great Cyclops and the Minotaur? All the other monsters? Surely, he didn't tell you the details of the dragons that were birthed, clawing their way out of their human mother's wombs and feasting on their flesh while still screaming in their labor travails?"

Jason swallowed hard, his eyes growing wide. "Uh...no. He must have left that part out."

CHAPTER 59

Azazel, the great warrior of the Nephilim, embraced his lord enthusiastically, both of them shedding warm tears of joy. He kissed both his master's cheeks and declared in his own language, "My great and gracious Lord Ptah. I never thought these aged eyes would see your precious face again, nor hear your voice, nor embrace you in my arms."

"Nor I," confessed the teacher. "I had no idea you were here in this facility. How were you released?"

Azazel shrugged. "I know not. I emerged from cryostasis as usual, and came here to the command center forthwith. The rest of your closest men are still in cryostasis below, Samiazaz, Tameil, Danel, Ezeqeel, Turel, and the rest of your officers. They only await your command to be released."

"We shall attend to them presently," the teacher assured his old general. "But an imminent crisis is upon us, and it is clear that the will of mother fate herself has brought you to my side once again for us to face it together."

"What is your command, Lord?" the warrior asked.

"Enlil is here," the teacher informed him.

Azazel took a step back, his face filled with alarm. "Commander Enlil is *here*? How many legions are with him? Has he the Forked Lightning in his hand?"

"Calm down," the teacher said. "You and I, and the goddess Helen here, shall confront him."

It was only then that the stranger took special notice of Helen. He gasped. "My Lord Ptah, I am overwhelmed. Who is this incomparable creature? Her beauty is beyond that of the great Isis herself. Is she yours, Lord, or may I lay with her?"

The teacher smiled in the wake of Helen's shocked expression. "She is mine, and not to be touched by any, by my word. She is your queen, Azazel, and you shall worship and honor her as such."

The naked warrior immediately prostrated himself on the floor, repenting with great deference and an avalanche of apologies. "A thousand pardons, my divine lady. I am your good and faithful servant."

Helen didn't know what to say. She just stared down at the stranger with a blank look on her face.

"Get up, General Azazel," the teacher commanded. "And listen to me carefully. I would not have you to awaken after so long a sleep only to see your life extinguished on that same day."

The obedient general respectfully rose and bowed his head. "As you command."

"Helen, my love," he instructed. "Draw near, and listen as well. All of our lives may depend upon your courage, your cunning and your strength."

Helen stepped closer, noticing how their new visitor humbly refrained from looking her directly in the eye. She took the teacher by the hand and told him simply, "I want to know."

"Fear not. I shall explain everything you need to do," he assured her.

"No," she stopped him. "I mean, I want to know about Else, of her fate. You challenged your brother to speak the truth about death. Of what happens to them when they die. She died seeking the answer to that question. You obviously know. Tell me what happens. Tell me the truth."

Azazel lifted his face, staring at the teacher with a look of confused apprehension. "She does not know?"

The teacher shook his head. "Before this day, she was one of the workers. I have purified her and transformed her entire being after our own image and likeness." He looked at Helen and gave his assent. "Yes, you may know the truth, my love. But you may not like all of what you are about to hear, for it may sadden your heart with respect to Else and others you have cared for in your life."

A nervous chill washed over Helen. "I want to know."

"Very well." He took a deep breath. "As I hope by now you have come to understand, the energy of sentient life is the most powerful force in the universe. It contains the sum of all forces of which it is a part. Verily, the tremendous velocity and inertia of the galaxies themselves are imputed to it and are a function of it. As I explained to you before, your very soul, that sentient energy which animates the vehicle of your body, functions either in the dark or the light. Your sentient energy is either polarized toward the light in concert with the Law of Creation, or diametrically polarized toward the force of the darkness, in concert with the Law of Entropy. This is not merely an abstract concept or philosophy, but an electromagnetic physical reality."

"Go on," Helen urged. "I understand so far."

He continued, "When physical biological processes cease, the life energy within the vehicle begins to dissipate, to literally be conducted out of the vessel, much akin to a capacitor in your science of electronics, transferring and releasing its power one cell at a time, discharging its energy from the individual intercellular mitochondria, vectored along the biochemical synaptic conductors of nerve endings to a reservoir in the cerebral cortex of the brain, which is often perceived by the deceased as a bright light drawing them near. In the first five or six minutes of death, little energy is lost and life can be retained if the vehicle is repaired quickly enough. Up to seventy hours after physical death the energy is in a stasis transformation condition, aligning itself magnetically according to its polarity within the cerebellum, assuming it is intact. If no reanimation occurs of the vehicle, or the cerebellum itself is destroyed, the energy is then permanently released."

"Just released?" she asked. "Like smoke from an exhaust pipe, diffusing into the atmosphere?"

"No," he replied. "That is why polarization is so important. Entropic polarized energy is either grounded, or it is merged with a sentient receptor."

"What does that mean?" She didn't like the sound of that.

"It means that it is either discharged into the earth itself, like any other electrical current, and effectively becomes inert, trapped and imprisoned, although it is still sentient and aware of its condition. Or it is collected by another entropic entity and assimilated, which through the ages of time, has become much more commonly the case."

"Assimilated?" Helen was starting to tremble again.

He nodded. "Every tale you have ever heard about creatures who seek to claim and collect souls, to actually feed upon them, to grow stronger in their destructive goals are shadows of this truth."

She felt a pang in her heart. "And those creatively polarized? Creatures of the light?"

"Their energy is discharged into the heavens." He lifted a hand upward. "Literally broadcast as a complex energy signal and translated into the physical architecture of the universe itself, to be one with the collective of all knowledge, all recorded engram patterns, all creativity, woven into the very living fabric of the divine of which we speak."

"And those are the only choices?" she was dismayed.

"Ultimately, yes," he said. "There is the odd, albeit rare, manifestation of mixed or neutral polarity. This is where a life's energy leaves its vehicle, but with insufficient polarization and is therefore temporarily neither grounded, collected and assimilated, nor translated. It happens more often when death comes tragically and violently, or restrained by the powerful personal desire to satisfy an unfulfilled purpose, or both. As strange as it may seem, many of these unfortunate souls simply fail to fully acknowledge the reality of their own deaths, caught in a state of psycho-logical denial in some cases, where the soul attempts to continue to function in life, albeit without its physical body. Sometimes they succeed for a time."

"Disembodied spirits?" she asked.

He nodded, "Yes. A miserable condition for any soul. But one where events typically sort out a final resolution of polarity over time, one way or another."

Helen tried to smile. "So there's no reincarnation to give them another try, if they don't get their polarity right in life the first time?"

"Reincarnation is a simple confusion over engram echoes," he said matter-of-factly. "It is merely an instance where a soul perceives the mem-ories of a distant life's energy, or many lives for that matter, picking up broadcast signals echoing through the fabric of space. This is where the soul erroneously believes that these memories are their own. It is a com-mon mistake. But the truth is, you only get one life of flesh, one opportunity to draw into the light, amplify your energy, and polarize your soul to become one with the spirit of creation itself."

"Is that true for both humans and your kind?" Helen asked. "You said before that immortality is organic, but you can be killed."

The teacher answered, "When those of my kind, which now includes you as well, meet our last day, the creative energy we have amassed over what can often be millions of years can be so great, that when we join the fabric of the universe, it is a spectacularly cataclysmic and visible event. It is a great and violent occasion, a celebration of celestial birth pangs. It is a succinct new act of creation unto itself."

And she suddenly understood. "The birth of a star. A new system of life, where it all begins again and again."

The teacher chuckled softly. "Yes. Exactly. Did you never notice that our entire universe is predominantly made up of circles and ellipses? That is by design. The circle of life is that which has no beginning and no end, where the alpha and omega are one, eternally orbiting and returning to the same orbits and destinies it has always traveled, expanding and contracting in an eternal dance."

"Yes," she whispered, staring off in thought. "I understand. It's so simple." She paused in awe. "I don't think I shall ever look at the heavens again in the same way. But tell me, is a soul's energy still completely sen-tient, fully conscious and aware, even after it is discharged or transformed?"

"Oh, yes. Very much so. The only thing a soul gets to take with it in death are its memories, its collection of engrams. It is the only true treasure worth having. It is such a pity more souls fail to place a higher priority on creating precious memories than striving for perishable commodities, placation of the appetites, or temporal positions of privilege and power. This is also why true seers and high priests seek to develop the skill of listening to the stars, and heeding the accumulated wisdom of their ancient voices, and not merely charting their alignments and paths." The teacher grinned, "But today is not the day I wish to give birth to my star." His smile faded. "That privilege, if at all possible, I wish to reserve for my dear brother."

That snapped Helen out of her mild daze. "You intend to kill him?"

"If I must." The teacher closed his eyes. "He leaves me with very little alternative."

Azazel stood tall and at the ready. "Command us, my lord. Only give the word and tell us what we must do."

The teacher looked lost in thought for a moment. "Indeed I shall. But first there is something important I must do, and must do alone." He started to leave the room.

"Where are you going?" Helen called after him.

He smiled back at her. "To make final preparations for all contingencies. And to procure the tools we need to do what must be done."

The teacher knew his errand wouldn't take long. He quickly reached the weapons storage chamber on level two. What took some time was getting through all the intricate security systems to unlock the shielded vault that contained the cache of small delicate golden batons. He extracted two more in addition to the one already in his possession, and was about to leave, but hesitated. There was one more important task of preparation to be done. He didn't want to do it, but knew it was the only way to ensure success.

Alone and in secret, with a heavy heart filled with apprehension, he knelt down on the floor, clasped his hands together, reverently bowed his head, closed his eyes, and established a high-frequency energy connection to the living, sentient fabric of the universe.

CHAPTER 60

"I'm not really sure who it was that attacked us."

As the three walked together, Jason still felt stiff from his neck to his waist, but he was breathing much easier. Emotionally, he was completely numb, half from his struggle to accept the reality of the horrible events that had just befallen him, and half from seeing for himself first-hand what had become of poor Dr. Markham and what was left of Andrew Duncan.

"It all happened so quickly. It was crazy. I was with one of the members of our group, a young woman I had only met this week. Someone very unique. Special. Her name was Christine." Recalling her name caused Jason to fade into a momentary daze. He blinked, and gathered his thoughts. "Uh...one second we were just talking about everything that had happened. The next second we're all over each other making love, like animals in heat. It was like nothing I've ever experienced. I mean, I completely lost control and couldn't stop myself, and her right along with me. It was like we both had OD'd on catnip or Spanish Fly. And then the next thing I know, this tall guy is there looming over us, with this Godzilla piece of firepower in his hand, apparently looking for the teacher, and he suddenly starts shooting. I still can't imagine how he got in here." Jason stopped and frowned with a sudden realization. "Come to think of it, how did *you* guys get in?"

Father Pietro smiled. "We followed you from the village down into the pyramid, and through the open door in the lower chamber."

Jason seethed in a penitent breath. "Oh, shit. I bet I forgot to close it. He warned me about that. That's probably how the other guy got in too."

"I don't think so," the priest said. "We were right behind you, and the door closed tight as soon as we came through. Your assailant must have had his own means of entry."

"I hope so," Jason replied. "I'd hate to think that all of this is my fault."

Father Pietro and Francesca stayed close to Jason as they ascended the stairs from level four to level three. The monsignor translated a synopsis of his conversation with Jason into Italian for Francesca's benefit. She only grew more and more visibly worried as they went along. They stopped at the third level landing, hugging close to the wall.

The priest discretely lowered his voice to library/church level as he peered down the quiet empty corridor. "But you didn't see this man harm the young woman?"

Jason shook his head, whispering, "No. I lost consciousness after I was shot. I don't know what he did to her. I'm hoping he just took her somewhere here in the complex and hasn't hurt her in any way."

But he means to hurt her, Jason.

"How do you know that?" Jason asked Pietro.

"How do I know what?" he replied.

"That he means to hurt her."

Father Pietro looked puzzled, "What are you talking about?"

Jason looked at the priest like he was crazy. "I said I hoped he wouldn't hurt her, and then you said, no, he means to hurt her."

"I said nothing of the kind," the priest denied.

Jason looked around, "Well, if you didn't say it, who did?"

I did, Jason. You must hear me. Please. All will be lost if you don't listen to me now, and listen carefully. My time is short.

Jason spun around, seeing no one but Father Pietro and Francesca with him, both of them staring at him as though he had lost his mind.

And then he saw it.

There, a few feet away, tucked back in a recessed alcove directly across from where they were standing was a familiar shape, a seemingly human shape, with a head, shoulders, arms, a torso, but fading out below the waist. It appeared to be made of a cloudy mist or moist fog, not entirely solid or stable, shimmering ever so slightly in the dimness of the light. A delicate fibrous web of silver lightning flashes gently rippled up and down it. The face, although somewhat obscured in shadow, was unmistakably that of Andrew Duncan.

•

The teacher handed both Helen and Azazel a golden baton identical to the one he held in his own hand, the same one he had used to deal with the two intruders in the astronomy gallery of the Rub Al Khali facility. Helen turned hers over several times in her hands, inspecting it carefully, somewhat surprised at how light it felt. She wondered if perhaps it was hollow.

The teacher explained to Helen, "This device is an energy accelerator. It works along the same lines as the staged lenses of one of your industrial lasers, that is, focusing and amplifying an energy source toward a defined point. It has many applications from a simple architectural cutting tool to a terrible weapon of great force. Today we must use it to deal with my brother."

Helen turned it over in her hands, fascinated by it. "If it's used to cut or to destroy, then it can't be creative energy you're focusing."

Azazel remained silent, looking uncomfortable.

The teacher nodded. "Astute observation. Which is why these devices are carefully guarded and rarely used. The energy source that must be conducted through these devices is entropic energy. It is very dangerous."

She looked him in the eye. "So must we avail ourselves to the darkness and not the light to use it?"

"No, not literally," he clarified. "The words darkness and light are metaphoric, referring to antithetically polarized electromagnetic concepts. Here we are talking about harnessing an incredibly destructive force, like humans have done with the process of nuclear fission. For us to be successful, we must create a field of harmonic resonance to that destructive force, much akin to a high-pitched sound wave harmonizing with the crystalline wave structure of glass and shattering it. In this case the goal will be to pool that force and create a barrier than Enlil cannot breach."

Azazel spoke up, adding, "We must physically surround him. The three points of harmonic discharge will create a triangulation field. Anything inside the field cannot escape it. Anything outside the field cannot penetrate it."

Helen frowned. "It repels matter?"

Azazel shook his head, "No, my queen, it vaporizes it, assimilating any available energy therein."

Helen was trying to picture this function in her head. An image immediately appeared in her mind's eye of a sphere of blue light marbled with red veins and tendrils of white hot electric discharges. "And can this field be defeated?"

The teacher answered, "Only if one of us falters. If so, then the field will collapse on two sides."

"Then we best not falter," she said. "And what do we do after we capture him inside this field?"

The teacher's tone dropped. "We diminish the field's internal volume. We come together until that which is within it has been destroyed."

"Show me how it is done," she said.

The teacher nodded and held his baton in front of him. "You must first clear your mind of all thoughts, save the necessity to be a conduit, a conductor of power. You hold the device in both hands, thusly." With his hands clasped together like a child in prayer, he held the baton in its middle with his thumbs wrapped over it, his fingers tightly interlaced below it, positioning it across his hands horizontally. "As Azazel and I do the same, you will become sensitive to the growing power near you. Your only thought, without distraction, must be to harmonize with the power, to let it resonate within you, and then to let it flow forth, like breathing in and breathing out."

"Can we practice it?" she asked. "Here, right now?"

Azazel concurred. "I think that is a wise idea."

The teacher shot his old friend a look of assurance. "Indeed. Although, I am confident that our queen will require very little practice to master the art. Go ahead, Helen. Try it by yourself. Get a feel for the energy flowing through you. It is important that you are completely comfortable with its operation before we attempt to wield it together as a group."

Helen held up the baton in both hands as instructed. She faced it toward a metal cabinet a few yards away. The simple thought of *RELEASE* flowed through her mind. With a loud crackle and a violent hiss two blinding white forks of lightning leapt from each end of the golden wand, engulfed the cabinet, bleaching out everyone's vision for an instant. She lowered the baton, blinked twice to allow her vision to clear, and looked upon a smoldering pile of white ash that stood where the cabinet once did.

The teacher applauded, "Well done."

She addressed him, "Why can't we just destroy him like that?"

"Because of the design of the weapon," he replied holding up his own baton. "He has one of these too, and I would be genuinely surprised if it is not with him at all times. The fact that it splits its power into two distinct discharges is from whence it gets its name, the Forked Lightning. When two devices are present, it is made to form a parallel cutting field, originally intended for cleaving metal or to sculpt large stones."

"Like the ones here in this facility?" she asked.

He said, "Surely you do not believe the great stones of our architecture were hewn with a mere hammer and chisel."

Helen smiled. "From what I understand, no one knows precisely how many great stones of antiquity were fashioned."

"Now you know," said the teacher.

Azazel pointed out, "The function of the two separate discharges is also why it is important to grasp the device firmly in the center, leaving the electrodes of both ends exposed. When a third device is present, the energy is automatically linked between the points of a triangle thus formed, allowing the two forks to align with the other two adjacent points."

"And if there are more than three devices present?" she asked Azazel.

He added, "Then you achieve more complex geometric configurations, but the same effect. The fact that the device has a maximum impact range of only a few hundred yards sometimes necessitates the use of many points to contain a larger area."

A thought suddenly occurred to her. "So what happens if he decides to join the configuration?"

The teacher nodded, deftly spinning the golden baton from a starting point on one end, rotating it over the back of his hand to a well-practiced and familiar grip in the middle. "That is why our task must be done before he realizes it is happening and can respond in kind. The triangular configuration must happen simultaneously. Otherwise he could indeed join the configuration and thus thwart our attack. Our advantage is my faithful Azazel here. Enlil undoubtedly has no knowledge of his release from cryostasis. Nor does he know that you are capable of opposing him in league with us. As usual, he will arrogantly believe that I alone am his nemesis. We shall also enjoy the element of surprise in our attack. It is his overconfidence in himself and underestimation of my resources that shall be his ultimate undoing."

Helen stepped back a few paces from the teacher and Azazel, grasping her golden baton in the middle with both hands once more. "All right. Let's try it together."

CHAPTER 61

"Why did you do that!" Christine shrieked. "Why did you kill her!"

The snub-nosed muzzle of the 357 magnum rose and swiveled in her direction, its menacing maul leveled directly at her face. Christine stood defiant. Jean-Marc Xavier tilted the gun on its side, his gaze piercing over the back of his hand. Neither of them blinked. Christine didn't breathe.

Xavier withdrew the gun with a playful grin, shoving it back in its well-worn holster beneath his jacket. "She wanted to know what lies on the other side. Now she knows. That's why."

"You murdered her," she spat.

"No, I saved her," he contradicted, "from a much worse fate. Don't mourn for her. Her life force was not without value. She was a good and faithful servant, for as long as I required her service. Without her assistance I certainly wouldn't have found you so quickly."

Christine was aghast. "She worked for you? As a spy?"

"I have eyes and ears everywhere, *cherie*." He was smug. "I see what I want to see. I know what I want to know."

"You intend to kill us all," she flatly accused him. "Don't you."

He shrugged. "As I said, I must do what must be done. You, along with any others who have been exposed to him, are a grave danger, to yourselves and to this world. Don't misunderstand. I take no pleasure from your suffering. And I am not without mercy. When your time comes, it will be quick."

"Why do you have to do this?" She was crying.

He bit his lower lip before answering. "Because even now, whether you realize it or not, you are being corrupted. You are being seduced, both physically as well as intellectually and emotionally. When I found you, rutting like rodents if I recall, it was clear the degeneration process has already begun."

Christine was suddenly perplexed. "What are you talking about? What degeneration?"

He leaned back against one of the metal tables. "I'm talking about tremendous forces locked within you that require enormous restraint and discipline and maturity and mastery to be wielded without extreme danger. Your kind has never successfully possessed this inherent ability, and I seriously doubt it ever will. At least not for millions of years. What my brother has fervently sought to unleash in your kind since the very beginning was that which was capable of destroying your entire species. It very nearly happened, and would have, had I not stopped it in time."

She scowled, "You mean you almost succeeded in your genocide plot with the Flood if it hadn't been for the one family he saved from your destruction."

He laughed. "Is that what he told you? He is the father of lies, you know. It was I who spoke to Ziusudra[27], or Utnapishtim[28], or the patriarch you call Noah from the Hebrew texts, warning him to save himself from the coming deluge, to build the watertight ship from available materials, to gather the menagerie, to secure his family, to save a seed of human life for the future."

"I don't believe you," she said.

"I didn't ask you to," he snapped, sending forth a terse spray of spittle. "I only require your compliance for the time being. Then you will know the truth, little girl, and which one of us is lying."

Little girl?

Christine's fear was being slowly eclipsed by a simmering anger. It was palpable in the back of her throat and twisting through her bowels. If she was going to die soon, then she resolved not to stand around like a lamb led to slaughter. She was determined to find a way to fight back, to do something, to react, to respond, no matter how futile the effort was. The presence of this creature repulsed her. She imagined him reaching out to touch her, and even the very thought of him laying a hand on her almost erupted from her mouth in a thundering scream. She glanced down at her bare forearm, to the exact spot where she pictured him trying to grab her if she made a run for it. One single thought scorched through her mind: *let nothing touch me.*

And then it happened.

Her arm began to swell and stretch in the place where she was looking, and then it vanished before her eyes.

At that same moment Jean-Marc was staring intently at the doorway of the laboratory—waiting, watching. He turned back to say something else to Christine.

She was gone.

His eyes frantically scanned the room as he reached behind his back

---

[27] The Sumerian name for the hero of the great flood.
[28] The Akkadian name for the hero of the great flood.

and withdrew a golden baton, holding it in the middle with both hands. "Oh, my petite mouse. Where have you crept off to? Come out, come out, wherever you are!"

•

Hot tears streamed down Jason's face, dripping from his chin. He reached out for the smoky mist in the alcove that was slowly fading away. "Andrew, I don't know if I can do it."

You have to. There is no other choice.

"What if it doesn't happen that way?"

It will. And you need to be prepared when it does.

"Does she know?"

No. She doesn't. And you won't have the opportunity to tell her. You must be prepared to do what you have to or all will perish.

"And if I fail?"

The apparition faded away without another word. Jason slowly turned around to face the horrified priest and confused young Italian girl clinging to his arm.

Pietro stammered, "He must be wrong. These things cannot be."

"You saw and heard for yourself," Jason sniffed and wiped his blood-shot eyes. "That wasn't special effects. Honest to God."

"It's madness," the priest muttered, clinging even tighter to Francesca.

"What's madness?" came Christine Jacob's urgent voice as she materialized standing next to Jason, just finishing a stride.

Jason's initial paralysis and shock at seeing Christine appear out of thin air lasted only a moment before he reached out and swept her into his arms, crushing her tightly against him, his tears running freely again amid spastic sobs. "Oh, my God, you're alive. Thank God you're alive."

Pietro and Francesca both gasped and backpedaled at this new apparition appearing before them.

"No, no, it's OK," Jason assured them with an outstretched palm, sensing their fear and seeing the look of fright on their faces. "She's real flesh and bone, all of her. I swear. This is the woman I was with when I was attacked. The one that I told you about. She's one of us." He leaned back, holding Christine by the shoulders and looking down into her eyes. "Oh, thank God you got away and you're OK." He smiled, "And...I take it you've learned a few of the teacher's tricks."

She leaned her cheek into his chest and shuddered. "And not a moment too soon. We have to find Helen and the teacher and get out of here. That maniac back there intends to kill all of us."

"I know," Jason nodded. "Been there, done that, put holes in my tee-shirt. Where is he now?"

She pointed toward the other end of the long corridor. "Way back there, inside the main laboratory. Looking for me now, I'm sure. And still waiting for the teacher and Helen to show up. Do you know where they are?"

"No." Jason let her go. "We just got here."

Christine suddenly blinked hard, and leaned back with a stunned sense of realization. "Whoa, time out. OK, two questions. One, who are these people? And two, how come *you're* not dead? I saw him kill you."

Jason managed a weary smile. "Answer one, this is Paulo and Frances-ca. It's a very long story, but the *Reader's Digest* version is that they're cool. Answer two, as far as my health and wellbeing goes, Francesca has the whole transmuted tissue regeneration and acceleration thing down pat. Trust me on that one."

"Got it," she nodded. "So what do we do?"

He took a deep breath and told her everything the remaining sentient energy of Andrew Duncan had just communicated to him.

•

"I see you are alone, Commander," came the stern voice of the teacher on the view panel in the laboratory. "Where is Dr. Jacobs?"

The laboratory was a ransacked shambles.

Jean-Marc stopped his frantic search and looked at the face of his brother projected on the screen. "She's around. But she doesn't matter. A trifle, I assure you. I will find her in time. If not today, another day, if not here, in another place. As it is with all of her kind. The only thing that matters is you and I. Why delay the inevitable, little brother? If we don't settle this matter today, it will only culminate on another day, with poten-tially much more devastating consequences for many more of their kind. I don't intend to make the same mistake you did of waiting too long to in-tervene ages ago. Remember? When there was but a single family left worth preserving? Do you remember how much blood was shed on that terrible day? Is that what you sincerely desire for your sweet little pets again this time?"

"I think not," the teacher sounded confident. "Actually, I have exactly what I came for in this place." The image on the wall panned back to show Helen standing by his side.

"Oh my..." Jean-Marc was genuinely impressed. "How lovely. Much better than the original, if I recall. The one you defiled. The original sin."

The teacher's jaw tightened.

Jean-Marc huffed. "You think I didn't know? I knew. I saw. I can only assume this one has already been treated to the venom of your forbidden affections as well."

The teacher ignored the taunts. "She is of our kind now, and that is all you need to know. And before you discover my whereabouts again, I assure you, there will soon be many more of us, ready to stand against you, and your reign over this world shall finally be at an end."

Xavier's eyes flashed with fury. "You would run from me like a coward?"

The teacher smiled. "A strategic retreat, I would call it. The better part of valor, as they say. Live to fight another day? My ship is prepared. It was very nice to see you again, Commander. Enjoy the time you have remaining. Until we...meet again."

"*No!*" Xavier bellowed in pure unadulterated rage as the image on the view screen went blank. Jean-Marc didn't miss a beat. He ran over to Else's twisted body, still lying in the sticky coagulated pool of her own blood. He knelt down and grabbed her limp hand. "Arise. I command you."

Her muscles twitched and her pupils constricted with life. She screamed in tortured pain.

"Where is his ship?" he demanded. "Where is it docked?"

Blood ran out of Else's mouth in coughing, choking spurts.

Xavier closed his eyes and his hands began to glow. Else began to suck in staggered gulps of air. The wound on her chest closed in a hiss of steam, releasing tangled wisps winding upward in thin vaporous ribbons.

"Answer me now, or I'll assimilate your energy into mine in my next breath. Where is his shuttle?"

She blinked several times, still completely disoriented, and stammered, "Level one. Beneath the Sphinx."

He pushed her back to the floor, leaving her gasping and gulping for air, still in excruciating pain and anguish. Once in the hallway he spied the spiral staircase at the far end and ran toward it at full speed.

•

Father Pietro and Francesca stayed huddled in the room right next to the laboratory. They heard a woman's screams coming from the lab, and saw the tall man with the white hair race by. Thankfully, he didn't see them. They knew from what they had been told precisely what they had to do. With no further sign of the tall white-haired man, they quickly made their way into the laboratory and found the woman with the short black hair lying on the floor, struggling and drowning in her own blood like a twisted dog hit by a car.

Francesca instantly knelt beside the woman and laid her hands upon her chest, positioned symmetrically on either side of the entry wound. The electric crackle of power filled the air, along with the rich pungent smell of cooking meat.

CHAPTER 62

In less than five minutes Jean-Marc Xavier reached level one and dashed headlong to the southeast end of the underground complex, picturing the geographic orientation of where the Sphinx had to be located overhead. He raced to the closed antechamber door and saw the hand sensor etched into the granite wall. The soft yellow glow pulsed beneath his trembling palm and the stone door began to grind back from its jam. The instant the opening was wide enough to permit his body to squeeze through he was past it. He stopped in the center of the room, momentarily confused. It was an empty stone chamber.

Then he saw the ladder carved into the far wall.

"There you are," he grinned. "Surely you haven't left me here all alone."

"I wouldn't think of leaving..." came a familiar voice behind him, "...without saying good-bye."

Jean-Marc spun around, his blazer billowing out as he turned.

At the same instant the teacher appeared in one corner of the room, shouting, "NOW!"

Azazel and Helen simultaneously appeared from behind their own photonic energy cloaks of invisibility, standing in two adjacent corners of the room, opposite the teacher, flanking either side of the ladder. Each held the golden Forked Lightning batons across their outstretched and firmly clasped hands. In perfect chorus the blinding white light arced from the ends of all three golden devices, forming a sizzling jagged triangle. Jean-Marc was fenced in on three sides. In the blink of an eye the field arched upward creating a shimmering dome of blue light above him, and draping down to the stone below, encasing him in a hemispheric chamber of living light. Just as Helen had envisioned it, the containment field appeared like a thin undulating membrane, translucent blue, marbled with a vibrant network of red veins of pure energy, buzzing and humming like a hundred megawatt dynamo.

Jean-Marc's reflexes were less than a second too slow, and that miniscule moment of surprise was all the teacher and his two companions needed to spring their trap. Xavier had been holding his baton with only one hand. His second hand flew to join the first, discharging two bolts of his own lighting, but his salvo impotently detonated into the triangulation field in front of the teacher. The teacher never blinked. The energy of Jean-Marc's blast only made the luminous blue skin glow brightly for a few seconds, then was assimilated into the containment field with a loud snapping buzz and crackle of power.

"You can't do this to me!" Xavier screamed in red-faced fury at the teacher. "This is high treason! You will be hunted down and slaughtered without mercy for even *thinking* of opposing me or daring to lift arms against me."

"And my other choice was...?" the teacher prompted, with a satisfied look of triumph.

Xavier lowered his baton. "To return to cryogenic exile, where you belong."

"No. Never again," he said. "I have too much work to do, a mission to fulfill. And it shall no longer be hindered by you."

"You're completely insane," Xavier sighed. "You'll kill them all this time...and not just thousands, but billions, in a cataclysmic war of such unfathomable carnage, that after seven consecutive years of barbaric fighting, they won't even remember how or why it started. Did you ever stop to consider that they no longer fight their battles anymore with slings and arrows and swords and spears, brother? Do you realize that? While you were sleeping they've devised much more lethal and effective means to slaughter one another. Is that what you want? Have you not foreseen the carnage? Have you no pity for what few might be left, for those who will be left eating the flesh and drinking the blood of their own children just to survive?[29]"

The teacher didn't respond.

"Well, well." Jean-Marc threw a glance over at Azazel. "And I see you have already revived your faithful Field Marshall. *Bonjour*, General Azazel. Are you really so foolish as to follow this fool again and tilt at his windmills?"

Azazel held his tongue, keeping his eyes fixed on the teacher.

Jean-Marc looked the teacher directly in the eye, taking a menacing step closer to him. "Can you possibly do it, brother? Can you finally bring yourself to shed my blood, the same blood that runs in your veins, the royal blood of our father and mother? Will it really be as easy as you think it will be?"

The teacher broke his older brother's steely gaze, glancing down at the

---

[29] Cf: 2 Kings 6:28,29

cold callous stone at his feet. "I do not relish your demise, Enlil. But your fate has become inevitable. I know you understand that. I wish there was another way. But what alternative have you left me? There is no possibility of truce between us. There never has been and never can be. You know it as well as I."

Their eyes locked, staring in anticipation of a moment neither truly relished.

"That wasn't always true," Jean-Marc said with a note of sincere dismay. "There was a time when we used to work together as one, you and I. Remember? We used to cherish the same goals and dreams. The same purpose. To cultivate and civilize this world. To make a new home here. To make it our own garden, our paradise."

The teacher sighed, as some of the cold ire in his voice melted away. "Yes, but unfortunately, we encountered irreconcilable differences on how that was to be done, and what was to be achieved in the process."

They both continued to stare at each other, tight lipped and breathing hard.

Helen spoke up, "Why didn't one of you just leave, and return to your own world?"

Jean-Marc laughed, keeping his eyes fixed on his brother, "Return? We couldn't."

She remembered, "Oh, right. He said you had come here from a dying world."

"Is that what you told them? That we came here merely to survive? What a noble sounding fiction." He finally broke his steely gaze at his brother and turned to Helen. "He's always been the cunning master of the half-truth. It's truly one of his finest talents. But contrary to what you may have been told, as we speak, our home planet is densely populated and thriving. More so than this one. Granted, everyone lives underground in an innumerable number of facilities very similar to this one, where they've been forced to live ever since he destroyed our atmosphere with his foolhardy experiments. The same way he shall ultimately destroy the atmosphere of this planet and kill every living thing on it if he's allowed to go free and wield his terrors unrestrained."

Helen searched the teacher's face. "What's he talking about?"

The teacher snapped, "More of his lies. He's stalling for time."

Jean-Marc huffed. "*I'm* stalling? Apparently, your naïve new disciples aren't aware of your convenient omission of a few of the more pertinent details about the true nature and effects of your work, little brother." He stepped toward Helen. "Oh yes, he can't deny it. He knows it's true."

"What's true?" she demanded.

Xavier replied, "What's true, my dear, is the simple fact that when sentient creatures, like humans, learn to access universal energy sources, and don't have the skills to fully contain its power, there are many undesirable side-effects."

"What kind of side-effects?" she asked, suddenly feeling very afraid.

"The first effect is pertinent to the individual who is mishandling the power, who begins to experience episodes of abnormal behavior, such as uncontrolled urges and rages, aggressive animal-like behavior, which can be intensely passionate, even obsessive, often expressed sexually, or sometimes taking the form of random acts of extreme violence or madness, or both. It varies among individuals. Your Dr. Freud labeled it the superego. But in this case we're talking about unleashing the basic antithetical drives of fornicating or fighting, creating life or taking it."

Helen was about to ask another question.

He didn't give her the chance. "And if that were the only problem, we might not find ourselves having this conversation. But unfortunately, these side-effects are also quite detrimental to the planet's ecosystem, specifically in terms of disrupting the earth's own gravitational field, which is the only force that keeps its atmosphere from floating off into space. The more random energy disruptions that occur, the more individual molecules of nitrogen, hydrogen, oxygen—literally the very air we all breathe—are allowed to drift away into space, along with the protective ozone layer that prevents cosmic rays from cooking every living creature on this planet." He looked back at the teacher, still addressing Helen, "I suppose he forgot to tell you about all of these little issues, didn't he?"

"Is he telling me the truth?" Helen asked the teacher.

The teacher licked his lips slowly. "He is merely reliving the tragedies of ancient history. What he speaks of can never happen again. Just like I promised the flood would never happen again."

"Liar!" screamed Xavier. "How can you say that?"

"Because it is true!" the teacher shouted back. "I told you. The code has been perfected. She is living proof of it. The genetic maturity to control the power and use it constructively is now active and growing within them as never before. The others of their kind will grow into it naturally, albeit at a radically accelerated pace. I have foreseen it. I will *make* it so."

Jean-Marc looked Helen dead in the eye. "The blood of six billion souls will be on your hands if you let him do this. Is that what you want? Is that your destiny, to be the mother of such violence and death? Your eternal legacy? Your contribution to the fabric of the universe?"

Helen felt that pang down in her gut, that sour acid-hot pang of bewildered confusion. She had no idea what to do.

The teacher sensed her fears. "He *is* lying, Helen. He is wrong. No matter what he says, you have to trust me."

Her eyes searched his, wanting to believe him, but she was plagued with conflicting doubts. She felt as though the fate of an entire planet was resting in the palm of her hands. Was it? Was the teacher's way the path to life and prosperity and rejuvenation, to benefit a confused and torn world, or was it a curse that would leave the earth as barren and lifeless as the red sands of Mars? Could they both be right, just looking at the problem from two different angles? Were they both wrong? My God, she thought, what do I do?

When it happens, climb the ladder as fast as you can. Don't look back. Whatever you do, don't stop to look back. Remember Lot's wife.[30]

Helen's breath stilled. In her mind she knew she had just heard the living voice of Andrew Duncan. Was he still alive? She had not seen his fate with her eyes, but somewhere in her heart she knew it, she felt it. The sentient energy of his body, his soul, was still alive, but no longer residing in the vehicle of his flesh.

"Drop your weapon," Xavier commanded Helen. "All of you. Now."

The teacher raised his voice, "Be strong, Helen. Begin moving forward now. Azazel, you do the same."

"Yes, lord," Azazel replied. "As you command."

The triumvirate pushed inward, collapsing the available space of the energy field, inch by inch, smaller and smaller, moving its sizzling walls toward the center of the room where Jean-Marc made his stand. As the field closed, the buzzing hum grew higher in pitch and brighter in intensity. Xavier didn't look terribly worried.

"Enough of this nonsense." Jean-Marc turned and addressed Helen. "If you won't listen to me, then your fate is that you, too, shall die here and now, like a diseased dog. Like your foolish friend, Dr. Friedrich, struck down at my pleasure." He whipped out his gleaming chrome revolver and aimed it directly at Helen's face.

"No!" the teacher screamed a fraction of a second before the hammer struck the firing pin, "Helen, it cannot—"

The report thundered through the chamber.

It was too late.

---

[30] Cf: Genesis 19:26

CHAPTER 63

The copper-jacketed hollow point round harmlessly vaporized the instant it made contact with the energy field eighteen inches from Helen's face, but she was hardly prepared for that. As was the case with all sudden loud noises, Helen flinched in terror, defensively throwing her hands up in front of her face. Her golden baton twisted free and fell, tumbling toward the stone floor below in what seemed like a tortured slow motion. Everything from that moment forward took on a slow syrupy pace, where every detail was clear and defined, yet moving in a shrill surreal blur. Helen could only watch the subsequent events unfold in mute wide-eyed horror.

Even before her golden baton clattered hard against the floor and shattered into three large useless pieces, two sides of the containment field instantly extinguished, leaving only a parallel energy connection between the teacher and Azazel.

Xavier was free.

The chrome-plated 357 magnum clattered to the floor as Jean-Marc grasped his baton with both hands and leveled it at Azazel's head, vaporizing it in a deafening discharge of destructive energy. The thunder of the blast reverberated throughout the chamber. The decapitated corpse fell to the floor in a twisted smoldering pile of arms, legs, and headless charred torso doubled over in two. Blood pumped from an open severed neck, spurting against the wall, until the heart seized a few moments later.

But before Azazel's body had even hit the ground two jagged bolts of lightning fired from the teacher's baton. The counterattack was immediately caught by Xavier's baton as he deftly spun around to face his younger brother. And there they stood, both of them, squared off a mere three meters apart, with two parallel bolts of silver lightning crackling and humming and sizzling between the ends of their golden weapons.

"It seems you miscalculated, brother," Xavier taunted. "And now you shall pay for it with your life, and the lives of all who are foolish enough to follow you. And at long last..." He let out a long weary breath. "...this insanity shall be over, and this mortal misfit world can go back to its less than perfect, but protected and preserved, humble little existence that I call home."

"Miscalculated? I think not," the teacher retorted, his jaw set firm. "Truly, this was not the outcome I would have preferred, but there were always contingencies. I foresaw this possibility, and am fully prepared for it. It is you who have miscalculated, Commander, and are about to leave this world once and for all."

Xavier's laughter dripped with contempt. "Bravely spoken, brother. But unless you have any more of your clever parlor tricks to play, I can sense your energy waning. The level of power you need to withstand what I am projecting at this moment drains you more rapidly that you can replenish. I can feel it. It won't take long. It's only a matter of time. Minutes, if not seconds." He huffed. "How ironic. A week ago, you had all the time in the world, and nothing but time. And now, time has become the precious tender of which you are all but bankrupt."

The teacher glanced at Helen, watching her sidestepping slowly and silently toward the bronze ladder. "Helen, I can hold him here, but not indefinitely. He is correct in that he has much more accumulated energy than I. So you must leave here. Now. Before it is too late."

"I'm not just going to leave you here with him," she cried out. "He'll kill you."

Xavier laughed again, taunting and cold. "So...she has made her choice. Oh, *c'est la vie*, *cherie*. How romantic. And how convenient. It will save me the trouble of hunting you down later with the others."

And that's when she heard it.

Helen heard a voice echoing through the fog in the back of her mind. Only, it wasn't the disembodied voice of Andrew Duncan's this time. It wasn't the teacher's voice, or Else's voice, but it was one she recognized. It was a young voice, a voice she hadn't heard in almost fifty years. It was the innocent sing-song voice of a small boy. Tears began to cascade down her cheeks. Yes, it was the unmistakably sweet and tender voice she'd never forget in all her days, the voice of a little boy named Aubrey. His words to his big sister were clear, and she cherished the sound of them, but she didn't want to listen to what he was telling her. It was too horrible to contemplate. But he told her the truth, and explained exactly what she needed to do at that precise moment, conveying the detailed instructions he'd been given, precisely as he'd been asked to do by the teacher when his spirit was summoned, just as Andrew's spirit had been summoned.[31]

"No," she pleaded to the air. "I can't. Don't ask that of me."

"You must," the teacher called out, his voice cracking with emotion. "You know whose energy it is that speaks to your heart, who sees you now,

---

[31] CF: 1 Samuel 28:7-15.

who has watched you from the heavens every day of your life with pride and affection and unyielding love. You know whose voice you could always trust, whose counsel to which you must now hearken, even when your fears cloud that which you physically see and hear. Listen to your heart, Helen. You've heard that voice so many times over the years comforting you in times of trouble, when you were most confused and afraid and drowning in doubt. You had no way in days past to know for sure who it was who watched over you, who comforted you in your pain, but deep down, you felt it, you sensed it. You know it for a certainty now."

"He's trying to deceive you, even now!" Xavier screamed. "It is a trick. Don't listen to any more of his ridiculous lies!"

The teacher sobbed openly. "Now, my love, my queen. Cast away your doubts. Do not argue! He is correct. Time *is* short. Even now my strength grows weak and is nearly at its end."

"There has to be another way!" she screamed.

"There is no other way!" the teacher bellowed though his tears. "Do it. If you believe anything I have told you, you have to do it. If you share any of the vision that was mine for you and for your people. If you have any love for me whatsoever, then do it. Do it now!"

Tortured tears streamed down Helen's cheeks. She could barely see. Her heart was breaking. How could this be? How could it all have come to this? In a single day she had found a new life, a new existence, a new love, and now it was all shattering to pieces right in front of her.

And yet, in that same moment, a new realization emerged.

With a flash of inspiration Helen understood the necessity of what he was doing, and that he was doing it all for her as well as for all of mankind, the multitudes of every tribe and nation and tongue whom he considered his own precious children. He was willing to make the ultimate sacrifice—to trade his life for hers, and for them. He was the living bridge from the past, the light from a distant star. And even if all his brother's fears were well-founded and the potential risks were catastrophic, she was the embodiment of his hope for the future, of all that might be.

How could she neglect so great a gift?

It's true, Helen. It's all true. You didn't know it when I was gone, when you were hurt, when you were laying there with me down there in that dark cold hole, so scared, telling me not to be afraid, not to worry, that you'd help me. I wished I could have told you then, if there had been a way. But you know now. You know the truth. You know what you have to do now. Don't be afraid any longer. I'm not. You taught me how not to be afraid anymore—a long, long time ago.

Helen clenched her eyes and choked back a wracking sob, the pain in her heart unbearable. Yes, the choice was made. A simple choice. A simple choice to believe, and to act upon that belief. A simple act of faith.

And then it happened.

Helen focused. She thrust her palm out toward Jean-Marc, her fingers stretched wide and quaking in a frantic *STOP!* gesture. He looked momentarily surprised by her unexpected movement. The shiny 357 magnum near his feet flew up off the stone floor into Helen's awaiting hands, as though it were magnetized.

Jean-Marc began to laugh yet again, his voice smug with condescension. "My dear, I assure you, that weapon is no threat to me. I have more than enough energy to assimilate its projectiles with scarcely a thought.

Hurry, Helen, before he realizes your intent and melts it in your hands.

Helen swiveled on the balls of her feet, aiming the gun directly at the hand sensor panel next to the entrance door to the complex.

She fired.

The air stung with the concussion and resounding echo of the gun's thundering report. The ancient stone fragmented in a cloudy spray of dust and gravel, leaving a deep penetrating gouge. A faint yellow light popped and fizzed and spurted a few dying sparks.

Xavier was completely mystified by her actions.

The revolver once more clattered to the floor.

A painfully familiar dull throbbing low-frequency wave penetrated the room, making Helen's teeth and sinuses hurt. She was sobbing almost hysterically, as she spun around and clambered up the access ladder as fast as she could go. The strength of her new body made the climb swift and sure, ascending two or three times faster than her original descent. The stone walls of the access chamber below her began to turn a light shade of green.

Still deadlocked in the Forked Lightning energy beams with the teacher, Jean-Marc's countenance suddenly fell with a dark pang of realization. "Oh, no. What have you done, little brother?"

"I have given them the chance you never would," the teacher replied, his breathing more labored and strained.

The two jagged beams continued to discharge between them as they sparred and parried for the next several minutes, circling, positioning, waiting, watching, angling for a single misstep that could turn into advantage. Yet neither gave quarter, instinctively knowing that the first one who blinked would be vaporized by the other in the next instant. Xavier's eyes frantically scanned the empty room, desperately looking for something to use, some strategy for escape. There was none.

The walls grew steadily brighter and brighter. The air temperature increased rapidly. Sweat streamed down both of their faces. Their gazes remained locked. The teacher's expression remained defiant and sure. Xavier's expression melted into a mask of sadness.

"You would kill us both for them?"

The teacher swallowed hard. "They are my children, my friends. I can think of no greater act of love for my friends than to lay down my life for them."

Jean-Marc coughed, his voice cracking and growing hoarse. "What if you're wrong? What if the disease spreads again?"

"I don't think it will. But nothing is certain. It might. And yet, in my heart, I know the risk is worth it. But whatsoever may come, whatsoever may become of them, I am confident of one thing." The teacher forced a smile. "The universe will compensate. The divine law will always rule and prevail. You know it as well as I. As it is written: for every action there is always an equal and opposite reaction. Balance will be found. If not in this age, then in one to come."

Xavier bowed his head, feeling his own limbs growing weak. "I hope for their sakes you're right." He coughed again, wheezing out a tired laugh. "You know, I would have taken your life swiftly, without pain. This is really starting to hurt."

The teacher began to stagger from side to side, quipping, "You always said my destiny would end with fire."

"Yes, I know. But I never intended to burn with you." Jean-Marc sucked in a scorching hot breath then coughed up a mouthful of blood and bile. As the skin on his face and hands began to redden and swell and blister from the intense heat and radiation, he abruptly dropped his golden baton. It shattered on the stone below.

The two bolts of energy between them disappeared.

Silence.

They stared deeply into each others eyes again, exchanging a long weary look that spoke millennia of words, words that could not be uttered, which no longer needed to be uttered, words of a final mutual understanding, a realization of personal futility and loss, but nevertheless redeemed by a shared hope for mankind's future they now would only witness from a great distance. It all culminated in a quiet look of resignation to the fact that it was really happening. The end was at hand.

"We came to this place...together. I suppose...it is only fitting for it all...to end this way for us." The teacher allowed his own baton to slip from his fingers. It clanged to the floor by his feet, broken in half. His robe was beginning to singe brown and blacken. The oppressive heat waves made it almost impossible to see anything but a wet wavy blur before him.

Jean-Marc took a few faltering steps forward as the steadily increasing deadly waves of gamma radiation continued to penetrate every living cell of his body, destroying them faster than his tissues could regenerate them, exactly as the facility's defense systems were designed. The teacher lurched forward as well, catching his older brother in his arms as their knees buckled in unison. They both twisted down onto the floor, their eyes glazing over, turning milky white and solid. Blood oozed from their gums, nostrils and ears. The teacher felt his brother's trembling hand slide up and tenderly touch his inflamed cheek. Their foreheads came together and touched.

They were both blind.

Jean-Marc leaned forward and softly kissed his brother's cheek, straining to whisper over his swollen, almost useless tongue.

"What will they do without us?"

With sizzling tears running down his blistered face, tracing the deep steaming lesions opening up on his skin, the teacher hugged his big brother tightly, protectively. As his robe caught fire and the hungry flames licked up around them, charring their skin, he wheezed his final reply.

"They shall live…"

CHAPTER 64

Jason flew the winged serpent craft exactly as he had been taught by the teacher, enjoying the experience immensely, despite the tragedy left behind. His hands were placed perfectly on the two circular navigation pads which glowed red beneath his palms. They were soaring high above the Atlantic Ocean, moving at three times the speed of sound. Christine stood next to the captain's chair, with her hand resting affectionately on his forearm, silently staring out the forward view panels at the dark waves of the sea beneath them.

Back in the passenger compartment Helen sat silently in the last row, in the same seat where she sat before, also staring out the view panels at the brooding ocean below. In the first row sat Paulo and Francesca. Else Friedrich was in the second row, sitting directly behind the ex-priest. Immediately after lifting off from the Sphinx they had flown to the north side of the Giza complex for a quick stop. Jason found the rest of the group waiting on the other side of the secret door of the Unfinished Chamber, just as they had been instructed by the soul of Andrew Duncan. It was Christine who had invisibly escorted him in, and the group out, undetected by the security personnel who were still searching for the tall stranger with long white hair who had mysteriously slipped past one of the guards earlier that night.

Of the entire group, Else was the one suffering from the greatest emotional distress, notwithstanding the fact that her gunshot wound had been completely healed by Francesca's ministrations. Nevertheless, the feeling of betrayal and abandonment still festered sour in her soul. She felt humiliated and stupid, like nothing more than a useless pawn. While they were waiting to be picked up beneath the Great Pyramid, a brief talk with Paulo was extremely helpful. He was a gifted counselor, but it was only a start. Many more talks would be needed before the healing process within her soul could ever genuinely commence.

Helen's legs were still a little sore. They had been slightly cooked in the last few seconds of her frantic climb up the access ladder, before the aperture on the Sphinx's back was closed and the lower hatch of the shuttle sealed tight. But her flawless alabaster skin healed itself in a matter of seconds as her accelerated tissue regeneration capability performed its natural organic function.

From the moment they finally launched from the plain of Giza, a stunned sense of shock and disbelief hung heavy in the air, painting an empty pensive daze on each face, like those who walked away from a fiery car wreck, or shell-shocked soldiers in the still aftermath of the last shot fired in a bloody battle. For several hours of flight no one said a word, just sat quietly by themselves, thinking, wondering, speculating, trying to grasp a reality that was as elusive as a drop of mercury.

It was Else who first broke the silence, speaking to Paulo. "It would seem the Sacred Order of the Eternal Light has lost its mission."

He almost found the strength to smile. "Yes. For us. Although, the rest of our holy brothers and sisters don't know the whole truth, and may never know, unless we tell them. That calling could be a life's work unto itself. Then again, many, if not all, wouldn't believe us if we told them, and would brand us heretics. I've seen many pay with their lives for far less."

Else nodded. "Perhaps." She turned to Helen. "So, my queen. Where are we headed?"

Helen looked at Else, flattered and somewhat comforted by hearing herself referred to by the title of Queen. It seemed to fit. "To the underworld. The southern hemisphere. To South America."

Pietro asked, "What's in South America?"

Helen turned back to the view panel and the vast brooding expanse of the indigo ocean below, remembering again all that she had been told. "There we shall find an ancient lake high in the mountains. Near a lost city. There, we begin our search."

Else frowned. "Search for what?"

"For their sister," she whispered.

Their sister?" gasped Pietro.

"She's in South America?" Else leaned forward in her seat. "You're sure she's even still alive?"

"It's what I was told," Helen muttered, only half listening. "She is likely to be found locked in cryostasis, just as we found our teacher. But we must find her. She's essential to our work and to our mission."

Else Friedrich and Paulo Pietro exchanged a wary glance.

Francesca asked Pietro in Italian what made his face cringe with such concern. He translated what had just been said. Francesca spun around in her seat, staring at Helen. It was going to take many long talks with Paulo, and with all of her new companions, with many more incredible secrets to learn before Francesca's own understanding would start to come in line with the new and unbelievable shared reality that she, too, was now facing.

Helen didn't say anything further.

She kept buried deep in her heart the very last thing the precious voice of her little brother had confidentially transmitted to her mind before she pulled the trigger of the commander's gun, sentencing both him and his own brother to death. All that she had just shared with them was true, even if it wasn't everything she had been told. It was indeed critical to find their sister as soon as possible. That's all they needed to know for now. When they found her, she would be the group's new teacher, and high counselor for a potential world war that was coming—but most importantly, to serve as aunt and nurse for the child already growing in Helen's womb.

EPILOGUE

As he sipped his morning tea in his office, Rabbi David Shemel's eye caught an article in his morning newspaper. It was an innocuous one-column story that most readers would probably skip, but one that pricked a faint memory within him for some reason. It had nothing to do with the disappearance of the leader of their Sacred Order of the Eternal Light, the mysterious Frenchman who masqueraded as an international arms dealer and financier. It had nothing to do with the death of his old friend Cardinal Giovanni Ricollo, who was buried quietly with little fanfare, nor with the disappearance of the cardinal's protégé Monsignor Paulo Pietro. There had never been any public mention whatsoever of the disappearance in the middle of the Saudi desert of an entire oil exploration site, along with its billionaire industrialist owner and its hundred man crew. No, what caught his attention was a tiny scientific article, unrelated to any of the events of the previous month in Saudi Arabia, Italy, and Egypt.

Essentially, the story was an innocuous announcement from the Mauna Kea Observatory in Hawaii about the discovery of a new binary star system in the galaxy. The scientists were perplexed as to why no one had ever noticed the twin star system before, being so visibly prominent and in relatively close proximity to the earth's solar system. It appeared in the heavens right between the constellations of Pisces and Aquarius. A few notable tabloid astrologers were quoted in the article as saying it was a sign of a dawning new age. Astronomers and astrophysicists disputed any mystical or metaphysical connotations in favor of a leading theory regarding dense gas clouds and electromagnetic space dust condensing rapidly around a dying star that had recently collapsed and split in two.

However, Rabbi Shemel had been taught decades ago in his training in the sacred order that upheavals in the heavens were often precursors or signs of imminent events about to take place on earth. He made a mental note to put in a few calls to others of his brotherhood around the world and see if any signs of trouble or other strange events had occurred which necessitated their swift attention and involvement.

These days the old rabbi was especially alert and vigilant. One Watcher had been found and was believed to have been discretely destroyed. Surely this event proved others could be out there as well. Heaven forbid if even one should ever be unleashed upon the world again.

"Religions die when they are proved to be true. Science is
the record of dead religions."

Oscar Wilde
*Phrases and Philosophies
for the Use of the Young*, 1891

"Science investigates; religion interprets. Science gives man
knowledge which is power; religion gives man wisdom,
which is control."

Dr. Martin Luther King, Jr.
Strength to Love, 1963

"The cosmic religious experience is the strongest and the
noblest driving force behind scientific research."

Albert Einstein
His obituary, April 19, 1955

ACKNOWLEDGEMENTS

Excerpts from *The Book of Enoch* are actual extra-biblical translations from the Aramaic version, *Enoch 1*, found in the Qumran *Dead Sea Scrolls*. All biblical verses quoted are from *The New King James Version of the Bible*, Thomas Nelson Publishers. All other direct quotes are cited as appropriate.

Many thanks to the British Museum's wealth of data on Egyptology and PBS's NOVA Online's most helpful virtual tours inside the Great Pyramids. While a few of the basic physics and biology concepts contained in this story are the fruits of this author's fertile and often wild imagination, most of them are factual, sourced from a wide variety of technical and academic publications (God bless the Internet!). Of great help was documentation regarding the Human Genome Project, sponsored by the US Dept. of Energy (www.ornl.gov) with respect to the fundamental workings and understanding of DNA and human genetics, fictional embellishments notwithstanding. Special kudos also go to www.howstuffworks.com, an invaluable online research resource.

A portion of the historical back-story of *The Mustard Seed* was drawn from the scholarship and research of Zechariah Sitchin's *The Earth Chronicles*. This highly controversial and much debated, meticulously detailed, multi-volume reference compendium, spanning decades of archaeological, linguistic, and historical investigative work, is widely regarded as non-fiction documentary evidence regarding the origins of many of the "gods." As has been aptly noted, if even ten percent of Sitchin's conclusions are valid, most of ancient history will need to be rewritten.

Inspiration for various integral elements of this tale were also drawn from the many works and theories of the likes of Albert Einstein, Carl Jung, Sigmund Freud, Jules Verne, Dante Alighieri, and a host of scientists, philosophers, authors and theologians to numerous to name. Of special note, it was at the tender and most impressionable age of thirteen that I first read a copy of Erich von Daniken's *Chariots of the Gods*, which first fascinated and intrigued me on the fanciful topic of ancient visitors to earth, and gave me cause to originally wonder, "What if...?"

Special thanks and sincere appreciation are due to this author's wife and daughter, Joanna and Tristina respectively, during the writing of this book for their unique patience with the author's intellectual obsessions and penchant for inflicting his often bizarre premises and convoluted conjectures upon them without warning, soliciting their input, insights, honest reactions, and constructive criticism.

This novel is, of course, a work of pure fiction[32]. But the basic question remains: "What if it all didn't happen exactly like they told us?"

---

[32] Or is it?

AFTERWARD

I repeat once more, this novel is a work of fiction. While its cosmogony is drawn from many fonts of imminent historical scholarship, archeology, ancient records, and contemporary scientific research, inclusive of broadly accepted and highly controversial theories extracted from the fields of biology, genetics, physics, astronomy, and numerous other scientific disciplines, its theological allusions, corollaries and metaphysical constructs are in no way intended to disparage or offend the strongly held and cherished values and beliefs of any group or individual. It is, instead, this author's sincere hope that while seeking to entertain and to intrigue the intellect, the flights of imagination contained herein might serve to provoke a measure of constructive reflection into why each of us believes what we do, and thoughtfully consider how we choose to apply those beliefs and corresponding values to our daily lives.

The search for truth regarding who we really are and why we are here on this earth has been man's eternal pursuit from the dawn of time. It is an ignorant man who can only blindly echo the views of others, ancient or contemporary, and can neither explain nor defend what he himself claims to hold true in his heart, and more importantly, why. It is a wise man who tries and tests every assertion laid before him with the fire of clear reason and honest facts, to burn away the chaff of ignorance and superstition, and thereby extract the pure gold of truth, whereupon he rests his faith.

REG